LIVE BY THE SWORD

Almost two centuries after the Linfield Horror, the trees were still stunted and sick, and black ruins stood where the castle had been. From a tangle of brambles, a pair of eyes watched him above a snout that looked more like a pig's than a dog's, although even a wild boar would not have had tusks that were so long and white, nor spittle that hissed and burbled where it touched the blackened earth.

Well, one thing you can say for the Sandoval is that he did a thorough job here.

I don't know that even you and I could have done it better.

The Khan seemed amused. Yes, it had been the Sandoval, and a knight of the Order. The feud with the Table Round had never really ended, and it had been far too close to its peak just before the Horror.

The rivalry was still there, it was just that the two rival orders tended to avoid each other. Knights of the Table Round, by and large, were more inspectors and couriers than anything else. In fact, when Gray had gone to New York to invite the duke to come to Londinium, the three Table Knights had been rude enough that he had been sorely tempted to have called one of them out.

But no. If he had challenged one of them, it would have been with his mundane sword, and not with the Khan. Pity.

No, not a pity, it was a necessity—one insult, one moment of loss of self-control by one knight of the Red Sword, and Linfield was the result.

BAEN BOOKS
by JOEL ROSENBERG

Guardians of the Flame
Guardians of the Flame: To Home and Ehvenor
Guardians of the Flame: Legacy

Paladins
Paladins II: Knight Moves

PALADINS II: KNIGHT MOVES

Joel Rosenberg

PALADINS II: KNIGHT MOVES

Copyright © 2006 by Joel Rosenberg

A Baen Book

Baen Publishing Enterprises
P.O. Box 1403
Riverdale, NY 10471
www.baen.com

ISBN 10: 1–4165–5562–5
ISBN 13: 978–1–4165–5562–9

Cover art by Kurt Miller

First Baen paperback printing, July 2008

Distributed by Simon & Schuster
1230 Avenue of the Americas
New York, NY 10020

Library of Congress Cataloging-in-Publication Data:
2006029918

Printed in the United States of America

10 9 8 7 6 5 4 3 2 1

Dedication:
This one is for the Slots.

This is what we do. This is who we are.
—Becket

PROLOGUE

The Knights and the Night

At least his feet had started hurting again.

It could have been worse, Edward thought. No matter how bad things were, they could always get worse. That was a simple fact of life, and he should be used to that by now, particularly on this cold, horrid night.

Pain was certainly safer than the numbness that had overtaken them the last time that Fat Harold had called for a break. Cold was dangerous; numbness was the beginning of the end.

It shouldn't be very far, he thought, although every step seemed to last forever, from the moment when he lifted a boot to when he set it down again, and the long, frightening moment after, until when he was confident enough that his forward foot could support him to before he dared lift the one behind.

There was no such thing as secure footing on the frozen trail; steady enough would have to serve, even though that kept their pace maddeningly slow, as rushing would be lethal.

It was, he thought, the night as much as the cold, although the cold was bad enough.

Edward didn't care for nights, generally. And particularly not for this one.

Didn't like cold, either.

The exposed tip of his nose had only stopped being numb and started being painful again when he had taken off a glove for a few moments, and warmed it with his hand, and then shoved his freezing hand back into what little warmth was left in the glove, and flexed his fingers, hard, until the pain returned as the blood began to flow through them.

There was a storm coming; far to the north, the clouds glowed with the dimming light of the moon, as they massed to overcome it. Darkness would triumph over the weak light, yes, but only until morning.

That was reassuring, he decided. Saint Albert of Leeds had written that only the impious would doubt that darkness would eventually fall to the light, and Edward de Vigny flattered himself that whatever his limitations and failings, he was not an impious man.

But piety didn't make him one whit warmer.

Better to fall forward than falling over backward, when his swords were strapped to his pack—even if he didn't tumble down the path, with Fat Harold watching helplessly.

Behind him, Fat Harold grunted. "Hope we can find the shelter before it hits," he said. "I'm not that fond of the cold, either, Butcher."

Fat Harold kept complaining, and Edward would have ignored him, if he could.

But he couldn't. God, in his infinite mercy, had not given the ears lids in the way that he had protected the eyes.

Fat Harold went on, and on and on: it was too cold; it was too high an altitude; they should have waited in the village; there was more than a hundred miles left on this long patrol anyway, and while, yes, they might need to take a side trip, they could do it in the daylight.

Edward wished Harold would just keep quiet. For a knight of the Order, Fat Harold—more formally, Sir Harold O'Reilly, like Edward, a knight, and therefore a priest of the Order of Crown, Shield, and Dragon—was far too much of a whiner.

He would have guessed that that was why Fat Harold had never been raised in estate to White or Red, but Sir Guy of Orkney—who, so Sir Guy apparently thought, was far too dignified to have a nickname—was a notorious whiner and complainer, something that Fat Harold was known to hold forth on at great length, on the rare occasions that Edward upbraided him, as though that was the key to such a raise in estate.

Edward thought it rather unlikely.

As to Edward, well, he would of course accept the honor if it was offered, but the live swords were rare and—at least until recently—thought to be utterly irreplaceable, and he would serve as best he could until and unless the Abbot and the Council decided that he was worthy.

His present status was hardly an indignity, after all, the present moment aside, which—as bloody uncomfortable as it was—was far more discomfort than indignity. He was, after all, a knight of the Order of Crown, Shield, and Dragon—and that was quite a rise in estate for a son of a butcher, eh?

Nothing to be ashamed about, and in fact, the sin of pride was a temptation.

He didn't doubt for a moment that he had fully earned his swords, but many men in this life failed to get what they earned, after all.

Even most Order Knights who made it to retirement, and the Reserve List, never went Red or White. If Edward was a jealous sort of man, it would have bothered him that when most Englishmen thought of Order Knights, they thought of the Reds and Whites, and often seemed to assume that there was something lacking with the majority of Order Knights who were never entrusted—or burdened, depending on whom you listened to—with a live sword.

When was the last time you heard a ballad about an Order Knight who wasn't a Red or White? Well, yes, there were all the songs and stories and talkes of the Final Battle at Bedegraine, but that was in the old days, long before the Age of Crisis, long before the live swords.

Then again, some song about Sir Edward freezing his toes off in this godforsaken place probably wouldn't be all that interesting, anyway. He tried to imagine some ditty—"he froze, he froze, he froze, and then he froze"—but couldn't come up with anything but a light tune that didn't either warm him or fit the words.

But the oath wasn't "for glory," after all. It was: "Service, honor, faith, obedience. Justice tempered only by mercy; mercy tempered only by justice."

In the meantime, while the Reds and the Whites served on His Own, or were sent—as Gray had been—to *have words* with important nobility or on missions almost as glamorous, the likes of the Butcher and Fat Harold got to make the rounds in what wasn't quite the most godforsaken territory over which the Crown held domain.

Quite.

But it was service, and obedience, and there was honor in that, and he would just have to have faith that he was being useful.

And he was, of course.

For one thing, it was a good thing for Crown subjects to see an Order Knight every now and then, and remember that whatever duke or earl or baron or headman or margrave that they mostly thought of themselves as serving, they were in reality His Majesty's subjects, and that the arm of the Pendragon King was long, and that the fist at the end of that arm every bit as lethal as necessary.

And, besides, with the Zone so close, and with rumors of more darklings south of Aba-Paluoja, it was important for them to walk the northern and eastern boundaries, and bless the ground. That was something that had to be done by a priest.

The country was rough enough that if the priest wasn't to be regularly expended, it had to be done by a priest who was also skilled with weapons, and all the better if the priest was an Order Knight, who would rarely find himself having to prove those skills to any sane man.

Darklings and other things from the Zone couldn't cross running water or hallowed ground—not without assistance, at least—and making sure that they never had a route to the south was as important to the Crown here as it was to the Empire, to the east.

Not enough rivers, and those too often frozen.

Yes, the blessings came from Him, but the unholy had their ways, too—defiling ground wasn't particularly difficult, if you didn't give a fig for your immortal soul.

It was a matter of intention—deconsecrating a church's sanctuary, so that it could, say, become a school, was a matter of proper intention every bit as much as the ritual, and would no more endanger your immortal soul than would building a school rather than a church on the same plot of land in the first place.

Defilement was another matter; the hezmoni used to rape Christian women with wine bottles—after, of course, raping them in other ways—then drink the wine and piss on the ground, which had seemed to serve.

There were, of course, other, less dramatic ways to accomplish the same effect.

The wind picked up, and off in the distance, a lone wolf howled his complaint over the cold, a complaint that Edward was sure that Fat Harold would have shared aloud, if he could have figured out a way to do so while puffing his way along behind Edward.

Edward had gotten awfully tired of Fat Harold's complaining, but even without that—even without having to trudge up the side of the mountain—he wouldn't have cared for this night in any case.

He had never liked the cold. Sir Edward de Vigny, despite his name, was no northerner. In fact, he was from Pinet in the south of Borbonaisse, a small village whose minimal fame was far overshadowed by that of nearby Mérifons. And, like Mérifons, Pinet was only a mile or so off the warm waters of the Bassin de Thau.

The only thing he had in common with the northern, noble Hautmont family of the same name *was* the name, and that was of dubious origin, and the one winter he had spent near Hautmont had been far too cold for his taste, colder than English winters, although not nearly as wet and damp.

This was worse.

Spring, *pfah*.

He would have spit if he hadn't thought that the spittle would likely freeze and shatter on the rocks.

What passed as a pitiful excuse for a spring night near Hostikka was no spring at all, and not just because it was more than six hundred miles to the north and east of the warm waters and gentle winds of the Mediterranean. Blame it on the cold waters of the sea to south, or the one to the west, or, if you liked, you could blame it on the Zone.

But blame on whatever cause, there was one thing certain: it was just too damned cold.

At least the fur leggings and long bearskin coat he wore over his Order robes kept the worst of it out, although whenever the wind picked up, the sleeves of the coat seemed to act like funnels for the wind, and would have chilled him to the bone if his pack's straps hadn't been so tight about his shoulders, preventing it from piercing him quite to the core.

For the moment. He didn't worry about his extremities, as long as they hurt—but his core was awfully cold as it was, and his testicles were trying to retreat up into his body.

He allowed himself a quick look behind, past where Fat Harold was huffing and puffing.

Half a mile below and miles further than that back, the lights in the village burned invitingly, promising warmth and food, and warmth. Their reception had been more than acceptable, which was just as well for all concerned, despite some apparent nervousness about the presence of two Order knights, and constant glances at their swords, with the unvoiced question never quite asked, and never answered at all.

The talk of the town was, of course, as it was all across the region, that the Blue Skolt Same were very late in their spring migration through, and should have been through sometime in York—a month which the locals irritating still called "Huhtikuu," although they spoke English well enough, albeit a formal, Church English—and here it was Marsey, already, or "Toukokuu," as they had it.

In spring, the locals would be trading with the Skolts for the leather and bone goods that the Skolts made during the winter; in the fall, it would be fattened reindeer. A good pair of Skolt Same boots were highly prized, and some thought that there was perhaps a little magic in their construction, rather than just careful sewing of the reindeer hide.

But there was no sign of the Skolt Same.

In a more civilized country, the local barons or earls would have already sent out search parties, but the Duke of Suomaland could barely be bothered to send taxmen out in the fall of the year, and he kept his subordinate earls—really minor court barons, in all but titles—close to him in Helsinki, as though afraid of revolt, although it passed human understanding as to why anybody would want to seize control of this misbegotten frozen wasteland.

So, unsurprisingly, the task fell to Order Knights. It was part of what their patrol was, more or less.

Most likely, the Blue Skolts had simply taken an alternate route to the south. Yes, they lived near enough the Zone as it was, but . . .

Well, they'd see.

"I still think we should have waited until morning," Fat Harold wheezed.

Yes, they could have waited until morning, and instead of climbing in the dark to the old shack at the top of the ridge, they would have been climbing in the light—through the storm—and reached the shack after dark.

At least, this way, they might have a chance for a distant view from the top in the morning, maybe even before the storm broke.

It shouldn't be much longer, and—

Ah.

He had been told by the village headman that it would be impossible to miss the cabin, and for once, a local had spoken truthfully, if only by accident.

The twisted pine that marked the crest of the hill really did look like the letter zed, even against the dark sky, and shelter was now just minutes away.

Whatever you could say ill about Fat Harold—and there was much that you could—he was a fast hand with a fire kit, and even if the headman had lied about the shack being faithfully restocked with wood in what passed for summer hereabouts, the hillside was littered with trees that had literally exploded during the worst of winter, and Fat Harold could make a good fire out of even frozen, wet wood, if necessary using a splash of the lamp oil to get it started.

And then there was the flask of good Scots whiskey in Edward's pack, wrapped with every bit as much care as the lantern, and for much the same reason. Once they had a fire going, it would warm him inside as much, or more than the fire would his outside.

He forced himself not to quicken his pace. It was always best to approach such things slowly, and not just because it would be a sad irony if, just as he was about to reach his goal, he tumbled back down the mountainside. It was, after all, not impossible that the shack would be occupied.

Not that a sane man would consider wintering up here, but Sir Edward had found hermits in crazier places, if not much crazier.

And there was always a chance that a bear had decided to make the shack his den for the winter, and that the bear would have sense enough to sleep through what the locals lightheartedly thought of as spring.

But, no. In the harsh moonlight, the drifted snow in front of the cabin was unbroken and unmarked, and both the door and the roof appeared to be intact. If there was anybody inside, they had been inside since the last snowfall, and with the lack of fire, that would mean

Edward and Fat Harold would find either vacancy and shelter, or frozen bodies . . . and shelter, too.

One thing you could say for building by laying stone upon stone is that it didn't rot—not that much of anything would rot in this horrid climate, not when it could just freeze solid instead.

The door, of course, was frozen shut, but it only took a couple of kicks for Fat Harold to break the ice loose, and knock it down—thankfully, without breaking the wood, which would have meant that they'd have had to fix the door in the morning.

"Turn around for a moment," Fat Harold said. For such a normally sluggardly man, he was preposterously quick in getting the lantern out of Edward's pack, and he knelt in the lee of the side of the hut with his fire kit, lighting it. Fat Harold was not quite as clumsy as he looked; he managed to manipulate the fire kit even with his gloves on, something that Edward couldn't have done.

"Give me ten minutes, Butcher," he said, his fat face grinning in the light of the lantern, "just ten bloody minutes, and I'll have a good fire going that will warm you, from toe to head, until you complain of the heat, and—"

His breath caught in his throat, and dropped the lantern to the ground, careless of the way that it shattered, sending flaming oil scattering about.

Silently, without even a whisper where their robes dragged upon the snow and dirt, two dark shapes glided slowly out of the hut.

The priest had promised. He had *sworn* that he had said the appropriate blessings at not only the four corners of the village, but had renewed the blessings from one end of the county to the other, including making the pilgrimage up here. Prayer could not kill such as these, but they couldn't cross water, or hallowed ground, not without help.

But they were here. Darklings, they were called. Were they really demons from Hell? Edward didn't know. What he knew about them was bad enough.

Here, so close to the Zone, they didn't even have weapons—they were themselves the weapon. Their touch would burn both body and soul, and while a live sword could kill them, there was little else in the world that could, not here. And certainly not the mundane swords that the two knights carried.

Fat Harold didn't even try to draw his swords from where they were strapped to his back; there was no time for that. Say what you would about him, Fat Harold was neither a fool nor a coward; they would be upon him before he could so much as turn and take a step.

He leaped at the darklings, his only words a shouted "Run, Butcher, for the love of God, *run*—" and his strangled screams were awful in the night.

It was Edward's only chance. An exorcism, this close to the Zone, couldn't kill them—but it could repel them.

All he had to do was run down the trail, run away, while the darklings finished with Fat Harold, and try the exorcism.

He could, at the least, flee—it wouldn't be cowardice; this should be reported.

No.

He was, after all, a knight of the Order of Crown, Shield, and Dragon; an emissary of light, not dark. The light was supposed to triumph over the dark, but there were no guarantees in this world.

Save one: what he would do was in his own hands, and those were the hands of an Order Knight, who would not abandon his companion.

How it would turn out would be in the Hands of God. He drew his swords and tossed his scabbards aside. He would make the sign of the Cross with his swords . . . and they had other uses, as well.

"I exorcise thee, thou foul and unclean spirit, in the name of God the Father Almighty, and in the name—"

Edward de Vigney died, his exorcism turned to screams in his own throat.

He never did see the plain beyond, where the bones of the Blue Skolt and their reindeer herd lay, still frozen on the hard ground.

CHAPTER 1

The Falconer

It was a glorious day.

Well, that was one opinion; the falcon didn't seem to share it. In fact, the hooded bird was annoyed, but that didn't annoy Mordred. He'd known that the saker was by nature irritable, and that the bird was more trying to claw through the thick leather glove than simply holding onto it wasn't surprising, and in fact he found it charming.

Falcons were amazing creatures, all of them, each special in its own way, not just as breeds but as individuals, as well. This saker was perhaps a touch larger than most, almost twenty inches long, and its dull brown color was relieved by the pale head, which emphasized the two dark brown stripes running down either side of its beak, which looked like mustaches even more than similar markings on the peregrines.

This one was a particularly tempery bird, and it was not happy. Even through the leather glove, even hooded, the bird could tell Mordred's hand from another, more familiar, one. This griping was just a mild reminder that he hadn't been handling the bird enough himself, leaving it to the old cadger and his apprentices. Falconry was, of course, the sport of kings, but kings had many demands on their time, and of the dozens and dozens of nights spent walking the birds, all but one of them with this bird had been left to Old Thomas and his apprentices.

It wasn't that Mordred V, by the grace of God Pendragon King of England, Scotland, and Ireland, among other places—as well as a score of other titles, including the obligatory Defender of the Faith—avoided the privileges and pleasures that came with the crown, any more than he skimped the responsibilities.

It's just that the responsibilities left him little time, and falconry, done properly, took much time.

Falconry had been a passion of his youth—no; it had been *the* passion of his youth—and these days he barely found time to occasionally hunt with the birds, and almost none for the endless work of raising and training them.

He loved it all. Every bit of it. Walking the birds; working with leather, shears, punch, and awl to make the hoods; winding the creances carefully around the spindles so that they could unwind smoothly and easily without pulling the bird out of the sky. Mucking out the mews, even, as strange as that would have sounded to anybody else.

A man had to have his pleasures, after all, and if others would have found some of those pleasures of his too common, well, that was a matter of contempt to Mordred, and he sometimes lied to himself that when Eric turned twenty-five or so, he would abdicate in his son's favor, and spend the rest of his life mucking out the mews and handling the birds. And, of course, hunting with them on every fine day, and a few foul ones.

It was a lie, and he knew it.

The Crown would pass to Eric upon Mordred's death, and with the traditional cry of "The king is dead! Long live the king!" and not some comical "The king has abdicated to go play with his birds."

Old Thomas cleared his throat, clearly to grab the king's attention, then frowned at the saker. "Not quite out of the molt, you know." He glanced back over his shoulder at the rest of the entourage, most of whom were back at where the woods broke on the clearing, and Mordred repressed a grin.

Old Thomas was worried about the damage to the King's dignity if the bird failed. Charming.

"I'm passingly aware of that," Mordred said, giving the gentlest of tugs at a loose neck feather, which immediately came away, and drifted off in the wind. "Tickle his feet a little, I think?"

"Bowse him a bit, I think," Old Thomas said, already pouring water from the lambskin water bag into the wooden bowl. He didn't wait for Mordred to nod assent before raising the bowl to just below the bird's beak.

The saker drank greedily; quite the little bowser, he was; Thomas quickly took the bowl away, lest he overdo it.

"And if anybody were to be asking me," the old cadger went on, "I'd say that he should best be flown on the creance today, and not hunted."

"Ah, yes, but then how would you expect him to get me a conie?"

Thomas smiled. "Well, there is that. But a conie caught by another bird would taste every bit as good, I'd guess."

"Not to me," Mordred said, smiling. "Not today."

This clearing in the King's Preserve, north and east of Pendragon castle, was for obvious reasons devoted to the king's own use, and the rabbits—although not the deer, probably for the reason that Mordred suspected but had deliberately decided not to take notice of—had become unwary and brazen. Even now, he could easily make out half a dozen munching on the greens that had been planted as bait at the far edge of the clearing, and while occasionally one would raise himself up and take a look at the humans hundreds of yards away, the rabbit would quickly go back to his foraging.

Thomas jerked a thumb back toward where his apprentices were situated, halfway back toward where the woods broke on the clearing. Three of the king's other birds were already hooded and perched on their blocks, and a half dozen more waited in their wicker cages.

"I'd still say," Thomas said, "that if it's a conie you're wanting, one of the peregrines would do as well, and quite likely better at that. Or the goshawk, the merlin—"

Mordred stopped him with a quick frown. "I've never had much affection for merlins."

"Your father didn't mind the name."

"My father wasn't named Mordred."

Thomas just sniffed, as though to say that only the most superstitious twit would worry that the handling of a bird with the same name would somehow bring back to life the legendary wizard of Arthur the Tyrant, and enemy of Mordred's ancient namesake. Mordred was the fifth Pendragon king to bear the name, and if he was the first such to find merlins not his favorite of falcons, that was among his many prerogatives.

Mordred would tolerate the sniff, but it was just as well that Old Thomas hadn't taken further liberties with his words. As his cadger, Mordred was far more interested in Thomas's opinions on the birds than he was in a private lack of decorum and proper acknowledgment of his station. After all, the late, unlamented Duke of York—Mordred's uncle—so history had it, had always been studiously respectful of his brother the King, to the point of obsequiousness . . . up until the moment that he'd tried to have Father and the then-infant Mordred assassinated, so that he could take the Crown for himself. He had come perilously close to success.

Had it not been for two knights—one of the Table Round, the other of the Order of Crown, Shield, and Dragon—Mordred wouldn't have reached his third birthday, and would have missed not only the endless responsibilities and duties that came with the crown, but, far more tragically, a gorgeous day like today, with nothing more to think about, at least for the next while, than whether the new saker would stay with his kill, return to the lure, or have to be chased into the forest.

As with the birds, dogs, and his servants—from the meanest of indentured serfs to the Crown dukes, even though the latter were Pendragons themselves—Mordred was far more interested in them doing their job well than in how much bowing and scraping they did while doing their job.

Still, the borderlines of propriety were sometimes fuzzy, and sometimes sharp—but Thomas had come far too close to taking a definite step over.

Mordred met his eyes for a quick moment, and Old Thomas looked away.

"Begging your pardon, Your Majesty," he said.

"Accepted, but not necessary," the king said. The gentle lie was not only a useful tool of state, but of other interactions, as well. Real steel always waited inside the velvet glove, after all.

Others were behaving much better. A short troop from the House Guard waited patiently just within the shade of the road leading into the clearing, as did the much smaller party accompanying Mordred's uncle, William, the Duke of New England—no soldiers, just a few servants, and, of course, Sir Joshua.

Patience was a virtue, but like all virtues, it could be overdone. Mordred had waited far too patiently for William Pendragon to take time away from colonial affairs to pay a call on and homage to his king; keeping Uncle William waiting, yet again, while Mordred enjoyed the morning seemed both fair, and a reminder.

It wasn't as though the duke had to wait alone, after all, or in discomfort; a small table and chairs had been set up, and since Mordred was far enough away that Uncle William wasn't officially in The Presence, he had chosen to sit, rather than to stand. If the wind had been blowing in the other direction, Mordred would have been irritated with him smoking his pipe, but it wasn't, so he wasn't. Besides, it was unlikely that tobacco smoke would startle these conies; they were very brazen.

The four Order Knights that served as the king's personal bodyguards were nowhere in evidence, which was to be expected. Assassination was always a possibility, and while the king made a point to take his excursions randomly, there were always concerns. A quick skulking through the woods at the edge of the clearing would serve better than the knights standing at the king's side to see if his back began to sprout bolts or arrows, after all.

Mordred tickled the bird's feet, just a little. It seemed to calm him, but not as much as Thomas's frown said that he would have liked to have seen.

"I always want your opinions," Mordred said, "about the birds. And that opinion would be that this one won't come back? That we—" He stopped himself. "—that you and the boys will have to go chase him down? Or that he might fly away altogether?"

Thomas took a long moment to consider his answer. "There's that risk." He seemed to want to say more, but only went on when the king made a beckoning gesture.

"Out with it, man. With no due respect for my station." After all, the borders of propriety might be fuzzy or sharp, but they were, after all, Mordred's to set, his and to move at will.

"It's just that, well, a saker is a common knight's bird. Seems unseemly that the king would have such an interest in it—particularly if it flies off. And never mind the kestrels, for the moment, much as I know you love them."

Has there been talk of that? he didn't ask. If he didn't know, he didn't have to deal with it. Backstairs gossip was, of course, commonplace, and unremarkable—as long as it wasn't brought to his attention.

Mordred actually preferred kestrels, particularly the New World one, which should probably have been named something else, although it would have been much to expect that the naturalists of New Eton would have thought that *falco sparverius* would have been of interest to a royal falconer, any more than *falco tinnunculus* was. Falconry had never seemed to take on in the New World, or most other of HM possessions, in the way that it had in Inja, say, and, besides, kestrels were considered appropriate for servants and children. Small, easy to keep fed, although the New World ones were a challenge to train—but they couldn't handle prey larger than a field mouse. But they were bright, clever, and easy to hand, and . . .

Enough woolgathering. The morning was getting no younger, and the claque of ministers and secretaries waiting back at Pendragon castle were probably doing just that—waiting. And then there was Uncle William.

"Different birds for different prey," Mordred said. "And I'm curious to see if this bird is ready. The only way to find out, I think, is to try him."

He unhooded the saker, and gave it a moment to settle. After a quick look around, its eyes locked on the conies across the field, as he had hoped. A good sign.

He raised his glove and released it. Its wings pinioning, beating hard against the air, the bells from its jesses jingling in a mad fandango, it beat its way high up into the air, then spread its wings, circling over the clearing, high above the west end of it, where the rabbits waited.

It was always an exciting time when you released a new bird, and the king could feel his heart thumping hard in his chest, as he readied himself for the stoop, and the kill, and the run.

The king's big Arabian gelding stood waiting patiently, a servant holding the reins, but Mordred had no intention of mounting it and riding just a couple of hundred yards across the clearing when he could run across the clearing as quickly as he could ride—yes, the horse was faster, but it would take precious seconds to mount—and retrieve the bird and its prey without assistance.

It would be every bit as fast and much more personal to dash ahead of Old Thomas—who wouldn't be able to run as fast—and the apprentices—who wouldn't dare run faster than the king—and get his hands on the bird himself, without the aid of a horse.

For a moment, the saker seemed to hesitate in the air, as though debating whether or not to flee, but then it dropped into a gorgeous stoop, and dove down—

"And now . . . " Thomas murmured.

And the bird swooped low over the ground, then beat its wings, climbing back into the air, its talons empty. It had missed.

It circled again, tentatively, as though considering making another try, but then it banked off and away; the jingling diminished in the distance as the saker flapped away, out of sight, over the huge elms that rimmed the far side of the clearing.

Mordred gave Old Thomas a look, and then clapped his hand to the old man's shoulder. "Well, it seems that my eagerness will cost your apprentices some work this morning."

Chasing down and luring an escaped bird was time-consuming, and the king, alas, had no time for it, although he would have loved to have spent the rest of this beautiful morning in that pursuit, or anything else involving the birds.

The old man had already turned to where the apprentices were standing, and pointed two fingers; the two boys he had indicated took off at a run for the far side of the clearing. "Don't think I'd trust that bunch of thumb-fingered dolts to coax the bird down. But they'll find him soon enough, and I'll see what I can do. I don't think I'll lose the bird for you."

"It was too soon to turn him loose," the king said.

"Perhaps." The old man nodded. "But it had to be done sooner or later. And there's always the risk, no matter how long you've trained him. We'll work him some more, and hunt him again. Maybe next month, or the month after?"

"Perhaps."

Without another word, the king walked back to where the others were waiting on the road. Unsurprisingly, as he reached the shade and cover of the tree line, the four Order Knights known collectively as His Own had quickly surrounded him, although remaining a respectful distance. Etienne of Marseilles looked much the worse for wear—it looked as though he had forced his way through brambles and nettles, which spoke well for his dedication, if not his woodsmanship. But, like Walter and the Beast—more formally, Sir Walter Davies and Sir Sebastian Cooper—he was where he belonged, and it was only a matter of moments until John of Redhook joined them, stepping out of the shrubbery as though he was walking out a door.

Mordred repressed another smile. Big John knew that section of woods better than most; even a woodsman with his skills wouldn't have been able to make it through the blackberry brambles beyond the stand of elms without doing some damage to his clothing. While the others had been making their way about the circumference of the clearing, Big John had stationed himself near where the Duke of New England was, able to get quickly between him and the king, if necessary.

The Order Knights didn't speak to each other or to anybody else, and their eyes never even met the king's.

Truth to tell, he liked the company of some of them, and not of others, but the tradition is that one of His Own on duty—whether it was watching believed-to-be-loyal nobility and long-serving servants in the king's Pendragonshire preserve, watching from behind or next to the throne at a formal reception, or sleeping across the king's doorstep—had no other obligations at all, not even so much as to acknowledge the other of their Order who stood a few careful paces away from the Duke of New England.

Mordred waved away a proffered tray of sweetmeats, but pointed at a goblet of water, and drank it greedily, wiping his chin with the back of his hand where it dribbled. Water only, dammit. He would not contaminate his personal ritual of a celebratory glass of wine—that was for a successful kill. It wasn't for when the only thing to celebrate was that the old cadger had, once more, shown that he knew his trade.

Oh, well.

Uncle William was smiling openly, as he took the stem of his long, New World-style pipe from between his tobacco-yellowed teeth.

"A nice attempt, Your Majesty," he said, perhaps a little too loudly, as though to make it clear that his smile was a congratulation for the attempt, rather than a comment on the failure. "For a moment there, I'd thought that you had him."

"For a moment, so did I."

William Pendragon wore his years well. While he complained, both in letters and more recently in person, that the affairs of New England were constantly occupying every waking moment of his time—and permitting little for even sleep—his appearance belied the claim. Beneath his tunic, the chest was still almost peasant-broad, and had not sagged down to become belly. His healthy color—which he had arrived in Londinium with, three months ago—was that of a man who spent a fair time outdoors. And while more than a few men his age blackened their hair, William Pendragon's vanity extended only to the perfect grooming of his salt-and-pepper hair and beard, and he kept his dull gray hair both dull and gray, eschewing both dye and pomade.

The queen had been very impressed with Uncle William, and Mordred didn't think it was just a matter of her trying to play on the jealousy that she knew that Mordred didn't have. She had her own court, in practice, and he had his, and as long as she kept out of politics and kept her affairs discreet and without issue, it was no concern of his. One very easy way for a courtier to lose favor with the king was to suggest, no matter how indirectly, that the queen's affairs were something that he should take notice of. All one had to do was read Mallory to know how badly that could turn out.

"Such things happen," the king said, turning to the man standing beside the duke. "What do you think, Sir Joshua? Old Thomas has had the bird in training for most of a year; was I too eager?"

He was watching the duke more than Sir Joshua Grayling as he asked, and noted with some satisfaction that the duke didn't seem surprised that Grayling didn't quickly answer with what no doubt all the others expected would be a quick denial that the king could ever make a mistake.

Mordred smiled. Uncle William had practically been dragged across the Atlantic by Gray, and knew him well enough by now to understand that, to Joshua Grayling, "Service, honor, faith, and obedience" included answering his superiors' questions honestly and bluntly, with less care for how things sounded than most, although with more care than a very few others that Mordred could name.

Sir Joshua Grayling was, as always, arrayed in the distinctive clothing of his order: a long, black, belted wraparound jacket over his white tunic, and that over loose trousers that had been bloused into his boots. The jacket was belted tightly across his narrow hips to support the two scabbarded swords that he wore, with their preposterously plain sheaths and hilts.

The leather cup that covered the stump of what had been Grayling's right hand rested near his waist, but not on anything, while the fingers of his left hand, as usual, seemed to keep themselves near the hilts of his swords, although, as usual, he didn't move to touch a finger to the metal of either hilt.

It didn't look protective; it looked like a challenge— there was something in his stance that seemed to suggest that he was constantly daring anyone else to take one of his swords, but perhaps the king was mistaken.

Not that any other man would have wanted to lay hands on the live sword. Even the whitest of White Swords would burn not just the body but the soul of the one who touched it, save for the one it was linked to. Once, as a boy—he had been far too impulsive as a boy—Mordred had deliberately reached out and laid a finger on the protruding hilt of the Goatboy, when Sir Alvin was guarding Father. While the wound had long since healed, the memory of the agony was as sharp and painful now as it had been on that day.

Gray's face was, as always, impassive; the nose too sharp and narrow; the eyes dark and recessed. Mordred had no doubt that the man could feel emotion, but had only once seen a trace of it on his face.

"Of the noble arts," Sir Joshua finally said, "I was never very much for falconry, Sire. Other activities have always occupied my time, and I'm a weak hand with the birds." Was that a shrug? "Makes me a poor judge of such things. I guess the only way to know was to try, and see, Your Majesty."

The king nodded. It was gratifying to hear that, from Gray, knowing that if Gray had thought that trying the bird had been a bad decision, he would have said so.

"It's that way with birds," the king said. And with other
creatures, for that matter. You had to, at some point, try
them out, and you could hope for success, but only a
fool would count on success. "Sometimes you find that
your judgment was right; sometimes wrong. Even if
you're king."

He was reaching out his hand for his own pipe, when
a cry sounded from far behind him, and he quickly
spun about.

Old Thomas, his legs moving with a speed that belied
his years, was running toward the far edge of the clearing,
whooping and hollering like a New World saracen.

Damn.

He had missed it.

He carefully set the goblet down on the outstretched
tray, although he wanted to smash it, and smash both his
uncle and the knight, whose conversation had distracted
him while the saker had circled back and made his kill.
A good strong kick to Old Thomas, who had not interrupted the conversation, was also a temptation.

But, no.

It wasn't their fault, but his. He had let himself get
distracted, and that the matters that he had been distracted by were of more importance than the hunt was
no excuse; this was supposed to be *his* morning.

Oh, well. He had invited the duke along, and it was
Mordred who had permitted the distraction, not the
duke who had insisted on it.

In a few minutes, Old Thomas was proudly marching
back across the field with the bird on his glove,
unhooded. It didn't rouse at all, but just glared angrily
at all and sundry, as though to express scorn for their

having doubted that it would make the kill—in its own time, in its own way.

Behind, one of the apprentices followed with the limp body of the rabbit, already properly gutted, fat drops of blood dripping onto the grass.

Mordred forced himself not to scowl. The bird had come back, and it had gotten the rabbit, and Mordred had missed both the thrill of the stoop and the kill, and the unalloyed pleasure of the mad dash across the field.

"Well, we eat tonight," the king said, mildly resenting the chuckles that echoed around him at the weak joke. Although it was only partly a joke—potted conie would be set before him at table this evening, or he'd know the reason why. "And we'll be sure to give a special tidbit or two to Cully, here."

At the mention of the bird's name, Gray's entire body seemed to twitch, but he didn't say anything.

The king just smiled at him. "All in all, I thought I named the bird appropriately—and the evidence of today makes me think I was right. He got the prey, but in his own time, and in his own way. A fitting description of Sir Cully of Cully's Woode; I think. Would you disagree?"

Eyes widened as Gray thought about it for a moment. "Incomplete, Sire, but fitting, certainly," Gray said.

"Now, if I were to name a bird after you, Gray, what breed would you prefer?"

Gray seemed to consider the matter. "Perhaps a saker, too, Your Majesty. Or one of lower ranking. A kestrel, say—the common one, rather than the New World one."

"Hmm." Mordred frowned. "I think of you and Sir Cully as very different sorts of birds, yes, but I'd hardly think of you as a kestrel. Uncle?"

"If you want similarity with Sir Joshua, I guess you'd have to pick a crippled falcon with one wing. Which wouldn't be useful." He said the words lightly, as though making a joke at the nonexistent bird's expense, rather than Gray's.

Mordred cocked his head to one side, controlling his expression as much as his body. It wouldn't do, he supposed, to slap the Duke of New England across the face. It would be something to discuss later, in private.

In detail. With short, curt words, many of them unsuited for polite company.

Sir Joshua Grayling had lost his hand in the service of the Crown; his stump was a badge of honor, not something to be mocked.

And it was not just his hand; he had lost more, perhaps. It was hardly a secret from those of the Order or from the king that Gray thought that his bearing of the particular live sword at his waist—a Red Sword, of course—had damned him.

Mordred had studied theology in his youth, among many other things, and he privately disagreed, although it was among many religious opinions that he kept to himself. Religious discussions were something that the king had best avoid, as more than two of his predecessors had demonstrated all too well.

This matter, in any case, had been muchly discussed and debated, for a couple of centuries after the creation of the live swords during the Age. The position of the Church of England was that whether or not the souls trapped in the Red Swords were damned, the use of them in support of the Church and Crown was laudable, if possibly a temptation to sin, and that God, in His

Grace, would surely not damn a knight of the Order even for taking something unholy to hand, if his goal was the support of the Church, and the Crown. After all, while Jesus had chased the moneylenders from the temple, and condemned the love of money as the root of all evil, even He had not condemned the use of money.

Mordred would, of course, make what judgments his nature and his position required; he tried to avoid others.

But none of the theologians who had written on the matter—nor the archbishops and kings who had made such rulings—had ever joined their own souls with a Red Sword, and there was something to be said for the notion that a knight who believed something from experience had knowledge that no amount of book learning and debate could teach others.

But it mattered not even a little if Gray was right—in Mordred's view, Gray's soul was every bit as expendable as his body was, in the service of the Crown. A saved soul was one's entry to Heaven, and that was all well and good—but Mordred was a man of this world, of this Crown.

But that sacrifice, were it real or honestly mistaken, was not something that Mordred would have mocked, and there would be words with the duke, in private, on that, and this mockery would not be repeated. And particularly not to Sir Joshua.

The Duke of New England's smile was in place. Good. Self-control was important in a ruler, and either Mordred had had the restraint to keep a trace of his fury from his face, or Uncle William the self-control to not react to it.

Gray's face hadn't changed in its lack of expression, but the fingers of his remaining hand had dropped to

touch the hilt of his uppermost sword, although not gripping it as if to draw it—he just touched a finger to the
metal. It was a common gesture among knights of the
White Sword, and less so among Red Knights. Communion with the holy was often reassuring; Gray's communion with the Khan undoubtedly wasn't.

"A saker, perhaps," the king said.

The Duke of New England nodded. "I like sakers
myself," he said. "A good choice for hunting conies. I
use them to hunt weasels, as well." He grinned. "And
even such a minor heir to the Pendragon name as a
Crown duke needn't worry about using a bird below his
status, eh?"

The king forced a smile. "There is, after all, only one
other present who could correct you on the matter. . .
and I enjoy sakers, as well."

William wasn't all that minor an heir.

The Duke of New England, as the king's eldest uncle,
was third in line, after the princes—and it was no accident that there were no New Englanders serving aboard
the *Tusk*, where Eric was a midshipman, and that both
he and John were guarded both carefully and separately.
Eton, where John was, was another matter, of
course—there were young New English noblemen at
Eton in abundance, over from the colonies. It wouldn't
do to be too obviously worried about some treachery,
and in fact, Mordred tried to worry about it as a matter
of policy, rather than out of some grounds for suspicion,
and most of the time, he was successful.

No. If this duke betrayed him, it would probably be
to declare New England independent from the mother
country, not a repeat of the York Rebellion.

Probably. But when the princes made a tour of the New England colonies—as Mordred had never done, although he wished he could have been able to do it—they would do it separately, not both at the same time, much less together.

Princes royal were, if necessary, expendable—but singly, and not en masse.

As were kings, come to think of it. But not now, not when Eric was too young to rule, if not to reign, and who knew who Parliament would name as regent? Perhaps even the Duke of New England? William was very popular at Parliament, and not just for the carefully selected gifts that had accompanied him, along with Gray, across the Atlantic. He had a smooth but not too-smooth way about him, and seemed to be able to moderate his New England drawl to precisely fit the circumstances.

Too good with words? Perhaps.

Well, leave that worry for another day. They all were waiting patiently for the king's next words, so he really ought to find some.

So Mordred just smiled at Gray. "Well, I've thought on it," he said, "I don't think a saker, or a kestrel. A gyr, I think, would be more appropriate." A gyr. A noble's bird, big, beautiful, and deadly—capable of taking much bigger game, and killing with dispatch before returning to the hand. "Always fit the bird to the task, eh?"

The duke didn't like that, but Gray's face was impassive. As usual.

Well, as long as he didn't grip the king's hand tightly, Mordred could live with that.

CHAPTER 2

Highlands

This is what we do. This is who we are.

—Becket

The two men stepped silently out of the darkness, and into the light of the dying campfire.

The night became quiet, instantly. Spring nights near Cannich tend toward the quiet and dark, and sounds never travel far in the thin air of the Highlands.

The apparently insatiable McGlennon brothers had still been taking turns with the girl, although Dughall didn't see much point to it, by now. Being the leader, Dughall had gone first. A matter of taste; old William

used to like to let some of the younger bucks soften them
up a little first, but old William was dead these three
months, and Dughall had different preferences. The
fresher, the better, was his way of looking at it.

When Dughall had taken his turn with her, hours
before, the girl had been so lively that it had taken four
other men to hold her down—although not too firmly;
Dughall enjoyed the squirming—but that had, after all,
been hours ago, and all of the fight had long since been
taken out of her.

Well, it wasn't as though they were going to keep her;
she'd end the night with her throat slit. Nothing else to
be done about it.

At least the sheep and goats could be driven over the
mountains and down the other side to be sold in Rhanich,
or perhaps closer, at Tean-ga na Dubhaird. It wouldn't
quite be impossible to sell a girl, and in fact they had
more than once ransomed one back to her clan and family, but not this time—she was just a crofter's daughter,
and her parents had been poor in life, and were dead
now. It was said that a man with the right connections
could sell anything in Rotterdam to a Guild trader, but
even if Dughall had those connections, Rotterdam was
a long way away, and he had never in his life come far
down out of the hills, and knew that he would be like a
fish flopping on a lakeshore if he tried.

"Stand easy," the older one said. Not in the mither
tongue, of course. English, with a heavy Sassenach
accent. "Put up your arms, the lot of you," he went on,
seemingly addressing all of the dozen raiders.

He was a wide-shouldered, squat little man, his head
bare save for a wreath of mussed hair. His voice held a
definite, almost comical lisp.

Michael Gwinnie, the stealthiest of them all, had been off to the edge of the clearing, wrapped in his cloak for the night, but he was gone now.

Good. Get them to talk while Michael made his way around behind them.

Dughall couldn't tell anything about his complexion under the bright moonlight that gave his face the same ghastly, ghostly complexion that it did everyone, but, even so, the older man had the look of the south about him. No proper beard; just a bristle of mustache, and no whiskers on his fat cheeks and many chins. He started to take a step toward the McGlennons, but desisted at a minimal head shake from the other one, and besides, young Davy had rolled off the girl, and was eying his gear lying nearby, something that the young one seemed to have noticed.

No weapons had come out, yet.

"In the name of the king," the younger one said, "lay down your arms and surrender, and I swear that you'll be given a fair trial before you're hanged."

He was even more of an outlander than the Sassenach; his voice held an almost musical lilt.

"I guess we have no choice." Dughall rose slowly, laid his own broadsword on the ground before him, and dropped to one knee. "I'll accept the king's justice," he said, formally. "Accept my sword as its token."

He hoped, for a moment, that the younger one was going to step forward, but the moment was gone when the older one snorted.

"And he should ignore the *sgian dubh* strapped to your hairy thigh?"

Well, it had been worth a try, although he hadn't much hope for the ploy. That was the traditional purpose of the *sgian dubh*, after all—to stick into the belly of some Sassenach demanding surrender or fealty, turning the moment of defeat into one of victory.

"Surrender now, or die now," the younger one said.

"Sounds awfully generous of you, under the circumstances." Dughall laughed as he rose and brushed himself off. "And I'd suppose that you've got a whole troop of Mordred's soldiers hidden in the woods?"

Granted, there had been a troop of soldiers—probably the earl's troops, but possibly the McPhee's—chasing them for the past few days. But once you got up into the rocks and the mist that you knew as well as you did the back of your hand, it was just a matter of letting them trail you through increasingly difficult country until they got tired of it, and went back to the lowlands.

The younger one shook his head. "No."

"That you're not just a couple of travelers who have stumbled into the wrong place, and are pissing yourselves in fear?"

The younger one didn't appear to move, but his cloak slid from his shoulders and fell about his feet. Beneath it, he was dressed in very strange garments: over his white tunic he wore a short black robe, split down the front although wrapped tightly about his chest. His leggings were bloused into his boots. The short robe was belted at the waist with a plain sash, and two scabbarded swords were stuck through it.

Two swords? And this outlandish garb? *No.* It couldn't be.

"There's much to be afraid of here, but not the lot of you," the younger one said. He let his hand rest on the hilt of one of his swords.

It couldn't be, but it was—the short black robe, the sash, the two swords . . . The only men that Dughall had ever heard of who carried two swords were knights of the Order, Mordred's—some called him King Mordred, but Dughall bowed before no king, and no clan chief, either—personal bodyguards and bullyboys.

"Sir Niko—"

"Shush, Nigel," he said. "They must be given a chance to surrender. Mercy."

Surprisingly, this Nigel chuckled. "As you wish, young sir." He leaned on his staff. "You're going to have to kill the lot of them, you know. And—meaning no disrespect, Sir Niko—you're no Cully of Cully's Woode or Gawaine the Legendary to take on so many with the sword that I resharpened for you just yesterday. You'll need the other."

It was hard to make out the Sassenach's words; he had a dreadful lisp that in other circumstances Dughall would have thought comical.

"Be that as it may." The young man turned back to Dughall. "You're the leader of this band of clanless scum?"

"Aye, although I'd dispute with any steel you care to name the—"

An arrow sprang from the side of the young man's chest. He looked down for a moment, as though he couldn't figure out what it was supposed to be, then wrenched it out with a quick pull.

"Bad choice," the one called Nigel said. "Should have gone for the head."

Dughall had never seen anyone move as fast as the young man did when he drew one of his swords and tossed the scabbard aside.

Red light, impossibly bright, flared, not just in his eyes, but in his mind.

And then it was all pain, forever.

Niko stood over what was left of the bodies, Nadide scabbarded, his hand carefully holding the scabbard, not letting his finger rest against her steel.

It got easier each time, he thought, and was vaguely disgusted with himself for that.

So be it.

When Niko first moved, Fotheringay had of course made a dash for the girl, and covered her with his own body, as Niko would have told him to, had it been necessary. It wasn't necessary, or possible, for Fotheringay to protect her from Niko and Nadide—but it would have been tragic if one of the bandits had managed, in his death throes, to fall upon her.

A wedge of surviving grass and shrubs marked the spot where the stocky little man was slowly working his way to his feet. Fotheringay was capable of rushing, when need be, but there was no need here, no need now: the rest was just destruction.

The bodies and parts of bodies lay smoking on the dead ground, ground where nothing would grow for years, if not forever.

Niko turned. The bodies of the five at the edge of the clearing were still smoking, and—thank the Good and

Kindly Ones, although never even think their names!—the awful smell of roasting flesh was carried away on the night wind. There were those who said it smelled like roasting pork, but they were either idiots or liars. It smelled like roasting flesh; utterly horrible.

He thought for a moment about chasing after the two others, the two who had managed to flee into the dark and mist. But there weren't more than those two left, not from this band, and they knew this strange land better than he ever would. No point in it. Landless, clanless men, outlawed . . . they were only dangerous when they were gathered together, with some leadership.

At least, that's what Becket had said. Among other things.

Still, he wanted to go after them. Justice was to be tempered by mercy, yes, but not by laziness, not by exhaustion.

It was hard for Niko to keep his feet beneath him. Using Nadide—using the sword was always that way, and it didn't seem to get any easier. His hands were trembling, but he had found that if he fastened his thumbs in his sash, the trembling wasn't perceptible to anybody else.

That would have to do.

"I'd not suggest we go chasing off after them," Fotheringay said from behind him. "We'd never find them, not at night, not even if they were blazing a trail, Sir Niko."

True enough. And in his woolgathering, he was neglecting his duty. He turned to where Fotheringay was kneeling over the girl. "Is she alive?"

"No." Fotheringay shook his head. "Sorry, sir."

Damn them. Damn them all. And him, too, for that matter—if only he and Fotheringay had been a touch faster.

"Not your fault, Sir Niko; the body's already getting cold. She was dead when we got here. Seems that they didn't know when to stop." He stripped off a kilt from one of the raiders, and moved toward the girl, as though to cover her with it.

"No," Niko said. No. Enough of them had touched her in life.

Fotheringay didn't protest. He rarely did. He just dropped the kilt to the ground, and stripped off his tunic, revealing the reticulated plate chest piece underneath, and laid his own tunic gently over the dead girl's face.

"Sorry, Sir Niko," he said. "Bled to death—I think one of them ruptured something . . . " He gestured awkwardly, " . . . inside."

It was hard to speak, but he forced his voice to obey his will. He could do that.

"I'll do what's needful." It would be better if Fotheringay could, but, of course, he couldn't. Fotheringay was a man of faith, in his own way, but he wasn't a priest, even in the limited, mostly false way that Niko was.

Niko dropped to his knees beside the body, and made the sign of the Cross, first on his own chest, and then across her forehead. It was warm to the touch.

"Glory be to the Father, to the Son, and to the Holy Ghost," he said. "As it was in the beginning, is now, and ever. Amen." There was no emotion or intensity in the words; he just spoke them quietly, quickly, as though trying to get them over with, as indeed he was.

The magic was, he had been taught, in the words and the office of the man who spoke them, not in the tonality in which they were pronounced. "Incline Your ear, O Lord, unto our prayers, wherein we humbly pray Thee to show Thy mercy upon the soul of this, Thy servant. . . "—his voice didn't break; he didn't let it—"Thy servant whose name we knoweth not, whom Thou hast commanded to pass out of this world, that Thou wouldst place her in the region of peace and light, and bid her be a partaker with Thy saints, through Christ our Lord. Amen."

The words didn't mean much of anything to him. The Order could require much of him, but not meaning, not sincerity. Service, honor, and obedience; yes. Faith, too, but faith in what? Yes, he had taken the oath, but his oath couldn't compel him in that, no matter how hard he tried.

Fotheringay hadn't said anything. Niko looked over at him.

"Amen," the older man finally said. "And for the rest?"

Niko looked at the bodies and parts of bodies strewn across the clearing. " 'Service, honor, faith, obedience. Justice tempered only by mercy; mercy tempered only by justice,' " he said.

"Yes, sir," Fotheringay said. "And how would you be applying that, Sir Niko? Leave them where they fell, in the name of justice? Or give them a decent Christian burial, in the name of mercy?"

"What do you think?"

Fotheringay shook his head again. "Not my place, sir. And, by and large, I do know my place, rumors to the contrary." His grin seemed forced.

"And if I pressed?"

"Then I'd let the crows eat out their eyes, Sir Niko. I'd put up a sign threatening the life of any who gave this lot a proper burial, or failed to piss on the ashes as he passed." Fotheringay spoke without heat, without emotion. "But I'm known to be more of a sentimental than a generous man."

"And if I said that we'll bury each one of them, properly? And give them last rites?"

"Well, then, I'll stand, head bowed, while you give them their rites, and I'll bury them for you. At your command, Sir Niko."

It would have been easy to just do what Fotheringay wanted to do. It was tempting.

But let their judgment come from Another, if he and Nadide hadn't already damned them anyway.

"We'll bury them," he said.

Fotheringay had already retrieved a camp shovel from the bandits' gear. "Aye-aye—I mean, 'as you wish, Sir Niko.'"

"Nigel—"

"I mean no offense, Sir Niko, and pardon me for the interruption, but if it can wait for later, Sir Niko, can you leave it for later?" Fotheringay's broad face was as impassive as it usually was, and his voice didn't seem to be overly controlled, but . . .

"It can wait."

They got to work, and took turns with the shovel, and for once Fotheringay didn't offer even the expected muttered complaint about how something as common as grave digging was beneath Niko's station.

The soil of the Scottish Highlands is hard and rocky, much like the people who live there; it was midmorning before they had finished, and at that they had buried the raiders only shallowly, in a common grave at the entrance to the clearing, as though leaving them on guard for the cairn in the center that held the body of the girl.

Fotheringay used the blade of the shovel to hammer a rough cross into the ground at the head of the cairn. He didn't look toward the south, but he gestured toward it. "A troop on the way," he said, then frowned. "Could have waited and let a bunch of McPhees do the digging, as it happens."

"Shut up, Nigel," Niko said.

Fotheringay gave him a toothless grin. "I've got my virtues, sir, and I'll be the first and p'raps the only man to swear to them. But if I was any good at keeping my mouth shut when I ought to, I'd still be sergeant in the Blue, sir, and not sweaty from digging a hole that a sergeant would have privates to dig for him." His grin widened. "Not that I'm complaining, mind you, but . . . " He cocked his head to one side. "Twelve, maybe fifteen horses."

Niko cocked his own head to listen, but couldn't hear anything.

This was such a strange land, all of it. The whole idea of being able to walk for days without so much as smelling the sea, much less seeing it, was something that he still wasn't used to.

And even when you did see the sea, it was different— dark, harsh, threatening, never the pleasant blueness tinged with dark that he had grown up with, that had been, save for a few bits of land, his whole world, back when he had been Niko the fisherboy.

It was frustrating. Everybody else seemed to understand things without effort that Niko couldn't duplicate, even with effort.

Michael, even without the aid of his gamekeepers or woodsman, could follow a boar's trail anywhere within a day's ride of Fallsworth, and that wasn't considered unusual for a young nobleman. And when the future baron turned his hand to a bit of blacksmithing, even the dour McLennahan would admit that he had a fine eye for color, and a steady hand with a hammer.

Niko's teachers at Fallsworth, both formal and informal, were preposterously skilled at their own trades. As Niko was with the one he had been raised in.

But there was little call for the skills of a fisherman there.

And it wasn't just the teachers. The two novices who acted both as Becket's attendants and, at least in theory, as Niko's fellow students, were accomplished at all of the knightly arts and crafts that Niko was utterly clumsy at.

Scoville—Niko kept forgetting and calling the boy by his first name—didn't seem faster than Niko, but he could score on him easily five-to-one, when they went at it with practice swords.

And never mind how useless Niko's hand was when he turned it to his letters, while both of the novices could turn out page after page in glorious quantity and quality.

And Fotheringay—Fotheringay had heard the horsemen easily a minute before Niko could begin to make out the faint clopping of their hooves on the hard ground.

Fotheringay had dropped his own rucksack at Niko's feet and pulled out a water bottle and some rags.

"I can wash my own hands, Nigel," Niko said.

"That's true enough, Sir Niko, but you can't see the dirt on your face better than I can, you being without a mirror, and the dirt on the back of your neck you can't see at all," he said, ignoring Niko's vague protests as he gave Niko's face a quick and not particularly gentle scrubbing, then pulled off Niko's tunic, letting him shiver in the cold air until he replaced it with a fresh one, then helping him replace his swords properly in his sash, finishing just before the first of the horses came around the bend.

Fotheringay congratulated himself with a brief nod that as much as said that he had, once again, made his master presentable in time.

It was good to have the fat old man at his side, and not just because Niko would have, more than likely, been too distracted to deal with matters that were, for reasons beyond him, important, but didn't seem important. Why an Order Knight should always appear to be fresh, crisp, and untouched was beyond him—although Becket certainly belabored the point, more than enough. There were some things you had to take on faith, and Fotheringay's attention to the right details was one of the easier ones.

Niko wasn't surprised to see the McPhee at the head of the party, although Fotheringay seemed to be, and if Niko could read his expression aright, Fotheringay didn't much like it.

"Sir Niko," the leader of the McPhee clan said, leaning forward to where his thick hands rested on the peak of his saddle, "it appears that we're too late to do anything, save congratulate you." From the back of his huge, Campbell-bred gelding, he seemed almost tiny, boylike in size, if not in age, what with the heavy scrub of red-brown beard that covered his face. "And, perhaps, inquire as to the clans that gave birth to the dogs," he said, as he climbed down from the saddle and dropped heavily to the ground. He stalked over to where fragments of kilts lay on the ground. "No tartans, of course—the dogs would have worn plaincloth," he said, fingering a singed scrap. "But I wonder if perhaps this was dyed dark? Be interesting to see if the dye could be removed, and find some trace of McGlennon or MacDonald beneath."

"Perhaps that decision should be left to Sir Martin," Niko said.

"I've no objection. Sir Martin's palanquin should be along shortly," the McPhee said, "although I can't see why he'd not want to know, too. I thought it better to move the rest of us along and see if we could be of some assistance, than to wait. In the meantime, it looks like the sheep and goats that the bandits stole are scattering?"

Niko hadn't given the animals a thought. "Yes, certainly— I . . . I can't see why you wouldn't want to have them rounded up."

The McPhee was a surprisingly small man, all in all, not what Niko would have expected in a clan chief. Thick-bearded and barrel-chested, the only thing that distinguished him in appearance from his clansmen-soldiers was that the cloth of both his blouse and his kilt was more densely woven than the others, coming from finer fabric; it was of precisely the same dense green-on-red pattern that Niko had learned meant clan McPhee, as opposed to the broader red squares of the MacGregors.

One of his soldiers said something to him in the local language, as though protesting, but desisted at a nod of the McPhee's head.

It wasn't fair, but life was often not fair. Knights of the Order were supposed to be learned men, as well as everything else, and while Niko of course spoke fluent Hellenic and enough Arabic, Turkish, and Shqiperese to get by, he was having enough trouble with Francaise and Latin, and understood barely a few words of Gaelic.

"In English, man, English," the McPhee said, with a quick glance to Niko, "and—"

As though ignoring the order, which he probably hadn't heard anyway, a soldier toward the rear of the troop called out something in that incomprehensible Gaelic.

The McPhee frowned. "Well, we've got a wee bit of a problem," he said. "One of the outriders"—he gestured toward a ridge to the north and east—"has spotted a party of MacDonalds coming up the . . . " He paused for a moment. " . . . up the Road Where Donald Gibbie Died Bravely—doesn't sound quite so grand in the English, does it?—and we've got half an hour or so before their arrival. Less if they flog their horses; more if they split their party and have one half swing about to cut off retreat. About forty of them, all in all," he said, with a frown. "Obedient to the earl's orders, I am, and a peaceable man by nature, but—"

"But this will not become a skirmish between the two clans," Niko said, as he knew he had to. That was why Becket and he had been sent here.

Minor feuding among the clans was, basically, inevitable, and could be handled by the local earl's forces, or

perhaps the Crown duke's, if it didn't start to spiral out
of hand too quickly, too dramatically. But the forces of
the Crown were stretched thinly across the world, and
far too many of the regiments had been seconded into
the king's service—the Kindallaghan Guard was keeping
the peace south of Vlaovic, while the Blairgowries were
just recovering from the disaster at Jelgava, where supposed bandits that everybody knew were really Imperials
had more than decimated the garrison.

Some cattle or sheep stealing? Hardly anything to take
notice of. But even a small band of bandits striking along
clan boundaries was the sort of thing that could easily
become much larger, and much more of a problem—and
sending in troops to put down open warfare between the
clans was always a bloody thing, and had been necessary
far too often, so Niko had been told. The Glengarry
Massacre of 1542 had become part of Scottish myth and
legend, as well as history.

Stopping problems while they were small was just pissing on fires, Becket called it, and it was among the duties
of the Order, and if Sir Niko didn't see any great glory
in such mundane matters, that would have to be his
problem.

Niko didn't see any glory, but it wasn't a problem.
Why Becket expected him to care so much about glory
was one of the many things that he didn't understand.

"Whether or not there is to be fighting, perhaps, is up
to the MacDonalds, Sir Niko," the McPhee said.

He knew what was required. "No. It's not. It's up to
Sir Martin, and to me. This will end here."

"Well, I guess we'll see as to the accuracy to that. You
won't mind, Sir Niko, if I make some preparations just
in case you're wrong?"

Niko had been about to say something—he wasn't sure what—when Becket's palanquin rattled into view.

It wasn't surprising that it had taken much longer for Becket to make it up the road, which was far too rocky and broken in places for any carriage or cart. His traveling palanquin was supported by two sullen dray horses, more suitable for plowing a field than for conveying a knight of the Order of Crown, Shield, and Dragon.

Niko hurried to where the lead rider was already dismounting, and managed to beat Scoville to the door.

Scoville kept his face studiously neutral, something he did around Niko except when in his cups, and usually even then. While Thomas Scoville was two years older than Niko, and far more adept at all of the knightly arts, he was still a shaved-headed novice of the Order, albeit a fourth-former, and Niko was not only Sir Niko Christofolous, a made knight of the Order of Crown, Shield, and Dragon, but a knight of the Red Sword, as well.

Michael Winslow, who was still at the side of Becket's palanquin, was easier to read, and upon not infrequent occasion less restrained in his muttered comments.

Niko touched his thumb to Nadide's steel.

I don't think he really hates you, she said. *But how couldn't he resent you?*

It wasn't competitiveness that had Niko at the door, and handing Becket down to the high-backed chair that Michael had quickly unfolded. It was just that, well, it was something that he knew how to do, and the fact that Becket's mostly limp body was closer to twelve stone of limp meat than further from it didn't mean anything more than a mild annoyance. Niko the fisherboy had hauled more weight than that up to the rocky beach at home—at his former home—in the nets, and his muscles had not been given the opportunity to go soft under Becket's tuition, after all.

"Hurry up with it," Becket whispered, almost limp in Niko's arms. "I've disgraced myself again, and I'd rather that the whole damn world doesn't share in it."

Sir Martin Becket was a human wreck. His service in the order had left his legs crippled and barely able to move. His shoulders, though, were massive, and his arms thickly muscled, although when his sleeve slipped open, the scars that had severed tendons and left his right hand useless showed, and he had retained only the thumb and forefinger of his left, beyond the stubs.

But then there was the face. His beard had been neatly and properly trimmed, and the cheeks shaved—although how Michael had managed to do that in a bouncing palanquin without cutting the old man's face to ribbons was something that Niko wouldn't have believed possible if he hadn't seen it himself, on more than one occasion.

But there was Becket's face. It was, still, the face of a knight of the Order, and it showed more in the eyes than the beard, eyes that missed nothing, and could see right into the soul of a man or boy.

Still, Becket smelled of piss and shit—his injuries had long ago lost him control of his bowels and bladder—despite the earliness of the day. Niko was vaguely familiar with all the details, although Becket had the novices attend to his needs, which included the sausage-skin tubes whose open ends had to be tied around the old man's penis, the tubes terminating in a former wineskin bag tied to a leg, and which Niko quickly concealed with a blanket.

Not that they could do anything about the smell at the moment, but the novices were quickly erecting the portable screen from the back of the palanquin. Given a few moments, they could give the old knight at least a modicum of a sponge bath, get him into fresh swaddling and clean robes.

But for now, Niko belted Becket into the chair, and tucked a blanket tightly around Becket's lap and over the restraining strap, and left it at that. Save, of course, for the final step—he quickly retrieved both of Becket's swords from the palanquin, and set them in the boot on the left side of Becket's traveling chair.

He was rewarded with nothing more than a glare from Becket's shockingly blue eyes.

Becket surveyed the scene. "Well, you handled it bloodily enough, I suppose." He cocked his head to one side. "Any idea of the clans of the bandits?"

Niko shook his head. There hadn't been any formal introductions. He didn't even know the Christian names of the men he had killed, much less their clan affiliations. "I'm sorry, but no."

"Hmmph," Becket said, his scowl making it clear he disapproved. "The thing about information, fisherboy, is that if you don't have it, you can't use it. You can't decide whether or not to share it, or conceal it, or—" He shook his head and snorted in disgust. "Well, I guess it was about to be expected. I know that the abbot's been none too impressed with my reports on you."

As always, Niko waited for the words he had been expecting for more than a year: *You'll not do as a knight, Niko. Go back to being a fisherboy.*

The abbot general, of course, would have supported Becket. Ralph Francis Wakefield, both archbishop of Canterbury and the abbot general of the Order of Crown, Shield, and Dragon, had no use for Niko, and particularly no use for Sir Niko Christofolous as a knight of the Order of Crown, Shield, and Dragon, and even more particularly no use whatsoever for the notion of Sir Niko being a knight of the Red Sword.

He had made that abundantly clear in their one interview, shortly after Bear's funeral, that one word from Sir Martin was all that it would take to have Niko stripped of his knighthood—and, of course, the sword—and that nothing that Baron Shanley, Cully, or anybody else could do or say would reverse that decision. His Majesty had decided to give Sir Niko a try—but the moment that Becket found him wanting, well, that try would have been accomplished, that moment would be his last in the Order.

But, once again, Becket just shook his head. "And now, with the MacDonalds on their way . . . there wouldn't happen to be precisely fourteen of them, would there?"

Also as usual, Niko didn't know what Sir Martin was getting at. "The McPhee said forty, not fourteen, Sir Martin."

"Forty." A quick nod. "Good. Or, rather: it should be good, and it should be a curb on the McPhees' temper, if the damned Scots were capable of being sensible. Which they aren't." He chuckled. "Pity that *prima nocte* has always been a ritual of loyalty for the past few centuries, rather than what it was in the Tyrant's time; with any luck, some English sensibleness could have been bred into these barbarians, and some of the young lasses are, well, delectable; it'd be a rare baron or earl who wouldn't enjoy the exercise. But enough of that." He shook his head. "I was thinking of the number fourteen? It's a number of some significance to our Order, and a second-year novice should have picked up the reference. I know you've studied Mallory; I watched you move your lips excessively as you read."

Niko didn't quite understand how Becket's eyes could become all distant and vague, and at the same time make it appear as though the old knight was reading from a book in front of him, but he did.

"Book XXI, Chapter IV," Becket said. " 'Then were they condescended that the false king, Arthur the Tyrant, and the true king, King Mordred, should meet betwixt both their hosts at the field of Bedegraine, and each of them should bring fourteen persons, and no more; and they came with this word unto Mordred.' Do you remember any of this?"

"Yes, Sir Martin." Niko nodded. "Yes, I remember." Yes, he had studied Mallory, although he didn't have the way of memorizing that Becket and the novices had.

Arthur the Tyrant and Mordred the Great had met between their armies, to try to make peace, as though such a thing was possible. Oh, there was a bargain: Mordred was to have Kent, and the Crown after Arthur's death—unless, of course, the Tyrant had managed, as all knew that he would try, to have Mordred assassinated and a bastard conceived by Lancelot the Damned on Guinevere the Whore, as he surely would have, and as he had been trying to do, to cheat his son out of his patrimony.

It was hardly the Tyrant's first attempt to kill his only begotten son, after all. The bargain would not have held, but Mordred the Great had seen enough destruction done to his people, and he was willing to make it, and deal with the consequences later.

There wasn't to be a later. The Tyrant could not give up on his treachery.

One of Arthur's knights—Niko couldn't remember Mallory well enough to have said which one it was; Dinadan, perhaps?—shouted that he spotted an adder in the grass, drew his sword, and made straightaway for Mordred, and had it not been for the fact that Mordred had chosen as his companions the very first of the knights of the Order of Crown, Shield, and Dragon, the Pendragon dynasty would have ended there in reality, if not in name, with Mordred dead on the field at Bedegraine, the impotent Tyrant unable to conceive a son upon his wife, and a battle for the Crown upon the death of the Tyrant.

But it hadn't ended there.

Yes, this was before the Age of Crisis, and the knights of the Order of Crown, Shield, and Dragon had no Whites nor Reds among them. And, truth to tell—for Sir Thomas Mallory had written the truth as he knew it, both for good and ill—when the fleeing Mordred had first found himself among them, they had been but a group of bandits from the Arroy, preying on travelers and villages beyond the Bedegraine and retreating into the Arroy when pursued.

They had little armor, and were probably even more clumsy with swords than Niko was, as banditry was accomplished with a bow and a dirk, not armed head to foot from the saddle of a warhorse.

But they were, after all, knights of the Order, the first of their kind, and while Mallory had never been clear on the point, how could they *not* have understood that what they did there would set the pattern for their successors?

Sir William Stutely had been to Mordred's right, and Sir John Little to his left, and Sir Arthur Tanner stood before the king, and as the two hosts rushed together in battle, they and the rest of the Order Knights had protected the king with their swords, and their shields, and their bodies, until tens of thousands lay dead about the field, leaving but Red Will and the Tanner alive amongst all the Order knights, and the Tyrant to face Mordred the Great, alone.

And while Mordred's blade had shattered on Excalibur, Mordred had still closed with the Tyrant, and cut his throat with the shards of the shattered sword.

Then, if you believed Mallory, Mordred had turned to his knights, his face full of black anger and red grief, and said to them, "With this sword I have slain my father, and am ever after a despicable parricide, despite the provocation, and no fit company for decent men, and you, my faithful servants, must leave me, and my service," and then threw the broken hilt upon the ground.

" 'And then,' " Niko said, quoting, for he owned at least some of the words, " 'Sir Arthur and Sir William knelt down before the king, and Sir William picked up the hilt of the broken sword, said unto the king, I beg of thee: 'swear that thou shalt send not thy servants from thy Presence, Sire, and if there be any burden from Your actions this day, we shall pray to God that they will be our burdens, not thine, for the one you slew was the

Tyrant Arthur, murderer of babies, and unfit to rule our land.' "

And the king took up the sword. Ever since, the Pendragon Kings had been crowned while holding the hilt of that shattered sword high above their heads, with no man standing closer to him than knights of the Order.

There the history ended, although not the legends.

Becket nodded, just as the sounds of hoofbeats reached Niko's ears. He called out to the novices. "Get this damned chair over there," he said, his good hand gesturing toward the road where the McDonalds were approaching. "Then stand back and aside, the lot of you."

"And let you face them alone?" the McPhee asked. "I'd not like to have word of that reach the earl, should things go badly."

Becket turned to stare the McPhee down. "You and your men *will* keep still," he said. "No matter what should happen." His eyes locked on the McPhee's until the Scot nodded.

"As you command, Sir Martin."

The boys quickly conveyed Becket's chair to the center of the road, then backed off, while the McPhee grounded the last of his men, with muttered orders in Gaelic that Niko couldn't follow, but had them clutching the reins of their horses with white knuckles.

Niko was never sure why the man at the head of the troop of MacDonalds halted just a few feet in front of the man in the wheeled chair, but sure enough, he did, although horsemen behind him started to spread out, fingers clutching at sword hilts.

Thomas, the elder of the two novices, stood by Niko's right side, while Fotheringay had taken up a position a little to his left, with Michael beyond them.

If it all fell apart, it would be up to Niko, and Nadide. Four men couldn't hold two troops of soldiers apart.

The foremost of the MacDonalds looked more French than Scottish to Niko's eyes—his hair was dark and straight, and he had a delicacy to his features that made him look almost pretty.

He said something in Gaelic to Becket. Gaelic, dammit. The McPhee had told *his* men to speak English, at least when Niko could overhear them. It wasn't just courtesy, Niko thought, but that the McPhee didn't want Niko thinking that they were planning any treachery, as though even Niko couldn't figure out that treachery could simply be planned in his absence.

Still, without being prompted, Thomas leaned over and whispered in Niko's ear. "He said, 'And what have we here? Do the McPhees have a new pet?'"

"Fair knight," Sir Martin said, "I pray thee tell me thy name." The formal language seemed to come to his lips naturally, although most of the time Niko felt like a fool when he practiced it.

That seemed to take the MacDonald back. "I'm no knight, but my name is no secret," he said, his Scottish accent thick and guttural. "I'm Donald MacDonald."

"There be many named Donald among the MacDonalds, and the ClanRanads of Cromarty are no exception," Becket said. "Art thou better known elsewise?"

Some of the men behind the lead MacDonald said something, and the leader nodded.

" 'I'm known as Donald Gwinnie, mostly, which means much to someone from Carlops, and probably little to you, whoever you might be,' " Thomas whispered. " 'An' so much the worse for you, or you'd know better then to speak so boldly to me, even if you weren't a cripple.' "

This Donald MacDonald looked across at the waiting McPhees. " 'Davy Bella, there, might be able to identify me, if that'd be a help to you; we've traded cows, and sheep—and insults and blows—on a few occasions. Not thought much of him, him being a McPhee, and all, but I'd not expected to find him standing over a fresh-dug grave that, I'll warrant, contains the body of my clansman's daughter, nor standing between MacDonalds and livestock stolen from my kinsmen.' "

Some of the McPhees started grumbling at that, only to be silenced by the McPhee himself.

The McPhee took a slow step forward. "At another time, I'd want some satisfaction over the slur on my kinsmen," he whispered, desisting at a be-still motion from Niko.

" 'And you are?' " Donald McDonald asked.

"I am Robert, son of William; I am the McPhee," the McPhee said. "We were in pursuit of the same gang of bandits that you seem to have been."

" 'Pursuit, eh? They raid into villages and crofts to the north and east in MacDonald land, and yet you pursued them from the south and west?' "

"You don't think they've been raiding only into Mac-Donald land, do you—"

" 'And why would a bunch of McPhees be raiding—' "

"*Silence!*" Becket thundered, his eyes on Donald Mac-Donald. His body was crippled, but his voice was strong. "I have asked thee thy name, Donald Gwinnie MacDonald of Carlops, and thou hast given it, as is only proper—but thou hast not asked me mine."

"Why would I want to know the name of an old cripple who conspires with thieving McPhees?"

Thomas had started repeating the words in Niko's ear, even though the rider had started speaking in English; Niko waved him away.

"That was most discourteously said, and I shall not abide it," Sir Martin said. "For no man, noble or common, kicks dirt on the name of Martin Becket without he be held to answer for it."

This MacDonald snickered. "Then let us have at it, Sir Knight," he said, slowly dismounting. "But if you think to distract me while your allies attack my clansmen, you'll have bought them but little time."

"A knight of the Order of Crown, Shield, and Dragon means what he says, and says what he means," Becket said. "I'm sure that after you've killed me, your men will fall on the McPhees, and that they'll give a good accounting of themselves, for McPhee is an honorable name, and they are honorable men.

"But you are forty, and they half as many. Still, you'll find the price of their lives high, and those deaths bought not easily, but dearly.

"As to me, you may find my life bought quite easily, but perhaps most dearly of all." He raised his good hand. "Bide but a moment, an' it please you. Sir Niko."

Niko was at the old knight's side in a moment. "Yes, Sir Martin." His hand was near Nadide's hilt, and his eyes were on the Scot's, not on Becket's.

"You're thinking to avenge me on these MacDonalds, when I fall," he said.

Well, yes, he assumed that was the plan, or close to it—that he was to draw Nadide and fall upon the troop, in the hopes that he would be in time to save Becket's life.

And to add another forty souls to his tally. The thought made him want to gag.

"No, Sir Martin," Niko said, "I think to try to see that not one of them so much as lays a finger upon the hem of your garment."

"No, Sir Niko," Becket said, shaking his head, "for that would be an unknightly thing to do. The challenge was offense that was given to me, not to you, and not to the Order. Yes, the offense is great, and it will become greater—and, as such, it must lay heavily not just on this one, not just on these two score, but on the clan they represent.

"You are not to save them from the dishonor that they bring, Sir Niko.

"In the name of our Order, I do charge you, as Mordred the Great charged Sir Thomas the Rhymer: make your escape; take to your heels; flee. On your honor, Sir Niko—you are to run away." He raised a hand and pointed to a nearby ridge. "Watch as I defend my name, and the name of our Order. Watch as these MacDonalds strike down not only a knight of our Order, but two novices, and then kill half their number of McPhees—all who are as innocent of these crimes as is Our Lord Himself.

"And let the king know, let all of our Order know, that Donald Gwinnie MacDonald of Carlops, leading a troop of MacDonalds, has struck down a knight of the Order of Crown, Shield, and Dragon, who but stood in a roadside, politely asking his name. Let the name of MacDonald be known for what it shall become: the name of coward, the name of bully, the name of the murderer of the innocent."

Donald MacDonald's face whitened, and his jaw clenched, and he started to say something, and his hand went to the hilt of his sword.

But Niko already had Nadide in his hand.

And the world changed.

It was always the same; it was never different, although he would never remember that later. It wasn't clear when he touched his finger to Nadide's steel, and they could talk with one another in the quiet words that nobody else could hear; it was only clear, it was only right, when he drew her from her sheath, and the two of them became one.

It was like recovering a lost portion of himself, of herself, of themselves. Colors somehow became much brighter, without being blinding; light itself pulsed redly through his tendons and veins. His own heart, which had been pounding like the tattoo on a navy drum, slowed to a *lub-dub*, *lub-dub*, that was so loud and strong that it should have been deafening painful, but he could barely hear, he could feel no pain.

No: *they* could feel no pain. They were one: Niko the fisherboy and Nadide the infant, sharing his body as much as the steel that either imprisoned or sheltered her soul. The sweet taste of the milk from the breast of She Who Smells Like Food was as utterly familiar to them as the weight of a net straining against the kicking of a madly flailing tunnyfish.

They were one; they were no different; they were as they always had been, always would be.

It was the rest of the world that had changed about them, and they were merely right with the world and more than right with themselves.

That part of them that was Nadide blazed brightly over their head, brightly enough that it would have dazzled human eyes more than the sun could, although not even the brightened sun could do so much as make him blink. It would have been trivially easy, a nothing, to step in front of Becket, to protect him and burn down not only the MacDonald before him, but all the other Mac-Donalds behind that one.

And why stop there?

They didn't know what the limits of their destruction might be, could be, would be.

Perhaps it could not be as great as that of the Khan that Gray carried, or the Sandoval borne by the false Knight Alexander Smith, but that was by no means certain. Burning down the bandits had been easy, and they could still taste the destruction not just of their bodies but of their souls, and it was a rich and heady brew, intoxicating in the way that milk of the One Who Smells Like Food had been, even moreso than the winter wine served at table at Fallsworth.

And these were mean men. They wanted to hurt.

They were bad.

Striking out at them would not only be right, but it would feel good. They, the part of them that was Nadide, had been hurt by the foul-smelling one, the one with rough hands, the one with the shiny thing that they now knew was a knife, and these mean ones had knives, all of them. No, they didn't smell the same as the foul-smelling one, the one with the rough hands, the one with the knife, but all of the men about her, about him, about them had knives, and would hurt, and they would—

No. There was that lullaby that they sang to each other. Not the one about the cabbages, the one that Niko sang that to her silently, on nights where they had trouble sleeping, and which eased both of them into dark, comforting sleep.

It was the other, the one about mercy. About honor and obedience.

They didn't understand much about honor, and it was hard for them to think about mercy; it was easier to just obey the one with the broken body and unbroken spirit.

So they ran. They ran past the first of the Campbells and right through the pack of horsemen, like a dolphin slipping through the water, barely disturbing the pack of sardines in its wake as it fed.

Except, of course, they didn't feed.

They didn't understand why, not really, but they were on their honor to flee, though it would have been so easy to just pause for a moment, to touch the fire of their steel to any of the men, but . . .

No. They were on their honor to run, and so:

They ran.

Niko never remembered releasing his hand from Nadide, although obviously he had; she was stuck through his sash, above the mundane sword that almost miraculously remained there. His breath came in gasps, and he had somehow managed to abrade the knees of his trousers, leaving them in bloody rags. His tunic felt pounds heavier, and was sweat-soaked beneath both arms.

He touched a finger—just a finger—to her steel.

Niko? You're hurting.

Not badly, little one. It's just a few scrapes, a little pain.

The pain was nothing he couldn't bear, but the exhaustion dropped him to a crouch, and then to the ground, the pain of the sharp rocks beneath his buttocks much less than that of the fire in his lungs.

In the clearing below, Sir Martin's chair still held his body, as the MacDonald stood before him, his men spread out an arc around and behind him, while the McPhees stepped forward. Over to the side, Nigel Fotheringay had gripped each of the two novices by the arms, pulling them away.

He—

No. Praise be to Zeus, to Athena, to Neptune, and to Jesus and all the saints!—Becket's good hand was raising his limp arm above his head, his fingers spread clumsily in what still was the sign of the Order, as McPhees and MacDonalds alike were busy stacking their swords and spears in two separate piles before him, watched over by Fotheringay, whose bald pate gleamed in the sunshine.

And, in a ragged wave, each and every man, McPhee and MacDonald alike, dropped to one knee before the knight of the Order of Crown, Shield, and Dragon, who sat in his wheeled chair, no doubt still stinking of shit and piss.

Niko just sat there, his breath coming in ragged gasps, watching the MacDonalds reclaim their mounts, while the McPhees reclaimed their own, and as the two parties slowly rode off in separate directions, the MacDonalds chivying their livestock ahead of them.

Sir Martin Becket sat in his chair until they were all gone, and then made a small gesture, and the novices rushed to his side, and pulled his chair from the road.

Niko shook his head, and when his eyes were clear, he retrieved his gloves from his belt pouch, and started to make his way slowly down the side of the ridge, careful not to let Nadide slip from his sash.

The night was chilly, as nights often are in the Highlands of Scotland, and the four of them had gathered about the fire that Fotheringay had built. The old sergeant was good with a fire kit, and almost preposterously adept at finding fuel, whether it was thumb-thick base roots from dead scrub, or the blocks of peat—where had he found a peat bog?—that now gave off a gentle, pleasant heat.

The horses had been watered and hobbled for the night, and fed enough that they'd not be tempted to wander far while grazing. Wolves were always a possibility, of course, but the night had been quiet, without any howling of a wolf pack, and the ruddy dray horse was known to be nervous, and particularly quick with an alarm.

Becket had long since been taken from his traveling chair, and lay propped nearer the fire than he should have been, although he made no complaint, despite the way that the sweat rolled off his forehead.

Niko had expected Becket to say something about the morning's events, but perhaps he should have known better.

Instead, Becket had had Michael pull a battered copy of Herodotus from the palanquin, and had him read a few chapters by the firelight, correcting his Hellenic constantly—Michael seemed to have much trouble with the pronunciation of "Alcmaeonidae," for reasons that escaped Niko.

It was an easy enough word, after all, but neither of the novices was terribly good at Hellenic, which was surprising, given how easy a language it was, and how fluent they were with much more difficult ones. He had offered to tutor them in it, of course, but Becket had dismissed that with a sneer. He had enough of his own studying to do, after all, Becket had said, and was making precious slow progress at that. Master his own skills, and then perhaps, someday, he might be able to teach others.

The day, or perhaps the single mug of wine that Becket allowed himself, had Sir Martin nodding off while Michael read, and he finally shook himself, fighting with his sagging eyelids. "Ah, I think I'm to bed," he said, and without a word, Michael closed the book, and the two novices rose and began to prepare his bedding, a few yards to the lee of the fire.

"And I think you might be well to bed yourself, young sir," Fotheringay said, rising.

"I'll tell him when he's to go to bed," Becket said, with a decided snap to his voice.

"Of course you will, Sir Martin." Fotheringay didn't hesitate. "And surely he'll obey you, as is his duty, as surely I'll prepare for him, as is mine," he said, choosing his words slowly, with obvious care.

"And you'll speak when spoken to." Becket's voice seemed to soften, as it often did when addressed to Fotheringay. He sighed. "And at other times, as well, I suppose."

"That's as it will be, Sir Martin. You may teach the young master as you see fit, and if much of that seems to be merely trying to run him ragged, you'll hear no complaint from the likes of Nigel Fotheringay, about whom not much good can be said, save that he knows his place. But when Sir Niko is permitted to go abed this night, he'll have clean blankets over soft grass to sleep on, and he'll have clean clothes to put on in the morning, as that is my place, Sir Martin."

"And if I tell him to sleep on cold stones, and tell him to put on the very robes I've soiled today?"

"Then he'll obey you, I'm sure, Sir Martin—but he'll do so with his own blankets, soft grass, and his clean clothes nearby. That would be your doing, Sir Martin, not me failing the young knight." Fotheringay drew himself up straight. "Knights aren't the only ones who know their duty, sir."

Becket gave a long stare at Fotheringay.

The truth, of course, was that being Niko's manservant was a matter of Fotheringay's choice, not an obligation. The old Marine sergeant could have, after the affair of Better-Not-to-Think-the-Name-of-Where, taken not only his Marine pension, but the OC that His Majesty had said was due upon his retirement; the only thing he had left Londinium with was the promise of Order of the Crown. He had gone back to the Fleet, only to show up at Fallsworth but a couple of months later, asking Niko for a position as "the dogrobber that a young knight such as yourself ought to have."

Niko had, of course, said yes, and while he had occasionally hinted at his obvious curiosity as to what had gone on that had brought Fotheringay to Fallsworth, his hat quite literally in hand, Fotheringay had never said. Niko found himself unable to ask, although he had his suspicions about Fotheringay having gotten himself in some trouble, trouble that Niko didn't want to officially know about. If he didn't know about it, he didn't have to cover for it, after all.

Maybe it mattered; maybe it didn't.

But he couldn't have said no.

He remembered not only Fotheringay standing next to him on Better-Not-to-Think-the-Name-of-Where, but later, on a windy Portsmouth dock, and Fotheringay stepping between Niko and a troop of soldiers, after a whispered, casual promise that he'd spend his life buying Niko the time necessary to get Nadide free from her sheath, ending with, *You can't count on much in this world, but you can count on that.*

It hadn't been necessary for Fotheringay to prove that he could do that; the soldiers had turned out to be their escorts to the king. It hadn't been necessary to prove that he would try to do that; Niko had no doubts, then or later.

But Fotheringay hadn't known what would happen, and Niko could still hear that whisper in his mind. Turning Fotheringay away? That had only crossed his mind as something impossible to do, disgraceful to consider.

Niko found the whole idea of others doing for him to be strange, certainly enough, but it was convenient. When it was allowed.

Becket insisted that Niko wash his own clothing, and maintain the two-room suite in Fallsworth that the baron called the "Red Suite," but Becket invariably referred to as Niko's "cell," and do all the rest of the work of maintaining his gear and equipment, just as the other—as the novices did, and Niko did that, and Becket insisted on constantly inspecting his work, to be sure that he wasn't slacking off.

Niko didn't. He was clumsy with most of the tools, and all of the languages, and all the rest of the usages of knights, but he wasn't lazy, and, truth to tell, the dawn-to-dusk regimen of a knight in training was less strenuous in most ways than what he had lived with, day to day, as a Pironesian fisherboy. Hours and hours of the work of a knight in training, after all, involved sitting at a table, reading—in the daylight!—when he should, by rights, have been deepdragging nets across a far-too-often rocky bottom.

Fotheringay, of course, had his own ideas about what was proper for a young knight, and was perfectly capable of taking a stack of clean tunics and trousers out to the laundry in the back of the keep, rewashing them, and then ironing them himself, and more than a few times Niko found that the often clumsy mending and patching that he himself had done, obedient to Becket's orders, had miraculously, overnight, been transformed into much finer work.

That hadn't gone over very well with Becket, of course, but Baron Shanley had taken him aside, and had a word with him. There weren't many men that Becket would hear out, but the baron was one of them.

Becket finally nodded. "Very well. You may be about your work."

Fotheringay didn't move until Niko nodded, but then he walked off beyond the wan circle of the fire's light.

With obvious discomfort, although no grunt of pain, Becket managed to move his body until he could face more directly toward Niko.

"Tomorrow, we'll start to make our way down to the coast. We can report to the earl on the way to the duke. Then, if there's no word waiting at Dunbeg, we'll see whether it makes more sense to head back to Fallsworth than over to Colonsay." He almost grinned. "The baron's to be summering at Colonsay, you know."

Niko was aware of that, and didn't need to be reminded that to Becket "*the* baron" was always Giscard, Baron Shanley. Who, of course, when he summered at his Colonsay home, would be accompanied by his wife, Grace, who, true to her name, was as gracious and gentle a gentlewoman as there was in all of England, Niko was sure.

Even though she hated him.

Which is why if the Shanleys were on Colonsay, Niko would rather have been going back to Fallsworth. It wasn't the baron, as much as the baroness—she blamed Niko for Bear's death, he knew, although she had not let a word pass her lips to that effect. In fact, she treated him with exquisite formal courtesy that would have seemed warm if the hate hadn't always shown behind her eyes.

But he didn't say anything.

"Not a bad day's work, eh? A few clanless bandits planted in the soil, and a clan war at least put off for another day, and probably much longer."

There was no question at the end of Becket's words; Niko knew better than to respond.

"Be slow in your Latin; speak French like the Hellene that you are who can't even lisp the word *monsieur* properly; bounce up and down on the back of a fine warhorse like a sack of potatoes; and, if you must, wear the robes of the Order as though they're some sort of St. Swithin's Day costume that ill fits you, no matter how well it's tailored," he said, quietly. "Perhaps you can still be a true knight, and fail in all of that even now; it can be learned, I'm told, although I'm still skeptical about that, when it comes to you. We shall see.

"But understand this, Niko: this is what we do. This is who we are."

CHAPTER 3

Lowlands

The right bait for a trap is always essential, whether it's cheese or lambs. If you want to trap a mouse, you use cheese; for the wolf, it's lambs. If the Lord won't forgive me for no longer baiting even the right trap with my own lambs, I guess that will have to be a matter He can take up with me.

The admiral, of course, has his own bait. And if that includes me, well, it's no worse than I deserve, and perhaps better.

—Cully

The night was too bright, although only a crescent of moon showed.

If Sir Guy had been a superstitious man, the crescent would have bothered him, as it reminded him far too readily of the Star and Crescent that waved above every city, town, village, and probably latrine of the Dar Al Islam, but superstition was one of the sins he was able to avoid.

Still, the further west on the Izmiri coast you went, the closer you got to Antalya, and Koosh, for that matter. Not the safest of waters in any case. The Empire still claimed sovereignty over all of what had been Turkish provinces, but that, as the saying went, when the emperor or his so-called pope spoke, it shook the ground in Constantinople, shook the knees in Cernivici, and shook the belly with laughter in Izmir.

Although maybe the laughter shouldn't have come quite so easily.

Even in its present, shrunken state, the Empire could have easily reconquered its way down to the Mediterranean, at least through Turkey. The Empire was not what it once had been, but it was nothing for a small former province to trifle with.

Still, such a move would have brought the Empire into conflict with both Crown and Dar, and while the so-called Emperor and his so-called pope were certainly fools, they likely weren't that foolish. Much better to leave it as a buffer zone, and eventually let the Crown and Dar fight it out, and hope to pick off the winner. That was the sort of cowardly thing you could expect from the Imperials.

"Do you think you're ready?" the admiral asked—and he asked Cully, not Sir Guy. At least he had addressed Cully, and not Kechiroski.

Cully shrugged. "As ready as I'll ever be," he said. "As soon as those clouds pass across the Moon."

And he shrugged again. If a man of as mild a temperament as Guy of Orkney could be irritated over a gesture, Cully's shrugging would have irritated him mightily. Even more than the admiral treating Sir Cully as though he was the senior Order Knight aboard, when Sir Cully carried merely two mundane swords—when he carried them at all—while Sir Guy was a knight of the White Sword, carrying Albert. Proper decorum would have required the admiral to be consulting with Sir Guy, who was, after all, in both law and fact, the senior of the two.

But, no; DuPuy was unfailingly polite to Sir Guy, but when it came time to ask a question or advice on a decision, it was to Sir Cully that he went, and that should have been utterly maddening.

But, naturally, it wasn't anything of the kind. Sir Guy was capable of sin, of course, but not that one; he was of a mild temperament. Still, without moving his thumbs from where they were stuck in his sash, he touched his little finger to Albert's steel, and was rewarded, as always, by the sense of peace that washed over him, as he imagined that a cold glass of wine would, although he was abstemious in that, too, and allowed himself no stimulants, save for his occasional . . . lapses.

He first tried not to think of those, then forced himself to. That was, after all, part of the nature of penitence: to remember the sins that had been washed away, to help him avoid their repetition.

Yes, Guy, it is. All is forgiven the penitent, but nothing is forgotten.

He let his finger fall away; a miserable sinner like himself didn't deserve the reassurance that came from the intimate contact with the saint who had voluntarily had his soul imprisoned in the whitest of White Swords during the Age, and had, as far as Guy knew—and no man living could know better; Sir Gustav had finally died the year before—not had the slightest regret in the centuries since of delaying his entry into Heaven to better serve both God and king.

Purity of the soul was hard enough to attempt to maintain, and sinner that he was, the attempt was all that was possible. Purity of the body was but a small step in aid of that.

Sir Guy failed, all too often. He still recalled the drunken night of debauchery in Pironesia, and it would have been tempting to blame Cully. After all, Cully had insisted that Sir Guy share a glass of retsina in the tavern, quoting St. Paul to St. Timothy: "Have a little wine for the sake of your digestion."

But, no. That one glass of wine had turned into many, and not one of the many had been forced down Sir Guy's throat, after all, and while he could not remember most of the rest of the evening, he did remember his shame upon waking up in the crib with the slattern.

At least, in Pironesia, there was an Anglian to hear his confession, and not just Cully. Cully would probably have, once again, insisted on too light a penance, rather than the self-flagellation that the Anglian had acceded to, to accompany the dozen rosaries.

Cully seemed to think of drunkenness as, at worst, the mildest of sins, and Sir Guy didn't want to know what he really thought of fornication in his priestly capacity, although to be fair, if Cully had been sneaking off to visit the whores, he had done so with great discretion; Sir Guy had been watching him for just that sort of lapse.

As least Cully was sober at the moment, and while DuPuy had quaffed at least three glasses of wine over dinner, he seemed to be steady-legged on the slowly rolling deck.

He didn't look like much of an admiral. He affected utilities aboard ship, rather than wearing a proper uniform, as though he was a dockside junior lieutenant running a crew of seamen stevedores. Worse—his utilities held not so much as a tab or braid of rank; it was an insult to call them a uniform.

The captain hadn't made a word of complaint about that, although Sir Guy had tried to draw him out, with no success whatsoever.

Well, at least the affectation didn't extend to DuPuy's aide, Lieutenant Emmons, who seemed to always be in a fresh uniform, no matter what the hour, although he really looked too young to be an officer in HM Navy. More of a midshipman, really.

Although not at the moment. He still looked like a midshipman, at least in the face, but he was dressed as the seamen in the skiff below were, save that he, at least, had the decency to be wearing a shirt.

DuPuy gave the lieutenant a nod, and Emmons hopped over the side and quickly made his way down the rope ladder to the launch below. Normally, of course, the launch would be propelled by its sails, but the mast had been shipped, and the crew waited by the oars. Even had the wind been onshore, rather than mostly offshore, it would still have been more discreet.

They were, once again, waiting for Cully to decide.

Sir Cully of Cully's Woode, *indeed*.

Not that he looked like much of a knight. If it weren't that Stavros Andropolonikos—more formally, Sir Stavros Kechiroski, KHMG, OC—didn't have the natural Turkish/ Hellenic swarthiness, they could have been brothers. They were built much the same, and dressed more or less identically as Kechiroski came up on deck, adjusting his trousers. With a woman aboard, the seamen had given up just pissing over the lee side whenever it took their fancy, and Kechiroski was a seaman by trade, if not his present trade.

He still looked like one, though. Not like a knight, either.

That didn't bother Sir Guy about the Hellene; granted, Kechiroski had knelt before the king to arise as a knight of His Majesty's Guard, but title aside, he had been and really was nothing more than a common Pironesian sailor, known as "Stavros Andropolonikos," because after he had been impressed into and successfully completed his term in HM Navy as common sailor, he had mostly worked his newly learned craft out of the southern Pironesian ports, where Andropolonikonians, or whatever they called them, were largely unknown.

Why Cully had asked Kechiroski to come along on the mission was less obvious than why Kechiroski had accepted. He could have been living back in Andropolonikos on the pension that came with the OC, but he clearly thought of himself as a knight, as though a tap on the shoulder had changed his status in the view of anybody who mattered.

But they both looked about the same.

Like Kechiroski, Cully was dressed like a Hellenic or Turkish peasant, in a stained and clumsily mended blousy shirt over short pantaloons secured at the waist by nothing more than a length of thin rope.

And he didn't look much like a knight from the neck up, either. He had allowed his thinning gray hair to grow into a sailor's queue, bound back tightly behind his head, and his beard was unshaven on the cheeks, in the local style. Of his two swords, he had only packed one in his seabag, and had insisted that Sir Guy permit the ship's carpenter to whittle plain sheaths and grips for both of Sir Guy's swords, and the armorer to—while wearing heavy leather gloves, to avoid the chance of touching a finger to Albert's metal—affix a plain wooden hilt to Albert as well as to his other sword, the fine saber that had been presented to Sir Guy by the abbot general himself.

Well, Sir Guy would report that, along with the rest of Cully's very unknightly behavior, to the abbot, when they returned to Alton. Which wouldn't be soon enough to suit him, for a fact. Pity that the workings of codebooks was a slight that Sir Guy had never quite been able to master; it would be best to have primed the abbot with an advance report.

He wasn't happy about his own appearance, either. At Cully's urging—insistence, really—Sir Guy had stopped shaving when they had set sail from Portsmouth, and Sir Guy had, shortly before their arrival off the coast, adopted a similar disguise himself, although he had, of course, seen to the proper laundering of his clothing.

There was no need to appear, even in disguise, with tears in one's clothing that could be mended, and every reason not to smell like the garlic that Cully popped, clove by clove, as though they were sweetmeats, until he not only looked but smelled like a garlic-eating Turk.

But Cully had taken on this . . . preposterous garb from the day that they had sailed from Portsmouth, and even insisted that Sir Guy dress in mufti when they made port along the way, although Sir Guy wasted no minutes in resuming the proper clothing of a knight of the Order of Crown, Shield, and Dragon the moment that he was back aboard, of course.

And the garlic? The garlic that Cully ate incessantly, just because the Turks did? The garlic that made Cully's breath smell like a pigsty?

Horrible.

Not that smelling like a peasant was Cully's only failure as a knight. A knight was supposed to have a certain dignity, and moderation was part of that.

Cully, on the other hand, despite his age, would keep up, mug for mug, with the most sodden drunks at the captain's table, of which there was more than an ample nightly supply. HM Navy had strict regulations against being too drunk for duty, and in Guy's opinion, even aboard the supposedly taut *Lord Fauncher*, they were enforced in far too loose a fashion, at least among the officers who dined at the captain's table, although presumably the ones who had the deck saved their tippling for after they were relieved.

Being treated as the junior of a drunk knight who was, in fact, junior to him wasn't the only thing that Guy found distasteful, at least within the confines of his mind.

Nor was the fact that he had been assigned as Cully's companion, for reasons that were surely good enough, as they had come from the abbot general himself, as unpleasant as the mission was.

All of it was, well, wrong, and the blame went through Cully straight to Admiral DuPuy. Given the admiral's assignment from His Majesty to manage the search for the source of the new live swords—and, more importantly, to extinguish that source—Admiral Sir Simon Tremaine DuPuy should have been in his offices in Portsmouth, where every report would quickly reach his desk, and ships and men could be properly dispatched in good order.

And, if not that—if he believed, as he apparently did, that the source was somewhere not too far north of the Med, and that rapidity of response would be in order—he certainly had the authority to set up his offices either at Gibraltar or Malta, or anywhere else he pleased. Napoli was wonderful this time of year—and almost every time of every year; that would have been a reasonable choice.

But he had done none of those. He had had a ship seconded to his service, with a full complement of clerks aboard, sending and receiving endless coded messages whenever they made port, or flagged down a ship of the line.

The *Lord Fauncher*. Bah.

If he had decided, as was apparently his prerogative, Guy supposed, to have a "floating office," he could have and should have seconded a ship of at least the second rank, rather than the *Lord Fauncher*, at best a ship of the Third.

Some people just didn't understand the matter of station, and DuPuy was worse than many, although not as bad as Cully. Somehow or other—despite his rank—the admiral seemed to be functioning as officer of the deck on more than one occasion, although not at the moment, when the master and commander, Lieutenant Winters, had the quarterdeck himself . . . although why the master and commander would need to take the deck with the ship lying at anchor was another thing that puzzled Sir Guy, as there was no good explanation.

It wasn't the only thing that was wrong here.

Sir Guy repressed a shiver, although he couldn't have said why he had to. Nights along the coast were balmy and clear, and the offshore wind brought distant hints of cook fires to his nose, and nothing more threatening.

Still, the nearest of HM ships of the line were off Rodhos, easily forty miles and ten hours away, under the best of circumstances, with a favorable wind. The *Lord Fauncher* would set no speed records, save perhaps for the speed it would sink to the bottom if a Dar ram managed to close with it.

Yes, the combination of the flinger crews and the Marine company could likely fend off any single-ship attack that the *Lord Fauncher* itself couldn't flee from, but it was itself too big a prize to settle for "likely," what with the admiral himself aboard.

And then there was the girl. Yes, of course, a wizard was obviously needed for this, but why couldn't it have been a proper man, preferably a nobleman, rather than a blousy young Injan thing who shamelessly flirted like a Northhampton trollop, with both officers and crew?

She was pretty enough, perhaps, in a dark sort of way, and that was probably why Cully had picked her, although seamen were notoriously unchoosy, and perhaps she did rather more than flirt, although—

No. That was an unworthy thought. And yet another thing to confess, and if he were capable of being irritated, he would have been more than slightly irritated that the only priest available aboard the ship to hear his confession was Cully, who had initially acceded with ill grace just this side of rudeness, at best.

Sir Guy lived in fear of few things, but one of those was of missing the specifics of a sin in his confessions. To give the old knight credit, Sir Cully finally had come around to agreeing to hear Sir Guy's daily confessions with what passed for good grace, and although he had initially resisted, he had eventually assigned almost suitable penances, rather than a token rosary or two that he clearly preferred.

And, of course, if Cully had so much as taken confession a single time since they had left Malta, much less Portsmouth, Sir Guy was utterly unaware of it, and doubted that he had, although Sir Guy had made the offer on more than one or two occasions even recently, although he had given up making the offer daily within a week after they had left.

Cully was eying the sky, as though he could read something more from it than how quickly the clouds were moving toward the half moon.

Below, on the seaside of the ship, the captain's launch was already waiting, along with its navy crew, although turning the ship so that it would be out of sight of land was, Sir Guy thought, just another one of Cully's overly cautious precautions; the Lord Fauncher stood at anchor easily a mile from shore, with all lights doused above-decks. Somebody sitting on the shore with a fine Arabian spyglass might—might—have been able to spot the ship, but only if they had the glass pointed in the right direction.

A massive puff of dark cloud was moments away from the moon.

Cully nodded. "It's time, I think."

"Two weeks?" the admiral asked, sounding hopeful. It wasn't the first time that he had brought up the subject of how long they'd be ashore.

"Unlikely. More like a month. If we have any luck. Could easily be more." He turned to the girl—to the girl!—first. "Are you ready, Sarila?" he asked in Turkish, his accent thick enough to spread on toast.

"Of course, Master Erdem."

Like Kechiroski, and unlike Cully and Sir Guy, her skin hadn't needed to be darkened with hours in the sun, or supplemented by the smelly oils that Sir Guy had had to apply to himself; with an Injan mother brought back by a soldier in the Mumbai Guard, nature had already done that for her. She didn't look Turkish, of course, but the slave trade had brought some injans to the area as slaves, mostly captured off of British merchantmen, and mixed breeding was hardly unusual for second- or third-generation slaves, for the obvious reasons.

"Ercam?" He turned to Kechiroski. *"Nisalsiniz?"*

Kechiroski grinned. *"Hayir,"* he said. *"Kirimizi sarap istiyorum."*

Sir Guy sniffed. Kechiroski wasn't well because he hadn't had enough wine?

Cully turned to Sir Guy. "And you, oh, Onan?"

Sir Guy forced himself not to wince at the name. It was a decent Turkish name, after all, although he was certain that was not the reason that Cully had picked it for him.

"*Nisalsiniz?*" Cully asked.

"Well, of course I'm ready, and—"

Cully silenced him with a raised finger. "The proper answer is incoherent mumbling. You're a mute, remember? Not a deaf-mute, mind you; just a mute."

Cully had found endless faults with Sir Guy's Turkish accent, and after repeatedly trying to get him to modify it, had announced that passing him off as a mute slave was the only alternative. The only reason Sir Guy had gone along with that indignity—as well as the indignity of the name that Cully had assigned him, and all the others—was that his initial protest to the admiral had been met with stony indifference, and followed up with one of Cully's powders slipped into his morning tea, and *that* followed the next morning by a thoroughly unknightly—albeit private—lecture on how Cully was going to obey orders to the extent that he could, but that he was perfectly capable of leaving Sir Guy behind, dead or unconscious, if he became a burden.

He was along, Cully had explained, because he was the least useful knight of a live sword that the Order had ever known, and while the abbot had not come out and admitted that openly, Cully said, interspersing his comments with common words that were as unknightly as unknightly could be, that was why Sir Guy had been foisted on Cully.

Had Sir Guy been a man of temper, he would have whipped out Albert and had at him. Even if Cully was still the swordsman that legend had it—something that Guy doubted—he could not have stood up to a live sword.

But that would have been murder. And, besides, the abbot general had warned Sir Guy that Cully would try to provoke him, as a way of getting rid of him.

That was not to be. He would just be patient, and bear up under the many indignities, until he could return to his proper life and proper station—preferably with His Own, although he had never been given that honor.

"Time to go," Cully decided.

He took his own bag and carefully dropped it over the side to the waiting arms of the seamen below, and then was quickly over the side himself, moving quickly and easily, despite his years.

The girl was next, and Sir Guy looked away by instinct—her shift had started to ride up, and no doubt both Cully and the sailors would be amusing themselves by looking up her full, native skirt, a sight that Sir Guy would not have been surprised was familiar to at least one of them.

And then it was his turn. He slipped the sword into his own bag, and lowered it on a line to Cully, then retrieved the line and dropped it on the deck for one of the sailors to handle.

But he was, after all, a knight of the Order, and even in his present disguise, the proprieties should be observed. He bowed toward the quarterdeck, where Lieutenant Winters properly returned his bow, and then to the admiral.

"Just get going," DuPuy said. "And come back alive, dammit."

Cully would, no doubt, have made some insolent comment, but swallowing his offense at the profanity, Sir Guy just turned and climbed down the ladder.

Beaching the launch wasn't possible, as Sir Guy had expected; the shore was just too rocky, and he wasn't all sure that Winters had read the charts aright, anyway.

What he was sure was going to be the worst of getting their gear ashore turned out to be the easiest—the tinker's cart, as it turned out, really did float when empty, and it was a matter of only a few minutes of soaking-wet sailors grunting and pushing to get it up on shore, followed by a stream of the rest of their gear, more or less kept out of the water by the sailors, at least most of the time. Unsurprisingly, it took two seamen to haul the anvil ashore, even as light as it was—for an anvil.

Sir Guy kept his voice low as he ordered the sailors where to put the gear. At least, with the warm western wind, his peasant garb had quickly dried.

Cully, by that time, had vanished, of course, just when there was work to be done. He had been first over the side of the launch, and had slipped off into the night, and only returned when all of the gear had been brought ashore, and that in the two bags that had leaked had been carefully spread out along the rocks to dry, at least for a while, and the last of the sailors had swum back to the launch, leaving only Lieutenant Emmons along with Sir Guy, the Hellene. The girl had started carrying the gear, or at least what she could manage of it, up the slope to the land above.

"I'd advise you to be careful, Sir Guy," the lieutenant said, his voice not quite a whisper, "but I know you're sensible enough to do that anyway." He grinned.

"And were I not," Sir Guy said, "I doubt that a lecture from a *lieutenant* in His Majesty's service would make me think otherwise, I'd expect."

"Yessir."

The moon had long reappeared from behind the clouds, but it was low enough in the sky that the rocky prominence above cast a shadow that covered not only where their gear lay, but spread far enough beyond the shore to cover the launch, as well, where the crew had stepped the masts, and rigged the sails, but not raised them.

Sir Guy looked out to see where the *Lord Fauncher* should have been visible, but it was gone.

Emmons, following his look, grinned again, the reproach forgotten. "We'll catch up with the ship, sure enough, and no worries on that."

Sir Guy furrowed his brow.

"Some men in a launch that looks enough like a small skiff making their way out to sea are smugglers, even if they're seen. Fair amount of opium traded locally—comes down out of the north, and makes its way to the New World," he said. "Black gold comes back as, well, *gold*. A launch heading out to something that looks like a Guild ship, well, that'd be fine; the Guild are known to be smugglers, and have as little respect for English law as they do for shariah.

"But a launch going out to what's obviously a ship built along English lines," Emmons went on, "well, that could be something else entirely, and rumors travel fast. About the only way to cover for that would be to impersonate a bunch of Seeproosh pirates, as they've captured one or two of our merchantmen recently—and that would mean that we'd have to raid a village, kill everybody who resisted, and make off with the women, children, and a few men, letting none escape. But then what would we do with them?"

"Of course, the admiral would never countenance such a thing."

"Yessir," he said, giving Sir Guy a dubious look.

Still, all in all, the lieutenant had a point.

If nobody along this admittedly lightly inhabited bit of shoreline had already seen the ship, or seen the boat coming in from it, there would be no problem. But their maps—to the extent that the maps were any good—showed that there was a major trading road along the ridge line a few miles to the north.

If they were in the right spot, it would still be there. It was an old Roman road, and whatever could be said about how the Romans had descended into the perversion and heresy of what was left of the Empire, it would still be here, unless the locals had carted away each and every stone.

Which was unlikely. One thing that Izmir was in no shortage of was stone.

Kechiroski was making his way to shore, a final leather bag held high over his head to keep it dry. As he emerged from the water, the way his leggings clung to him made it clear that he wasn't wearing any undergarments whatsoever; Sir Guy averted his eyes.

Kechiroski staggered up above the waterline and dropped it with the rest of their gear. "That should do it, I think, Lieutenant," he said. His English was very good; Sir Guy had to give him that.

"Time for you to be off, Emmons," Cully said—from right behind Sir Guy, startling him. Sir Guy hadn't heard him at all, although how he had made his way down the slope without being seen or heard was another one of his woodsman things, Sir Guy supposed.

"Good luck and fair winds, Sir Cully."

Cully briefly clasped hands with the boy, and then beckoned to Kechiroski. "The cart's going to be the worst of it. Let's get it up the hill. Sir Guy, if you don't feel like grabbing what bags you can manage, I'd appreciate it if you'd at least dry off what's here."

It was more than an hour later, soaked with sweat, that Cully gestured Kechiroski toward the handles of the cart, and they set off across the barren ground, looking for the road.

They found it at first light, and headed east, walking as quickly as possible.

Sir Guy took his turn at the arms of the cart. Yes, it was undignified, but Cully just shrugged at his initial mild protest, and offered him a drink of water.

He knew better than that.

He drank from his own water skin.

A Sore Temptation for a Formerly Honest Former Sailor

The most useless things that the world has ever known are male teats, women's tears, and a man who used to be a sailor.
                                        —Sir Simon Tremaine DuPuy

He was holding onto the wheel, but he wasn't a sailor.

Not anymore.

Officially, of course, he had been placed on the Retired List at the pleasure and for the convenience of HM the king, and he doubted that it was accidental that the wording of his orders had been as little like those of a beached officer being put on the Inactive List and half pay as was possible. His Majesty was a kind man, when he could be, after all.

But the truth was that DuPuy wasn't a sailor anymore. The best thing to do would have been to let the damned steersman do his own job—which, at the moment, would have probably been locking the wheel down, rather than holding onto it—but the truth was that, as frustrating as it was to be what he had become, the feel of the spokes of the wheel in his hand was an unadulterated pleasure, and gave some balance to his humiliation. You could feel the sea through the wheel, after all; holding onto it made him a part of the ship, if only for the moment.

The steersman stood by, carefully not watching the admiral, having apparently interpreted an order of "stand easy" to mean "assume a rigid brace of parade rest," and it didn't escape DuPuy's notice that the steersman was but a quick lunge away from the wheel, ready to take over his responsibilities the moment that the useless old man stopped playing sailor.

Well, enough of that. "You may resume your post, Steersman," he said.

"Aye, aye, sir." As DuPuy stepped away, the steersman took the wheel, and gave a quick glance at the locking pedal, but didn't either touch it or ask permission.

Hmmph. It was like the boy was afraid of him, or something equally preposterous.

Simon Tremaine DuPuy—he had had to continually remind himself not to think of himself as *Admiral* Sir Simon Tremaine DuPuy over the past year, and was finally getting the hang of it, despite the almost constant, false reminders to the contrary—stalked the quarterdeck like a, well, like a plump, soft, old, useless man.

Which he was.

Emmons was standing by, just below the quarterdeck, waiting. He had, as usual, risen before DuPuy, and was quite properly arrayed in his Second Class uniform, entirely suitable for a naval officer at sea, even if he wasn't technically in service aboard the ship, but seconded in service to Commissioner Sir Simon Tremaine DuPuy. If the uniform was just a touch threadbare at the knees of the trousers, that was something that only a superior officer would take note of, and not a despicable old man who merely carried a title had any business noticing. Besides, it was preposterous what the cost of uniforms could to do an honest officer's finances, and if DuPuy wasn't sure how honest Emmons would be under the right temptation, that temptation had clearly not happened while Emmons had been serving DuPuy.

DuPuy shook his head, scowling to himself. It wasn't as though there was any suggestion aboard the ship of his shame.

Quite the contrary, and it shamed him all the more.

Whenever he came up the ladder from what should have been the captain's quarters, "Admiral on deck!" was always sung out by whoever—officer or man—noticed first, and DuPuy had as of yet never managed to actually plant even so much as a single foot on the wood of the deck without hearing those words.

On the rare occasion that he could bear to approach the quarterdeck, he always made it a point to ask for permission to mount the deck, of course. The *Lord Fauncher* wasn't his ship, after all; it was Winters'—and, also of course, the permission was always granted, whether by whichever officer or middie had the deck, or by Winters himself.

And if it was Winters who had the deck—and Winters took the deck himself routinely, quite possibly not aware of how that relatively recent tradition had entered HM Naval custom—DuPuy tried to stay below, as Winters always seemed to be looking for an opportunity to invite him up, and more than once had asked if "the admiral" would be kind enough to take the deck.

That was something Winters surely had the right to do, and a request from a captain was only a hair's width away from being an order, after all. Hell, the man could have explicitly ordered it, just as he could have ordered DuPuy to take sand and stone to the main deck, although, of course, he never even suggested such a thing.

If he had, DuPuy would have had to comply. Although, of course, there could be an accounting later on. While it perhaps would not have been a trivial thing for Commissioner DuPuy to have had Winters relieved of his command—the *Lord Fauncher* had been seconded into the commissioner's service, yes, but it was still, by God, a ship of the royal navy, and part of the Home Fleet, not DuPuy's private yacht—if that could be done, it could be done in Portsmouth, not here.

In law, DuPuy was every bit as much at the captain's command and under his authority as the meanest, lashed prisoner-at-large seaman mucking out the lower hold while still groaning from the fresh weals across his back.

DuPuy wasn't quite sure why he found that thought as pleasing as he did. Maybe it was just because of the rightness of it.

Winters emerged from the for'ard hatch, and mounted the ladder to the quarterdeck without so much as a by-your-leave, as of course was also utterly appropriate. The captain didn't require permission to mount his own quarterdeck, after all.

"Morning, Admiral."

It was a fine point of etiquette. Nobody else aboard ship had the right to correct the master and commander; it was a matter of privilege, and Winters had never explicitly granted DuPuy that privilege.

A good man, Winters, more or less.

"Good morning, Captain," DuPuy said. "Request permission to go below, sir? There's some paperwork I should be doing."

"Of course, Admiral," Winters said, formally. Give him that; he was unfailing cooperative. "I have the deck, and I thank you for taking it for me, sir, to give me a little time below." He patted at his stomach. "I think that last night's mutton didn't quite agree with me, sir."

DuPuy didn't respond to that. If he had still been an admiral, he would have pointedly suggested that a ship the size of the *Lord Fauncher* should have had easily a dozen officers and middies capable of taking the quarterdeck while out at sea, with no shoaled waters to worry about, and no other ships in sight—and, to be fair, it did—and that there was no need whatsoever to rely on a useless old man who had once been a sailor.

But, of course, that was the sort of thing that even an admiral would have been on legally shaky ground to address directly to a master and commander, and DuPuy was not an admiral any longer.

Winters, of course, called him "Admiral," although DuPuy would have much preferred to have a stick stuck in his good eye instead of being addressed by the rank that he no longer held.

Retired. He could have billed himself as Admiral Sir Simon Tremaine DuPuy, *Retired*.

Well, at least His Majesty ordered him to take retirement, along with his new post, instead of merely putting him on half pay and beaching him. And he couldn't complain about the salary, either, not even to himself—HM had explained that if the post paid a shilling less than that of any minister of the Privy Council, the word would get out, and it would encourage a lack of respect for the post, and—

Ah. To hell with the money. He should have been enjoying this, not thinking like a Marseilles wine merchant, gloating over his riches.

There was something about the particular way that the rolling of the ship felt from the quarterdeck that was as much a drug for him as opium would have been for a weaker man.

He forced himself not to give a last, longing look at the wheel, but let himself walk down the steps, make his way aft, and down to the captain's quarters, past the two Marines who came to attention, but quite properly didn't open the door for him.

Nothing had changed, of course.

The last mail call had been in Pironesia, and while they'd flagged down the *Cowperstown* just as much for resupply as for the possibility that it was carrying a copy of the scattershot dispatches that chased the *Lord*

Fauncher everywhere it sailed, the only dispatches has been duplicates of the ones that had been picked up in Pironesia, and didn't even require decoding, just—careful—disposal.

He put the duplicates into the wooden box that Emmons—more reliable than Scratch—would take up to the deck to burn, and then stir the ashes before throwing them overboard. The chances of some useful fragment washing up on the wrong shore were small, and the chances of them falling into the hands of somebody who could make sense of the code was even smaller, but what of that?

He uncovered the map that he had hung on the captain's wall, after quickly checking that the wax seals were still in place before breaking them.

The map covered the Med, from Gibraltar to Seeproosh, and a bit beyond. Yes, the source of the new live swords could in theory have been anywhere, but there was plenty of evidence that it was somewhere east of Pironesia, and west of Syryah, and—at least so he hoped and thought—north of the Med, rather than in the Dar itself. For all he knew—as opposed to concluded—the wizard who had figured out how to create live swords with the souls of infants could have been quietly ensconced in a flat in East Londinium, or somewhere in New England, or Darmosh Kowayes, or Inja or any other godforsaken place, but there were hints to the contrary.

Many hints. The race of the girl, Nadide, whose soul had been imprisoned in the sword that that Hellenic boy carried; the words of al-Bakalani's servant, who had been placed as a spy, giving a lie to the cleverness of al-Bakalani; the location of the one lost sword that had been brought to shore by a fisherman in that offshore Pironesian island, the one marked with a red pin—none of it was proof, but all of it were clues.

And not the only clues, at that. When given this assignment by HM, DuPuy had as quickly as he could seconded every available beached officer on half pay, had Dougherty put them on full pay, and sent them across the northern arc of the Med to try to investigate, doing the best he could to have them assume local garb and disguise, although a scant tenth of them, if that, spoke any of the local languages.

It wouldn't have been what he would have wanted to do, but in this life, a man made do with what he had. He would have preferred to have a thousand spies, each well-trained in the local usages, speaking a dozen local languages, each with a well-developed background—say, as merchant trader seamen—that would have given them some protection from being identified as what they indeed were, as many had.

Some had managed to make it back to a Crown port; many hadn't.

The blue pins on the map showed where men had been sent to. Whenever a new batch of dispatches showed a report of one of his spies coming back, they were replaced by green pins. When a report was more than a month overdue, the blue pin was replaced by a yellow one, and a month after that, by a red.

What did it all mean? It meant that DuPuy had sent men ill-equipped for any task but to be stalking horses to their deaths, but that wasn't important. They were, to use the technical term, expendable, and DuPuy had expended them. DuPuy had, in his lifetime, expended many more men than that. Seaman—able and ordinary—officers, supplies, rigging, launches, and even ships themselves were all expendable. The Crown was not.

But that the men had died was not important; it was where the deaths occurred that was perhaps indicative.

The black pins were even more interesting. Darklings hadn't been spotted south of Aba-Paluoja in more than a generation until recently—now reports of them were springing up from eastern France almost all the way to Inja, but spottily, as though they kept a low profile until they moved southward far enough from the Zone.

But as much as DuPuy tried to apply some system to his investigation, it was all haphazard and improvised.

Deviousness didn't come naturally to the English, alas, and deviousness was what was called for. Crown Intelligence, such as it was, had traditionally been involved in keeping track of ship and troop movements. You could tell quite a lot about what somebody was planning by where he put his soldiers, and his ships.

That was easy enough, and there was no deviousness required. British merchantmen made calls on all the open ports, of course, and there were few such ships with at least one officer who didn't have a naval portfolio, and an assignment to log ship names and movements. An officer might be beached on half pay for any number of reasons that wouldn't make him unsuitable as a sailing master or loadmaster for a merchantman.

Very good for keeping track of others' ship and troop movements, and utterly useful for this, whatever this really was.

Yes, there were spies of all sorts operating out of Crown Intelligence in Londinium, but their traditional brief was to supplement the ambassadors in the various courts. The Frisians were, of course, technically allied with the Crown, but there were constant intrigues around the Ostfriesische Landschaft, and they were no better than the damned Portugees—pity that the assassination attempt on Henriques IV had failed—or any number of other supposedly aligned or neutral states where the flag of the Crown didn't fly.

And not that that was the only problem, of course. Intrigues weren't unknown in the lands of the Crown itself, and it was DuPuy's opinion that His Majesty should have long ago invited Monsieur Le Duc du Borbonaisse to take up regular residence in the Tower, an opinion that he had not been asked to share, and hadn't.

The really interesting pins were the gold- and silver-tipped ones.

Those came from al-Bakalani.

Details? Al-Bakalani was preposterously generous with details, apparently working under the theory that a new source of live swords—and who knows what else?—could end up being as much of a threat to the Dar Al Islam as to the Crown. If the smooth-faced bastard was capable of being frightened, the affair on Pantelleria had frightened him mightily.

As it would have any sober man, and most drunk ones. A sword with the soul of a saint or a sinner trapped within it had great power, even so long after the Age.

What could such a sword with what passed for the Soul of the Wise have done?

DuPuy was sure that al-Bakalani had no more idea on that than he himself did, other than it could be incredibly bad, for Crown, Empire, and Dar, and everybody else. Expand the Zone? Restore Avalon? Make the horrible magics of the Kali-worshipers in the Kush seem mild by comparison?

What?

Well, if they could find and extinguish the source, they'd never have to know.

His opposite number from the Dar—more or less—the despicable Abdul Ibn Mussa al-Bakalani, seemed to have ample spies able to work from at least Syryah to Gibbie, and he had deviousness to spare. From his quarters in Londinium, where he had been, alas, accepted as an exotic oddity among society, al-Bakalani had received reports from the Commission for the Prevention of Vice and Promotion of Virtue from all around the Med, as well. Coded, too, DuPuy presumed; certainly the two cases that DuPuy had had intercepted had been coded, and indecipherable by both Crown Intelligence and His Majesty's College.

It would take years—decades, perhaps—for a well-hidden spy to search out every village and croft (or whatever the accursed local called their crofts) even along the northern coast of the Med, but al-Bakalani had reported some similarities to DuPuy's own researches.

Izmir. It pointed to Izmir. Better than half of the men DuPuy had sent out had eventually reported back—with information that might have been useful to Crown Intelligence on other matters, although not this one.

It was the silence that was deafening. Izmir. Southern Izmir, to be specific. That was in accord with the Turkish ancestry of the girl Nadide, who had been imprisoned in the sword, and while the late unlamented Efik had claimed to have come from Anatalya, DuPuy took what he had said with rather more than the traditional grain of salt.

None of the men DuPuy had sent into that territory had returned. One explanation of that is that the Izmiri were a particularly violent people, suspicious of strangers who they would, no doubt, generally suspect as advance scouts for the pirates from Seeproosh. Seeproosh seemed to treat much of Izmir, Antalya, Balakazir and Koosh as a harvesting ground for slaves for the New World. Yes, in theory, Musselmen were prohibited from enslaving other Musselmen, but that was only theory, and, after all, Izmir was under the theoretical control of the Empire, and Musselman worship, when it happened, a secret affair. In any case, the plantations of Darmosh Kowayes were filled with slaves taken from at least theoretically Musselmen kingdoms along the African coast, and it was the rare Darmosh Kowayes *reis* who wouldn't find an Izmiri concubine worthy of purchase; the frequent local combination of black hair and blue eyes seemed to be almost irresistible there. It was hard to imagine that all of the agents DuPuy had sent in had run afoul of Seeproosh pirates, after all.

It wasn't just DuPuy's agents. Just a few weeks before, al-Bakalani reported that the Commission for the Prevention of Vice and Promotion of Virtue had lost agents in that territory, as well—and had done so without it being a confirmation of any of DuPuy's previous suspicions, which made it more likely to be true. DuPuy had a grudging respect for al-Bakalani, but trust was another matter entirely.

There was a knock on the door.

"Stay," he said, and covered up the map with its sheet. Then: "Come."

It was just Emmons, with a mug—a mug, thankfully, and not a cup and saucer—of coffee. Emmons carefully latched the door behind himself, then set the coffee on the appointed spot on the captain's—on DuPuy's desk, then drew himself up to a stiff brace.

"Oh, sit down," DuPuy said, as he always did. "And feel free to light your pipe, if you're of a mind to," he said, taking up his own.

Emmons was probably too young to take up the pipe—he should really still have been a midshipman, rather than a junior lieutenant; DuPuy was to blame for that too, among his other sins—but it had been almost a year since he'd been seconded as DuPuy's aide, and it had taken him but a day or two since he had first been given the offer to acquire a pipe, and little longer to acquire the habit.

He fussed about for a few moments with his pipe and pouch, and DuPuy busied himself with his own pipe, and the coffee. Good navy coffee it was—brewed strong enough to peel barnacles off a hull, and with a pinch of sea salt—and it went well with the tobacco.

"Rail talk?" he asked, as he always had before.

"None first hand, sir," Emmons answered, as usual. "To the extent that Tiptree's accurate, there's been quite a lot," he said, as he set his pipe down and started fiddling with the admiral's clothes, pointedly setting out the Class

Two uniform that DuPuy had no intention of wearing, with or without his medals.

Emmons didn't need to mess with the chamber pot; he had emptied and replaced it at daybreak, and without a whimper of complaint.

In addition to his other duties as his clerk and aide, Emmons served as DuPuy's valet. An ordinary seaman would, of course, snoop if given the opportunity, and it was a lot more convenient to station a couple of Marines at the door to the cabin than to, every time that he took the air topside, lock away every bit of paper that DuPuy wouldn't want to share with every manjack aboard the ship—and probably from Hull to Mumbai, indirectly.

DuPuy handed over the last of the packet of dispatches. "See to them, please," he said.

"There's one left," Emmons said. "Begging the admiral's pardon."

"I know. I'll handle it myself."

It wasn't actually a dispatch, not really. It was the latest letter that was the source of the unmarked pins on DuPuy's map.

Randolph. Still Randolph. Formerly Lieutenant Lord Sir Alphonse Randolph; formerly the second son of the Earl of Moray; at present the likely heir to Moray, what with his elder brother having died in what was believed to be a hunting accident.

Randolph, who had sworn on Pantelleria to track down and kill the traitor knight, Alexander Smith, now known as Abdul Ibn Mahmoud, who now served the Dar with presumably better bought loyalty than that which he had served the Crown.

What was most interesting in al-Bakalani's own dispatches was the singular omission of any reports on where Smith was, or what he was up to. It was a virtual certainty he was on what trail there was leading to the source of the swords, but the only word that DuPuy had had come from Randolph, who was on his own, very personal crusade, a matter that no doubt had been less than well-received in the Earl of Moray's court.

He started to pick up Randolph's letter, but changed his mind. He had already memorized it, after all. How Randolph had managed to avoid capture during his travels throughout the region was something that he hadn't detailed in his uncoded letters, of course, and DuPuy just chalked it up to what a fat purse could do. Noblemen tended to have more money than sense.

Which was unfair, but DuPuy didn't mind being unfair.

No.

It was time to face his daily temptation again. He removed the thin chain from around his neck, and brought the key over to the strongbox. A duplicate of the key hung on the wall, but anyone who used it would have had quite a surprise when he turned it in the lock that had been prepared by a senior wizard of HM College of Wizardry.

He turned it slowly in the lock, and opened the strongbox.

There the letters were. Dozens and dozens of them. Written by His Majesty in his own hand, and sealed with his own seal, they were uncoded duplicates of the coded, sealed orders that had been passed to every master and above in the Mediterranean, as well as to the every subject court across the coast, with the strict admonition that the seal would be checked, repeatedly, even though the code sheets for their contents were in this very box, and without them the orders would be incomprehensible.

If action were to need to be taken, it might well need to be taken as quickly as was humanly possible, and HM had given DuPuy authority that no man subject to the king should have: to commandeer any man or force, royal or ducal, navy or army, into service under the command of Grand Admiral Sir Simon Tremaine DuPuy, by the Grace of God and Appointment of His Majesty, Mordred V, the Commander in Chief of all of His Majesty's Forces.

"Use the tools you need to do the job, Admiral," the king had said. He hadn't mentioned that to pick up this set of tools would have huge risks, and horrible consequences, even if they were properly used. Strip away what there was of the Med Fleet? Take the King's Own and Red Watch from Gibraltar and leave Gibbie ripe for the plucking by the Portugees or the Dar—or possibly the Portugees *and* the Dar? Strip away the Duke of Napoli's forces and thereby persuade the Sharif of Tunisia that he could now conquer his way up the peninsula, planting his filthy foot on Crown territory and reinforcing with the endless swarm of soldiers that the Dar had at its disposal, while the Empire swept down from the north?

Any of that could happen.

Any of that could be why al-Bakalani was being so bloody helpful.

No. DuPuy would continue as he had, as long as he could, until he had more than clues and suspicions, but certainty, and a way of dealing with that certainty. And that he had sent more and better men than the likes of Sir Simon Tremaine DuPuy to their deaths bothered him, and would again, well, if that interrupted his sleep, that would be his problem.

DuPuy locked the box, trembling, then put the key back around his neck, downed his coffee, and spent the annoying moments covering and sealing the map before he went up to take the air.

The damned cabin, despite the good salt air flowing through the portholes, was too stuffy.

Again.

CHAPTER 4

The Saracen

The English have a saying that necessity makes strange bedfellows. There are times when I worry that my brothers in لجنة نزع السلا themselves worry about that with regard to me.

My only instructions were to watch and report, and I have watched, and reported where I can. Since we left England, I have seen the markings that show that there are messages waiting for some brother or brother in half a dozen ports, but both in Malta or Pironesia, while I did see signs, there were no messages for me. Please, if you would, I ask again, as I asked in the message left in that

place in Londinium that I'll not commit to this writ-
ing: let me know what your will is with regard
to me.

There is no reason to worry, my beloved broth-
ers. Yes, I think of myself as Stavros Kechiroski,
Sir Stavros the Hellene, almost all of the time, as I
was trained to do. It's even more necessary these
days, for reasons that I trust you will understand.

But I remain, at my heart and soul, the one who
I have always been.

—Nissim Al-Furat

It was a delicate balance.

Even in Cully's absence, while bargaining over the teakettle, Stavros tried to do it well, but not too well. That would be suspicious, in and of itself. Andropoloniki weren't Athenians, after all, renowned as hagglers—although not even the best of the Athenai that Stavros had ever met was at most a patch on the robes of the least of the olive merchants in the *souk* of Tikritzia when it came to haggling.

It was all a delicate balance, Stavros Kechiroski decided, not for the first or the hundred-and-first time. He had spent the trip from Portsmouth thinking of little else.

"At that price," he said, keeping just a trace of a hellenic drawl in his *türkçe*, "it would hardly have been worth my master having me haul this up even the hill to this miserable village, much less all the way over from Antalya, where I know he paid better than ten times the pitiful two bice that you insist on insulting him with."

The old woman sniffed. "Then I guess that he must have paid for it with the gold that litters the streets of Antalya, because it's worth not more than three here."

"And perhaps you'd rather another tinker mend your pot?" he asked, pointing to the growing pile of work, where villagers, hearing of the tinker, had come to the market, always carefully negotiating a price and examining the tinker's other wares before leaving. Like most of the stack, this particular pot—more of a small kettle, really—was the sort of thing that should have been mended by a blacksmith, but the nearest one was two days away, and the patches showed that it had been, as the English said, "tinkered with" endless times before, and would now be, once again.

Steal it?

Turks would steal soiled swaddling clothes, if you let them—but a tinker who absconded with goods left for repair would find not only that his reputation preceded him to the next cluster of hovels, but peasants were dropping their work to hunt him down. When Cully had said before he had departed, as though he had said it a thousand times before, that Onan and Erdem were to guard goods left for repair with their lives, that had not been taken as a figure of speech, not in the marketplace.

"No, no, I'll be back for that tomorrow," she said.

Pots sprung leaks, after all. Of such was a tinker's fortune made.

She started to turn away, slowly, and for a moment, Stavros considered telling her to turn back, the way an Athenian would, but—

He just shrugged, and let her walk away, rewarded by the smallest of nods from Sir Guy.

"I know, Onan," he said. "Better not to sell, than to have Master Erdem beat the two of us half to death for selling too cheaply."

Onan—Sir Guy—just grunted. He was actually quite good at that.

It was slow today, here, it being a Sunday.

Saturday was *the* market day in this village, although in every one of the villages that they had passed through, every day seemed to be a market day, even Sunday. The Church forbade trade on the Lord's Day, true, but Izmir was far from Constantinople, and even cassocked priests could be seen in their robes and crucifixes, moving from stall to stall, seeking bargains. Stavros was not sure what could possibly be a bargain on the basket of poorly salted-down smelts that might—might—have been almost fresh the day before, but surely were good for nothing but feeding to the hogs now, if that, as when the wind changed and blew the smell this way, it turned Sir Guy's face almost green. Stavros had no difficulty in stifling his own smile at that; he had smelled it, too.

Fortunately, the wind changed, carrying the stink away from them.

The fishmonger shrugged an apology, and stepped out from under the shade of his stall. "Ah," he said, "that's the trouble with Istia. Too close to the sea, and too far from it, at the same time."

"Eh?"

"Doesn't pay to smoke it or pickle it," he said, "as we're too close to the sea. And by the time that the fish is properly gutted and washed, I've practically got to whip my asses half to death in order to get the lazy fellows to make the trip overnight for Saturday market."

He shrugged. "And then, of course, with my luck being notoriously bad, yesterday had not a cloud in the sky, and I could practically watch it all spoiling before me."

Well, while there still was a large pile of smelts, most of the rest of the fish had gone; the fishmonger was just complaining for sport or, more likely, as an opening for some negotiation.

He was an amazingly fat man, although he moved nimbly enough, and he kept his eyes on Stavros's while his fingers toyed with the teakettle, no doubt much more interested in the set of knives that had been laid out on the boards. Decent working knives, bought in Pironesia, not good Sheffield or Damascus. What would itinerant tinkers be doing with anything so fine? Sir Guy had argued in favor of better equipping themselves—after all, he'd said, even though they had to lower themselves to do all this, that didn't mean that they had to lower themselves any more than necessary.

He turned to Sir Guy. "Onan, I find myself thirsty. Be so kind as to fetch more water."

For a moment, Sir Guy hesitated, then sagged his shoulders in an overly dramatic demonstration of resignation, picked up the bucket beside the table, and stalked off.

"Hmm . . ." the fishmonger said, eying Sir Guy's retreating back. "Seems to me that that other slave of your masters could do with a clout or two."

Stavros grinned. "That was my thought, as well—but don't tell it to Master Erdem Tenekeci. It was his clouts about the head that cost poor Onan his speech." He pointed at the knives. "I see that you find these of interest."

"Hmmmph. Possibly. Depends on the price. Which must be large enough to satisfy your master, I take it. Is he due back soon?"

"Well . . . " Stavros chuckled. "I doubt it. Not with his new girl still new to him. Amazing endurance, Master Erdem has, for a man his age, and he's got a feeling about how a quick servicing while the irons are cooling makes the day go better, if not faster. My guess is that she'll be hauling more than his shoes and hammer before they're back."

Peasant farmers would rarely shoe their children, but their horses were a different matter, and while many itinerant tinkers were also farriers, it was likely that few were as good as Cully, all in all, nor as quick, and the reputation of Ercam the Tinker was quickly spreading from village to village. Of all that a Turkish peasant owned, his dray horse was more important than his children, and there was always work for a farrier, even if the local blacksmith—when there was a blacksmith— resented the competition. Three days in Istia, and there could easily be a dozen more horses to be shod before they moved on.

"Where I was born," Stavros said, "it was customary to purchase a knife before slipping it into one's robes." He made to rise up, as though to cry *thief*—a call that would bring others from all over the market—but the fishmonger simply set the knife down and put three copper coins next to it.

By the time they finished negotiating, Sir Guy was back, and took no note of Stavros's glare at him as he carefully put all five coins in the leather pouch that hung about his neck.

The fishmonger grinned. Obviously, Stavros/Ercam had thought to pocket one of the coppers himself, risking the beating for having sold too cheaply to line his own purse.

He didn't mind being thought obvious; that was just fine with him. What all three of his persons—Ercam, Stavros, and Nissim—were doing was, for once, one and the same. Listening for gossip. This part of Izmir was where so many of the admiral's agents had disappeared, and the locals seemed neither more nor less dangerous than anywhere else.

Less so, if anything. Slave raiders from Seeproosh rarely made it this far inland. The *reis* hardly had much of a standing army, but raising a company of peasant bowmen was something that could be done quickly, and, whatever else you could say about the cursed Turks, they were accurate with their short bows, if only from endless shots at wild animals poaching on their fields.

But . . . wait.

It was just a muttered curse exchanged between two women who were walking by, and a quick gesture at a hilltop toward the north east.

Büyüleyici kadýn.

Witch.

Now, *that* was interesting.

INTERLUDE

Seeproosh

During my time teaching at Alton, many of the other knights developed the belief that I could, at a glance, determine which of the novices would eventually kneel before the king to rise as Order Knights.

Among my many sins is this: I began to believe it myself.

What did I miss about Alexander? I can still remember standing in the door, over Bedivere's body, holding off the traitor duke's soldiers, while Alexander and Gray held the king back, ignoring his shouted demands that he be allowed to join me in the door.

*If somebody that day—or any other day until
the moment that he murdered Lady Mary and stole
the Sandoval—had suggested to me that there was
some serious failing in Alexander, I would have
called him a liar. If somebody had suggested that
he could have turned traitor, I would have called
him out.*

What did I miss?

—Cully

There he was.

By God, there he was!

Lord Sir Alphonse Randolph—or Hakim Ibn
Muhammed, as he was calling himself these days,
although he couldn't really think of himself by that
name—forced himself not to quicken his pace as he
made his way through the Limmasol markets. Too much
speed would seem suspicious; the cut of his flowing robes
and muted blue-and-black *agal* marked him as a Darmosh Kowayes merchant, and why would such a man be
hurrying here, when he could take his time and spend
his money at leisure?

The *agal* got occasional glances, always followed by
shrugs. Merchants from the Dar New World were not
unknown on Seeproosh, but rare, rare enough not to
escape notice. That was acceptable, and a necessary risk;
here, his accent would likely be seen as simply exotic,
rather than suspicious. He would have preferred, of
course, to have found his quarry at the Guild *kontore* at
Kyrnia, on the northern edge of the island—but that had
not been the case.

Now, to kill the bastard. And, if at all possible, get away after.

It was all he could do not to whip out his sword, shove his way through the crowd, and make for Smith.

But, no. That would have been pointless. The idea was to kill Smith, and to—if at all possible—cut off his head and lay it on the grave of Lady Mary, and that called for patience, stealth and more patience, not bravado. A shout, a cry, a sudden movement would draw attention, and whatever you could say about the traitor knight, he was devilishly fast, even without drawing the Sandoval. Randolph had seen that for himself, on Pantelleria.

A direct, immediate attack would have been both suicidal and futile. Patience, as difficult as it was, was called for.

It didn't bother him at all. Patience? Bah. That was nothing. Trickery, deception, lying—that was hardly the worst of what he had done so far, and successful or not, it was likely to be nothing near as wicked as what he would have to do before this was all over.

A shame to his family? In one sense, absolutely.

Not by resigning his naval commission. Even Father had had no objection there.

Alphonse would have had to do that anyway, after the death of Francis during that horrible boar-hunting accident. Francis should have been the next earl, and while Randolph had as a boy always envied his older brother that part of his patrimony, he had found the navy to be a calling rather more suited to him. He had never expected to be the next Earl of Moray, although he had been quite confident that an admiral's flag had been somewhere in his future.

The navy was a good choice of a career for a second son, particularly one who wasn't dependent on a lieutenant's three crowns six every payday, nor worried about what being put on half pay might mean to his personal finances, as unlikely a possibility as that had been.

Instead, he always had been able to concentrate on rather more important matters, particularly after being given a ship—like being damned sure that the *Redemption* or the *Lord Launcher* were always ready for service, even when that meant that he'd had to dip into his own purse to restock his ship's stores more quickly than the navy could, or bribe an openhanded shore officer, something that he had done repeatedly, and with no regrets. If other masters couldn't have afforded to do the same thing, and if some resented him for it—and, of course, most couldn't have; he hadn't known or cared about the resentment—well, that was their problem, not his.

But that was gone, vanished in a tumble from a horse. A quick death, yes, but a tragedy not only for Father and Mother—and, of course, poor Francis—but for Alphonse Randolph, as well.

He forced himself not to grin. There were few people who would have much sympathy for his position, after all. Becoming the heir to Moray was not what most men would have considered a tragedy, or even a mild disappointment.

By most lights, he should have been back at home, helping Father manage the earldom's affairs, mainly in aid of preparing himself to take the earldom upon Father's death, and not—to quote the Earl of Moray— "chasing off after that bastard Smith across the face of the Earth." He should have gotten himself married to some likely noblewoman—the future Earl of Moray would not have found the search difficult, after all—and had her pregnant with an heir.

On a clear day like today he should have, say, been riding out in a carriage to pay a call on one of the local land barons, properly escorted, properly attired, properly shorn, and carefully bathed, not stalking through a marketplace in these godawful robes, wearing a full beard, his skin darkened by endless hours lying in the hot sun, and sweating beneath his robes in a way that still reeked in his own nostrils.

He forced himself not to quicken his pace, or to change his stride. That had been one of the hardest of the skills to master, after all. Walking erect, his shoulders set with the dignity of his family and his training as a navy officer, would have been a far better clue that he was out of place than a few shades off of his skin color, and while the government of Seeproosh, such as it was, was a council of pirate captains, they were known to be quite efficient at disposing of those thought to be spies.

Not too efficient, of course; like any other kind of common merchants, pirates couldn't afford to scare off too many customers, and it wasn't only Guild traders who used Seeproosh, after all. Traders of all sorts made their way to Seeproosh, usually breathing a sigh when they got within sight of the island, where by order of the Council, merchantmen were every bit as immune from attack as they were when sailing away, under the everchanging flag of protection that was invariably cast overboard at the first sight of a navy ship.

Truth was, a man with money—and particularly gold, and most particularly gold from Darmosh Kowayes—

could buy damned near anything he wanted on Seeproosh, if he was willing to root around, and have at least a reasonable expectation of being able to keep it, as long as he took passage to and from there on the right ships. Guild ships were, of course, the safest—and Randolph had taken passage to Seeproosh on a Guild ship for just that reason, despite the absurd high cost for deck passage. While a flotilla of Guild ships had no immunity outside of Seeproosh waters, Guild ships were renowned for giving pirates a good fight, and as a matter of clan honor scuttling themselves, with all hands aboard, rather than be boarded and taken. To the extent that one could be safe on a merchant ship in the eastern Med, passage aboard the *Lubeck*, the flagship of the Lubeck clan, was as close as you could come to it.

Despite the cost.

Still, the gold he had, and plenty of it, and he kept it on him; it added a good ten pounds to his weight. A very small portion of it—just two of the coins—were in the pouch at his waist, along with silver and copper, and he deliberately kept his hand on his pouch, as was commonplace. There were always pouch-slashers about in the most decent of places, of which this surely wasn't one.

Other than a few left more as bait than anything else at the bottom of his bags in his rented rooms, the rest was in the pockets of the vest that he wore beneath his robes, each tiny coin in its own tiny pocket, so that they wouldn't jingle, and each pocket close enough to each other that, in an extremity, the vest might serve as a minimal sort of body armor—useless against an arrow or bolt, unlikely to stop a thrust, but quite possibly able to put paid to a slash.

He kept his grin inside. Father had been, well, Father: he had made his position clear, he had chided Alphonse up one side and down the other—and then, when it was clear what was going to happen, Father had gone to some trouble to procure a preposterous number of the small golden coins issued by the Sharif of Darmosh Kowayes, for fear that Alphonse would find that exchanging good English golden crowns would be something that would expose him.

Randolph would have been careful, and it wouldn't have happened—his plans had included doing the exchange through two intermediaries in the City, lest the banking establishments had been compromised by Dar spies—but he had been touched by Father's concern.

Father had his flaws, yes—but unless Alphonse was seriously mistaken, the extra pains that Father had taken had every bit as much to do with a sense of pride that it might be a Randolph who would avenge the murder as it did with simple concern for the safety his son. Not that it couldn't be both, or more than that; Father was a complicated man, and Alphonse was not indispensable to the continuation of the Randolph line.

After all, there were still his two younger brothers and a half score of nephews who could have assumed the title, if necessary. Philip was married, and his first child a son. Father was not a cold man, but he had to be a calculating one, and part of that calculation had to include the possibilities arising both from Alphonse's failure or his success in this, and taking pains to prepare for both eventualities.

That sort of attention to detail ran in the family; Alphonse had gone to some trouble to make himself appear as other than he was.

It wasn't just the clothing, or the Arabic lessons. While the curved Seeproosh pirate saber that he had taken as a personal prize in the same battle that had gotten him the scar on his right cheek now hidden by his unshaven beard was at his waist, he had taken the precaution of having its plain hilt replaced with an ivory one. Smith—whatever he called himself these days, he was still Smith to Alphonse Randolph—might catch sight of him, and anything that even hinted at his real identity had to be changed, or discarded. Smith had never seen the blade, alas—Randolph devoutly hoped that it would be quite literally the last thing the bastard would ever see—but he had seen the hilt, and plain though it was and unlikely as it was that Smith had found it memorable, he would not see it again.

Smith stopped at a *shashlik* vendor's booth, and produced a coin, and after a very brief bit of haggling— Randolph wondered why Smith haggled at all, then decided that he had simply gone native in that—walked away with a heavily-laden piece of the local soft flatbread wrapped around the slices of lamb.

Losing sight of the bastard was, of course, unacceptable, but Smith wasn't walking quickly through the marketplace—he was taking his time as he made his way toward the docks, as though he had a particular destination in mind, but no particular sense of urgency in getting there.

So Randolph stopped and produced a copper coin, engaged in a quick few moments of haggling—Seepriots were as fond of haggling as was the greediest of a dockside Londinium fishmonger—and then walked away, chewing on the same meal that Smith had selected for his own, careful not to worry about how the drippings soiled his robes.

Randolph's mouth watered, and he forced himself to eat the *shashlik* slowly, despite his hunger, just as he forced himself not to quicken his pace. Dripping the sauce on his robes was more difficult for him, but Darmosh Kowayes traders were famous for such sloppiness.

Not exactly how he had been brought up, and not exactly the way that the future Earl of Moray would act, which was just as well, under the circumstances.

Father had not only been unhappy when Alphonse had taken his leave, closer to a year ago than farther from it; he had been visibly unwell. Was it just a passing case of the flux, or something more serious?

He wondered, from time to time, if he was the Earl of Moray, or if he ever would be.

Not that it mattered. Lord Sir Alphonse Randolph had, if not more important issues to deal with, ones that were more pressing and immediate, and far more personal.

Unsurprisingly, there was a slave auction going on dockside, and Smith stopped to watch, while Randolph stopped to watch Smith, while being very careful to seem to pay attention to the offerings on the platform.

The last of the compact but muscular Turkish male slaves had been sold off, and walked away quite meekly, keeping close to his new owner, without so much as a thin rope to lead him along—understandable, given the scars that crisscrossed the man's back; he had apparently taken quite some taming, but it seemed to have taken—as the first of a string of young women was brought up.

Again, all clearly Turkish. The raids on the southern coast had made the Izmir in particular the most common local source of new slaves, and they brought higher prices than Africans, for obvious reasons. Even here, thick-lipped African women were a drug on the market, and much less valuable than the light-skinned and often stunningly beautiful mulattoes imported back from Darmosh Kowayes.

For that, on Seeproosh, the Limmasol markets were the obvious place.

There was much trade in the Guild *kontore* at Kyrnia, of course, but none of it in human flesh. A man who was resolved to think kindly of what remained of the Hanseatic Guild would have said that was because they had long since disavowed such trade; a more reasonable one would note that HM Navy's policy had long been that the immunity of Guild traders was conditional, and a Guild ship outfitted for slaving would be quickly adjudged to have violated the conditions of its immunity. It was in the interest of Crown, Dar, and Empire that the flow of grain, timber, furs, tar, honey, and flax from Europe be echoed by an inflow of spices, gold, steel, and cloth from the Empire, Dar, and the colonies—but the Crown was hardly going to let the Guild supply new breeding stock or recruits for the Dar's janissaries troops without more than protest, after all.

And, besides, while trade was a lowly profession, and often a dirty business, slaving was the dirtiest of trade.

Smith watched with obvious interest, and perhaps hunger, as one young girl—she could not have been more than fifteen or so—was strung up by her wrists and then slowly stripped, as the bidding went on. She was wearing rather finer clothes than Randolph would have expected for a peasant girl, and rather a lot more of them—probably provided by the seller just for that purpose, although the auctioneer only hinted that she was of some of what passed for Izmiri nobility, rather than declaiming upon her ancestry.

Simply yanking off a simple peasant girl's shift wouldn't have gotten the same effect, Randolph supposed.

He was irritated that he found himself more aroused than disgusted by the sight of her nakedness, and forced himself not to look away, although he didn't bid. He considered it—but he would have had to do that carefully, for fear of winning the auction. And what the hell would he do with an Izmiri slave girl? Still, it might have been worthwhile to put in a bid in an early round, just to blend in, but while he hesitated, her price went quickly up, cutting out much of the hopeful early bidding.

She was remarkably shapely, at that; Turkish girls seemed to blossom early, just as they wilted young. But Smith just watched her, and waited. Whatever he was here for, she wasn't it. Unsurprising—no doubt, back in Qabilyah, he was able to maintain his own *harim*, with a variety to suit whatever his preferences were, stocked and probably regularly restocked by a grateful caliph.

Bidding was brisk, and a half dozen of the Turkish girls were quickly auctioned off.

"And we do have a surprise for you, noble bidders," the auctioneer said. "An Englishwoman, with hair the color of spun gold, freshly captured, and—but why tell you about her when I can show you her?"

Smith was watching with great intensity as a young woman was dragged up to the platform, stumbling both because of the rope around her slim neck, and probably because she was hooded. Like the Turkish girls, her wrists were quickly taken up and attached to a hook on the overhead beam.

Well, she certainly was dressed like an Englishwoman, although Randolph was suspicious. Not that it was unknown for Englishwomen to fall into pirates' hands, or be valued—apparently quite a few of the so-called nobles of the Dar Al Islam liked variety in the *harim*, and humiliating Christians undoubtedly but added to their enjoyment—but one would expect that her clothes would have been soiled, or at least ripped, in the ordeal.

She was dressed in what Randolph would have called a travel outfit—a tweed vest over a shockingly clean white blouse, that over long skirts that matched the vest.

The auctioneer ripped the hood from her head.

She was stunningly lovely, and, indeed, thoroughly blonde. Her golden hair fell about her shoulders, gleaming in the sunlight, as though it had been carefully brushed and somehow arranged to fall just so when the hood was removed, as seemed likely.

"Please, would somebody help me?" she cried out, silencing herself when the auctioneer's fingers went to the whip at his belt, much to the amusement of the crowd.

He wished she'd had a chance to speak longer; he couldn't quite place her accent. Brigstow, perhaps?

"Do I have an opening bid?" the auctioneer asked.

It didn't surprise Randolph that Smith made a gesture with his fingers, and the bidding picked up briskly, getting more so as she screamed when the auctioneer began to unbutton her vest. She tried to kick out at him, but he easily turned, and caught the kick on his thigh, then gestured to one of his assistants who quickly reached under her skirts, and bound her ankles to one of the U-shaped clamps on the platform.

Other than the fact that it was an Englishwoman, and the bidding steeper, it proceeded like the rest, with each garment being removed, one piece at a time. Either the auctioneer was much stronger than he looked, the clothing less well-constructed, or the hems had been deliberately weakened—the vest came off with a single yank, as did the skirt, leaving her dangling in her shift and underthings, her long legs bare from the knees down. Like the Turkish girl, her legs had been shaved; the sight of those long, porcelain-pale legs seemed to inflame the crowd, and the bidding grew more brisk, but for every bid that anybody else made, Smith simply nodded and gestured, and the auctioneer waited until Smith was the high bidder before removing another garment.

By the time that she hung from the ropes, stark naked, her eyes glazed, as though trying to pretend that she wasn't there, the bidding had reached two golden *reis*.

It wasn't the first time Randolph had seen a naked woman, although it was certainly the first time he had seen a naked Englishwoman in the daylight, with filthy smiles leering at her.

And the filthiest, of course, was Smith's.

At the sound of another bid, Smith made a gesture. "Four *reis*," he said, quietly, too quietly. "My final bid.

The final bid of Abdul Ibn Mahmoud, servant to the caliph himself—may Allah grant him wisdom and long life." His Arabic had a strong English accent. "Would anybody care to bid further against me?"

There were gasps from the crowd, and then silence. There were rather a lot of men named Abdul Ibn Mahmoud in the Dar Al Islam, but one with an English accent? One who dropped the name and rank of the caliph?

The auctioneer seemed displeased, for just a moment, then studiously put a neutral expression on his sweaty, thick face.

"Seeing as there are none," he said, "the girl is yours, Noble Sir."

Smith walked up onto the platform and handed over four small coins to the auctioneer, then reached into his robes and produced a preposterously plain leather collar, which he quickly fastened about the girl's throat, then another set of leather cuffs, with which he fastened her wrists behind her.

She was wild-eyed.

The auctioneer came forward with another one of the thin cotton robes, but Smith waved it away. "No," he said, "I'd much rather walk her naked through the streets." He smiled, as he took her chin in his hand. "Always a pleasure to humiliate an enemy, isn't it?" he asked, in English.

The girl looked away, and didn't answer. He took her chin in one hand as he produced a thin chain from his robes, and snapped it to the collar, then turned, leading the girl away.

She cast a glance over her shoulder. "Is there no one here who will help me?" she cried.

Smith gave a cruel yank on the chain, much to the amusement of the crowd, and Randolph forced a smile and a laugh to his own lips.

Randolph watched as Smith led her away, but walked slowly away in the other direction.

Very nicely done, Smith, he thought. Just a little too pat, a little too easy. Any red-blooded Englishman spy in the crowd would have been sorely tempted to rescue one of his countrywomen, and while this was obviously not the time or the place, it would be a terribly easy matter for Smith to have planted men to watch and see who followed, no matter how far back.

He was tempted to look behind him for the eyes that were no doubt watching for somebody following, but didn't give into that temptation.

A nice trap, at that, he decided. Only a few false notes in it. Save for a fresh welt across her bare buttocks, the girl's skin had been unmarked—no hint of the sort of intensive beatings that it would have taken to have broken the spirit of an Englishwoman, although she had silenced herself at just a quick gesture from the auctioneer.

And a cry—in English—for help and succor? Smith had smiled too easily at that.

No. It had been a trap.

Probably a general-purpose one, rather than one set for Randolph in particular. Smith was up to something, certainly, and was making sure that his back trail was clear, at least clear of any decent man, who would out of simple decency do what he could for a poor English girl who had fallen into such foul hands, no matter what the cost.

Not today, he decided. Maybe not ever. And if that made him other than a decent man, there wasn't any alternative.

Whether the girl was exactly what she appeared to be, as Randolph doubted, or something else, there was nothing that he could do, and therefore nothing that he would do.

But he would definitely pick up Smith's trail. The talk of a naked blonde English girl being marched through the markets behind Abdul Ibn Mahmoud would mark it well.

Patience, he cautioned himself. Patience.

CHAPTER 5

The Witch

The details are important, but it's easy to get lost in the details. That was as true when I was teaching my students at Alton, and allowed myself to get caught up in the day-by-day aspects of teaching, as it is now.

I have much to answer for. If I had a conscience, the blood of my lambs would weigh heavily upon it. But if I had a conscience, I couldn't have sent all my lambs to the slaughter, could I? My poor lambs—I do murder you all, don't I?

At least, now, I rarely have to set foot in England, where I'm widely known as the great hero, Sir Cully, who sent an army of novices into the meat grinder of York's soldiers. Two survived; Alexander became as black a traitor as could be, and I'd not save his soul if I could.

And Gray I can't save. Even She can't. My poor boy; I grieve for you much more than Bear, even.

And the worst of it? I think that most, if not all of them, would forgive me without being asked. I know that Gray does.

I'd thought to escape, but it's not possible for such as me. So be it. I'll be Sir Cully of Cully's Woode until the day that I die.

Or, perhaps—just perhaps—longer. It's a harsh punishment, but it's deserved.

—Cully

Her name was Penelope.

That was important, at least to her.

At her birth, Father and Mother had, so they said, agreed that she should be given a proper name, although they had argued, long and hard, as to what a proper name was. Mother had thought perhaps she should be Priyanka, and Father—who, unusual for a sergeant in the Mumbai Guard—had learned to speak Hindi fluently, always said that if she had to have a goddamn heathen name, it should be Parmeshwari, because as an infant she squalled and screamed like a demon goddess, but there was no sense in discussing it further—she would have a good English name, and enough of any nonsense to the contrary.

So she was Penelope. Penelope Priyanka Miller. Father always addressed her by her name, as did Sir

Michael, although Father did, when in his cups, occasionally refer to her as "my beloved little bastard," as he had married Mother in a church in Brigstow, not in Mumbai, where she was born.

Mother did call her Priyanka, when she thought that nobody else could hear. A few times Father had heard, and—out of sight or hearing of the captain, of course—had cursed his wife in a combination of English and Hindi that would have peeled paint.

But he meant well by it. That was one good thing you could say about Father: he really did mean well.

He was so different than many soldiers, in so many ways.

More than a few of HM soldiers took "native" concubines, and of those many, almost all of them left their half-breed children along with the concubines on the docks when their ten years was up, and their ships set sail from the docks of Mumbai. It was just a matter of economy; it was only a little cheaper to have one's own whore than to rent the usage at the brothels that sprung up around the compounds, after all. "Even a bloody private's miserly pay goes far, very far, very far in Mumbai," as the barracks song said, and more than a few soldiers slept outside the walls, awakening only in time to put on freshly washed uniforms for morning formation, perhaps after a quick servicing.

And Father had, she suspected, done most of that, although he had used the perquisites of his rank to have his own "girl" tend his private quarters, inside the walls.

But leave Mother and Penelope on the docks when he sailed away? He had, so he had said—drunk and sober—never considered it.

Not Father. He was, in his own way, every bit as stiff-necked as you'd expect from a sergeant of the Guard, but when it came to Mother, and to Penelope, it was as though he was another man entirely. It had taken all of his legitimate savings and probably most of the graft that he had taken as the regimental quartermaster sergeant, but he had shipped both of them to Brigstow the week before he left for, for home, and met them at the docks with a most uncharacteristic display of affection, interrupted only when he set Penelope down with Hemashri, and turned to administer a remarkably savage drubbing to some longshoreman who had made a comment that Penelope hadn't heard, and probably wouldn't have understood then, although she would later.

He had taken a position with the captain—Captain Sir Miles Weatheral was always "the captain" to Father, whether present or not—as his butler, and if late nights at Everwood often found the butler and his master in the library drinking and even singing, none of the rest of the staff took official notice, despite the upstairs gossip. She wasn't sure whether it was Father's influence or the captain's natural tendency that while Father was always addressed as "Miller," and mother as "Cook," she was always "Penelope" to the captain, who would always—always—ask permission from Father or Mother before taking her upon his lap, permission that was always granted, and a practice that had stopped when she reached her womanhood, although she had missed it, at least at first. The captain was a bachelor, and as a girl she had had dreams of him asking Father for her hand, although that had never happened, also of course. She was, after all, just a servant girl, and if the captain showed her more affection and respect than the other children of the staff, that had little to do with her and much to do with Father.

Still, when the upstairs houseboy tried to . . . take liberties with her, it was the only time that she had ever heard Father and the captain argue, although that was only because she had her ear pressed to the door. She wasn't able to follow all of it, but the final result is that the houseboy had, bruises and all, been sent packing, and she had been called into the captain's study, where he had stuttered and hemmed and hawed in a way quite unlike his usual self as he asked her what he called a favor, which she had of course granted, and then to swear to him—on the Bible that he had produced—that should *any* man *ever* give her such insult again, she would come directly to him, and to none other.

And it was one of the captain's acquaintances, for there always seemed to be younger men paying calls on him, who noticed her serving, and who asked the captain if he might have a word with her privately.

She hadn't thought much of it at the time; she had just assumed that he was in need of a girl, and that the captain would turn him down, perhaps after consulting with Father.

The young man, as it turned out, was a full fellow in HM College of Wizardry, despite his age, and Sir Giles had seen, so he said, a "spark" in her, and that would require testing.

Father had been appropriately shocked, but Mother just smiled, and Penelope had soon found herself in Glymphtown, before a "board." Master Hollingwood himself had made the preparations that showed her spark, but it was clear that all the other masters and mistresses could see it without that, and while it was really several weeks later she remembered it as being days at most before she had found herself sleeping in a dank cell that was most depressingly unlike the much more comfortable servants quarters at Everwood in every respect.

Glymphtown, naturally—not, of course, the Residence of the College in Oxford. That was for finer folk, as HM College of Wizardry was largely a noble affair. But both ordinaries and fellows were always in need of clerks, and clerks who could not only read and write but help with at least basic preparations would always be able to find themselves a position in at least an ordinary's shop in a small village.

Most of the rest of the students were English, of course, and being English, to them she was just another Injan, of which there were several, as though there were no differences between Hindi or Sinds or Tamils that were worthy of note, them all being little and brown.

It was unpleasant, in all respects, save for two: the teachers, and the work. Magic was more than the laws and the "spark," particularly in these days when the sparks of the Great Wizards had long since been quenched, and it was more study than anything else.

Languages, ancient and modern; alchemy; glassblowing; pottery; heraldry—there was still much power there, if you knew how to look for it. And then there was woodsmanship and natural science, for the difference between a spotted salamander and a speckled salamander would not show in the liver, but only in the efficacy, and while, as tradition had it, there was indeed much use for the "eye of newt" in various preparations, it had to be the right sort of newt, as errors could be and were often disastrous, not the least of which was trying to use the death of even the most humble of creature as a source of power, as she was certain was what had gotten at least two students killed. The Dark Arts could, so it was said, be turned to noble purposes—the Red Swords were but an example—but that was a matter for the Great Wizards, and at best risky for the lesser ones of a lesser age, and utterly unsafe for a clerk-to-be.

The unsupported "spark" of a Glymphtown student could hardly do much damage by itself—even the spark of a senior fellow had to be carefully tuned and directed to be of much use—but she was fairly sure that what killed poor David was an attempt at a love potion that had gone bad, and she was always most careful, something that Master Hollingswood would occasionally remark upon to others of the students.

Which would have left her very lonely, if she was capable of loneliness, something that she denied to herself just as much as she looked forward to her occasional holidays at Everwood.

Her life's path was clear to her. She would become a clerk to a wizard, an apprentice in name who would never become more than that, and she hoped to one who would appreciate that a woman clerk would be of more use than a man during part of the month, and less during others, and not beat her too often for her inadequacies.

It was all very clear until the day that the old man in the robes of a knight of the Order had walked into the dining hall during dinner, spoken briefly with Master Hollingswood, who argued, argued some more, read the paper that the knight presented, argued yet again, and then threw down the paper and stalked from the room as the knight walked down the tables to where she sat, wondering what this could possibly be about, and stood before her, and said, "My name is Cully. I'm very sorry, but you're to come with me."

And now she walked through the bright Izmiri night behind the two knights, with the third knight behind her, in search of a witch.

At the thought, the wind began to pick up, and while the night was warm, she still found herself shivering.

A witch. Mother had told her tales of the *moha karana*, and they were similar enough to the English stories about witchwomen as well. Usually more than half-mad, unsystematic to say the least, and more often frauds than not.

More often; not always. Skills could be learned in other places than Glymphtown, after all, and could be passed down from mother to daughter. The Church didn't burn witches, and hadn't for centuries—although that couldn't be said for the Inquisition, where the Empire ruled. In England, the College did most of the policing of such, at least in southern and eastern England, although much less in Scotland and Ireland. Witchcraft—as opposed to wizardry—was always a matter of suspicion, as the arts could easily turn black, and there was power to be had in the necromancy that, when it was just a matter of a newt or bat or even a cat, could do quite a lot of harm, and much more so when it was something with a soul. Through Inja, the Kali cult was still being suppressed, although in fifty years the administration had made little more than a dent in it.

The Kali worshipers were, well, systematic. Not the same systems she had been taught in Glymphtown, of course—and woe to the student there, or at Oxford, who tried his hand at necromancy—but both the letting of blood and the killing without bloodletting each could be the source of much power. It was the only thing that did explain the new live swords, after all.

She was skeptical, though, and thought that Cully shared her skepticism. The source of new live swords being a Turkish madwoman witch? That didn't make sense, at least not to her.

No.

But. What else did they have to go on at the moment, except for exhaustion? They had spent the rest of the afternoon and most of the evening doing the tinkering that Cully had promised for the next day, and carefully hidden the completed work along with the rest of their gear. If this turned out to be the nothing that her mind told her it was likely to be, there would be questions asked in the village the next day, and when all the questions were the same, the answer would be that they had been doing something other than the tinkering.

So that had to be done, and sleep would have to wait.

Sir Guy, of course, grumbled a little—well, much—accepting Sir Cully's reproach with his usual ill grace.

About the only good thing about this was that this was the right time of the month for her. She could feel her spark burning just a little more brightly in her belly, as the part of her that was a woman said that it was time to create life, supporting the part of her that would some-day be a wizard, at least of sorts, urged her to channel that otherwise.

There was no road up into the hills, just a winding path, but that didn't matter. A cook fire—or a fire of some sort—was burning somewhere up it, and that gave a direction, even if it didn't provide a map.

As they neared the top of the hill, Cully held up his hand, and she and Stavros stopped immediately, although Sir Guy walked on for a few more feet before turning back.

"What is it?" Sir Guy whispered.

"Shush," Cully said. "There's a shack of some sort, just through those trees." He turned to Penelope. "Can you sense anything?"

His hand went to the hilt of his sword, then dropped.

If the smoke rising slowly into the night marked it, the shack was a full hundred yards away, at least. A full fellow of the College would likely not have been able to spot the spark of an adept—even a powerful one—at this distance.

While this time of the month her own spark glowed more and more warmingly just above her womb, and her senses of such things were as acute as they could be, she certainly couldn't have.

If she had been where she ought to have been—sitting at a bench alongside the other students at Glymphtown— she could no doubt have detected the sparks of the boys as far as two or three seats down, and perhaps the girls even further, if they were at their peak.

But not across even a tenth this distance.

But she shook her head. "There's nothing that I can sense. We're not close enough, even if there's anything there."

He nodded. "Which means if there is, it's nothing of much power."

For a man who seemed to be smart and clever about most things, Cully was being amazingly stupid at the moment. "It means nothing of the sort, Sir Cully," she whispered back. "It just means that I can't feel the spark from here. It doesn't mean it's not there."

She could more feel than hear Cully frown in the dark, but it didn't feel like a reproach.

Sir Guy snorted. "Is there anything you *can* do?"

Well, of course she could. The tinker's gear wasn't the only thing that they had brought from England, and the bag that Master Hollingswood had given her was strapped to her back.

"Yes, Sir Guy. It will take me a few moments to prepare." Detecting a spark or the use of the Powers wasn't particularly difficult, and just a technical matter. She couldn't feel it with her own, but she certainly had the tools available.

"Why not just walk up and see?" Sir Guy asked.

In the dark, she could more feel than see Cully rolling his eyes. "Do what you can," he said. "But quickly."

Sir Guy waited with as much patience as he watched the girl, kneeling on the path. It seemed much of a production for something that could have been, and presumably should have been, settled by merely walking up the path and knocking on the door.

He let his hand fall to Albert's hilt.

Patience, Guy, is a virtue.

Well, as always, what Albert said was more than true enough, but patience for *this*?

Coming all the way from England, lowering himself by pretending to be a mute slave, hauling a cart up and down the hills of Izmir, and now watching as a little Injan girl knelt on the ground, her shift riding dangerously up her thighs as she spread out her candles and potions, and because there was a rumor of a witch?

Patience is a virtue. Are virtues only virtues when your life is one of convenience? Are they to be practiced only when it is easy to practice them? And only when your own station in life is shown the respect that you believe it deserves?

Guy bowed his head. Saint Albert of Leeds, despite his noble birth, had taken a beggar's and a hermit's life. It was a matter of God's Will, Sir Guy was certain, that the rigors of that life had found Saint Albert dying in a hut outside of Almsbury, just at the right moment when his soul could, at his death, be sealed within the sword.

And the rumors that Morrolyst murdered me? You've never given those much credence.

Well, of course not. How could a White Sword be created by murder? It didn't stand to reason.

Albert said nothing further on the matter; it was hardly the first time it had come up.

Perhaps another time. In the meantime, it might be best to concentrate on the present. There's always the possibility that it holds some peril, you know.

He let his hand drop from the hilt of the sword. It wasn't the first time that Sir Guy had the feeling that Albert looked down upon him, and he didn't much care for it, truth to tell.

But, as usual, Albert had a point—granted, there were all those agents of the admiral's who had disappeared in the area, and maybe that meant something, or maybe it didn't.

Well, at least, the girl did seem to know something—if not necessarily her craft in the way that a fellow of the College would have, at least in terms of the contents of her bag and the basics of her trade. She had scratched a circle in the dirt of the path, and set out candles that she had insisted—almost silently—that she had to light herself, even though Cully was far handier with a fire kit.

With the candles in place and lit—and they were each of a different color and shape; Sir Guy assumed that there was a reason for it—she dribbled several somethings from several of the vials just inside the inscribed circle. He was sure that one of the vials contained frankincense—that was a familiar enough smell—and perhaps the other another spice, but was the third really urine? It smelled like . . .

She murmured something, then took a knife from her bag and cut at the inscribed circle in four places.

"*Davetsiz misafir,*" a voice said, out of the darkness. "How interesting."

Sir Guy raised his head, and reached for Albert, stopping only when Cully gripped his sleeve with strength that a man his age shouldn't have had.

"Stand easy," Cully said, rising. "We likely mean you no harm."

The dark shape stood on the path above them, and laughed. "I have heard that before," she said—and not in Turkish, but in English, and that with a smooth accent that would not have seemed out of place in a West End drawing room in Londinium itself.

"Interesting," the voice went on, "that you should appear here, sneaking about like thieves in the night, and tell me that you mean no harm."

"I didn't say that we mean you no harm," Cully said. "What I said is that we *probably* mean you no harm. It depends, I suppose, on who you are, and what you're about, more than anything else."

Another laugh. "Ah. Sir Cully of Cully's Woode— always one for honesty, except when it suits you to lie." More laughter. "Well, as long as you keep your *kamýp* in your trousers, you'll do me no harm, and likely give me no pleasure." The shape extended a dark arm. "Ah. And here we have a little girl playing with little toys." A quiet snicker. "Well, let's make it easy for you."

A murmured word, and the flickering flames of each of the candles grew brighter and brighter, until Sir Guy had to throw his arm over his eyes to avoid being dazzled.

And then the light dimmed—but not the quiet flicker of the candles that had barely illuminated the circle where the girl still crouched. The candles were still lit, and burned more than halfway down, but their light seemed to permeate the air about them.

With one exception. The hooded figure in front of them was still wrapped in darkness, and the light seemed to stop just short of her robes, save only for the eyes.

It would have almost have been reassuring if the eyes had shone red or yellow in the darkness, but they were just eyes, with the rest of her features hidden.

"You will come inside," she said, and Sir Guy found himself in lockstep with the three others, following her through the scrub brush, unable to do anything about the way that the brambles clawed at him as much as he was to ignore it.

He tried to turn his head to meet the others' eyes, but his body wouldn't obey him, any more than it would when he tried to clamp his hand to Albert's hilt.

CHAPTER 6

Gray

I'm told that, often, there comes a time in the life of a knight of the Red Sword when he finds the sword more of a blessing than a burden.

I am, I am sorely afraid, coming to that time. I can no longer sit in judgment of the Khan, I think; it was impious of me, perhaps, to ever think that I could, from the moment I took him in hand. Bear used to talk about how it was Vlaovic that changed all that, but that there still and always was the opportunity for all, even including me, for hope and repentance, even after.

Bear was not merely my companion, but my friend, and I mourn his death every day. But I'll

mourn him in my own way, and do him the honor
of thinking of him in death as he was in life:
In this, my beloved friend was entirely on sound
theological grounds.
But he was a fool.

—Gray

Getting permission had been faster and easier than he
had thought it would be. He hadn't had to go directly to
His Majesty—Gray had just had a page send a note,
which had come back within a surprisingly short hour
with a short "Do as you think best. I'll handle the duke.
Godspeed. M.R." scribbled on the bottom of it.

Which may have been why the abbot general had
immediately sent word that he would receive Gray, when
he had begged an audience, also via the proper channels.
King's Messengers were not exactly in short supply at
Pendragon castle, and the use of them a prerogative of
the Order, and while the best writing that Gray could
do with his remaining hand was none too good, it was at
least legible, and he hadn't had to find a scribe to do
for him what it was only right and proper that he do
for himself.

And waiting gave him more time to practice.

He would, of course, never again be the swordsman
that he once was, not with his right hand but a stump,
but left-handed swordsmen did have some advantages
when foining, after all, as most swordsmen, right- or left-
handed, had difficulty adjusting.

He would never be able to tie his own boots again,
but he could give a decent account of himself with his
mundane sword.

The best of it, though, was the hand-to-hand. The soldiers of the House Guard were always on a one-in-six guard schedule, which left plenty of time for practice at the skills of their trade, which included unarmed as well as armed combat, and if an Order Knight asked a guard captain to provide him with a few opponents, it was hardly surprising that he had had a half a dozen of the larger, tougher privates and one barrel-bellied sergeant reporting to him every morning.

It felt good to hit people, and the being hit never bothered him. Hurt, yes; bothered, no.

Truth to tell, on average, the best of them were almost the equal of Order Knights in most respects, save only for the swordsmanship. Hacking at an enemy while maintaining their ranks wasn't something that Order Knights spent any time at all on, after all—but hand-to-hand, like swordsmanship, was a skill that had to be built over years and maintained for a lifetime, or it would surely wither even more quickly than the slow way that age would rob them of it.

And, in that, he found that his stump was every bit as useful as a fist—more so, perhaps, as it seemed incapable of pain, not that pain would have slowed him down.

Cully had always said that it was a strange thing that a knight of the Order had the right—not merely the privilege—to walk into the presence of the king himself without let or hindrance, but had to apply for an appointment with lesser men, like the abbot general, although he couldn't remember Cully referring to him by title, except when in his presence, and then only grudgingly.

So, of course, Gray had sent his request for an audience by royal messenger, and it had been less than a day later that a tired rider had appeared at Pendragon castle, and even before Gray could order a horse saddled from the stables, word had arrived from the king that, yes, Gray was to do as he would, but to keep His Majesty personally informed of his whereabouts, something that His Majesty had said over the preceding months on more than one occasion, and which Gray hadn't needed to have repeated.

As Gray rode slowly under the elm-lined road, noon had given way to afternoon, and dark, oily clouds loomed in the west, promising a downpour.

Alton, as both the home and school of the Order, was always busy, with Order Knights not on mission or leave in residence, both to keep them under the eye of the abbot and to keep them available for assignment. And since skills when not practiced grew rusty with disuse, whether it was polishing their languages or their fighting skills, Order Knights resident in the North Tower worked every bit as hard as the novices living at the school buildings did, and often at much of the same things.

And, truth to tell, the majority of the knights of the Order were from common backgrounds, and unable to maintain a household of their own, although in the village a few miles to the east, several of the better-off maintained town homes. If Gray's cell in the North Tower was unavailable, he would not have to go hat in hand or find a place in a stable to sleep; Swift or Linsen or the Beast (if he was in Alton, which was unlikely) would have seen to his lodgings, and if there was more than one of them in residence, they would have vied for his guesting with them, playing at draughts for the privilege, more likely than not.

Knighthood in the Order of Crown, Shield, and Dragon was, in financial terms, no more well-paying than that in any other holy order was. Yes, it was far more expensive to the Crown to equip a knight than it was for the Church to robe an Anglian, but the Order was appropriately miserly when it came to disbursing personal funds. Yes, ample Crown funds were available on mission, but they were for duty, not to line a knight's own purse. Those who came from noble or merchant families, like Bear or Sir Robert or the Beast, of course, always had stipends and such from their families, but that hardly applied to Gray.

Still, a knight of the Order missed a meal only out of duty, not poverty; the Order provided.

He forced the horse not to canter up, trying to enjoy the moment as much as he was capable of.

It was coming home, after all. A man should have a home, and while the dockyard orphan called Grayling had been lucky to find an alley to sleep in unmolested, the novice Joshua Grayling and the knight Sir Joshua Grayling had always had Alton.

It could be argued that his life really had begun the day he had walked, barefoot and ragged, through these gates, among the gaggle of boys that Father Cully had gathered up, but that was an argument that Gray would not have made; his life had really begun on a dark, miserable night on the docks, when through the pain and humiliation that he had become resolved to accepting as his lot in life, he had heard a quiet voice saying the words he would hear again, and again: *Not while I breathe.*

But it wasn't a moment for remembering; it was a moment for trying to relish the familiar, and the right.

Over near the edge of the woods, a trio of knights armored cap-a-pie were working out with blunted swords and bucklers, while the *clang-clang-clang*ing sounds and the smoke from both chimneys of the smithy spoke of others polishing their blacksmithing skills.

If Gray had been the sort to be amused by such things, he would have found very amusing the four squares of mixed knights and novices over by the stables going through some complex estampie while a single lutist— also in knightly robes—plucked away at a tune, his timing far more precise than his fingering. The novices wearing red sashes about their waists that proclaimed that they were taking the women's roles weren't as clumsy in their movements as usual, which was just as well, and the novices absent the sashes seemed to move as featly as the knights themselves, although from this distance, the only knight he could make out was Sir Daniel of Farmount, and that only because of his great height and immense belly.

Still, they were all doing quite well.

In Gray's time at Alton, that hadn't always been the case, at least among even the senior novices. He still remembered his very first ball at Kent, where he'd managed to step on the foot of some young noblewoman whose name and face his memory was weak and generous enough to have blotted out at the moment, although both name and face, no doubt, would return to him sooner than later.

Gray vaguely recognized the moves, which seemed elegant enough to be French while broad enough to be

Neapolitan; apparently it was some new variation that was popular in some court or courts. Being able to mingle among nobility was simply another of the skills that Order Knights were expected not merely to learn while novices, but to maintain their mastery of as knights.

The novices were already out in force, as well, in their short tunics and blousy trousers. Shaved-headed first-form novices trimming the hedges and shrubbery under the eyes of not just their upperclassman monitors, but of old Sir Robert Linsen, who was dressed not in the particularly ordinary robes that he donned on formal occasions, but a carefully tailored, finer set, with what Gray assumed was a deliberately short sleeve for the left arm that displayed the old man's naked stump. Shorter than Gray's; Linsen had lost his arm above the elbow, but at least it had been his left.

Linsen, a twinkle in his eye, raised the stump in a quick greeting that Gray ignored, as the abbot himself was walking quickly down the front steps of the keep, clearly heading toward where Gray was just dismounting; Gray's intention had been to let the horse cool off on his way to the stables.

Two novices trailed in the abbot general's dignified wake. Without a word one held out a hand and ducked his head, asking for the reins to the brown gelding, then quickly led it away while the other handed Gray a goblet of icy-cold water, waited for Gray to drain it, then accepted it back, then quickly made himself absent as well.

"It's good to see you, Sir Joshua," the abbot said, as soon as the boys were out of earshot. He offered his left hand for a clasp with Gray, and briefly clasped his right hand over their joined ones before releasing him. As always, his grip was firm and strong, and while the heat of the day had sweat running down his bald head and into the collar of his robes, it didn't seem to affect his dignity.

Sir Ralph Francis Wakefield, by the Grace of God and Order of His Majesty the King not only the archbishop of Canterbury, but the abbot general of the Order of Crown, Shield, and Dragon, was arrayed in his plain Order robes, the only concession to his other office a large golden cross on a thick chain. His sash was, as you'd expect with any Order Knight, belted tightly across his hips, keeping both of his swords in place, although Gray tried hard not to look at them, and failed.

The basket-hilted rapier was easily distinguished from the other sword, above it.

Jenn. The White Sword that Cully had carried, and which now decorated the abbot general's waist. An utterly plain cutting sword, with a simple wooden hilt, carried in a simple wooden scabbard.

It was hard not to hate the Abbot for the friendly smile, the apparent sincerity of which was somehow more maddening than any falsity would have been.

"Well, you've clearly had a long ride," the abbot said, taking his arm—his right arm, as though to leave the left free. "Let's see to getting you freshened up, and properly fed. And you will, of course, stay the night." He grinned. "I think you'll find your cell as you left it. If there's so much as a cobweb there, it's been spun since this morning."

"I'm at your service, Sir Abbot," he said, addressing him properly. If the abbot had been wearing his surplice and carrying his miter, it would have been "my Lord Archbishop," of course.

"Not quite as graciously spoken as I'd have hoped for," the abbot said. He pursed his lips for a moment. They seemed somehow redder than they should have, like a wound in his well-trimmed white beard.

"Then I humbly give apology," Gray said.

"Accepted, of course, of course. You've had provocation enough, I'd say." The abbot waved it away, then stopped, and looked around, before he spoke. "I'm not your enemy, Gray. And I'm not just your superior in the Order, either, although I am that.

"Sir, Father, and Brother Joshua Grayling," the abbot said, formally, "I am a priest and brother of the Order, just as you are, and . . . " he patted at Jenn's hilt, "a knight of the White Sword, as you are of the Red." He cocked his head to one side. "And if you were to tell me that Jenn should properly be in the sash of Sir Cully of Cully's Woode, I'll neither voice agreement nor disagreement, but remind you that he lost the honor of carrying Jenn by his own decision, not mine."

For a moment, the Abbot's face clouded over, but then he took a deep breath, and his expression became, if not as friendly as it had been, not hostile.

Gray didn't know what to say. He knew that Cully utterly despised the abbot, and of all living and all the dead, he loved Father Cully above even the Order—and above He Who should have been in Gray's mind and spirit above the Order—as sinful as that was.

But love is not agreement, and loyalty was to be informed by thought and insight, not practiced in reflexive blindness, and in the battle over Gray being given the Khan, it had been right that Father Cully had lost and the abbot had won. Perhaps it was possible for another man to mix his soul with the Khan's and avoid damnation, although Gray had his doubts.

It certainly wasn't possible for Gray.

But if ever there was a man who deserved Hell, it was Joshua Grayling, and the abbot had chosen wisely when he had ordered that the Khan be belted around Gray's waist.

Let Cully fault the abbot for that; Gray would not.

"Are you here to be asked to be relieved of, of it?" the Abbot asked.

A foolish question, for anybody who knew Gray, but the Abbot really didn't know Gray. "No, Sir Abbot, it's—"

"No. Gray, I—no." He stopped himself with a peremptory hand. "*It*—whatever *it* is—is a matter that can, unless you tell me otherwise now, wait a few hours, that's what *it* is, although I've my suspicions. You're a knight of the Red Sword, Sir Joshua, and arrived at the home of your Order, but you've as yet been met with scant hospitality, and for that I hold myself responsible, and beg your forgiveness. Can it wait until you've bathed and dined? Can *you* wait?"

"Yes, of course, Sir Abbot."

"Then let's see to that hospitality, first," the abbot said, picking up the pace with a cheerful bounce to his step. "You'll join me at table tonight, I hope? If you can remain for more than a day or two, it's only appropriate that you sit table with the rest, Sir Joshua. But if you'd be willing to go along with an old man's preference, as I hope you will, we shall dine alone this night."

"Yes, Sir Abbot; I'd be honored."

"But first, let's get some food in you. And if ever I've seen a man who would benefit from at least a little strong drink, I'm looking at him right now."

"As you command, of course. But there is one favor I have to ask. I'll bathe before, at your orders, and if you insist that I drink, Sir Abbot, I'll drink."

"And that favor is?"

He swallowed. "Will you hear my confession?"

If the abbot seemed surprised, it didn't show. "Of course. But your sins, no matter how grievous, surely can wait for an hour or so until you've cleaned yourself. I've always thought that cleansing the body goes well with cleansing the soul, in any case, so I guess we're both for our baths."

Which was fair enough. Gray tried to prepare his body as well as his mind when he heard confessions. It wasn't a theological necessity—the sacrament, thankfully, didn't depend on the cleanliness of the body or the mind of such as Sir Joshua Graying—but it was what he had been taught.

"Thank you," he said.

The Abbot's eyes met his. "I shall hear your confession, Sir Joshua, and assign such penance as I think just and proper. But . . ."

"But?" Was there some condition? How could that be?

The abbot shook his head. "You misunderstand me. I'm not a common tradesman, bargaining with you over your barrel of oats and mine of groats. I'm your superior in the Order, and neither no more nor no less a priest than you yourself are, Sir, Brother, and Father Joshua Grayling. I shall hear your confession, Sir Joshua, as is my duty to you, and to God, and I shall do that without reservation, and without condition." His eyes were fierce, and the fierceness was a comfort to Gray, although his words were not:

"And you, Sir Joshua Grayling," he said, and there was no hint of indecision in his voice, "you *shall* hear mine."

Dinner was quiet, and private, in the abbot's study—not his office. The difference was mainly a matter of degree than of kind; both study and office were lined with bookshelves, and each featured a large desk near the outside window. But the study had a table that could seat perhaps six, with ample room about it for the servants to move about and serve, without bumping into anybody.

There were true servants at Alton, of course—it couldn't have gotten by without cooks and bakers, stablemen and cobblers, coopers and smiths and all the other necessities—but all of what would have been the common domestic service in a great home was done by the novices.

Which was only right and proper. Many of the novices were from middle-class or lower families, but more than a few were of noble lineage, and if there was a better way to learn humility than emptying chamber pots and doing other scullery work, Gray couldn't think of it. Unless, of course, it was something specifically unpleasant like, say, mucking out then stoning a stable, just to pick one example not entirely at random.

There were differences, of course. In a noble house, one would hardly be introduced to the staff, save perhaps the majordomo, or butler, or the maid assigned to one's rooms. One would be given their names, perhaps, depending, but that was merely so you'd know how to call them.

But each of the novices had been formally introduced, and Gray tried hard to mark each of their names, and use them, and if he tended to be a touch more friendly to those of lower origin, well, that was only because it was far more common for a lowly born to make it all the way through the training and Alton, and to kneel before His Majesty, to arise as a knight of the Order of Crown, Shield, and Dragon.

The boy who had been introduced as William McGowan gathered up the dishes. A well-made boy, by the looks of him, although Gray would not have made him as a Scotsman. It was sometimes difficult to tell the origin of a novice who had gone beyond his first couple of years, as traces of their local accents had been carefully extinguished, just as the orphan boy who had been called Grayling, after the fish that he supposedly resembled, had lost his dockside drawl more years ago than Gray could remember.

"Thank you, William," the abbot said. "Stay a moment." He turned to Gray. "If you don't mind, Sir Joshua?"

"Of course not. Should I excuse myself for a moment?"

"Not at all; please stay. Now, as to you, William . . . ?"

The boy didn't answer; he simply ducked his head. Silence was the rule under such circumstances, except for responding to direct inquiries.

"Sir Aloysius," the abbot went on, "tells me that you're coming along remarkably well in all of the martial arts, that your table manners are unexceptionable, to say the least, and that your memory of the missal minor is as good as he's ever seen—"

The boy's face brightened.

"—but that you can barely get through a passage of Agesilaus or *The Art of Horsemanship* without stumbling, that your penmanship is sloppy, and that you seem to be particularly hard on that Injan boy in your cohort, almost to the point of bullying, while you let a spot of insolence from Lord Wellington pass the other day with no more than a word of caution. None of that is acceptable."

The boy's face fell.

"I'll see you here after morning prayers," the abbot said, pausing, "one month from today, on the fifth of York. We'll decide what to do about you then. If that suits you?"

"Yes, Sir Abbot," the boy said, his face a stony mask.

"You may leave."

When the door shut behind the boy, the abbot let his face split into a grin. "I'm of the opinion that he'll shape up. He's really not quite as bad as all that; just needs to behave a little better with some of his juniors, really, and spend more time with his books." He sobered. "Besides, Jenn's of the opinion that he's got the heart of a knight of the Order," he added, as he brought his free hand up to the table and clasped it on the other in front of him.

Gray hadn't seen the abbot's hand dip to the side of his chair, where both of his swords stood in a boot lashed to the chair, as did Gray's own. A knight of the Order of Crown, Shield, and Dragon was, in at least a theoretical sense, always on duty, and while there were rare occasions when that duty prohibited him carrying his swords, those were rare.

Gray had not been tempted to touch his finger to the Khan's steel until now, but he found himself doing so.

Hmmm. The Khan was unimpressed. *I've never understood why you people think that washing feet and mucking out thundermugs has anything to do with being a warrior. Better training would be to have the boys ride down a few peasants—and a few peasant girls—to see if they've got the stomach for conquest.*

It was an old argument, and one Gray didn't feel like continuing at the moment, particularly since he well knew that if he did mention to the Khan that there was much more than fighting to being a knight, the Khan would only bring up Vlaovic, among other things.

So he touched his thumb again to the Khan's steel anyway, and said as much.

The Khan was amused. *Vlaovic. Szebernica. Dunladen. Pironesia. Pantelleria—should I go on? If you had the heart and the manstick for it, you could burn your way from—*

He pulled his thumb from the Khan.

"Yes." The abbot nodded. "A heavy burden, indeed, the Khan. Probably more than the Sandoval; certainly more than the Tinker, say, or Croom'l. And the boy Niko seems to find his new Red Sword less than a heavy cross he must bear, eh?" He sipped at the single glass of wine that was all that he had allowed himself through dinner. Moderation in all things, the abbot preached, and at least appeared to practice, most of the time.

He seemed to be choosing his words carefully, as though to see if he could arrive at what he had been told in Gray's confession otherwise.

No, that was unworthy. The abbot respected the seal of the confessional as much as anyone, if not more, and if he could not help letting his thoughts escape into the rest of his mind—and Gray doubted that anyone could—he would not go further, not without the permission that he would not so much as hint a request for.

But the permission could be given without a request, after all.

"Please, Sir Abbot," Gray said. "We're alone; what . . . what I said to you before, please feel free to refer to it—or need I repeat it here?" The begging sounded despicable in his ears.

"*No.*" The abbot was firm. "Those sins which God has forgiven are not yours any longer." He raised a finger. "I can't make you forgive yourself, Gray, but I can tell you that as much as you repent of the sin of pride, as much as you repent of your sin of despair, as much as you continue to repeat those sins, you continue to endanger your salvation." His face was grim. "But your sins of the past, Sir, Father, and Brother, are in other Hands than yours, and borne by He who can bear them all, and He can bear them lightly; do not trouble yourself more with them. I've done what I can, and will do what I can, and not merely because you are my Brother, Sir Joshua. I've served you badly." He shook his head. "My predecessor should have had you in this office, years and years ago, while your head was still shaven, and sent you away. Not that you've served badly—quite the contrary. You should never have been a knight of the Order. I had my misgivings, but in those days, Cully was capable of persuading me, and he did—my predecessor listened to both Sir Cully and to me, and well, you were quite the hero in those days, even as a novice, eh?"

Gray ducked his head, accepting the reproach.

"*Lift up your head*, Sir Joshua Grayling, and conduct yourself as a knight of the Order of Crown, Shield, and Dragon, in private with me as you do so well in public, when you're among others. I'm not criticizing you, boy; I'm criticizing myself. It was my fault, just as much as Cully's—I listened to him, fool that I am, and I put my misgivings aside." His voice softened. "But I'm always overcritical, I'm told. I'm always worried that each time that I let a boy kneel before His Majesty I've helped him create not a knight, but a monster—but that's not my worry with you, Gray. It's not now, and it wasn't then.

"It was your relationship with Cully. I could say that I don't understand it, or I could say that I do—but it doesn't matter: the truth is you've always loved him too much." He shook his head. "We serve God, the Crown, the king, and the Order—and we do so in that order." He held out both of his hands, palms up. "If I were to put the life of Sir Cully of Cully's Woode in your left hand, and that of the king in your, in another hand, which would weigh more heavily upon you?"

"The king's," Gray said, instantly. It hadn't required thought. That wasn't the point. Of course he would turn his back on Cully to protect the King, as he had as a fourth-form novice, during the York Disgrace.

To the end of his days, he would still see the late king's screaming face, demanding to be turned loose and given a sword, and he would hear Cully's cries of pain from behind him as he held the door by himself, Sir Bedivere having fallen moments that felt like hours before.

He had not wavered, not for a moment. He would have turned from the king only if Father Cully had fallen, and not a moment before. And, although he was then only a novice, he would have taken up Father Cully's borrowed sword. And yes, he would have died there, beside Cully, but that thought had not frightened the young Grayling in the least.

Would he do it again?

Of course he would.

How could he face Cully if he did otherwise?

"Yes," the abbot said, nodding. "And is it because of your oath?" He shook his head. "We both know better than that: it is because you know that Father Cully would want it that way, that he would, once again, order you to protect this king rather than himself with your own body, if necessary, as you did the king's father?" He raised a palm. "Don't answer. Don't even think about it."

"Yes, Sir Abbot. I'll try."

The abbot took a long breath. "You haven't asked it of me, but I'll tell you: I'd relieve you of the Khan in a heartbeat if I thought there was another better able to wield it.

"But I don't. Neither does the king. That's why you bear it.

"Of the worst of the Red Swords, do you think that I'm such a fool as to not consider with utmost care which knights should be trusted with them? It wasn't accidental that my predecessor put the Sandoval in Lady Mary's hands and . . ."

He stopped when Gray ducked his head and murmured a brief prayer, then sighing, joined him, and was silent for a moment when he went on.

"Yes, our Mary, our lovely Mary, was no accident, any more than it was when Abbot Oakley begged His Late Majesty to make her a knight, even though it's an unwomanly thing. I worry about who is given White; I have nightmares about you Reds, and about the Khan more than any."

He made as though to pat at Jenn's hilt, but stopped the motion. "The Reds are more common, and usually of less power, which is as it should be; evil should bow before the right. The Whites, rarer though they are, are much safer; they mainly tempt those of us who carry them into pride, and a few days on one's hands and knees with brick and sand in a stable is a good remedy for pride," he said, smiling. "As I'm about to have a reminder of, over the next few days. You give a sound penance, Father Joshua, if not a light one. Well, it'll be good for my soul, if not my hands and knees. They'll heal, even at my age." He leaned back and folded his hands over his belly.

"But you've come a long way for a not particularly good meal and a much-needed confession. I'd say I'm honored that you chose me as your confessor, but I'm not. You came to ask me something, something you could have asked the king for."

Gray shook his head. Yes, Order Knights had unlimited access to the Royal Presence, but that was for the king's benefit, not their own.

He said as much. Asking the king for leave, via messenger, was entirely proper; going into the king's Presence for the purpose of asking the king himself for a personal favor was another matter.

"True enough. We have access to him for his sake, not our own, and it's rare that an Order Knight abuses it." The abbot nodded. "I think it was as much because of that as anything else that His Late Majesty didn't even consider acceding to Cully's request, the time he came to him over you." He frowned. "Although, to give the devil his due—and none of that; it's just a figure of speech, Sir Joshua—I think that Sir Cully went to the king out as much out of a sense of duty toward the Order as because he thought you too weak to bear the Khan." He cocked his head to one side. "You could have done the same as he did; you could have gone to the king. But you didn't do that. Instead, you quite properly come to the abbot general of the Order, and ask . . . ?"

The abbot already knew. How?

"There's loose talk in the palace—Admiral DuPuy thinks that he's on the track of the maker of the new live swords, and . . . "

"And you think you ought to be there. You want to be there. And since His Majesty hasn't ordered you to stay at Pendragon castle, and you haven't been sent away on leave or mission, you come to me and ask that I put you on mission and order you to join him." The abbot sat silently for a while, then chuckled. "You're different from Cully; I'll give you that. He'd have taken a note from the king like the one in your pouch and used it to commandeer a fast ship, even though that wasn't the intent of it.

"But, instead, you come to me, and you ask.

"And you ask that knowing that I've little faith in Sir Cully's good sense, that I think him reckless and foolish, and you hope that I'll think that you'd be a steadying influence on him, rather than him tempting you into sin or excess."

Yes, there was that. And there was more. Cully understood how close Gray was to the breaking, how he always had been, and how, with Bear dead and the Nameless in another's hands, the only check on Gray and the Khan was Gray himself, and that that could easily not be enough.

He remembered the screams in Vlaovic, and the Plaza of Heroes in Pironesia, and he knew that there would come a time when he would draw the Khan, and would have to be stopped, for the unified person that was the Gray Khan was far too dangerous to be allowed to live for long, if at all.

And perhaps there would be no one who could stop him.

Service, honor, faith, and obedience. He was bereft of faith, and a murderer of thousands was a man without honor. His obedience was merely subordinate to service. If he had slipped out of England, the Khan in his hand, how many other knights, Red or White, would have had to be dispatched to chase the traitor Gray? How much service would go undone while the likes of Big John, or Sir Walter, or the Beast, or the Saracen hunted Gray down?

No.

"There is another option," the abbot said. "And I know it's one you've thought of. Lay the Khan upon my desk, surrender your vows, and walk out. No, I'll not demand that you surrender it—but I'd not stop you. I'll allow you to leave the Order. I'll find another to bear it. I'll have to, eventually." He gestured toward the door. "Perhaps Sir John de Ros, although I worry about his corruptibility. Perhaps Sir Niko, who you seem to think so highly of, would be of more use with the Khan than with that little Red of his." He gestured at Gray's stump. "But then, you think to yourself, how much aid could you be to Father Cully with but the one hand? Instead of leaving the Order, perhaps you should simply surrender the sword and let me put you on the Reserve List, like old Becket. But that wouldn't serve your purpose, would it?"

"No, Sir Abbot, it would not."

"Well, I'll tell you: I think it's a bad idea. Not the worst in the world, mind. Cully needs a steadying influence, and I'm none too sanguine about the possibility of Sir Guy being that. If I thought it were up to me—if it were up to Ralph Wakefield, not the abbot general—it would be easy. I'd say no. I'd say to hell with that arrogant bastard, Cully of Cully's Woode, and hope that he manages to get himself killed before he does more damage than he already has, because where Cully goes, destruction always follows in his wake, even though salvation has been known to, as well. But ever and always the damnable destruction accompanies him." The abbot's voice was barely under control; he took a moment to calm himself.

"But . . . " The abbot rose from the table and walked to his desk. There were two sheets of parchment sitting under the same paperweight of plain stone that Gray remembered from his novicehood. The abbot sat down behind the desk and put the papers before him, signing both in turn, carefully pouring blotting powder on each in turn before tipping the excess into the stone bowl.

"But I think if I did that, you might well resign, and leave the Khan on the table, that I would lose the combination of you and the Khan to the Order, and His Majesty is of the opinion that, as he says, 'the combination is near perfect,' and like you, I'm the servant of the king.

"And there's another reason, which I'll get to in a moment.

"So here," he said, "is your authority. This is for you. Guard it carefully. You've held a paper like this once before; it grants you my own authority, as both abbot general and archbishop of Canterbury, and it's been signed with my coded signature as both. Yes, as my vicar, it makes you Cully's superior in the Order, once more, although scant good that's done or will likely do. Don't expect it to move DuPuy, though. His authority comes from the king; mine comes *through* the king.

"The second paper is a dispatch to His Majesty; it will leave Alton within the hour. It informs him that I've sent you out again—after the live swords, yes, but to use your own judgment as to where that may take you. And it's not just for his eyes; there'll be copies to Admiral Dougherty, as well as to DuPuy, and my suspicion is that there'll be a fast ship waiting to convey you to wherever you think you need to go when you reach Londinium, without you having to go through the rigmarole that you did the last time.

"Of course, if and when you find Cully, he will tell you that this is all merely a machination of mine. He'll say that I'm simply relaxing to the inevitable, and have taken advantage of the situation to try to keep him under some sort of control, as you're one of the few that he will ever listen to—although not much, alas—and that

I've seduced you by my kindness tonight, which you'll long remember, Joshua, as you've seen scant kindness in your life.

"And that will be true, too," the abbot said, nodding to himself. "Life is full of contradictions, after all, and there's few times in my life as abbot that I'd done a thing for one reason and that one reason alone.

"But there are other truths, as well," he said, taking up the third sheet of parchment. Unlike the others, it was small, and folded over several times. "You'd best read this, although I'll want it back after you do. It arrived a week ago, and I've been dreading the each day ever since. One of Her damned crows dropped it right on my desk." He chuckled. "I'd take to closing my windows, but I doubt that would inconvenience Her.

"Still, I wish She had been more specific; I'd been expecting that it would be Cully riding onto the grounds, and I was almost embarrassingly relieved to get your message that it was you who wanted an audience with me." He made a get-on-with-it-gesture with his right hand. "Well, read it. Read it."

Gray unfolded it. The parchment was ragged along the edges, and not even vaguely square, and a few clumps of wool still clung to the edges, as though it had not been properly scraped before being dried.

The words were written in red.

Not the ruddy brown of dried blood, or the cheery crimson of colored ink, but the too-deep red of fresh blood from the heart, though the letters were dry to the touch, and unsmeared, even though the parchment had manifestly been folded and refolded many times.

I bid you: do as he asks. Salve his soul if you can, although I hold little hope there. Do as he asks. But tell him to come see Me first, they said.

"She has sent for you, Gray." The abbot ducked his head. "Do give Her my best wishes." He started to speak, then stopped.

It wasn't necessary, for Gray knew what the abbot wanted to say, although he wouldn't. For once, long ago, the abbot general had been the boy Ralph Francis Wakefield, the novice whose last task before being knighted was to go into Arroy for a private audience with Her, and he had fallen in love with Her because all the boys always fell in love with Her, because that was Her nature, after all.

How could you not fall in love with the Queen of Air and Darkness? How could you not ache to lay your sword or your life, or whatever She wanted, at her feet?

Was that the origin of the hatred between the abbot and Cully? That She loved Cully more than him? Or that Cully loved Her more than the likes of lesser men such as Ralph Wakefield and Joshua Grayling were capable of?

Everybody knew that the abbot was jealous of Cully, but Gray had always thought that it was the fame and the legend that had grown up around the York Disgrace, of the stories of Sir Cully raising an army of novices that had delayed the traitors almost long enough, and of the final moments, of Cully standing in the doorway over Sir Bedivere's body, while the two surviving boys and the prince's nurse stood behind him, Mary murmuring soft lullabies to the infant prince, quieting him, while Gray and Alexander held the king to one side, of the promises of riches and titles that came through the doorway as

much as the arrows and swords, of oaths sworn on all
that was holy that all save the king and prince would be
spared, and be rewarded, if only the door would be
opened, and if the knight would stand aside . . .

And the knight who would not stand aside, and the
quiet whisper, of *Not while I breathe.*

The abbot could be jealous of that, but, no. It was an
unworthy thought. All of it was unworthy.

The abbot folded the parchment twice, very carefully,
and if he touched it briefly to his lips before he tucked
it into his robes, Gray didn't have to notice.

But there was one last surprise, in what was said, if
nothing else.

The abbot met Gray's eyes. "Oh, and yes, do send Her
my love."

It wasn't a request.

CHAPTER 7

Baba Yaga

Weapons. Knights spend far too much time thinking about weapons, as though it's the sword that prevails—the sword, the bolt, the spear, the ram, the catapult—and that it's merely a matter of having more and better weapons.

And there's some truth to that. You could have asked the Duc d'Artois if was Thomas II's bowmen that stopped him at Crecy in 1246. Was it? Yes, the battle was decisive, or so the histories say, but was it the weapons, or was it the will of Good King Thomas, who promised death and destruction on one hand, and pardon for the Capétien Rebellion on the other?

I'm not suggesting an answer. I do suggest that you think on it. And make up your own mind, have your own opinions. But it is not a matter of opinion, but of a matter of history, that when Phillipe rejected Good King Thomas' terms, it was his son Louis who cut his own father down, surrendered to King Thomas, and insisted on being tried and hanged as a parricide, quite properly, under Artois law.

Is it the weapon, or the man?

And who won that battle? Could it be both?

The French have not rebelled since Crecy, true—and it's also true that more than half of the queens since then have come from d'Artois lines.

One thing you can say about the Pendragons is that they remember.

—Cully

"Sit down," she said, and like the others, Cully sat. He would have fought the command, but there was nothing to fight. His body was simply under her control, not his.

She threw back her hood, but didn't let the dark robe fall from her skinny shoulders.

Beneath the hood, her face was preposterously ordinary. Her hair was a mare's nest of gray, her face lined and withered, and her thin nose was a sharp knife over thin lips that smiled only at the edges.

The smile didn't reach her eyes.

"Ach," she said. "I'll have to give you a little freedom, won't I?" A withered finger, the knuckles swollen with age, raised in admonition. "But I'll have no nonsense," she said, pointing the finger not at Cully, but at Guy. "You're to keep your hand off the hilt of your sword—of both of your swords. You're not to throw anything at me, or move so much as an inch closer toward me than you are now—and that goes for the rest of you, too."

She aimed a thin-lipped smile at Penelope. "And if you think to try one of your pitiful little cantrips or glamours against me, feel free—but feel even more ready to suffer the consequences." She smiled more broadly, and her withered lips revealed teeth that, at first glance, looked dark as to be almost rotted away. But, no—they were made of iron, vaguely rusted. "I can promise you that you won't care for the consequences," she said.

Cully found himself able to move, at least a little. He planted his feet on the floor, and his hands against the arm of the chair. When she turned past him toward Guy, again, he could be able to move—

But no. She did just that, the witch, the bitch turned past him toward Guy . . .

. . . and his traitor body refused to obey him. To move out of the chair would be to move toward her, and she had forbidden that, in a way that he couldn't so much as lift a finger to disobey.

Inside, the hut appeared to be much larger than it was outside. The floor was not the dirt that he had expected, but freshly strewn straw, although the sputtering ashes and flinders from the open hearth died the moment that they touched it, without a hiss of quenching.

An ancient stone bathtub, of all things, stood in one corner, the water steaming slightly, and curled up against one of the thick legs of it, a black cat watched a mouse hole with intent interest.

A waist-high pile of bones lay in one corner, up against the pillar, all of them bleached white. There was no question about what kind of bones at least many of them were; the human skulls were distinctive.

She dropped her robe about her feet, in a gesture far too reminiscent of an Order Knight. Beneath the robes, she wore peasant clothing, but not local peasant clothing— a blouse and long skirt, rather than a shift.

Her neck was decorated with a multilayered necklace that at first glance looked like raw pearls. But, no—they were teeth, bleached as white as the bones.

"So, now, Sir Cully of Cully's Woode," she said, addressing him, as though the others weren't there, "you've found me. But you don't seem to recognize me. Curious," she said.

"I don't," he said. Talking seemed to be one thing he could do. No reason not to, he supposed.

"Jenn would have." Her smile was neither cruel nor gentle, just amused. "She would be of the opinion that she killed me, although quite some time before you and she were joined." She cocked her head to one side. "What's it like being married to a sword?"

He didn't answer. It wasn't just stubbornness, although it was that, too. There just wasn't an answer, and while he had long since given up his White Sword, that didn't mean that he had given up all longing for it, just as Gray, perhaps, still missed his right hand.

Or Sir Guy his brains, for that matter.

"You'd best release us," Guy said.

It was when he turned his head away from Guy that Cully finally really noticed the corner pillars of the hut. They weren't wooden uprights, although that's what he had assumed that they were when he had only seen them out of the corner of his eyes.

No. They were vaguely cylindrical and rippled, and familiar-looking, like the legs of a bird.

A witch who lived in a hut supported on chicken legs.

No wonder nobody had returned from this part of Izmir.

"Oh, had I best?" She started to sit, and a wicker chair quickly whisked itself across the hay-strewn floor and was under her before she had finished sitting. "You hardly seem to be in a position to make threats, any more than demands." She gestured at Cully. "He, at least, has worked that out. And has probably figured out who I am, as well."

Cully nodded. "Baba Yaga, I assume," he said. "You're rather far south of where you should be. And apparently somewhat more alive than you have any right to be."

She should be dead. Back when Jenn had been carried by Sir Edward, he had killed her. That's what the Annals said. Sir Edward Williams—known as the Horseman, although Cully didn't know the origin of that nickname— had hunted her down, and killed her.

Cottage witches were one thing, and toleration of them had gradually increased over the centuries. But wherever the Crown ruled, magic of the blackness of that of Baba Yaga, or the Kaliites, or the Ghost Dancers, or *zerostiva* was wiped out, mercilessly, whenever it surfaced. It had taken generations to wipe out the hezmoni, but they were finally gone.

As Baba Yaga should have been. But even if she wasn't dead, she shouldn't have been here—she should have been up north, in Vezalukis, near the southern border of the Zone.

"Not only less dead, but rather more alive than I should be, am I not?"

"That, too."

"Well, I can tell you in truth that that's as much a surprise to me as it is to you. Not the being this far south, of course—things near the Zone are far too . . . interesting, these days, for even the likes of me." She shook her head. "But I'm neglecting my duties of hospitality. You've come a long way to find me, and you're all quite filthy. Time to clean you up." She turned to the girl Penelope. "You'd best bathe yourself, my dear. Now, if you please."

Without a word, the girl rose from her own chair and walked over to the steaming tub, dropping her clothing about her as she did.

Guy averted his eyes, as though looking away would make any difference. Cully had seen a naked young woman or two in his time, and while under other circumstances, he would have found himself aroused by the sight of the remarkably full young breasts, crested by nipples that were darker than he would have expected. He was, of course, an old man, but he wasn't a dead one.

But even when she bent over to grip the edge of the tub, he found himself utterly unmoved, in any sort of sexual sense.

Guy was blushing, even as he kept his head turned, and Kechiroski watched the girl with a visible hunger, something that he should have been too scared to feel, and the sight of which should have disgusted Cully.

But Cully found himself utterly, surprisingly, devoid of any sensation, any emotion, even any feeling of horror at the pile of bones in the far corner, and as the girl began to wash herself, he watched the witch trimming carrots and turnips and tossing them into the bathwater with a strange sense of detachment.

She was going to eat the girl. And she was going to make the three of them watch, until it was their turn.

"Quite so," she said, responding to either his head movement or his thoughts. "And a tasty morsel she'll be indeed." She smacked her lips. "Do you know how hard it is to find a virgin hereabouts?" She sighed. "Oh, for the old days, when I could get a stepmother to send one to me, when I was able to at least tolerate some daylight."

The cat looked up at her. "If you asked me, I'd say to just eat your food, and not play with it first," the cat said.

She snorted. "And a fine one *you* are to talk, and you with your mousies."

"That's my nature." If a cat could shrug, it would have. "It's not that I care much, one way or the other, but there's something to be said for a clean kill and a quick meal. It's not like you're teaching kittens how to hunt, you know."

She walked over to where the girl was bathing and brushed at her hair with a bristly brush that Cully had not seen her produce. "But it isn't just the meat. Can you feel her fear?" She seemed to grow larger in the confines of the hut. "Tasty. Powerful."

"Not nearly as much as that last English fellow, though." A pair of small eyes peeked out of the mouse hole. "Now, if you'll excuse me, I've got my own kill to attend to."

"Do as you please." She laughed, and turned back to the girl. "Scrub yourself thoroughly, my dear," she said, as she walked over to the fireplace. She took a buried stone from the ashes with a preposterously ordinary set of tongs, then carried it over. "I think that the water is chilling you—let me help with that," she said, plunging the stone into the water.

It burbled and steamed, and when the girl started to scream in pain, the witch laid a withered finger across her lips, and all she could emit was a whimper, although her eyes were wide in terror.

She eyed Cully. "It would be much more of a pleasure right now if you still had Jenn with you. Hurts, doesn't it? More than if it were your own flesh scalding?"

"I've seen pain before," Cully said. "And felt it."

"Oh, very brave, Sir Cully of Cully's Woode—when it's another's pain. We'll see how you fare when it's you in the pot."

"Why don't you tell me what's going on?" he asked. Anything to delay, and besides . . .

She laughed again, as she busied herself with adding another stone, and yet another, to the water. "And just after I've been chastised by Bubastis for playing with my food? I think not."

It was all wrong.

This shouldn't be Baba Yaga; she was supposed to have been dead for almost three centuries, and almost a thousand miles away.

Talk, he thought to himself. Stall.

"I don't think you're really Baba Yaga," he said. "I've read the Annals. Sir Edward wrote that he killed her, and he was a knight of the Order."

"And knights of the Order never lie?" She was amused. "You, of all people, should know better than that, Sir Cully of Cully's Woode. Collect up your silly sins; sort them as you please, and you knights have committed far larger than simply bearing of false witness."

The girl was still unable to open her mouth, but she was more screaming than whimpering behind her sealed lips, as the water simmered about her.

"I don't know very much about Order Knights," Kechiroski finally said. "Or about Baba Yaga. Although I have heard it said that the greatest of all the witches was Circe, of course, but perhaps that's just—"

"Circe." The witch practically sniffed in disgust. "You might as well bring up the *litae*—those tired old biddies, who can do no more than bind a wound or two."

Kechiroski was thinking, although to what effect—

Yes. Keep her talking, get what information that they could from her, and bide their time, waiting for an opening to do something, something useful. Like flee.

Of course. He was compelled by her words, in combination with whatever spell she had worked on them. When her mouth was full, perhaps they could flee, and he could put his hands over his ears to keep the words out.

All Cully would have to do was watch as the witch boiled the girl alive, and hope and pray that he was the last, and not the next—that he could find a moment to break away.

It was all sensible, and cold-blooded, and the right thing to do. Whether this really was Baba Yaga, or something else, that was important, and getting word of it out far more important than the lives of all four of them, or more than that. Darklings south of Aba-Paluoja; new live swords; an attempt on the Wise in Pantelleria—those were all pieces of a puzzle, and this game of puzzles was being played for high stakes.

And, besides, there was nothing that he could do except wait and watch.

Bile rose in his mouth, and spewed out over his chest.

No. There might be a way. He might be able to—

The witch was opening her mouth to say something. The right thing to do, the only thing to do was to wait and listen, and if he survived this, the muffled screams of the girl would haunt his dreams, but they'd have company aplenty, after all.

And—

The witch turned away, ever so slightly, to drop another slice of carrot in the stew pot.

Sir Cully of Cully's Woode kicked himself backward and sideways out of his chair, not toward the witch, where his traitor body would have refused to go, but toward Guy, tearing at his own tunic as he did, to give his hand at least some protection.

Sir Guy of Orkney, bearer of the White Sword Albert, sat wide-eyed.

Faster, old man, faster, before—

She was turning, murmuring something, as he reached Guy's side.

The right thing to do, the safe thing to do would be to clamp Sir Guy's hand on the hilt of Albert, and force him to draw it, but Sir Guy was decades younger than Cully, and stronger, and even Cully's desperate strength might not be enough to overcome Guy's obedience to the witch's command. Willing spirit could not always overcome stubborn flesh, after all.

So it was simple.

He snatched up the scabbard and drew the sword himself.

Sir Guy had averted his eyes, although there was nothing that could be done about his ears, and the calmness of the witch was even more frightening than the screams of the cooking girl.

His hand ached for Albert's hilt, and he cursed himself for the weakness of his body and spirit that kept his hand away from the hilt.

And not just to kill this witch, although he hungered to do so with a passion that astonished even himself.

It was the fear. Yes, he had made confession that evening when they had finished their work, and for once Cully had had no complaint. Surely whatever sins he had committed since then were of a venial nature, easily forgiven. He had, after all, averted his eyes from the disturbing sight of the naked girl.

But it was the fear of dying that had turned his bowels to water. Not the fear of pain; pain was a frequent companion.

But of dying.

How could a good Christian knight not go to meet his maker with eagerness? Yes, suicide was a sin, but there was nothing that he could do here. He had carried Albert for years; surely, the calmness of the saint should have rubbed off on him enough to treat this, his end, as fitting. It wasn't as though he was some stumblebum like Cully, after all, who had made a life of doing what he pleased, whether it was leaving the Order when it suited him, or tricking Sir Joshua—and the king himself!—into bringing him back into service.

No. Sir Guy was, after all, on mission, and knights of the Order of Crown, Shield, and Dragon died on mission all of the time.

So why was he trembling in fear? Why? It was absurd, but it was.

And there wasn't a thing he could do about it, or about—

And suddenly Cully was at his side, a scrap of cloth hastily wrapped about his hand, reaching toward his waist and drawing Albert.

Cully was trying to turn away, as though to hack away at the witch, but . . .

But it was all wrong. Cully? Yes, if he touched flesh to metal, Albert would burn not only his flesh but whatever Cully had left of a soul.

But it was preposterous. Cully had no right to a live sword in his hand, be it the reddest of the Reds or one as White as Albert.

Yes, they were all to die here, but that was the way of it, and for a moment his fear was washed away with fury at the wrongness of it all, and he reached out to stop the indecency.

Cully's face was twisted into a mask of agony, and he didn't resist. But as Guy reached for him, he clapped his hand—the hand with Albert in it!—to Guy's.

It was all pain.

It was always pain, and worse, and, as always, they could remember it only when they were joined.

Two souls, welded into one for the moment—how could it not be agony? How could Guy's insufferable arrogance and pride not grind painfully against Albert's sharp, grating humility? How would it not be possible that each wrong that each of them had done would not be laid bare before the other, disgusting the both of them?

Touching his hand to Albert was a reassurance; taking him in hand was something that they would both blot out of their memories.

Later.

They had heard that for some of the others of the Reds and the Whites, the world became gentler, laid out in pristine black and white or in deep, rich colors, with the light of the sword a beacon of clarity. They hoped and they prayed that story, that myth was true for the others, and surely that was possible—but it never was so for them.

It was all ugly. It was always ugly. Not just in sight, but in touch, smell, and taste. The foul stench of their own sweat was overpowering, reeking of ancient, unforgivable sin, and they could feel every tiny foot of every single one of the lice burrowing through their body hair.

The witch was the worst, perhaps, but the best was still awful.

Still, the power, the fire was there, the purifying fire that had Cully's hand still afire, still smelling like a pig on a spit. It hadn't been enough to purify that spawn of Hell, but that would be a simple matter.

It was all a simple matter, after all: all life was sin, all life was foul, and they had the power to cleanse it.

The witch, though, was worst of all. The sweat dampening her armpits stank not just of humanity, but of human flesh, and the fire burning within her was no cleansing flame, like the white flame that burned within them, threatening to consume their own sins.

It was a dark and ugly fire, a smouldering reeking.

She was far more fire than flesh; he could see that now, and it was all that they could do not to recoil in horror from the hellfire that clung to her bones. She stank not only of human sin, but of sulphur and brimstone, beyond any power to cleanse, but only possible to destroy.

So they lowered the part of them that was the burning sword toward her flame, and met it head on.

But it all stank. They brightened their flame, careless of the damage it was doing to Guy's body.

There was no heroism. There was no dignity, nothing ennobling about it.

It was just a matter of fighting the stench.

Stavros's mind had been spinning—but no, he wasn't Stavros here, he was Nissim. He had to sound like Stavros, but not act like him. Sir Stavros Kechiroski, OC, was a hero, and that he had earned the Order of the Crown trying to do what Nissim al-Furat would have been doing was merely a coincidence.

Here, a hero of the Crown would have stayed and fought—and died.

He wasn't afraid of death; that would be as Allah willed, as it always had been. It was the notion of failure that frightened him—failure of service.

When the White Sword flared into brightness that dazzled not only his eyes but his mind, he kicked himself out of his own chair, and out through the door into the night. Let the knights win or lose to the witch; that didn't matter as much as him getting away. The nearest place that he knew he could make a report was Pironesia, and he would work his passage there, no matter what he had to do in order to get that done.

What did this all mean?

He didn't know, and it wasn't his to know. It was enough to know that this was important—this wasn't a matter of some Tikritzian village crone who made vile potions that probably did a little more harm than good, for she would always end her supposed spells with *inshallah*, as was only proper.

No. This was a witch like something out of the old fables, the sort of power that the Caliphate, just as much as the Crown and Empire, had hunted down, and for much the same reasons that the afrits and djinni had been killed and confined by Suleiman the Magnificent.

There was no living with such as these—except that there she was: alive.

The caliph and the sharifs, of course, had their own court wizards, in much the same way that the Crown had its College. Those were different, working along the boundaries of magic and alchemy to cure lesions, or clarify sight, and if some dabbled in the Black, well, such things always happened, and the officers of the Caliphate were always firm in their resolve, and the headsman's sword was always thirsty.

But this? You could bargain all you would with one of these, but it was like bargaining with shaitan—the bargaining in and of itself was impious, and a repudiation of faith. The best thing, of course, would be to kill her, but doing that was beyond the abilities of Nissim al-Furat and Stavros Kechiroski alike.

So he ran.

The girl was screaming in pain, her hands scrabbling at the rim of the stewing tub, unable to find any purchase, while Sir Guy and the witch stood locked, her darkness warring with the light of the live sword.

Cully's legs tried to refuse to support him, and his right hand was useless, but he forced himself to his feet, barely able to keep his balance, as though the hut itself was rocking from side to side.

Ignore the pain, he told himself. It was important that he ignore the pain.

It didn't matter how much it hurt. Even with Albert in hand, Guy was by no means the superior of Baba Yaga—not in her place. The walls, which had seemed preposterously far away, began to close in on them, and the hut itself rocked back and forth, splashing the witch even more than Cully with the scalding water from the stewing-tub, splashing him from leg to hip in agony that seemed to exceed that of his hand.

But his body was his own again. Concentrating on Guy and Albert had caught the witch's attention, or distracted her power, turning it away from him.

The right thing to do would be to launch himself at the witch, and ignore the dying girl in the boiling water. Even if the sword had not lit up the hut with its actinic brightness, he could see that Penelope's skin was all blistered and broken; she'd die anyway.

So he reached his good hand into the boiling water and yanked her free from the tub. Her skin was blistered and burned, and she couldn't stop screaming, but as he turned to leap upon the witch's back, she was at his side.

His fingers reached out into the blackness that wrapped itself about the witch, and in that there was surcease from the pain, at least in his hands. They were numb and insensate, and he wasn't even sure that he was reaching into anything at all, except for the cold darkness.

Which popped like a soap bubble, and he found himself astride the old woman, his hands around her neck, the hut motionless, and with a whimpering girl at his side, Kechiroski gone, and Sir Guy passed out on the straw floor.

"Wait," she managed to choke out. "Please stop." Was he hearing her with his ears or his mind? He wasn't sure. He was gripping her throat as hard as he could, and she shouldn't be able to croak out anything more than a gasp. He wouldn't have waited, but his hands just weren't strong enough to wring the preposterously thin neck, although he tried, as hard as he could.

Was it that her neck was too strong, or that he was too damnably weak?

Her fingers clawed at his face, trying for his eyes, and he shook them off, leaning harder on his hands, ignoring the pain as her nails clawed his forehead and cheek, until they fell away; and when he opened his eyes her lips continued to work, and he could still hear her—not with his ears, in which the rush of his own blood would have drowned out her whispers, but in his mind.

The roaring grew louder and louder, and it deafened him. It was all he could do not to take his hands from that neck and clap them about his ears, but no.

Not while I breathe, he thought.

I know something, some things you need to, Cully. And you've won—I'll tell you. Just let me have the girl.

I need her—that, that sword did me in almost as much as your Jenn did Mother.

So she wasn't really Baba Yaga?

Yes, I'm Baba Yaga, daughter of Baba Yaga, herself the daughter of Baba Yaga, and your beloved Jenn and that horrible Sir Edward killed Mother, but they didn't get me, and—

What do you want?

What do you want? It's yours for the asking. Anything. You have but to ask, Cully.

She raised her withered hands to touch at his, and at first he thought she was trying once again to break his grip, but, no: the blistered flesh from his injured hand sloughed away, leaving pink, fresh skin behind.

I can do more than that, much more. Make love to me, Sir Cully, and with your manhood touching my womb and my tongue in your mouth, I'll lengthen your life. The aches, the pains that you wake with will be gone. I can make you forty again. Or twenty, even. No seeming; it's just a matter of adding life to life.

And all you want is me to mount you, and hold my nose while I do?

No, no, you fool—I need the girl. I'll cook the life out of her, as I must; I'm badly hurt—but I'll share that life with you. Drink of her broth, with me. She's young, and of a strong spark, and a virgin; she's not just a tasty meal, like what I've been living on, but prepared properly, she's a banquet. You can share at that banquet. It will fill you beyond your imagining.

Not a chance.

But there's more—I know. I know what you're looking for; I listen to the wind, and it brings me many tidings. I'll tell you. After. Just give me the girl.

Tell me now, and I'll let you live—for now. I swear it on my soul.

Pfah for your soul; you'd sacrifice that in a heartbeat. Would you swear it on Joshua's? Would you swear it on your love for him, or for Her?

Yes, I'd swear on all that and more—tell me, and I'll let you live this day.

Yes, he would let her live—and then he would hunt her down, and kill her.

She seemed to laugh at that possibility.

I'm unworried about that. But you'll give me the girl? It's of little import; she'll probably die anyway, burned as she is, and if not today or tomorrow, soon—you ephemerals live such short lives. Give me the girl—help put her back in the pot, and I'll tell you. I need the girl.

Tell me first.

And then I can have the girl?

"Of course," he said. "I swear it on my hope of salvation," he said.

And you swear it by Her? By Joshua's soul? Do you bind yourself by the hope of his salvation to help me in this?

Of course he would have lied; She would have forgiven him the lie, and Gray would have forgiven him the truth. Lying had always come easily to Cully; it was the truth that was hard for him to see, to speak, to accept.

She could have produced a stack of Bibles, and he would have sworn on them, without regret, and then betrayed the devil's promise in a heartbeat.

But what if his oaths had power here and now? What if his word could bind his body as tightly as her magic had, moments that felt like days ago? No need to worry about what She would do, or feel—She was far more powerful than he was, and his words could touch Her only if She so chose.

No. If words could bind his body, his body would now be bound.

But . . . but what if his words could bind Gray's soul? A just God would not have permitted that, save by Gray's own choice, perhaps.

But Cully knew full well what Gray would have chosen, for it was a choice Gray had already made.

For himself, by God, he could solve this if needs be, for while his life was not always in his own hands, his own death was. And if God would hold him accountable as a suicide, that was His choice, not Cully's.

But for Gray? What of the risk to him? Could Cully's oath breaking endanger Joshua's soul? It was against all sense and logic, against all his training as a priest—but so much in life went against all that.

What if it was true?

It was a risk Joshua would have insisted he take. Put it all in the hands of God, and trust to His mercy. Perhaps he would not condemn Gray for Cully's impiety, Gray would say, and it mattered not a whit if He did, Gray would have said, for he was already damned, and it didn't matter if he were not.

He knew what Gray would have said, were he here: *As you love me, Father: say you what needs be said, and then do you what needs to be done.*

As you will, Joshua.

"I so swear," he said. "I swear it on Joshua's soul; I shall do as you say."

Liar. You'll kill me the moment I tell you.

"Of course," he said, for he could bear no more, and if all it would take to compel the Baba Yaga were his hands on her throat and his words in his mouth then it would already have been done.

But, no, he would not sacrifice the brave girl. He loved her too little, and too much, for that.

He tightened his hands and bore down, his hands clenching with all the strength that they had, more than he would have thought he was capable of.

Cully bore down for a long time, until he noticed that he could hear again, and that the wind was whistling through the trees.

Sir Cully of Cully's Woode found himself kneeling on dead, wet leaves, with Sir Guy passed out beside him, and the girl whimpering in pain as she writhed on the ground.

Kechiroski was nowhere to be seen, but that was understandable; they were no longer on the hill that they had climbed, but in a clearing, hills and mountains rising in the distance.

How far away from the hilltop? He couldn't recognize any landmarks, not in the dark, and the moon and stars overhead were no clue at all. The hilltop could have been among the dark mass rising off in the distance to the north, but he wouldn't swear to it.

Maybe. The familiar smell of the sea was strong in his nostrils. He must be much closer to the sea than the hilltop had been.

The only thing in his hands was a scrap of cloth, and of all that had been in the hut of Baba Yaga, the only things that remained were four preposterously ordinary chicken legs, stuck upright in the dirt, and over by the trees were the eyes of a cat, reflecting the moonlight.

For just a moment.

And then it was gone in the dark, and he was alone with the screaming.

CHAPTER 8

Colonsay I

It would probably be best, all in all, if I left Colonsay to itself. The McPhees, as is true for all of the clans, certainly resent having any part of the land of the clan be tributary to an English noble— even one with a good Scots title, like the Earl of Moray, as the Morays have married far too much into English families for local tastes.

And while I doubt that there's the resentment of my family that the mainland McPhees have over Moray's tight hold on his Scottish lands, whenever we arrive to summer at Kiloran, I wonder in the back of my head if perhaps I should petition His

Majesty to let Colonsay lapse back to Moray when I'm gone. At least he's a Scot, if one of diluted blood.

I know that Michael would make no protest. He's a proper English land baron, and will, no doubt, resent leaving Fallsworth when it's necessary to go to Londinium, when it becomes his turn, and while he came willingly to Kiloran as a boy, remaining behind in Fallsworth is something that he always chooses these days, and likely would have preferred in his younger ones, as well, although I can't remember him protesting.

He'd have no trouble with me giving away Colonsay.

I doubt that the Colonsay McPhees would prefer it if all McPhee land was tributary to the same English lord, though, although there would be some advantages to them. When the Colonsay McPhees send their one-in-twenty to take service with the Crown, there would be advantages to having them serve under the earl's banner, rather than under His Majesty's alone.

And there was a time, of course, when the Barons of Shanley raised their own companies, and maybe some would have preferred to serve under that, although perhaps not if they'd known me during my army days, or the later navy ones.

Still, knowing the McPhees as I do, I have my own suspicion that, sooner or later, were that the case, the rampant Shanley griffon would find itself wearing a bright red-and-green tartan, with strands of bright white and yellow. The McPhees have a way of having things their way, after all.

And while I trust I reign over the island rather
more than I rule it even when I'm there, I'd still
stay away, if I didn't love Kiloran so.
But I do love it so, after all.
                              —Giscard, Baron Shanley

The drunken singing and laughter poured in through the
open windows.

Closing them would have lost Giscard the breeze, and
done little to cut down on the noise, alas.

And, besides, while the singing was one thing—who
could enjoy the sounds hundreds of drunken McPhees
singing, each in his own key?—and although he wouldn't
have admitted it aloud, Giscard enjoyed the laughter.

Not just that of the children—though it had been too
long since not only the laughter of children had filled
the house at Fallsworth or here—but that of the adults,
as well. Laughter was better in the throat than a fine
whiskey, and better in the ears than any music.

And if the price of the laughter was the drunken Scots
singing, well, he could bear that, as though it was a trade
and he was a tradesman. It had been too long since he
had heard laughter, and he couldn't remember the last
time it came from his own lips.

Or from hers.

He looked across toward the foot of the table where
Grace sat, picking at her food, seemingly oblivious to the
sounds outside as much as to the care with which Cook
had taken with the pottage pig, which was—which had
been—one of her favorite dishes.

These days, she had no favorite dish; her plate was still annoyingly full. She hadn't had more than a polite bite or two when they had put in their appearance at and after the wedding, although she had made a point to taste everything, even though he knew for a fact that she utterly despised mutton, and would willingly tolerate lamb only when it was very young and fresh.

The wedding party was easily a hundred yards outside, on the beach, partly under the tents, although the sounds of laughter and the singing—all in Gaelic, naturally— flowed through the open windows with a volume that clearly irritated Grace.

Then again, Grace was more than a little irritable these days, although the baron flattered himself, and he hoped her, in that none other would be able to see it but him, or perhaps Becket.

Becket's eyes weren't what they had been, long ago, but his sight was still keen, in most ways, and they had had the honor of Becket as their guest in happier days, as well as these ones.

Becket gave him a glance, and the slightest of shrugs, as though to say, *what can't be cured must be endured*.

"Sounds like a fine party outside," the priest said, smiling. Father Olafsen certainly didn't seem to be able to detect her irritation.

The priest had presided over the official ceremonies— well, the marriage, at least—and had, as he always did, accepted the baron's invitation to dinner and to stay the night. The road up to Scalasaig, after all, was hardly the sort of thing one could expect an old man to walk in the dark, as it was far more path than road, although the natives seemed to manage it with few falls, all in all. The priest was not a native to Colonsay.

He couldn't really tell about the boy. Sir Niko was quiet at table, as he usually was, and his table manners, under Becket's ungentle instruction, had become impeccable. About the only thing that remained from his early days was his tendency to eat as though there would be no food tomorrow—in quantity, these days, although not in rapidity of the early days that had earned him more than a few tongue lashings from the older knight that the baron had admired the craft of, even if he had affected not to hear them.

The time that Niko had spilled soup across the front of his tunic, Becket's use of words had been particularly . . . colorful. Excessive, perhaps, but, well, that was just Becket being Becket, he supposed.

The five of them were dining alone in the cottage, as while they had all been invited to the wedding, it was really the sort of affair that went better with the lord merely making an appearance, save for the obvious, and a priest would have shed almost as much of a pall on the party.

He shook his head. Cheap folks, the Scots—all of them. While he was in residence, weddings seemed to wash up on the beach at Kiloran bay more often than the ever-arriving driftwood on the Oronsay flats. It was always some father of the bride, anywhere from Priorty to Balnahard, and always with the same pretext—and always in English, as though the laird couldn't understand Gaelic: "And since you'll need to be exercising your permer nockter rights and all, milord, will you be joining us?" And, as always, having no desire to either leave Kiloran or find himself stuck in some black house up near, say, the well-named *Sguid nam ban Truagh* for the night, he would always offer the use of the beach—of *his* beach, dammit—for when the day's revelry was done, even when it didn't last through until dawn, all would be far too drunk to make their way home.

Of course, those from Oronsay could cross the Strand only at low tide. But it wasn't just them—the revelers, Colonsay proper and Oronsay, would sleep it all off on the beach under the stars, enjoying the shelter of the hills around Kiloran from the harsh winds that blew even during summer, only to arise, one by one in the morning, clean up the detritus of the previous night—they did that religiously; he had to give them that—and stagger their separate ways home.

And if he hadn't offered at least a sheep or two for the wedding dinner, and not supplied a keg or two as well as enough bottles of good Scots whiskey to toast the bride and groom, he'd have found himself feeling more like a guest than a host in his own home, and likely end up being known across the island as *Tòicear* Shanley or perhaps Laird *Sgrubaire*, rather than the much less insulting Lord *Eachdranach*, which he didn't particularly mind.

Of course, he'd have his own little celebration, such as it was, and a damned silly one it would be.

Just as well, actually. He had, of course, made his proper appearance at the ceremony itself, and even in his young and randy days—and, despite legends to the contrary, Lieutenant Lord Giscard Shanley of the *Gaheris* had had his randy days—he would not have found the bride tempting. This Rebbecca McPhee—called

"Becka" to her face and "Becka Calum Peter" behind her back to help distinguish her from all the other Rebbecca McPhees in Balnahard—was not only dark enough to remind him that the original name of the clan was *Mac Dubh Sith*, and that *dubh* was Gaelic for "black," and either had developed a small potbelly, as uncommon in young McPhee women as it was prevalent in the older ones . . .

Or, of course, she was already expecting, as he expected was the case. He doubted that many brides hereabouts made it to the altar as virgins, and at least some as pregnant. That was often hereabouts, and no doubt the subject of much gossip, none of which would reach the ears of the lord, unless he made some effort.

He doubted that McPhee fathers actually told their daughters, come early spring, to lay with their intended and force a wedding at the time when the lord would be in residence, but perhaps he was being overly generous. Certainly, if a Colonsay McPhee could have gotten his daughter's wedding to be hosted by the baron while she was flat on her back screaming in pain, pushing out the baby while attended by fretting midwives, he no doubt would have.

"So what did you think of the ceremony, Sir Niko?" the priest asked.

"It was very nice," the boy said, after a short pause. Presumably he spoke freely in front of Fotheringay, but his servant was probably the only one. Becket reported that the novices didn't find him at all talkative in private, and Giscard certainly had not.

"*Nice?*" Becket snorted. "You think it *nice*, what with all the hollering and whooping and yowling like a bunch of New World saracens?"

He gestured toward the open windows. Beyond the windows, flames roared up from the driftwood fires on the beach, the crackling of the wood and the *whoosh-whoosh-whoosh* of the waves gently breaking on the beach beyond, to the extent that one could hear them over what was probably the eighteenth repetition of "In Praise of Morag," which appeared to be, for some reason, tonight's favorite, although Giscard couldn't imagine why.

Yes, it was better than porcine Prussian drinking songs, certainly, in principle—but Prussia was far, far away, and this was here.

Well, at least they were only singing it now, rather than trying to have their voices compete with the *ceol mor* piping out the same tune. Enjoyment of the pipes were either an acquired taste or more likely the result of calluses of the ears built up from birth, and Giscard had acquired neither the taste nor the calluses.

Becket smiled at Giscard. " 'In praise of Morag' is the sort of thing that goes better without the lyrics, and at a distance," he said. "It's sort of like a dead skunk—I actually find the smell somehow pleasant, if it's far enough away. Doubt that I'd enjoy it much if the skunk were hung out the window any more than I care for this."

He was slurring his words more than usual; Becket was thoroughly drunk, which Giscard noted without faulting him for it.

Becket turned back to Niko. "And you don't find that the dignity of the sacrament is sullied by this sort of drunken revelry?"

No pause this time: "No, Sir Martin," the boy said, meeting the older knight's eyes. "I do not."

Giscard hid his smile behind his napkin. One thing
you could say about the boy: he was learning. Becket
would upbraid him for the disagreement, no doubt, but
he would have been far more severe with compliance.
Perhaps Niko couldn't win with Becket, at least not in
the short run, but he could minimize his losses.

"We'll speak on *that* later," Becket said. "And without
that blasted Fotheringay of yours to try to distract me."

The priest chuckled as he leaned forward, toward
Becket. "You can speak to *me* later on it, if you'd like,
Sir Martin, as I fully agree with the young knight. The
singing, the drinking—none of it does any harm." The
priest took a long pull at his own glass, and nodded,
careless of the way that he was dribbling down his beard
and onto his cassock. Anglians! "The sacrament, of
course, remains untouched, and while it should be shown
due respect, the respect was paid when it was performed,
and while I think the groom was less than steady on his
feet, that may have had more to do with the father-in-
law than anything else I can think of. A celebration after,
even a bit raucous of one, does the sacrament no disrespect, and no man can do it harm. Very standard theology, Sir Martin," he said. "As you should know."

Becket glowered at him. Being reminded that, as a
knight of the Order, he was a priest as well, was the sort
of thing that Becket would be certain to take offense at.

Time to say something. "I think the wine for communion was quite good," Giscard said, and not just to
change the subject, but, so he hoped, to provoke a
response from Grace. He had provided the wine, out of
his own cellar here—a Burgundian claret that had aged
very nicely, although perhaps a little too tannic.

Certainly expensive; at least arguably too expensive. She wouldn't quibble with the expense, but there was a time when she would argue about the necessity of providing a particularly good wine for Communion, it being a sacrament and all, and not possible of further ennobling.

And he would argue back.

It was one of his favorite arguments with Grace, and for a moment, he thought he saw the light back in her eyes, and that they would launch into this, perhaps his favorite one of the fierce arguments that both of them had so dearly loved, despite how the fury of them would horrify strangers. There were no strangers here, and he could remember many an evening when, when their arguments flagged, Becket egging the two of them on, switching sides whenever one or the other would seem ready to drop the matter.

But it was just for a moment. The light in her eyes dimmed, and she pushed herself back from the table with a quick gesture for them all to remain in their seats, a gesture that Niko ignored; he rose instantly.

"I'm sorry," she said. "But I feel a touch unwell. Please don't end your evening on my account," she said, as she turned and walked out of the room.

Well, that ended the evening, as surely as if each and every candle had been blown out.

"Just sit down, boy," Becket said, eyeing the door. "The lady's unwell; leave it at that."

The boy sat.

The priest looked at the door for a long time. "Well, in truth," he said, into the silence, "I find myself more than a little tired, as well. If it won't offend the baron,

I'll take to my bed, as well, and give the—and give you more privacy."

"Of course," Giscard said. "And my apologies for cutting the evening so short."

"Ah, it's not necessary that it be short," Becket said, gently, as the priest walked away. "I'm sure you've got a bottle of something interesting somewhere about, and since I can't sleep while all this yowling and yammering goes on outside, I think I might prevail on you to find that bottle, and share it with me, after I get the novices to refresh me, for an hour or so, if you follow my meaning. After, of course, you've performed your own duties."

"I'd be grateful for the company," he said, as he always did, and always meant.

Instead of reaching for the bell cord, Becket banged his fist three times on the table, and the two novices, who had clearly been waiting just outside the hall, quickly rushed in, and wheeled him out of the room, leaving Giscard alone with the boy.

Giscard forced himself not to push back angrily from the table. Anger was what was called for when a wife misbehaved, be she a peasant's or a king's, and Giscard tried, to the extent he was able to, not only to conduct himself as was appropriate, but to feel that which was appropriate.

But the truth was, he felt no anger at her, and if he displayed it in front of the boy, the boy would have misunderstood, more likely than not.

"And you, Sir Niko?" He forced a smile. "Will you abandon me, too?"

"No, sir. I'll stay with you, if you'd like." The boy was stopping himself from saying something. He simply rinsed out his fingers in the finger bowl, and then care-fully dried them on his napkin.

Out with it, Sir Niko, he could have said, and the boy would have done as ordered, or at least affected to.

But, no. It was not right to compel him to talk.

On the other hand . . . "What with the wine and the noise, and my . . . responsibilities of later this night, I find myself desirous of some air at the moment," he said. "Will you keep me company?"

"Of course."

He thought for a moment about going to his room and changing from his dinner clothes into something more appropriate for a walk up and away from the beach, but decided against it.

Perhaps . . .

Perhaps what? Perhaps Grace would be in his room, rather than her own? Perhaps in the act of changing his clothes he could bring some light back into those dead eyes? He forced himself not to sigh.

"Let's go out through the kitchen," he said. "I've some rough clothes out in the woodshed." It wouldn't be the first time that he had gone out into the night, after all, of late, whether here or at Fallsworth.

It likely wouldn't be the last.

Giscard led the way, under the light of the flickering torch.

The road up into the hills and then down to the lake was rough and ill-traveled, as were all three of the roads coming into Kiloran. Truth to tell, on the rare occasions when Giscard wanted to or had to go somewhere else

on Colonsay, he tended to use the launch, over Grace's
protests.

Surely, a man who had taken the deck of the *Gaheris*
herself could, with a little help, manage a single-masted
launch beyond the edge of the cove, and if he would
head perhaps a touch too far into the Firth of Lorn than
was strictly necessary to make his way out past the shoal
waters around the point on his way to Scalasaig, it was
decidedly more pleasant to have a few hours out on the
water than to go tramping through damp heather and
the peat. And it was probably quicker, all in all.

But there would be no skiff tonight; the distance was
small, and the destination uphill, not shoreside.

The moon was full enough that they needed no light
after their eyes had adjusted from inside, and he carefully
extinguished the torch in a boggy spot by the side of the
road before throwing it off into the heather.

"It's just over the next hill," he said.

"The lake?"

"Yes. The lake. What there is of it. I'd call it little
more than a pond, mind you, but *Loch an Sgoltaire* is
what it's named. Every pond, every hill, cleft, valley,
cave, and half the rocks have a name hereabouts. At least
we're not up in the hills, where the cattle browse, where
half the stones seem to be named after a *gruagach*." He
forced himself to chuckle. "And if you're up near Garvard, don't be surprised if you find that most of them have
spoiled milk in them."

"*Grugrach?*"

"Gruagach. One of the Old Ones. Well, one of many;
each to her own place. She watched over the cattle, and
the milk, and if you didn't leave her an offering of milk,

all of your milk would spoil, and your best cow would
be found dead in the morning. I'm sure that there's much
the same sort of thing in Pironesia, even these
days—didn't you tell me about some goat sacrificers on
one of the islands?"

Niko nodded. "Yes."

He looked like he was going to say something more,
but stopped himself.

Just as well. Giscard didn't want to know if, back on his
island, they'd still sacrificed bulls to Jupiter or the like.

But most of the Old Ones had gone with the end of
the Age, and the rest were quieter; and it was a far tamer
world, now, thankfully, than just a few hundreds of years
ago, a man might worry that if he walked the Scottish
lowlands, he might find an old woman at a ford, washing
a shirt, and have to forebear asking whose shirt it was,
lest she answer, *Se do leine, se do leine ga mi nigheadh*;
it is your shirt, your shirt that I am washing. And he
would know that it was the shirt he was shortly to be
buried in.

Or, worse, when the *Cailleach bheara* would still be
seen washing her own clothes off Jura, and riding her
night mare through the dark.

But a tamer world? he asked himself. Here he was,
walking side by side with a knight of the Red
Sword—and a newly created one, at that, and—

Perhaps things weren't quite so tame these days,
after all.

"Do you fish—" He stopped himself, and forced a
laugh. "Now, there's a silly question for a knight who
was raised as a Pironesian fisherboy, eh? You're probably

better with a stick and hook than—" No; he stopped himself, then went on. "—than I am."

"I'd doubt that, my lord," Niko said. "I've never hunted fish with a hook, just with nets. Spear and gaff, at times. Traps, too, for the crabs. But mostly nets."

"But where would be the sport in that?" He shook his head. He was being a foolish old man. "But then, you didn't fish for sport, but to eat, and for trade. A rather different thing, I'd suppose."

Niko nodded. "Very, I think. But I can learn this kind of fishing, if need be."

That seemed to be the boy's response to everything.

"Hmmm . . . of all the arts and usages that a knight of your Order needs, I'm not sure that hook-and-line fishing is among them."

Niko nodded gravely, but happily; it seemed to reassure him that there wasn't another skill he would have to struggle to learn.

Giscard led him up the hill and down to the rocky shore of the pond. He would call it a lake out loud, but not in his own mind.

At the waterline, there was, of course, the large, mostly flat-topped boulder that he remembered well, although he had long since forgotten its Gaelic name, which would no doubt roll off out of the throat and off the tongue in grandiose syllables, and end up meaning something like "the big, flat rock where John of the Sea used to fish."

If you stood atop it, and held the fishing pole and curled line just so, you could cast out near the middle of the pond, where the larger trout seemed to spend the heat of the day, coming up only to the tangle of weeds at the waterline at dawn and dusk.

It made for a good spot to fish, easily roomy enough for a man and a boy, as he knew from experience, and through most of the year it was high enough out of the water that one could sit down on the edge and dangle one's legs over it without getting one's boots wet.

They sat there in silence for a while, and he took out his pipe, and filled it from his tobacco pouch, toying with it, although he had no fire kit in his rough jacket, and even if he had, lighting it would have been too much of a bother. If he'd wanted to smoke, he should have thought of that before he extinguished the torch.

The wind brought only occasional hints of the drunken singing down on the beach, most of a mile away, although sparks rose in the night, only to be taken and snuffed by the wind, and he had to remind himself that this was damp Colonsay, and not like Fallsworth in a dry autumn, where fires, while unavoidable, were to be managed carefully. Here, the problem would be to keep a fire lit, not to worry about it burning down the heather.

"So," he finally said. "Sir Martin tells me that you're coming along well."

Niko didn't say anything for a moment, then: "He's not said that to me, Your Lordship." He hesitated, as though afraid to speak. "He's not much for praise."

"True enough." Giscard grinned. "That said, I don't think I've seen him enjoy himself so much in years. Standing down a clan war? You've given him the opportunity to do that, and more."

"It wasn't me, Your Lordship." Sir Niko shook his head. "He did it himself."

"No man does anything himself, Sir Niko. Not even Sir Martin."

Could he explain to Niko that, under all the bluster—real and affected—how grateful Martin was for that one last chance to be a knight of the Order once more? No. The boy wouldn't understand.

Niko just cocked his head to one side as though to say something, but didn't.

"Come now, Sir Niko," he said. "The idea was to get away from the noise and the unpleasantness for a while, and walk and talk. You've done the walking part; do I have to hold up the whole conversation myself?"

"I'm sorry, Your Lordship. It's just that . . . "

"Well?"

"She blames me for Bear—for Sir David."

Giscard closed his eyes. "Do you remember what I said when we first met? Something about how I knew that David's brothers in the Order always called him Bear?" His forced chuckle rattled in his throat. "An understandable nickname; he was a large baby, a big boy, a larger man, and looked little like a Shanley. I wouldn't be surprised if there were some who thought me a cuckold, eh? Or, in the old days, hereabouts, there'd be suspicion that my real son was stolen by the Good Folk, leaving one of their own in his place.

"But, no, he was my son; I've never had a worry on that score. And to me, he'll always be David; to you, he'll always be Bear, and please do me the courtesy of continuing to refer to him as you knew him. And please do him that honor. He deserved that, from his brothers, and his friends."

And you were both, Sir Niko, he thought. No. It was not enough to think it.

"You were both his friend and his brother in the Order, Sir Niko. Yes, it was for but the short time that was accorded you, true, but no less a brother and friend for that."

The boy reached down and touched at the hilt of his sword, a gesture so familiar from David's infrequent visits home of recent years that Giscard found himself unable to speak for a moment.

"She blames me," the boy finally said, again.

"Which she would that be? The One whose name you never seem to speak?"

He knew full well what Niko was saying, but for reasons that he couldn't quite understand, he needed to have it said aloud, to have it said explicitly, as though the words themselves would make a difference.

"No. Not Her. The baroness. For, for Bear."

Which Giscard already knew. It couldn't be the Queen of Air and Darkness; Niko had never met Her, as he had not made the trip into the Arroy; Becket said that would happen when he, Becket, thought the boy was ready. Damned if Sir Martin Becket was going to send the boy to Her when he still found his skills wanting, albeit improving.

Betwixt and between, Niko was—not quite a knight, despite the Red Sword and the title; and not a novice, mainly because of the sword and the title.

And a certain something else, perhaps.

There was an . . . intensity to the boy. It wasn't just that he went through all the work that Becket set him to with energy and without complaint; it was as though, even when he was doing something as ordinary as throwing charcoal into a forge, or setting to work on a leather gauntlet with pincers and awl, he was utterly dedicated to the task, not for the sake of the task itself, but because it was what a young knight in training ought to be doing.

Not that Giscard thought himself any judge of such things. After all, when he had had David sent to Alton, it was mainly to prepare him for a military or administration career. Michael was the heir to Fallsworth, after all, and Matthew next in line. He had thought that a year or so at Alton would leave David with the ring of the former novice, and a good start in life. A year or two at Alton was . . .

But he was woolgathering to avoid the subject. A bad habit, and one that he would not have tolerated in himself in Parliament; it was little better here.

"I could tell you that that isn't so," he said, "but I'm not sure that you'd believe me."

"Yes. I'm not complaining—"

"Well, you damn well *should* be complaining, if that's what you think." He bit hard down on his pipe stem and tried to take a deep draught of it, irritated with himself when he remembered that it was unlit. "You should be complaining to me about my wife's misbehavior, if that's how you see it. I'm her husband, boy; I'm responsible for her."

"I've . . . I've no complaints." He shook his head. "If I'd just been a bit better, a little faster—"

"If you'd been a fully trained knight, instead of a fisherboy who Sir Cully had found it expedient to be equipped with that Red Sword, and if luck had been with you and Bear and Sir Joshua and Sir Cully, and all the rest, yes, David might still be alive." He waved his pipe stem. "And don't you think that a day goes by that

I don't think that, too, and wish that it had been the case." He shook his head. "But blame *you*? No. Not her, not I. It is a . . . signal honor to have a son rise before the king with two swords in his sash, and it's an honor that's granted to few fathers. And then, for him to be made a Knight of the White Sword?" He rose. "It was as proud a moment as a father could have," he said, "until the moment His Majesty said of David, 'He was a good and kindly knight.' " He kept his voice low, not permitting it to crack. "And did you think that his mother and I did not know the risks that he had undertaken, of his own, stubborn will, and with pride? Yes, Grace aches for the loss of her son, as do I. That's as it should be. But blame you? No. Not her; not I." He shook his head. "Have you nothing to say?"

Niko shook his head, too. "Just that I hope you'll forgive me, too."

Giscard sighed. He was supposed to be quite a speaker, at least, that's what was said in Parliament. He had obviously left the boy unconvinced.

In a way, he supposed, that was as it should. The world should ache for the loss of his son, as he and Grace always would. But of all the world, why this boy? Why?

Well, at least he had tried. He would try again, should the occasion warrant.

"Well, we'd best be getting back," he said. "I've got some duties yet to perform tonight. *Prima nocte*, and all." He grinned.

Niko looked puzzled, and it took him a moment to work out the Latin, and then to remember what it was supposed to mean. "First night? You mean that you really—"

"Of course not." Giscard sniffed. "It's a ritual, that's all, and largely a way of the McPhees getting me to help pay for the wedding. I'll be sitting up with the bride, this evening—yes, in my bedroom—while her mother and father and one of her cousins bear witness both to the fact that, as is my right to insist—and as the McPhees do their best to insist on me insisting—she spent her first married night in the bedroom of the lord, with her husband noticeably absent, and also to bear witness that I not so much as laid a finger upon her." He shook his head. "It's not the silliest thing that a man of my station has to do, although I can't think of a sillier one, not at the moment." He shrugged. "An hour or so of polite conversation and a few 'drops of his own,' and I can be done with it, and down by the fire sharing a bottle with Becket."

He would have said something about how each man had his own duties, but this one was an embarrassment, and the evening had already held enough embarrassments as it was.

With another to come.

"Let's go, Sir Niko."

"Yes, Your Lordship."

It was the screaming that woke Niko.

He had had no trouble falling asleep, of course; he never did. When he had returned to his rooms, Fotheringay had already had his bed turned down, and had warmed it with the bed iron that Niko had never seen the old sergeant take from the fireplace.

This whole notion of wearing clothes to bed still seemed strange to him, but after setting his swords down beside the bed, he undressed and carefully folded his clothes onto the bureau next to where Fotheringay had already set out fresh clothing, and carefully laid out his next day's clothes and his boots beside his bed, as always.

While he had been inconsistent in ringing the waking bell while on Colonsay, Niko knew that if he did, Niko had better be down the stairs and out onto the training ground behind the house before Sir Martin could count to twenty. Sir Martin was not patient with "dawdling," one of those trade language words that Niko had never quite understood.

But it was the screams that woke him up. High-pitched; frightened.

He was out of bed and out the door, into the hallway, with both his swords in hand, Nadide still in her sheath, before he quite knew what he was doing.

Lanterns burned in their niches, flickering light casting weaving shadows.

The screams continued—they were from down the hall. Her rooms.

Somebody's hurting Bear's mother.

There were sounds of footsteps behind him, but he didn't look behind as he dashed down the hall, and into the room.

The only light in her room came from the fireplace, and in it, some dark form was over her bed, holding her down, his fingers reaching for her throat.

The right thing to do, the knightly thing to do, would have been to draw his sword—his mundane sword; drawing a live sword was something too dangerous to be done without necessity—and run the dark shape through.

But he found himself dropping both of the swords, leaping on the other, his forearm coming across the throat, as he had been taught. He would have told himself that he was doing that out of fear that his sword might hurt the lady, but the truth was that it was that he wanted to, he needed to get his hands on whoever it was that was hurting her.

Hurt Bear's mother? he thought. *Not while I can get my hands on your throat.*

Blunt hands reached back for him, but he shook them off. *Concentrate*, Sir Martin had told him—*concentrate on what you're doing, boy.*

He did. His whole world shrunk to his right arm, and where his knees found purchase on the larger man's back.

There were sounds around him, and others were shouting, but that wasn't part of his world, part of his universe, nor were the words that the woman in the bed were saying.

No. None of it mattered. One thing at a time, Sir Niko, he could almost hear Becket say. Concentrate, damn your eyes, concentrate.

He squeezed, and pulled, and ignored the blows and the cries, even when the body went limp.

He became aware that there were others in the room, and that Fotheringay was standing over him.

"Easy, young sir," the old sergeant said. He had a lantern in one hand, and a dagger in the other. "You've done for the bastard." He handed the lantern to somebody who Niko couldn't see, and made his dagger disappear. His gentle fingers were strong as they pried Niko's arms loose, and helped him to his feet.

Fotheringay was undressed only in the sense that his buttons were unbuttoned, and his boots unlaced; he, as usual, had slept in his clothes as his nightclothes, and had not taken time to do more than step into his boots.

They were all there, wide-eyed servants, the priest in his cassock, and Becket, with the two novices—including the baron, in his own nightshirt. He should have looked preposterous with the nightshirt falling only to mid knee, and his skinny legs protruding beneath them. But he had a sword in his hand, too.

While Becket was more held up than supported by the two novices, he was the only one who seemed to have any dignity; he was in his robes, and his good hand clutched a sword, although he let the point drop.

"Roll the bastard over," he said. "I want to see what's left of his face."

Fotheringay—faithful Fotheringay—looked to Niko, and waited for his nod of confirmation before he dropped to one knee and rolled the man over onto his back.

It was a McPhee, of course; the clan tartan was distinctive.

The dead man's face was red and swollen, the cheeks already blackening. Niko doubted that he could have recognized him in life; he certainly couldn't now.

Niko took a deep breath, and wished he hadn't; the McPhee had fouled himself in death. He picked up Nadide, and tried to put her away in his sash.

But the sash wasn't there. He was just wearing the silly nightshirt. He stood there, wondering why he didn't feel as foolish as he no doubt looked. It just didn't seem important.

Fotheringay shook his head. "Recognize him? Anybody?"

It was so like Fotheringay to take charge when everybody else was simply standing around.

"Calum McPhee," the baron said. "Calum Peter Michael, he's called. Oldest brother of the bride. Not one of the . . . guests in the bedroom." His voice was unnaturally calm as he stood in the doorway. "Get the other McPhees in here, and now," he said, to somebody out in the hall.

"No, no—leave them where they are," Niko said, and the baron, after hesitating only a moment, made a waving-away gesture to whoever he had spoken to, and shook his head. "Please," Niko said, "just go to your wife, milord."

Becket started to say something, but desisted at a gesture from Niko.

"Please, Sir Martin." He turned back to the baron. "Get her out of here, sir. Now, please. She doesn't need to see this."

"Better not for either of them to leave the room until we've got a better idea of what's going on here, young sir," Fotheringay said. "If you asked me, which I don't recall you doing."

Niko forced himself to stop listening to the pounding of his own heart. Yes, Fotheringay was right. A drunken McPhee staggering up the stairs and trying to rape the baroness? How had he gotten past the servants? And why? Were there more of them? What was going on?

The baroness had gathered her bedclothes about her. The straps of her nightdress were torn.

Niko, at least, knew what to do about that. "Fotheringay—the lady needs a robe."

"Yessir." From somewhere, Fotheringay found a robe, and didn't quite elbow the baron aside as he draped it over the baroness's shoulders. "Easy, now, Lady," he said. "Let's get you out of the bed, and maybe over to the chair, where you don't have to be bothered by the sight of that."

"No." She drew the robe around her, and rose from the bed. If it weren't for the fact that her knees seemed ready to buckle beneath her, Niko would have said that he'd never seen a man or woman so dignified. Her mussed hair, the growing bruises about her face—they didn't matter. "I was here for the worst of it; I can stand to see what's here." Her knees did buckle, then, and she sat down on the bed trembling.

"Grace. Do as the sergeant says."

"No. We shall do as Sir Niko says." She looked over at Niko. "Thank you," she said, quietly.

"You're welcome, but you've nothing to thank me for, Lady," he said. "Just doing my duty, that's all."

It was all he could do not to kick the body.

Lay a hand on Bear's mother? The bastard was lucky that Niko had gotten to him first. Gray, Cully, any of the others would have done worse than killed him. Niko would have, too, if he'd had time to think about it.

Becket was starting to say something, but Niko waved him to silence.

"I don't like this at all," Niko said. His own voice seemed to come from far away. "It's not . . . it's not right."

"I can smell the whiskey on him from here," Fotheringay said. "He probably should have had a dram or two less."

"Shut up, Nigel." He shook his head.

No. A drunk McPhee, invading the lady's bedroom to assault her? That was the obvious explanation, the simple one, but it wasn't enough. There had been drunken McPhees at every wedding on the beach, the baron had implied. Why this? Why now?

He would get the explanation. But get the family safe, first.

"Nigel—get the drapes drawn, and quickly now."

"Should have thought of that myself," Fotheringay said, moving to do just that.

There were sounds from outside, but nobody had—yet—come in through the door. Fotheringay quickly drew the shades, and helped the baroness out of her bed and into a chair up against an outer wall, over her quiet protests.

Niko looked to Becket. "Sir Martin? What do we do?"

"Not mine to say." Becket shook his head. "Your mind isn't cluttered by drink, as mine surely is, and you've handled this well enough so far; you're in charge, Sir Niko." His grin wasn't friendly. "As you seem to have already decided."

There would be no arguing with Becket; Niko knew that from experience. So he turned to the novices. "Get Sir Martin on the bed, and then go dress and arm yourselves— have the servants keep the McPhees in the lord's bedroom; you guard the bottom of the stairs."

Too many doors into the house; this was built as just a residence, not as a castle, or a keep. But at least the foot of the one staircase should be defensible, if need be. "Now," he said, "if you please."

Becket nodded. "Do it, boys, and quickly, now, and never mind my aches and pains—just chuck me on the bed and we'll worry about my dignity some other time, if I ever happen to acquire any again."

Despite Becket's growling, the novices lay him down carefully albeit quickly on the bed before running from the room.

Niko took one quick look at Sir Martin, who shook his head, as he lay sprawled on the bed.

"Nearest earl's soldiers in Oban," Becket said. "Be midafternoon before we could have any here. Get the baron and baroness in the skiff and go, you think?"

And what if there was some danger waiting at sea? Or between the house and the dock? No. Better to defend the house, if necessary.

Niko shook his head. "Get the skiff going, yes—but for help."

"Makes sense, it does." Fotheringay nodded. "The downstairs valet is ex-navy; served on the old *Lord Davy*—should be able to handle a skiff, with or without some help. From the house staff."

"You could do it."

"Meaning no more than my usual impertinence, but my place is here, Sir Niko, with you. Unless you got a lot more men you can trust at your back that I've not been hearing about?"

There were voices being raised down the hall, but Niko wasn't going to leave the baron and baroness to investigate; he gave Fotheringay a quick glance, and the sergeant stalked out of the room, his short knife held

against the flat of one arm, while another one clutched
a length of thick kindling wood that Niko hadn't seen
him retrieve.

The baron was still standing next to his wife, his sword
still in his hand. "What do I do, Sir Niko? I'm not as
young as I was, but I'm—"

"You're the baron, and a husband, sir. Please, sir, just
stay here, with your wife."

"He can get paper and pen from that writing desk,"
Becket said, gesturing. "The word of some Shanley
retainer will go over better and quicker in Oban with a
note from myself and one from the baron."

"Do that," Niko said. He found that he still had Nadide, scabbarded, in his hand, and tried to slip her into
his sash.

But the sash, along with his clothes, was back in his
room, and he wasn't going to leave this room, not now.
Still, there were sounds outside, and they weren't the
drunken sounds of laughter that he had heard.

"I hear it, too," the baron said, shaking his head. He
had brought the bedside writing desk over to Becket,
who was scribbling madly.

"Sir Niko," Becket said, "I think the baron can be
trusted to go to your cell and get your clothes."

"No. I'll be fine." He didn't want to let the baron out
of his sight. Close, Niko could get between him and
danger, without leaving the baroness exposed.

He hadn't seen her rise, but the baroness was kneeling
in front of a deeply carved bureau, and had the bottom
drawer slid open.

"Sir Niko," she said, her voice as flat and emotionless
as always, "this is far too large, but it will do for now,"

she said, taking out a tunic jacket and sash. She rose and approached him. "Please."

He allowed her to help him on with it—with Nadide's scabbard in his hand he could hardly have dressed himself—and then she knelt to belt a thick Order sash about his waist. The trousers, undertunic, and boots would have to wait, at least for now, but at least he had some way to get both hands free without dropping the sword again.

"Stand back, please, all of you."

He went as far across the room as he could, and stepped behind the curtains. They were heavy enough to block out daylight, for when the baroness would take to her bed during the day. He looked out toward the beach and the sea, rather than up toward the hills.

Too many lanterns had been lit in the bedroom; it took him a few moments for his eyes to adjust to the dark.

The wind had picked up outside; the hills around Kiloran were only partial protection, after all.

It took the burning embers from the bonfire and drove them both to the east, and high in the air, showed no signs of extinguishing it. If anything, the bonfire still burning on the sands, seemed much larger, and people were still gathered on this side of it, but it wasn't the merriment and celebration of before. Lit by the burning flames, the crowd of more than two hundred was swaying, back and forth, as though moving to a slow dirge.

But the pipers were gone. Beyond the fire, mostly obscured by the flames, a dim figure swayed back and forth, but instead of the *ceol mor*, the bagpipes, he seemed to be playing a syrinx—two or three simple reed pipes, and while it was hard to hear much of any of the tune over the roaring of the wind, the few sounds that reached Niko's ears made him dizzy.

There was no drummer that he could see, but a harsh, monstrous drumbeat thumped in time with the beating of his own heart, and as the pace of the drumbeat slowly, inexorably increased, so did the sway of the dancers.

And his own heart.

At the edge of the crowd, piles of naked bodies writhed, and he forced himself not to force his eyes away.

There was nothing even vaguely erotic about all of it; children, adults alike in a mass of coupling that seemed to have no sexuality to it.

The wind began to die down, and the sound of the pipes reached his ears more clearly. He found himself painfully erect, his body swaying in time to—

No.

No.

No.

He forced himself to clap his hand to Nadide's hilt.

Niko? Niko. Niko!

Help me, Nadide.

He was never quite sure whether it was him or her that let him stagger back through the curtains, not quite falling. They seemed to deaden the sound, at least a little, but it was still hard to put his feet down where they belonged. His whole body wanted to sway, to give in to it.

But the wind picked up again, driving the last traces of the pipes more from his mind than his ears.

He was having trouble breathing, and his eyes refused to focus. There were too many people in the room—

Niko, come back to me.

He forced himself to focus.

There were too many people in the room. In addition to the baron, the baroness, and Becket, Fotheringay was standing behind four of the McPhees: the bride, her mother and father, and another young McPhee woman whom Niko couldn't place.

All of them had their hands clasped behind their backs, as though inspecting him; all were wide-eyed, and couldn't stop from looking down to the body on the floor, and up to Niko, from where they stood, pressed up against the far wall of the bedroom.

"They're not going to be doing any harm, young sir," Fotheringay said, as he rose from tying ankles together. "Not without pulling their thumbs out of their sockets, or falling flat on their faces." His expression was every bit as calm as always, but there was an edge in his voice. "Just a precaution, given that I'm only one, and all."

"There's something going on out there," Niko said. "A piper—he seems to have everybody under a spell."

Shanley grunted. "Not that that's any excuse—but, Sir Niko, are you . . . ?" He didn't seem to have the right word.

"A piper?" It was the McPhee father—Calum was his name, although Niko didn't remember what he was usually called. He was a big, thick, stout man, easily a head taller than Fotheringay; but the old sergeant seemed to handle him with ease.

"But the *ceol mor* does nothing of the sort." His voice was higher-pitched than Niko would have expected, and his face was greasy with sweat. Niko could smell the reek of the whiskey even over the charnel house smell of the body on the floor; this McPhee had apparently had more than a few "drops of his own" before the screaming began.

At Niko's nod, Fotheringay pushed Calum McPhee forward. "Well, let's see about that," Fotheringay said. "Seems to have taken the young knight ill—let's see what the sound does to the likes of you, shall we?" His left hand gripped the McPhee's hair, and from the way that the bigger man rose to his toes to comply, Niko was sure where the knife was.

"I think that nobody else goes outside," he said, as he shoved the man through the curtains, and Niko quickly pulled them back around his arms, to keep out what he could of the piping sound.

From behind him, there was a crashing sound downstairs, and cries of pain.

"Just two," came a shout from down the stairs, "but there's more coming."

"Hold them, as long as you can," Becket said.

"They'll not hold them alone, by God." The baron dashed for the door, sword in hand, ignoring Becket's curses.

Becket beckoned to the baroness. "Come, Grace, get a chair in the door and get me to my feet, what there is of them," he said, trying to rise. His sword slipped out of his fingers and fell to the bed, but he ignored it and used his good arm to pull him to his feet, standing wobbly.

"Of course, Martin," she said. She was surprisingly strong for such a slight woman; she slid the huge dressing chair near the foot of the bed across the room, not glancing down at either the body, or how her gown fell open, then half supported, half carried Becket into it, and placed his sword in his hand.

"I can't hold many in the doorway long, Sir Niko," Becket said. "And I can't go chasing off after the baron, either."

Niko nodded.

Fair enough. Keep Fotheringay with the baroness, and he could join the baron—

"Wait." Fotheringay had dragged Calum McPhee back through the curtains.

His eyes were wide with madness.

"Amadan Dubh," he said. "Amadan Dubh." There was spittle at the corner of his mouth, and he shook his head as though to clear it.

But his eyes stayed wide.

Fotheringay dropped him to the floor with an economic foot sweep. "Just what we bloody needed, eh?"

Niko shook his head. "I don't understand."

"If you'd been reading your Celtic history more," Becket said, his back to Niko, his voice back to its usual calm, scornful self, "you'd know that he's talking about the Black Piper, the Fairy Fool, the Dark Piper. A *sidhe* supposedly, but not a halfling like Our Lady is—full-blooded, ancient, and crazy. Passer-on of madness, through his damned pipes."

But the sidhe were long gone, so it was said; all of the Old Ones were, with but a few remaining, like the Wise on Pantelleria, and the Queen of Air and Darkness, and but a few others.

I'm not sure what it is, Nadide said. *But it's time. This one will hurt Bear's mother, and his father.*

"That may be so," he said, as much to himself as to her, "but not while I breathe."

He drew the sword, and the world changed once more.

CHAPTER 9

She

The last task before a novice goes to kneel before the king, to rise as a knight of the Order, is always the same: it's a visit to the Arroy, and to Her.

Why? I don't know; I won't even guess. I do know what others say.

Some say it's because She provides a final temptation, as She surely does. The road to an Order Knight's swords is pitted with temptations, and if this is the final one, that's not unfitting, and while most return from the Arroy, some do not. How did they fail? I have my suspicions, but that is all: I suspect that She looks into their souls for one thing, and one thing only, and either finds it or finds it wanting.

Others say that she's lonely, and desirous of company. I think that unlikely, myself, but I'm not made to understand Her, and my thoughts of likelihood and unlikelihood should be given the weight that they deserve.

Still others say that She's simply looking out for Her family, and wants to have one last look, in person, at the candidates for the Order that will protect her family.

And if you listen to the brothers of our rival Order, you'll hear another theory—that it's yet another example of the favoritism that we receive from Her, and yet another slight for them to properly resent.

As to me, I have no opinion. I've sworn to service, honor, faith, and obedience; to justice and mercy, but not to wisdom, and not to understanding.

She sends for us; we come to Her.

That has always been enough for me, and it always shall.

—Gray

Gray took the straightest path.

He went both quickly, and rapidly, stopping only for the sake of his horse, and to rest himself when necessary.

And, yes, he rode—Gray rode toward the Bedegraine, and the Arroy hidden within it, although he knew that Cully would have walked, even though the straightest

path would have taken him through Linfield, as it had
Gray.

Cully wouldn't have walked around it, either.

Gray wished that he felt that he could. Gray had had
quite enough of Linfield for one life, and he didn't see
any harm in going through it as quickly as possible,
although he hadn't seriously considered riding around it.
That would have been cowardly.

Say what you would about Joshua Grayling, and you
would likely have not said enough that was condemnatory—
but he was no coward.

Almost two centuries after the Linfield Horror, trees
in Linfield were stunted and sick, and black ruins stood
where the castle had been. There were still remnants of
peasants' dwellings, strangely enough; in more than one
field, the rusted remains of a plow were still mostly standing, the wooden handles still sticking out, as though they
had been preserved as well as blackened.

It was hard to look at what had been an apple orchard.
The trees seemed to be covered with some sort of green
ichor, rather than moss. The apples themselves were too
large—they were easily fist-sized, even though it was but
spring—and far too red and perfect.

Not that he would have been tempted by them. Some
had already fallen to the ground and split open, revealing
their blackened insides, with the maggots writhing in
pleasure and agony.

At the edge of Linfield, some fool had planted a field
of what undoubtedly looked like New World maize, but
it had turned, too; the husks on the short, withered stalks
had sprouted eyes, which watched him as he rode by,
hiding themselves among the leaves when he returned

their gaze. The rotting carcass of what appeared to be a rabbit, and a few white shards of bone showed that this perverted maize had more that it shouldn't than just eyes.

The plants were bad enough, but it was the animals that bothered him the most, and for once he was glad that he wasn't the woodsman that many of the other knights were, and he knew that his eyes missed things in the forest and on the ground that others could see plain as day.

Which was more than acceptable to him here.

The occasional sight of a squirrel rooting among the misshapen acorns beneath the twisted oaks was bad enough. They weren't gray or red, but a sort of deep taupe, so deep as to be almost black, but without the honesty or sheen of a true color, and when they rose to watch him as he rode past, their chittering was a serpentine hissing, their teeth too long and sharp, and their looks far too bold.

From a tangle of brambles to the right of the road, a pair of eyes watched him above a snout that looked more like a pig's than a dog's, although even a wild boar would not have had tusks that were so long and white, nor spittle that hissed and burbled where it touched the blackened earth.

Well, one thing you can say for the Sandoval is that he did a thorough job here.

I don't know that even you and I could have done it better.

The Khan seemed amused. Yes, it had been the Sandoval, and a knight of the Order. The feud with the Table Round had never really ended, and it had been far too close to its peak just before the Horror.

On the other hand, when was the last time that one of those Table Knights chose to give offense to an Order Knight? The lesson seemed to have been learned.

The rivalry was still there. It was just that the two rival orders tended to avoid each other. Knights of the Table Round, by and large, were more inspectors and couriers than anything else, these days, spending their time in subordinate Crown courts, like Napoli, Borbonaisse, Saxony, and, of course, the various earldoms of New England, and, in fact, when Gray had gone to New York to . . . invite the duke to come to Londinium, the three Table Knights had been rude enough that, if he had not been on mission, he would have been sorely tempted to have called one of them out.

But, no. He had been, and that was that. And if he had challenged one of them, it would have been with his mundane sword, and not whipped out the Khan.

Pity.

No, not a pity; it was a necessity—one insult, one moment of loss of self-control, by one knight of the Red Sword, and Linfield was the result.

No. It was important to be honest, with himself. This was just the remnants of the result, just the leftovers. It had been much, much worse, and the last of the Linfield deodands had only been put down a few years before.

Now, that *was fun. I do have my uses.*

A shadow passed over him, and Gray looked up.

High above him, no trace of light leaking through his broadly spread black feathers, a death kite circled, as though waiting for an opportunity. He carefully slid his hand back on the reins so that he could rest his hand on the Khan's steel.

I hope it tries, the Khan said.

Yes, the Khan would like that, if it forced Gray to draw him. Not likely, though; his mundane sword would do, if anything would, and death kites were unlikely to attack something larger than a child, anyway.

Of course, you could try to shoot him down.

True enough. His crossbow was tied to the front of his saddle, and a year of practice had gotten him to the point where he could, albeit clumsily, manage to cock it with the small hook that projected out of the leather that covered the stump where his right hand had been. Not quickly, though, and he would never be a decent shot with his left hand, although he practiced as much as he could.

Not much of a loss; he had never been much of a bowman, anyway. One life was too short to master all of the arts, and back when he was a novice at Alton, his clumsiness with a longbow had been the source of much amusement among the other novices, and quite a frustration to Sir Alex.

He had handled the first problem with singlesticks.

He hadn't been *quite* unbeatable, even among the other novices, but he had been resolute, and Father Cully had carefully ignored his tendency to pick as his practice partners those who had mocked him, and he had made a point to bruise them repeatedly and severely, and after a while, all of the mockery had stopped—but, still, he had never become much of a bowman.

If his abilities with the sword hadn't eventually become exceptional, it would have been entirely possible that he never would have graduated.

Anything rather than think on Linfield, eh?

He removed his hand from the hilt of the Khan. That it was true didn't mean that he wanted to be reminded of it.

He rode on, forcing himself to look at the horror he rode through, while, high above, the death kite banked away, looking for more likely prey.

Ahead, the boundary between Linfield and the relative sanctuary of the Bedegraine was sharp, as though it was a green curtain, beyond which lay sanity and comfort.

The big bay gelding had keener senses than Gray had; without being spurred, he cantered toward where the green giants of the Bedegraine towered, and Gray let him, only pulling him back to a walk when they were under the cover of the trees of the Bedegraine.

Yes, out of the light of the noonday sun, it was cooler here, but he felt warmer inside. Here, the trees were just trees, and within a few minutes he saw a squirrel, high in an oak tree, that was just a squirrel.

After Linfield, the ordinariness of the Bedegraine was almost luxurious.

No forester tended this part of the Bedegraine—it was too close to Linfield—so what paths there were were largely deer trails, and heavily overgrown, making for slow going in most places, and often forcing him to turn his head to protect his eyes from branches.

The floor of the forest was littered with rotting humus, but it was a comforting, homey smell, and the crashing through the brush that brought his hand near the Khan turned out to merely be a massive buck deer, with a huge rack easily of twenty or more points, who gave horse and man a quick look before dashing across the trail, and off into the brush, disappearing with barely a sound.

He was never sure quite how far he rode into the Bedegraine before he reached the Arroy that it contained; the border between the encompassing Bedegraine was by no means well marked, and no mapmaker had ever been able to map it out.

Best not to try—things tended to happen in the Arroy to any who came without invitation, and even some who had been invited. Not always good things; not always bad things, but it was known as the Forest of Adventure for good reason, after all, and adventures were something that a wise man or woman would try to avoid, if possible.

But slowly, very slowly, the forest changed about him, becoming darker and quieter. No trace of sun peeked through the overhead canopy of green, and the chittering of the squirrels and the chirping of birds was but a memory. Other than the slow, muted clopping of his horse's hooves against the ground, the only sound he could hear was of a creek burbling, hidden ahead of and below him by the twist of land and thickness of the forest.

Yes, it was dark and quiet, and if he had taken a different route, he might have found it disturbing.

But not today, or any day that he came from this direction; it was, after all, the dark and quiet of the Arroy, not the black and silence of Linfield.

The trail grew too steep for him to be sure of the horse's footing, so he dismounted, and wrapped the reins about his stump, leading it down the slope, waiting—as he always did—for the trail to fork, finding—as always— that it never did, not for him.

He didn't understand that; Cully had always talked about how one thing he liked about visiting the Arroy was that it didn't matter which fork in the trail one took, as it would bring you to Her, in any case. Gray had always found that there were never forks in any trail, no matter which he took into the Arroy. They had, for him, always led directly to Her.

It probably didn't make any difference, even if it was true. Was it that the choices that you made entering the Arroy didn't matter? Or was it just that there were no choices? What was the difference?

He shrugged. It was probably just Father Cully using a story by way of making some sort of obscure point, one that would have gone over the head of the wretched Southampton orphan boy called Grayling just as much as it still did over the head of Sir Joshua Grayling.

He just followed the one trail.

At the bottom of the gully, the trail crossed the stream, and there didn't look like a better place to ford, so he did just that, wrapping the reins around his stump so that he could lead his horse while holding both of his swords high, to keep them out of the water.

The water was bone-chillingly cold, and soaked him from waist to toes. But his boots had long since shrunk as much as they could, and they would dry, eventually. He had a spare pair in his horse's pack, but lacing and tying boots was something that a one-handed man could do only with great time and trouble, and, after all, he had been summoned to Her. Damp feet would not be allowed to delay him in that.

He was so occupied in getting his swords back where they belonged as he was walking the horse up the bank, that he almost missed the rucksack lying on the large, flat rock on the bank of the stream.

"Hello?" he called out. "Is there somebody here?"

There was no answer.

Strange. He thought for a moment about stooping to examine the rucksack, but that really was a job that would have required two hands, and he had but one—and while in most places, there would be no reason to worry about his horse wandering off, this was, after all the Arroy, and even so minor a quest could turn out to be far more interesting than he had any interest in.

So he walked the horse over to a tree and tied the reins around a low branch, not trusting to it to stay ground-hitched, then walked back to the rucksack.

He dropped to one knee next to it. Very strange. There was a cake of soap on a piece of waxed paper, lying next to it. He touched a finger to the soap—it was dry, as though it was waiting for a bather.

He looked around. The creek twisted through the vale, and it was only a few yards before it twisted out of sight. There might easily be a deeper pool beyond, downstream, where a traveler might bathe, if they were of a mind to.

He could, of course, just leave it there.

He was no thief—well, he hadn't been a thief for many years; a Southampton orphan boy got by as best he could—but there was something strange about all of this. The rucksack couldn't have been lying there very long, after all; while the ground was littered with dead leaves and fallen branches, the rucksack lay atop them, as though the owner had left it there but minutes ago.

Leave it here? Had he frightened the owner of the pack, and run him—or her—off?

Perhaps the owner was hiding, and watching him from some nearby cover. Far stranger things had been known to happen in the Arroy, after all. He peered at the greenery, but couldn't see a place where somebody could be hiding, although with the way that the creek twisted through the gully, somebody could be just a few tens of feet away and be utterly hidden. And, besides, he wasn't much of a woodsman—there were probably places within his sight where eyes could be watching him.

"I am Sir Joshua Grayling, of the Order of Crown, Shield, and Dragon," he said, loudly, trying to make his voice carry without actually shouting. "I mean no harm to most."

He had to be careful what he said; if it turned out that this was the rucksack of some outlaw, say, he would not promise him safe passage.

On the other hand, this was the Arroy, after all, and in the Arroy, finding a noble girl fleeing to escape an unwanted marriage was the sort of thing that could much more easily happen than in most other places. And if the noble girl had paused at a stream to bathe herself, and hidden her nakedness from the arrival of some traveler, that, too, was the sort of thing that was more likely to happen in the Arroy than anywhere else he could think of, and probably most places that he couldn't.

He had been summoned to Her presence, but if necessary, of course, he could and would tarry long enough to see to the safety of some—

"No, there's no naked maiden hiding among the leaves," She said, chuckling. "Just Me. I'm quite decently clothed, and not hiding."

244 Joel Rosenberg

He turned.

She stood there, high on the bank, toying with the gelding's reins.

And She was, of course, utterly perfect, from toe to head.

Her naked feet rested on arched sandals that seemed to have no straps. Each toe was perfect, undeformed by shoes and boots, its nail unmarked, unsullied by color or polish.

She wore a simple shift of white linen, only a few shades paler than her own creamy skin, drawn in tightly with a silver belt at her narrow waist, before it fell immodestly to just above the knee. On anybody else, he would have found its clingingness, its briefness, utterly shocking, but he simply could not see Her in that way.

"I know," She said. Her voice was sweet without being cloying, and loud in his ears, although She spoke barely above a whisper.

The horse whickered, and started to shy, but She laid a finger on its muzzle, and it immediately quieted, and stayed quiet, standing in place, turned its head to watch Her and him with its huge eyes when She dropped the reins to the ground and walked over to him.

"No," she said, turning her head for a moment toward the animal, "we'll have no adventures with you today, if you please."

Her black hair flowed like shadow across Her shoulders, and fell behind Her, held in place by a simple silver band. Her lips were red as freshly shed blood, and parted in a smile that revealed teeth that were even and white.

"Hello, Gray," She said. "I won't ask you to kneel, you know. If I put you in a position where you must defy

Me, or break an oath, it will be over something more important to Me than that slight courtesy. Stand if you please; I'll take no offense."

He had sworn, long ago, never to drop to his knees other than by his own will. He had done so many times since, but always by his own choice, by his own will.

Yes, She knew everything there was to know about him, so it was through his own will, his own sense of what was right and proper, that he dropped to one knee before Her, using the leather cap on his stump to sweep his swords properly up and behind him.

"As you wish. Please, Joshua," She said. "Rise, and take my hand."

He did so immediately, and once again, as before, at the moment he touched Her hand, he knew why they all loved Her so, why he couldn't help it any more than any of the rest could. Her hand, small in his, wasn't just warm and warming; it was intoxicating, even more than the way that her eyes, behind the long lashes, looked unblinkingly into his.

It wasn't just the physicality of it, although he tried to ignore how he had become suddenly and painfully erect, and how Her scent filled his nostrils, for the moment driving away not just the pains of the body, pains that he only noticed by their absence, but those of the spirit. His shoulders had been tight, and painful, and somehow or other he had gotten a scrape on his left cheekbone. He had ignored those things, as was only proper, and now only noticed them because they were gone.

But it was more than the aches and pains of life. For the moment, he felt whole, and decent, and it was the touch of Her hand that had done it.

It was as though the weight of all of his many sins had been lifted from him, and though he knew that their weight would return the moment that Her touch left, he felt good and worthy and whole for the moment.

But, even without that, even if the touch of Her hand had burned his flesh instead of lightened his heart, how could he not have loved Her?

Her smile broadened. "Yes. But you'll let go of My hand nonetheless, won't you?" she asked. "And you'll not take Me in your arms and crush Me to you, My mouth warm upon yours, even though you know that I would make no protest?"

She took a step closer to him. She smelled of wild-flowers and musk, and if there was a hint of the reek of the rotting humus of the forest floor, it only added to the intoxicating effect—to Her intoxicating effect.

"No, Lady, I would not," he said. It was bad enough that such as he touched Her hand; he would not sully Her with more contact than that, save by Her command.

"And would you resist Me, if I tried to force Myself upon you?"

He didn't have an answer for that, although it was not the first time that she had asked him that question. "I still don't know, Lady. But I will, once again, beg You not to think of lowering Yourself so."

She smiled. "And, once again, you dodge the issue. But, be that as it may, I'd not do so, save in necessity."

Necessity? What could make that necessary? He didn't ask; if She wanted him to know, She would have told him.

"Yes," She said. "I would." She nodded, slowly, and in a quick blink She was an arm's length away from him, his hand no longer touching Her.

And all the weight of his sins fell back upon him, and he wept.

"Gray," She was saying. He didn't know how long he had crouched there, weeping like a child. It could have been a moment, or a year. Time seemed to do strange things around Her. "Please stop."

He let a breath out in a ragged sob, then drew another one in.

"Of course, Lady. You have my apologies," he said, as he rose, noting with no pride, albeit some sense of accomplishment, that his voice was steady and calm, suitable for a knight of the Order.

"Apologies? You've nothing to apologize to Me for," She said. "And if you need to draw strength by touching the Khan, though, please do so."

No. Not in front of Her. She could see into the foulness of his soul, yes, but he would not add to it. Not now, not in front of Her. Later, perhaps—no, later, certainly; Gray would be honest with himself. But not before Her.

He hooked his thumb in his sash.

"At most, you can only be once damned, you know," She said, shaking Her head, slowly. "And that is avoidable. But it doesn't feel that way, does it?"

No. It didn't. He could not have served his king, and his brothers, as well if he had not taken the Khan into hand, to mix his soul with the surely damned one of the Khan trapped in the Red Sword, but . . .

"No, it's not that." She frowned. "Even if it's as dark a sin as you think it is, it's forgivable, as all are, to those of the faith you profess. It's the despair that you will not release yourself from that's the sin, Joshua."

Will not, or can not?

He didn't ask. He would like to pretend to himself that it would be otherwise, but he remembered, each and every time that he drew the Khan, what he had made of himself, and what he would make of himself not merely when next he drew the cursed sword, but took a breath without repenting of the necessity of it, a repentance that he could not feel, and would not lie about, to himself or to others.

"Such arrogance, from a man of such modesty." She cocked her head to one side. "Who are you to say that your God cannot forgive you?"

Always the same questions; always the same answers.

"I'm a man who has sworn to live by mercy tempered only by justice, justice tempered only by mercy," he said. "I'd not ask for mercy for myself that I think would be tempered by no justice at all."

Yes, Christ had died, offering to take the sins of the world with him; yes, forgiveness was available, to all who confessed and repented.

But how could a just God forgive the unrepentant?

"The world," she said, "is a stool that rests on three legs: faith, wisdom, and justice. And which of those is most important?"

There was, as always, only one answer to that ancient riddle. "It's as with any other stool—the weakest leg is the most important, Lady, of course. And justice is, always and ever, the weakest. Wisdom there is, although never enough; and faith, while sometimes lacking, is always available. But justice? There's little of that. Of all my failings, Lady, of all my sins, of all that can be said about me, please let it not be said that I begged God to weaken the most important leg of the stool on which the world rests."

"Gray—"

"Please, Lady, may we speak on this no more?"

She sighed. "A stubborn one, you are. More so than most, and your Order is a stubborn lot, all in all. Would you rather speak about the rucksack?"

In Her presence, he had forgotten about something so mundane.

"If it pleases You, yes," he said.

"It's Cully's; return it to him, if you would," She said. "He left it here his last visit." She actually chuckled. "Most of you, I would chide for leaving your laundry for Me to do, and I guess I should make no exception in his case. But I shall, anyway, and tell you not to chide him on My behalf. In fact, I tucked in a hairbrush for him—he forgot to bring one with him last time. Don't mention that, either; let him discover that for himself." She cocked her head to one side. "Are you not going to ask?"

"Ask what, Lady?" He didn't pretend to understand Her. You didn't need to understand Her in order to love or worship Her, after all.

"Are you not going to ask if I had you sent all the way here just to pick up Cully's rucksack?"

She wanted him to, so of course he did: "Lady," he said, "did you have me sent all the way here just to pick up Father Cully's rucksack?"

"And if I did?"

"I make no complaint."

Seeing Her was always pleasure, always pain, and there were times when he wasn't sure that he could sort out which was which, but that wasn't important. Obedience; service; faith; honor; justice and mercy; mercy and justice, yes. His own agony, physical or otherwise, simply didn't measure on that scale.

"No, you'd not complain." Her voice grew sharp. "Well, you should, if that was the case. You should be complaining much. You should be complaining about Mordred, and about Cully, and about the abbot, and about Me, for that matter. Let's start with the king. He treats you like an archer treats an arrow—to him, you're just a tool, just a weapon."

"As is his right, Lady," he said. "And as he's said, in so many words. And if among my sins is the pride that I'm a good weapon for him, I'll not repent of that, either."

She snorted. "You're as unrepentant an inveterate penitent as I've ever known, Joshua."

He didn't answer; he didn't know if one was called for.

"And then there's Me. You should be angry at Me. I sent you off to be knighted, suspecting what might happen to you." She frowned. "Not a Sight, no. Just a suspicion. But even if I'd had a Sight, do you think I'd have not sent off such a promising young knight-to-be to serve My family? You were quite the hero in those heady days, and you've further distinguished yourself since, on more than several occasions." She cocked her head to one side. "The Khan is quite dangerous, as much as the Sandoval, I think—but I also know that you'd not drop your iron self-control for a moment; there'll be no Linfield Horror created by the likes of Joshua Grayling."

"Not without necessity," he said, carefully. "Not over mere anger. I've done awful things, as You know better than most, but not because I can't control myself."

"And that's one of the things that makes you such a useful weapon for the king."

"I'm honored, Lady."

"Not angry, but honored." She nodded her head. "And I made you love Me."

At that, he smiled. "How could I not?"

She smiled back at him, and Her smile warmed him more than he could have said.

"Oh, yes," She said, "all the boys love Me, and in My own way, I do love them, though there are those who think that I love all of them in a fleshy sense, and not in a chaste and proper way. In the villages around the Bedegraine, you'll hear whispers that I bed all of them, too, that the reason that the final test for entry to the Order is the trip into the Arroy is so that the novices can satisfy the carnal needs of the insatiable Queen of Air and Darkness, and that those who fail to do so are left as empty husks, sucked dry of life."

He had never heard such a thing. Of course, he wouldn't—if someone were to speak disparagingly of Her, it would not be even a whisper where the likes of Joshua Grayling could overhear. Not twice.

Nor, for that matter, would any do so twice around any other of the Order, including the abbot general.

"Ah, yes, Ralph," she said. "Another one of those horrid romantic triangles my family seems to find itself in. Although this one has more than a few angles to it; triangles linked in a chain—did you never wonder why the abbot general carries Jenn?"

Cully had carried Jenn, and surrendered the White Sword when he had left the Order. Yes, Jenn belonged at Cully's waist, not the abbot's, but—

No.

He shook his head. No. It wasn't for the likes of him to judge his betters, and the abbot was a good man. He was. And if he differed with Gray about Father Cully, that was not only his privilege, but his right, and—

"He played you like a lute, Joshua, and I can hear the distant song even now. 'Hear my confession,' he said, and then he emptied his heart out to you, withholding no trace of sin, for he is devious in his directness, as he knows that you're the most pitying pitiless man that he's ever met. He gulled you with sincerity, and you fell for it."

"To what end?"

"To make you doubt. He has good intuition, that one—and I *would* think that, since I share it. He thinks that Cully's irresponsible, and reckless, and that there are things happening where Cully may well be near the center and the heart, and that you'll be a steadying influence on him, if only Ralph can persuade you of his own wisdom. The abbot thinks that, in the final analysis, he can trust you, for he has given you his trust, confessed his sins and failings without reservation, and he knows that utter honesty can be far more manipulative than even the cleverest lie, more effective than can be even the most carefully constructed deception, Gray."

But Father Cully *was* irresponsible, and reckless. He always did what he thought best, and only bowed to superior authority out of necessity—when he saw the necessity—not with the giving heart and oath of a knight of the Order. He ruthlessly used the tools given him, and never counted the cost until after, if then.

"And you love him for it, and if I could promise you that you could die horribly, in great agony, at his side, protecting him, you'd bless Me for that promise."

"Of course, Lady," he said. He would love Her no more for that promise, because that was impossible. But he would certainly try.

"But, yet, you should be angry with Cully—he took you in, as a child, yes, but he abandoned you."

"He did *not*." Yes, Father Cully had left the Order, and England—but it was not an abandonment, it had been an attempt to save Gray's soul, to prevent the king and the abbot from giving him the Khan.

That Father Cully was wrong wasn't a betrayal; he had been trying to protect Gray. How could Gray be angry with him for that?

"You used to be," she said, answering his thoughts, rather than his words.

"Then I was a fool, as well as damned." He could not stop Her from speaking as She saw fit, and he wouldn't have if he could have, but he would not hear Father Cully accused without defending him, not even—no, *particularly* not when the awful words fell like bright jewels from Her lips.

She picked up the rucksack, and handed it to him. "Well, I'm not telling you that you'll die by his side, protecting him; I have neither the power nor the desire to grant that, and no Sight to foretell it." She sighed. "Just tell Cully that I tried, if you please."

"Tried? I don't understand"

"Just tell him. He will understand; it's something between him and Me." Her hand reached out toward him, but She drew it back. "And be careful, Joshua," She said. "There is something awful going on."

He would have asked if there was more that She could tell him, but She would have, if She could.

"Yes, I would." She nodded. "I'm not keeping anything from you, Gray. I have fear, but no understanding of it. It's feeling, hints, worries—and you've enough of those latter without Me burdening you more."

"I make no protest, Lady," he said. He would bear his burdens as best he could, and without complaint.

"Well, you should." She shook Her head. "Darklings in the south are only part of it. The new live swords? Another piece of the puzzle, and the one thing I'm certain of is that those aren't the only pieces. You've heard about Hostikka, and that was hardly the only missing piece.

"And so I send you, yet again another one of his lambs, out to find more pieces, and help put them together. And if it's to the slaughter I send you, as it might well be, what would you have to say to that? What would you have to say to Me?"

Of lies, there were no limit; there never were. But of the truth, there was only one answer:

"I would say: I thank you, Lady; I bless you, Lady; and I love you, Lady, for the honor that you bestow upon me, unworthy of it though I am."

She sighed. "Then I'll say this to you, Joshua: follow your heart and your head. Look for the right thing to do, even when it doesn't mean self-sacrifice. I will not say that I trust you to do the right thing, because I am not sure that you will know the right thing any better than do I.

"But let Me say this: when it comes time to decide, listen to others, and accept their counsel, if you think it wise. But listen with an open mind, and an open heart, and as you love Me remember this: it was you whom I sent for, and you to whom I have said this, and not the king, and not the abbot, and very much not Cully, much though I love him.

"I said, truly, that I have no Sight in this, and that concerns me, but I have a feeling, Joshua, and My feeling is that the stool of the world may not rest on faith, or wisdom, or justice, not this time: it may, indeed, rest on you. What have you to offer, Joshua?"

And, as always, there could be only one answer. "Service, honor, faith, obedience. Justice tempered only by mercy; mercy tempered only by justice."

"Obedience? You've been set out on your own, Joshua, to do as you think best: that is your obedience. Your whole life is service; that can give you no clue. And if you should see that faith, wisdom, and justice are insufficient, and since you believe with all your heart that you are a man who has sacrificed his soul, and are without honor, that leaves you one virtue left."

"Mercy, my Lady. Mercy tempered only by justice, but mercy nonetheless."

"Mercy, indeed. And may it include mercy on yourself, Gray."

He bowed stiffly, and when he raised his head, he was alone by the bank of the creek, his horse snorting in impatience. It was difficult, working with one hand and his stump, to strap the rucksack to the saddle, but he did it as rapidly and thoroughly as he could, then gave a quick tug on it, to be sure that it was securely bound.

And then he was quickly on his way.

There was, of course, only the one path.

He followed it.

CHAPTER 10

Colonsay II

*I will learn, but I'm not sure that I can believe all
that I'm taught.*

*We're taught that White Swords contain the
souls of saints, voluntarily putting off their entry
to Heaven until the rest of humanity can join them.*

I'll try to believe that.

I think I can.

*And we're taught that Red Swords contain the
souls of sinners. We're taught that some think them
already damned, and merely being given an opportunity to delay their punishment, while others think
that a Red Sword is merely Purgatory on earth—a
last chance for repentance and salvation.*

I'll not speak of the Khan or Croom'l, or the Sandoval, the Tinker, or any other of the Reds. But Nadide was just a baby, plucked hungry from her mother's breast.

What sins had she to repent of? What just God would damn her?

Perhaps, although I'll not speak of it in front of others, the answer lies in the question itself.

—Niko

The world was supposed to slow down; it had happened every time before.

But it didn't.

Yes, the world had changed about them. Yes, the red light coursed through not only the air around them, as though the lanterns and candles had become darker but more powerful; the light flowed into and through their shared steel, their shared bones and muscle and eyes and mind.

The demands of the body became distant and irrelevant, although the feel of the body was sharper, more distinct, from the blister on the sole of his left foot that had split two days before, to the small scratch over his right eye—it was all there, all present in their shared mind and body, but it just wasn't important, any more than her thirst for the sweetness of She Who Smelled Like Food was.

It was the pounding heart.

They could hear the beating of Niko's heart, but it wasn't the slow, desultory *lub-dub* of the other times; his heart was pounding fast, in time with the fast drums that kept pace with the piper's manic tune, a tune that the curtains could no longer keep out of his ears, and together with the pounding of the drum and his heart, drowned out all other sounds.

As he pushed past Becket into the hall, he could see Fotheringay's mouth working, and knew that the older man was shouting something out at him, but he couldn't manage to make sense from the words.

The baron was halfway down the blood-slicked stairs, his sword in hand, tentatively probing for some way past the two novices near the foot of the staircase, and into the McPhees clawing at them. There were now more than a dozen in the house, battling with the novices.

It was horrible. War, battle, fighting were supposed to be between men, and that was awful enough—but there were five women among them, and one child who couldn't have been more than five or six, who didn't even scream when Winslow kicked her away from where she was grabbing at his foot, trying to bite it, and back into the crowd.

She fell beneath the feet of the other McPhees, who didn't so much as look down, but just stepped on her as they made their way toward the foot of the stairs.

It should have been easy, a one-sided fight, despite the numbers—the shuffling McPhees were wide-eyed in madness, slow and clumsy, and armed only with their hands. It was like the distant piper was a distant puppeteer, sending them as fingers to grab and to clutch, and not caring one whit about the fingers themselves.

Most still wore their clothing—although it was filthy, sweaty, and disarrayed—though two of the men and one of the women were stark naked. But the naked and the clothed shuffled forward in unison, their clumsy feet trying to keep time with the drums, reaching out, not deterred by the blades hacking and slashing and stabbing at them, not even trying to evade the steel, ignoring everything, just to try to reach the men who blocked the stairs.

And, sure enough, they bled when cut, as the novices slashed with their swords. Thomas Scoville slipped the tip of his sword into the chest of one man, then kicked him off the blade and into the others, knocking three of them down, as blood spurted, spraying the stairs.

The one who fell stayed fallen, but others clambered over the body, simply rising again as they slipped on the blood-slickened stairs, and then rose again, and again, ignoring their wounds, and clawing at each other as they tried to reach the two novices.

One of the heavier men in front fell when the point of Thomas's sword found his knee, and Michael kicked him away, while the baron used the opening to reach through the two and put his sword into a bearded throat, then lightly brushed aside the withered dug of a naked old woman before his blade found her heart, too.

The baron's eyes were wide, too, but not with madness, but with something that Niko and Nadide had no name for, and his jaw was set.

There was something magnificent about him—blade in his right hand, he stood on the step with his left hand on his hip, as though in a gesture of disdain, and from moment to moment, seeing an opening, he would drop in full extension, recovering with a wet blade.

He turned to shout something to Niko for just a moment, but Niko still couldn't make out words, and the

staircase wasn't wide enough for him to make his way
past where the baron and the novices stood. The pipes
and the drums didn't have a grip on his mind, not here
and now, but they had enveloped his ears, driving all
outside sounds away.

It was all wrong. There were hundreds and hundreds
of the maddened McPhees, and eventually they would
overwhelm the defenders, even if the bodies were piled
so high that they would have to climb over them.

It was all wrong. He—they were all wrong.

Where was the speed that they were supposed to
have? The incessant drumbeat from outside felt like it
had anchored them in slow time, and without that they—

No.

Without that, they were still not powerless. They were
still Niko and Nadide, welded together, and there was
more than enough power in that.

They lowered their point, and reached out and in:

—in, for the fire and ice that lay at juncture of their
fused souls,

—and out, past the baron, past the novices, for the
souls of the maddened men and women.

To the part of them that was Niko, it looked and felt
like silent thunderbolts crashed from the tip of the sword
and into the McPhees; to the part of them that was Nadide, it was as though the jagged light was coming in to
the sword, feeding a hunger that they had not even
noticed that they had, but feeding it in a way that made
them even more hungry.

And with that, the McPhees—the men, the women,
and the children—died with horrid screams that diminished as they were eaten by the sword, the bodies falling

limp and lifeless to the floor, leaving the baron and the two novices standing on the slickened staircase, drenched in blood and sweat.

Looking to him. Talking to him, although he could not make out their words.

It wasn't done. Still, the sound of the pipe and the drumbeat pounded outside. Still, the shouts and cries of the baron and the novices were drowned out in his ears and his mind.

It was only the other sounds that were absent, denied to him.

The baron was shouting something to him, to them, but they pushed past, and shoved Scoville aside. But the toe of their boot slipped on a patch of blood on the steps, sending him falling too fast, too hard to catch themselves with his free hand; it was all he could do to hold onto Nadide as he fell among the bodies, cursing himself for falling across the body of the little girl.

They would feel about it later.

Perhaps they would feel justified; perhaps they would be horrified; most likely both.

But they forced themselves to their feet and ran—too slow, too slow, still stuck in real time, anchored by the drumbeats—and out into the night.

The music had been intoxicating in Niko's ears, but that was before he had drawn Nadide.

The world was different now. Out here, the tune of the pipes was, at least, just a tune, one that they could barely hear—they could feel it wash madness over the McPhees on the beach, both those coupling on the ground before them and the others, who were quickly turning to face them, but it didn't wash into their minds, into their shared soul.

It was the drums that did that, and not only didn't the tune infect him, he couldn't understand—

No—he was wrong.

It didn't infect him, but he understood it all, even though he knew none of the words.

Outlanders invade the land that is ours, the tune said. *Rise up, sons and daughters of the* sidhe, *throw off your chains of mere humanity.*

It is their shirts, their shirts you are washing.

A glissando on the pipes was a mocking laugh, as the piper swayed in time with his own music, notes splattering madness across the sand.

Look at the boy and the girl, the music said. *Curse them as the invaders that they are. Grab them, hold them down, mount them again and again until their flesh lies in pieces on the sand.*

They ran and ran, toward the left side of the crowd, trying to make their way around them, toward where the dark piper stood alone, but the tune picked up, and the crowd moved in unison to block them.

No. Where was their speed? It was stolen, stolen, stolen by the drum, by the drum, by the drummer before him, and they would have to kill all of them before they could get to the dark piper, and silence his tunes of madness.

The drums, the drums—the drummer was off to his right, his face sweaty in the firelight, as he sat on a stone, his hands blurring with speed on the head of the drum.

Niko ran across the sand toward him, ignoring the crowd behind.

No, the part of them that was Nadide said. *Drink them all. I'm hungry, and I'm only getting hungrier.*

It should have been a mad, rapid tattoo that they were hearing, but all that they could hear was the rapid *thrum-thrum-thrum* in time with the pounding of their shared heart.

No chance to make their way around the crowd to the piper—

The drummer.

They reached out their fire toward him, the lightning flashing from the blade, or the soul being pulled into it, or both.

The drum burst into flames, and the drummer rose, his face sweaty in the firelight, his mouth wide in a scream—

That they could hear, as their shared heart, broken free of the tyranny of the drumbeat, fell into the slow *lub-dub, lub-dub, lub-dub* of a body trapped in real time, heart pounding as fast as it could, while they had their speed back, once more.

The nearest of the McPhees was reaching out for them, but the McPhees were all trapped in the slow time that clawed at their resistant body—

And beyond them, the piper played.

Now, it was as easy as something impossible ever was—they sped across the cold sands, past the crowd that was moving to block their way, both to the right and the left: men, women, and children moving so slowly, but so many of them, and across the bonfire the piper played.

It is their shirts, their shirts you are washing.

One path, and one path only . . .

They ran to and through the bonfire, toward the piper, running up the burning cinders, neither knowing nor caring what the flame did to their body.

It didn't matter.

The hooded piper was caught in the same slow time as the rest were. Just a matter of getting close enough, then letting their flame burn him, burn him, as it had burned the others. They hungered for the taste of his soul, and reached in, and out, as they had before.

Lightning crashed—

And the pipes and robe dropped to the cold sand.

They poked at the robe, but it was empty.

Quickly, as quickly as their reluctant body could turn, they spun around. Where was he?

Gone.

The *lub-dub, lub-dub* of his heart had started to miss beats, their shared mind noted, as though it was something important.

Yes, yes, it was important. They had been together too long, and their body—Niko's body—was starting to fail.

So be it? Perhaps. Perhaps the thing to do was to turn the part of them that was Nadide upon the part of them that was Niko, and weld them together, forever. Be one with each other for eternity, not for this brief moment that was all that they could allow themselves.

But, no. Perhaps another time, but not now. There was work to be done, yet, before that.

So the part of them that was Niko stuck the part of them that was Nadide through the piper's empty robes, and into the sand, and then released their grip on each other.

And then he was just Niko again, shrugging out of the burning jacket, the pain present, but his fingers vague and clumsy, as though he was outside of his own body, and not, once again, trapped within it.

All around him, voices were raised in screams and cries of pain, and he found himself falling forward, into the warm blackness, not wondering or caring if he'd ever emerge.

That was better. The blackness was a place of no pain, no fear, no hunger, and it went on forever.

"Easy, young sir." It was Fotheringay's voice, of course, dragging him out of the dark. "Let me be helping you up." Strong hands raised him to a sitting position.

Where was he? His eyes were open, but they refused to focus, and stung as though he had opened them under water. It was worse than trying to see underwater; at least, underwater, you could make out vague shapes and colors, blurred though they might be.

His eyes refused to focus, but his hand reached down to find Nadide. His fingers gripped only sheets.

"The swords—both your swords—are right next to you on the bed, young sir, where they ought to be," Fotheringay said. "But I think, just perhaps, you might want to save that for a while?"

He blinked, and tried to force his traitor eyes to focus on Fotheringay's face. But it wasn't Fotheringay's—it was Becket's. He closed his eyes and opened them again.

Yes, it was Becket, sitting in his chair next to Niko's bed, and Fotheringay was on the other side of the bed, half supporting him.

Becket gave him a nod. "Was starting to wonder if you'd wake up at all," he said, reaching out his good hand to touch the blanket that covered Niko. "You've got some minor burns here, here, and here," he said. "They've been cleaned and dressed—you're probably in for a spot of fever, but you should survive."

His mouth was dry, and it was hard to speak. "The Shanleys—" he croaked out.

Becket silenced him with a snort. "Do you think I'd be sitting here, watching you sleep, if the baron and the baroness weren't safe? They're in the next room, and they're both unhurt, which is more than I can say for you, or the boys. Scoville had his right leg pulled half out of him, before it all came apart, but he can stand, as long as he has something to lean against." Becket jerked a thumb up, toward the ceiling. "Should have some of the earl's troops landing in a few hours, and I've got the novices up on the roof with bows, ready to warn any of the locals to stay away, although the only ones who haven't fled are the dead, and there'll be plenty of work burying them." He shook his head. "And it seems the two of you managed to do for the Amadan Dubh, eh?"

His mouth was dry, and it was hard to talk, but he shook his head.

"No. At least—" His hand found Nadide.

Niko. You're hurting.

Never mind that—the Amadan Dubh, the piper . . .

I wish we'd killed him. He was making the people do mean things.

"No," Niko said. "I . . . we just chased him away."

He expected a harsh comment at that, but Becket just nodded. "Well, it's not what I'd have hoped for, but it's better than any of the rest of us did, at that." He leaned back in his chair, and again they were teacher and student. "So what is the right thing to do now, Sir Niko?"

Niko shook his head. "I can . . . only see things that aren't as wrong as others. Get the Shanleys out of here, certainly; get the earl's troops and leave them in place, yes, but . . ."

"And about the attack?" Becket's face was impassive. "There were literally hundreds of McPhees trying to kill their liege lord last night. What would you recommend to the Baron? Trial? Execution?"

"No. Blame it on the one responsible," Niko said. "The piper. Find him, and kill him."

"You think you're up to that?"

"I'd certainly like to try. I'd much rather like to try that than to have to deal with the baron putting all of the surviving McPhees on trial, Sir Martin." He tried to gesture with his free hand, but it just flopped. "Is he considering that?"

"And if he is?"

Some things weren't difficult to answer. "We can't allow that. 'Justice tempered by mercy,' Sir Martin— there'd be no justice, and no mercy."

"True enough," sounded from the doorway.

Niko looked over. The baron was standing there. His left arm was bound up in a bandage and sling, and his face was pale, but his voice was as calm and quiet as it had always been before. "I'm sure I can say that I don't understand what went on, but it was no rebellion, just a madness—a madness which seems to have passed."

Becket grunted. "And the sooner that we get you and Grace off of this accursed island, the better I'll feel about it staying passed, or not hurting you if it returns."

Niko nodded. "I think we know what the source of it was—the piper."

"And your recommendation, Sir Niko?" the baron asked, as Becket had.

"To hunt him down. Bring him to ground, and kill him." That was obvious. Niko's stomach churned over the killings that he had done during the night. He would pray for the souls of each and every one of the McPhees he had killed, most with just a wave of Nadide.

But he knew where the blame was to be found. It wasn't in the souls of those whose minds had been captured by the pipes and the drums, but in the one who had sent them on their bloody path.

"And do you think you can manage it?"

"I don't know," he said. "I do know that I can try."

"Yes, you could." Becket nodded. "A knightly enough answer, at that, but—"

"But the matter has already been decided, and I don't know why you're bringing it up, Martin," the baron said.

"I'll thank you, Lord Baron, to let me test my own student in my own way," Becket said, a snap in his voice. He met the baron's gaze for a long moment until the baron nodded.

Fotheringay quickly turned his eyes away from that, and grinned at Niko. "Well, perhaps we can try after we get back from Londinium, or Windsor, young sir. If we're sent back here."

"Londinium? Windsor?"

"The king could be in residence in either place." Becket nodded. "For one thing, if a knight of the Order is to go messing about with any of the Old Ones, it's something that he should have sense to avoid deciding himself. Beyond that, if you're going to go hunting one of the last of the *sidhe*, you're going to need more than

Fotheringay to act as your hound. And you'll need a lighter load on your back than the likes of me."

"Or, for that matter, the baron and his lady," Fotheringay said. "Can't watch out for them while he and I and whoever else are out hunting a mad piper, Sir Martin."

Becket glared at him. "You're not one who knows his place, Fotheringay."

"I think I do, Sir Martin." Fotheringay didn't quite shrug, and he met Becket's glare without flinching. "Just trying to do my job, Sir Martin, and watching the young knight's back is that job, and I'll do it, whether it's keeping it from sprouting daggers, or bearing too heavy a load for the task—and speaking of which, Sir Niko, if you'd do me the courtesy of just lying back for a while, there's a tray of bread and meat here that's not doing you any good lying on a plate, when it should be warming your belly."

"Fotheringay—"

"Listen to the man," Becket said. "He's got the right of it. Eat."

Niko forced himself to eat, but every bite was ashes in his mouth.

CHAPTER 11

Rhodos

The York Rebellion had a certain directness to it. Kill the king, take the throne, and be done with it. I can't say that I admire it—and if there's really a Hell, I'd like to think that the late duke is burning in a particularly fiery pit, with hosts of demons poking him up his backside—but at least it was straightforward.

It's not that I'm always a great practitioner of straightforwardness, of course; but I do prefer to see it in others.

—Cully

The admiral beckoned him outside.

That was fine with Cully.

Guy started to rise, but DuPuy waved him back to his seat, next to where Penelope lay in her bed.

"I would very much appreciate it if you'd watch over the girl," DuPuy said.

Guy started to open his mouth, but then wisely chose to close it. He simply nodded, and resumed his seat, touching one hand to the hilt of Albert, and another to the wrist of the girl, from where she lay on the narrow bed, under the fresh sheet. They would have to change it shortly, again. While most of her skin had scabbed over, it kept breaking in spots, particularly around the joints, and those needed not only to be kept clean, but not allowed to bind to the cloth.

For a man who clearly liked being on a ship more than anything else, it was strange that DuPuy had met them ashore, rather than having them brought out to the *Lord Launcher*. If Cully was a more generous man, he would have attributed it to concern over moving Penelope more than was necessary.

That said, he did have Kechiroski aboard the *Lord Launcher*.

The night was clear and calm, with only a sliver of moon above the three ships lying at anchor in the harbor. They rose and fell with what remained of the swells that made it through the breakwater.

Rodhos tended toward the quiet at night. Oh, there was some singing coming across the water in one of the dockside taverns, and the familiar tunes of the navy drinking songs making it clear that the admiral had allowed some liberty ashore, but that was about all of it, and about all one could expect. Managing the tricky channel into the harbor—or out of it—was something for daylight, and the masters of the other ships that had been in the harbor that morning had found the arrival of the three navy vessels good reason to leave prematurely. Either that, or it was the sort of coincidence that Cully didn't believe in, as a matter of experience.

"I don't like any of this, Sir Cully," the admiral said. He put his pipe between his mouth and took a puff. "Not that that much matters."

"No. What matters is what to do about it." Cully shrugged.

"Should you be going back to Izmir, perhaps?" the admiral asked. "Obviously, you can't take the girl, but . . ."

"I don't think so." Cully shook his head. "It was the Baba Yaga that was the problem there, and—"

"And that means that the source of the live swords can't be Izmir?"

The admiral was being an idiot. Probably on purpose, to draw Cully out. So be it.

"No," he said, "it means that if it is—and it may well be—we're still no closer to finding them there than we were before, and I don't see how Kechiroski, Guy, and I could manage to function there. Erdem the Tinker disappeared, along with the household goods he was supposed to repair."

"You're worried about being identified as spies." DuPuy nodded. "Fair enough."

"I don't care whether the problem is us being hanged as spies or stabbed as thieves—it's not only likely to hurt, but more to the point, either would render the three of us useless."

That said, Guy and Albert could fend off most of those sorts of attacks easily—but not quietly, and not without drawing attention.

Cully shook his head. "I've no objection to you sending me in as bait, to see what takes to my trail behind me, admiral—"

"A way you've used yourself before."

Cully nodded. "But then I had Gray and Bear on my trail, and some reason to think that the two of them could handle whatever it was. Right now, all we've got is pins on your map, and some reason to think that they point to something else." He deliberately allowed a trace of irritation to creep into his voice. "And I've got the most useless knight ever raised to the White Sword in my way, more than half the time."

"So what do you recommend?"

In the two weeks it had taken them to make their way across the coast and take ship to Rodhos, he'd been thinking of little else. Kechiroski had caught up with them there, as prearranged—and Cully could hardly fault the man for making it there more quickly. When Kechiroski's courage had returned or his good sense abandoned him—Cully wasn't sure which—he had gone back to the hilltop to find them gone, along with the hut. Even if the hellene had wanted to try to find them—and he said that he had, although Cully couldn't think of why he would—there was no obvious way he could have done that.

Well, he might as well get it out into the open. "We've tried the clever way. That hasn't worked. There's something to be said for a cruder approach." He cocked his head to one side. "You think it all points to Izmir?"

DuPuy nodded. "I think so. But I don't know so."

"And if you wait for knowledge . . . "

"Then it may be a long wait indeed." The admiral nodded. "Possibly too long a wait. So: we send the *Hind* and the *Antelope* out with dispatches, telling the admirals on Gibbie and Malta to put together every ship and man that they can, send the same word to the Dukes of, say, Napoli, Sicilia, and Ancona, and mount an invasion of the Izmiri coast, hoping to kick something up. Is that what you're advocating, Sir Cully?"

"I'm not sure I'm quite advocating anything," Cully said. "Not at the moment. But don't you think that would flush the game, if it's there?"

"And if it's not? Or even if it is? Look at what else it might do." The admiral took another puff at his pipe, and frowned when nothing came out. "Damn me if we're going to do that—and double damn me if we do that without need." He shook his head. "I wouldn't be at all surprised if that smooth bastard, al-Bakalani, has alerted his masters to just that possibility. We send tens of thousands of soldiers chasing around the waste of Izmir, and then we'll have hundreds of Dar ships set sail from Sfax, for Sicilia, and Italy—and before we know it, they've got a foothold on the Continent." He spat. "We need to war with the Dar, yes, and if it were up to me, we'd be raising the troops now—for that. But we're not."

"You've probably got that authority," Cully said. "Sealed orders, sent to every captain in His Majesty's

Navy, ever administrator, every duke—Crown or otherwise—and half the land earls?"

DuPuy shrugged. "I wouldn't make assumptions about what's in those orders."

"I would," Cully said. "I'd hazard a guess that among your papers is a military commission, quite possibly one that hasn't been given in centuries. I'd not guess at the title, but it would be something like grand duke and commander in chief of all of his majesty's forces— whatever it is, it'll be intended to make any man, noble or common, military or civilian, hop about at your command. His Majesty's a smart man—he doesn't expect you to solve this with a few hundred spies, an aging knight, and an idiot." He forced a grin. "Or even with those, plus the girl and Kechiroski, and the other spies you've sent out. Not in any sort of final way."

"No," DuPuy said, "he doesn't. But he doesn't expect me to strike out like a child having a tantrum, either. My brief is to find the source of the live swords, and whatever else is involved with that—not to declare war on the Dar Al Islam."

Well, that wasn't surprising. Cully wasn't as impressed with DuPuy as His Majesty obviously was, but he really hadn't expected much different. DuPuy would use his authority as directed, not as he wished to, although his hunger for a war with the Dar Al Islam was almost palpable.

Which was probably one of the reasons His Majesty had picked DuPuy in the first place—at this point, the Dar was no more eager for an all-out war than the Crown was, and the threat of that could act as a spur for the

Caliph's cooperation, via al-Bakalani, on the matter of the live swords, and whatever the hell else was going on.

And there was another possibility, too.

"You don't think the swords are at the heart of it?"

"I don't even think I know what the bloody hell *it* is, not anymore," DuPuy said. He shook his head. "There's those other reports—more darklings in France, and the number of merchantmen disappearing in the Atlantic seems to be growing, and the dead outside of Hostikka. Tell me how some hidden swordmaker in Izmir is behind that, if you please."

Cully shrugged. "As far as I can tell, there's only one way to find out, at least only one way to find out quickly." No, that wasn't true—they had gone a year beyond *quickly*.

DuPuy nodded. "Just as there's only one way to find out for certain if sticking a sword up your backside would hurt. Maybe it wouldn't, but I don't see you squatting on one to find out." He shook his head. "I don't have any objection to doing something precipitous, as long as I've got sufficient reason to believe that it's the *right* precipitous thing. A land invasion of Izmir isn't that, right now." He shook his head. "I'm having more spies dispatched there, and elsewhere."

"And for me?"

"And for you, and for me, we're homeward bound," DuPuy said. "Londinium, by way of Portsmouth, perhaps after a stop in Marseilles. At some point, we'll rendezvous with Sir Joshua, since—"

Cully's voice caught in his throat. "Gray?"

"Sir Joshua has been seconded to me—well, more to you. By order of the abbot general, of all people. I'm not sure where he is at the moment, but I expect him presently—he should have both the codes and the authority to read any of my dispatches as to where you are." He sucked for a moment on his unlit pipe. "And Marseilles? There's been some reports of goings-on north of there." He reached into his jacket and pulled out a folded dispatch. "And then there's this. From His Majesty."

Cully read through it quickly. Even filtered through His Majesty's careful use of the language, Becket's words came through. "First the Baba Yaga, and now the Amadan Dubh, eh?"

"And the new live swords, and darklings where they shouldn't be, and other stirrings, other places. Some of the Irish barons reported having heard cries of *Imeacht gan teacht ort* as they rode off for Parliament." The admiral took a pull on his pipe. "And it's not just where there's noise and trouble where there ought not be—there's also a lack of troubles where, perhaps, you might expect some. The saracens in New England aren't becoming much more troublesome, I think, although there's been a new . . . batch of Ghost Dancers out on the plains. And, yes, there's still troubles with the Kaliites in the Kush, despite what a swath Sir John cut through them not so long ago. But all that's been ongoing, not new—not like this—this, whatever it is, is something new, or the rebirth of something old. Be interesting to know if there's similar stirrings outside of Crown territory, wouldn't it?"

"Al-Bakalani has been—"

"Silent on the matter. On all of it. Curiously silent. I think that I—that we—need to speak with him, and see if we can pry some information out of him. And, meanwhile, see if I've got enough authority to prevail on Crown Intelligence that the sort of spy system that the Dar has is something we'd damn well better emulate."

"That's all well and good, but . . ." Cully shook his head. "That's a matter of years, at best."

DuPuy shrugged. "And if we have years, the sooner we start, the better. If we don't, then it does no harm."

"Unless we are—unless *you* are—diverting resources that could be better used."

"And if I had any bloody idea of how they could be better used, I'd use them for it."

"There is that. So, it's off to Londinium, and to see the king?"

"And that Arab bastard. For me. I don't know about you, not yet." DuPuy nodded. "For now, let's see to the girl."

They went back inside, and at their approach, she started to rise from her bed.

"Stand easy, girl," DuPuy said. "You're to rest, not tire yourself."

She had been a pretty girl, in a dark sort of way. The combination of her Injan mother and Cumberland father had given her a vaguely Mediterranean look, close enough to pass for Hellene or Turk or Arab. But that was before.

Her face was bad enough. There had been only splashes of the boiling water on her cheeks, and while each and every one of those splashes had left a burn that would become a scar, they had mostly healed. But from the neck down, she was a mass of burns, mostly scabbed over. Cully wasn't sure whether it was innate stubbornness, the preparations that, even in her agony, she had made from her kit, or something else, but he thought that she would live.

He cursed himself every time he saw her horrible wounds. She would not ever draw a breath without pain; brave men would turn their faces away from her rather than gaze on the wreck she had become; and instead of her daily agony, he could have simply put her out of her pain.

As he would have, had she asked. As he should have, out of mercy.

Guy rested one hand on Albert, and another on her hand. Once more, her whole body seemed to relax.

Guy nodded. An idiot he was, yes, but he was doing as well as anybody could for the girl. Holiness could be comforting, and if the comfort came from her belief in the touch of Sir Guy and Albert together rather than any innate ability of the combination of the two, that was fine with Cully.

"Brave girl," DuPuy said, nodding. "Credit to your father."

"And to your mother," Cully added, "and your College." He ignored DuPuy's glare.

"Well," the admiral said, "let's pretend that I've come to a decision. Let's say that I'll take the girl back to Londinium with me, in the *Lord Launcher*—and that you can have your choice of *Hind* or *Antelope*, and your choice of destination." He tapped at the dispatch. "Would it be Marseilles?"

Cully shook his head. "Pantelleria. And I want to take the girl, and Sir Guy, and Kechiroski with me. If you can get dispatches out—"

"And if I can't, I'd want to know the reason why."

"—I'd appreciate it if you would pass the word on to Gray, if you can. If he can rendezvous with us in Malta, he can join us."

DuPuy's mouth barely twitched. "I thought as much. And after that?"

Cully shrugged. "We'll see where things lead. If we get some hint on Pantelleria as to where to go, I'm not disposed to waste time sending dispatches to Londinium, and waiting for your response."

"On that, I'm undecided." DuPuy took a long pull on his pipe. "How much good would it do for me to tell you to check in with me after Pantelleria?"

"That would depend on what we find there. If anything." Cully shook his head. "I'm not sure that the Wise will be of any use—but I can't think of anything more useful. Can you?" He eyed the admiral levelly. "If you're thinking to pull rank on me, I'd suggest that you consider, first, if you really want to."

DuPuy was silent a long time. "And then I'd have to consider the fact that you will do as you think best anyway, and decide if I want to be an impotent old man who gives orders he knows won't be obeyed, except by coincidence." He looked toward the door as though looking out toward the ships in the harbor.

Yes, he could order Cully aboard one of the ships, and yes, he had enough Marines with him to make that order stick—even if Guy wouldn't have supported the admiral with glee, and even greater glee if the admiral's orders were to clap Cully in irons and haul him, willy-nilly, back to England.

What would Cully do if that happened? He didn't know. He knew that he felt that it was wrong to leave the Med right now, that whatever his role in this thing was, it was here, but he had far too often been the sort of fool who had let his feelings overrule his good sense.

Would Cully do that again? The question was whether or not to. How to do it was a simple matter, really—just kick a chair toward Guy to distract him, then follow that up with a short punch to the admiral's midsection to drop DuPuy, and then he could be out and into the night, and away.

There would be something gratifying in all of that. Not just beating that idiot Guy—as pleasant an exercise as that would be, on one level—but shaking off the chains of another's commands, of returning to doing what he thought best.

Would he?

He hadn't quite decided when the admiral nodded. "Well, then, Sir Cully, the *Hind*'s the fastest of the three—it's at your disposal." DuPuy's mouth split into a grin. "Or, of course, I'm lying, and I'll have you thrown in the hold the moment I get you aboard, even though I'll give you my word that that's not the case."

"You'd break your word, Admiral?" Guy seemed shocked. The idiot.

"Of course, you fool. I'd do it in a heartbeat—if I thought it necessary, or even advisable," the admiral said. "My word and my honor are expendable; hardly the most valuable thing I could expend." He turned back to Cully. "But I don't see the need, not here and now. You've got your crew; you've got your ship." He raised his voice. "*Emmons.*"

If the young lieutenant had been lurking about the door when Cully and the admiral had been outside, Cully hadn't seen him, but it was only a matter of a moment until he was inside.

"Sir."

"Pass the word to Captain McGinty—he's at Sir Cully's disposal, until further notice. Sir Cully will, I'd expect, want to raise sail at first light. Longboat ashore, along with a crew—Miss Penelope will need assistance."

"Aye-aye, sir." Emmons was gone even more quickly than he had appeared.

The admiral turned back to Cully. "Guess I've saved Sir Guy and myself a beating, as well, eh?"

"I'm not sure," Cully said, truthfully. He hadn't decided, after all. "But quite possibly."

DuPuy just smiled.

CHAPTER 12

Windsor

I have this unfortunate tendency to speak my mind. Granted, His Late Majesty was tolerant of that, mostly, particularly in private, but I think I came close to pushing it too far the time that, obedient to his order, I told him what I was thinking, something to the effect of that he should remember that even when he was sitting on the throne, he was still sitting on his ass.

—Cully

The small door in the massive gate to Windsor castle wasn't all that small, really. Ten men could have walked through it, abreast. It just seemed dwarfed by the massive gate to the castle.

It opened instantly when Niko dismounted, and a troop of the House Guard emerged from the nearby, slightly smaller door in the main gate, and took up a formation next to it.

The captain at the head of the Guard drew himself up to a stiff brace, immediately echoed by the rest of the Guard troop. Just into his forties, with what had been a massive chest threatening to sag into becoming a massive belly, although at Becket's glance, he sucked it in and came to an even straighter brace.

"Well, let's get to it," Becket said, as the novices who brought Becket set him down into his traveling chair.

"I'd be grateful if you'd but give me half a moment, Sir Martin." Fotheringay adjusted the shoulders of Niko's jacket, then gave the jacket a slight tug at the skirt, pulling all into place. He gave an approving nod. "There. That'll do, Sir Niko."

Becket had taken the indignities of being cleaned and re-dressed while the carriage was moving with his usual equanimity, which wasn't much. While the carriage had been intended to seat eight, that was eight for travel, not for doing anything more. The carriage had been crowded, what with the five of them. Both Niko and Fotheringay had had to crowd themselves into opposite corners to give the novices enough space to work on Becket, then carefully gather up the leather tarpaulin that they had set on the floor and tie its ends together. It had only taken a minute or two for the stench to disperse itself through the shuttered windows, and only a minute or two more for Niko, with Fotheringay's assistance, to change his own clothes.

Niko pushed the wheeled chair through the gate, past the guards who, if anything, came to an even stiffer brace.

There was a protocol to be observed, but it was a strange one, even for Niko, who had become used to strange protocols over the past year.

Fotheringay and the novices had to wait at the front gate—although there was little doubt that they would be summoned. But they would have to be summoned, while the Order Knights just walked right in.

There were no gardeners or servants working on the grounds inside the gates, although the roadway was free of dirt or dust, as though it had just been freshly swept, and the rose beds to the right and left of the roadway were lined with an explosion of red and yellow and gold, with no petals either wilting, or lying on the ground.

There was no sign of the House Guard barracks; that was, Niko had been told, beyond the castle itself, but well within the walls, and while guards marched atop the walls, only a pair of guardsmen and one sergeant stood in front of the massive oak door atop the front steps.

And as Niko pushed Becket's traveling chair up to front steps, not only was there no challenge from the soldiers of the House Guard, but the sergeant on duty bellowed a command, and immediately a pair of almost preposterously large men in the black-and-white livery of palace servants appeared through the open doorway, running down the stairs to lift the chair, and convey it up the steps, without so much as a challenge or a question.

They were met at the top by the lord chamberlain of the household.

The Earl of Somerset was a slim man, elegantly dressed in black and silver, the only other color the golden necklace with the pendant that marked his station, which matched his only other visible piece of jewelry: the signet ring on his right hand.

"Sir Niko, Sir Martin: welcome," he said, with a quick bow. He stood aside, as though to make it clear that he was greeting them, not barring their way, and then gave a quick nod to the two servants, who immediately set the chair down.

"Sir Niko can push my chair," Becket more growled than said, and the servant who had taken up a position behind his chair and gripped the frame leaped away as though the wood had burned his hands.

The chamberlain didn't appear to notice. "His Majesty is in his small study," Lord Henry said, leading the way down one long hall, and then to the right, down another. For whatever reason, the lord chamberlain kept his slippered feet off the red carpet that ran down the middle of the corridors, and Niko mimicked him.

This was strange enough as it was, and he was in constant fear of committing what probably would have been a solecism of some sort.

It was, as Becket had explained, simply a matter of protocol. Commoners and nobles, knights and ladies, waited upon the king's pleasure, or for his summons, as was only fitting. As a matter of law and tradition, knights of the Order had the right—no, the obligation—to go to His Majesty's side as they saw fit, and it had been that way ever since the final battle of Bedegraine. Yes, like any other of His Majesty's subjects, an Order Knight would be obedient to a summons; what was unique about their station was that they could be, well, self-summoning.

Becket chuckled, as the wheels of his chair made *clickety-clickety-clicking* sounds on the marble. "It's perfectly acceptable to roll my chair down the carpet, you know," he said, quietly. "Be bold, Sir Niko. Don't pussyfoot into the Presence—we've the right, and good enough reason."

The chamberlain gestured toward the door to the study before he gave them a slight nod, then walked away.

He needn't have bothered indicating which room it was; it was well marked. It wasn't just that His Majesty's study was just past the throne room: it was where John of Redhook stood at his ease, leaning up against an ancient tapestry—Niko assumed it was ancient, from the way that the colors of the greenery surrounding the fauns had faded—as though utterly unconcerned, but with his eyes missing nothing.

Those eyes swept across Niko and Becket, and Sir John gave just the barest of nods, as he raised his right hand in the Sign: thumb tucked into the palm, four fingers spread.

He was a big man, taller by half a head than even Bear had been, but long and lanky, without quite being skinny. His ruddy brown beard, thick and full but neatly trimmed nonetheless, framed a face that seemed to smile almost all of the time, but never too much, and as he stood, leaning against the tapestry, he seemed utterly in place, and at his ease, something Niko couldn't help but envy.

That didn't seem to be an issue for Becket, who snorted.

"In my day," he said, his voice too loud, "when a member of His Own was on duty, he was far too busy seeing to the safety of His Majesty to greet even members of his own Order, and far too much concerned with his duty to be lolling about a hall, leaning on a wall."

"Well, it was not much of a greeting," Sir John said, his thumb resting on the hilt of one of his two swords. "I meant only not to delay you. But since you apparently have the time to talk with me, Sir Martin, rather than hurry to His Majesty's side, I'll take the time to greet you properly." He gave a quick, stiff bow. "Sir Niko; Sir Martin. It's good to see you." His beard split into a wider grin at Becket's gasp. "Oh, be still, Sir Martin. I'm not on guard at the moment; the Beast is. I just decided that I'd sit in on your audience."

As was, of course, Sir John's right, every bit as much as it was theirs to have the audience in the first place. "We generally run a one-in-four in the castle," Sir John said, "except when himself has visitors." He grinned again. "You're not really a visitor, and His Majesty isn't alone."

"Inside, Sir Niko," Becket said.

Sir John followed them in.

Mordred V, by the grace of God the King of England, was much as Niko had seen him the first time: seated in a large, comfortable-looking chair, with a pile of papers on a table at his side, and a team of four scribes at a longer table behind him.

It was Sir Sebastian—the Beast, he was called, although Niko didn't find the nickname apropos; he was a handsome man, and looked entirely like a proper Order Knight—who stood over near the open window, and he didn't greet them with even a glance and a nod.

Niko stepped to the side of Becket's chair, and dropped to one knee, sweeping his swords properly up and behind him, while Sir John knelt on the other side of the chair, and Becket started to struggle out of it.

"Sit, Sir Martin," the king said. "That's not a suggestion."

Becket immediately sagged back into his wheeled chair. "Then may I make a request, Your Majesty?"

"As long as it's not something to the effect of you kneeling before your king, well, then, yes."

Becket just sat silent.

The king frowned. "Well, say *something*, man."

"Then the only request I have to make, Your Majesty, is that you tell these others of my Order to speak widely of my shame, as it's clearly deserved, coming from you, Sire."

The king looked at Sir John. "I told you he'd say something like that." He made a quick beckoning gesture with his fingers, and both Niko and Sir John quickly rose to their feet.

"Your Majesty is usually right," Sir John said, smiling. "But not always—I was thinking that age might have mellowed him."

"Hardly." The king shook his head. "Well, then . . . " He turned back to Becket. "No, Sir Martin. I'll not order that your brothers speak of it or not speak of it, as there's no shame involved. But if you must cause yourself pain in order to greet me as you see fit, then do so." He shook his head. "And the next time that I find myself irritated with a grouchy bird, I promise to think of you, and I can assure it will not be in a particularly kindly way."

Becket didn't let so much as a grunt of pain loose as he levered himself out of his chair, and to the floor beyond, catching himself on his hands to prevent falling flat on his face. His face grew red as he forced himself up to one knee, and let a deep breath in and out before he spoke.

"Thank you, Sire," he said.

Niko started toward Becket's side but stopped himself, until the king made the same gesture he had before, and both he and Sir John quickly had Becket up and back into his chair.

The king waited, patiently, not even holding out his hand for his pipe until Becket was properly seated.

"You've come a long way to see me," he finally said, finally reaching out his hand, into which a waiting servant quickly placed his pipe. "Probably in need of some food and rest—well, the lord chamberlain will see to your needs when we're finished here." As a servant produced a lit taper, he puffed his pipe to life. "But in the meantime, if you would do me the favor of sitting, I'd much appreciate it—I'm hurting my neck looking up at the two of you."

The only chairs available were heavily padded, and deep; Niko removed his swords, and placed them across the arms as he sat, noticing with some satisfaction that Sir John had done the same thing.

"So," the king said. "You want to go hunting the Ama-dan Dubh." Niko had expected His Majesty to lead up to it, but Becket just nodded, as though unsurprised that he'd gotten right to the point.

"And you come to us," the king went on, "rather than to the abbot, because it was faster to get from Colonsay to Londinium, and then to Windsor, than it would have been to Alton? Was that it was quicker to ask us than the abbot?"

"Yes, Your Majesty," Becket said. "It is faster, at that. And, more to the point, I think that something this . . . unusual and serious is more a matter for Your Majesty to decide on than any lesser man, even the abbot."

The king snorted. "Sir Martin, you're not quite lying to me, but you're coming very close, and I don't much care for it. There's something else going on. You're not afraid to brace the abbot and tell him that you didn't follow his instructions to run Sir Niko out of the Order, to find him sufficiently lacking enough to disqualify him. Are you?"

There. It was out in the open. Niko had always sus-pected it, but . . .

Why hadn't Becket obeyed his orders?

"I'm not much for fear, Your Majesty," Becket said. "And it was at your orders that Niko was sent to me, and you made it my decision. Not the abbot's."

Sir John chuckled, then silenced himself after a quick glance from the king.

"Oh, never mind—speak up," the king said.

"Well, he's spoken a truth, Your Majesty," he said.

"Yes, but it's not the whole truth." The king eyed Becket levelly. "You would have told Ralph what?"

"I'd have told him, as I'd tell anyone, that the boy—that Sir Niko needs much more education. That he's slow in learning his letters, barely a fair hand in the armory or smithy, and weak in all the rest of the knightly arts. But I'd also say that when it all breaks apart around him, I've twice seen him act as a knight of the Order ought, with both courage and good sense, and he's taken to the, to the important part of what an Order Knight is as though he was born to it—and by God, I'd say that he was.

"If he's cast out of the Order, it won't be any of my doing."

"I see." The king nodded. "And that's all that you'd say to him?" He tilted his head to one side.

"No," Becket said, "I'd likely say more. I'd remind him that, in the final analysis, it's you who decides how you are to be served, and I'd say to him that if you wanted Sir Niko cast out, you'd hardly have sent a spy to watch over him, and to watch over me."

A spy?

Fotheringay?

The king grinned, and Sir John chuckled.

"I told you he'd figure that out, Sire," the knight said. "And I'm capable of being other than wrong, too. Meaning no disrespect for your station, Your Majesty, but you'd have made a great smith—you really do fit the tool to the task, and not use a single weld when you can arrange two. Or three."

"Whenever I can." The king nodded, then turned to Niko. "A falconer—I prefer the falconer metaphor to the smith one, and I'm accustomed to having my preferences served—finds that he uses different birds for different things. I don't know all of my Order Knights as well as I could—as well as I wish I did—and all I had on you, Sir Martin, was other men's words. I know that Ralph was none too fond of this whole thing, and that he can be very persuasive; it's one of the things that makes him valuable to us." He raised an admonishing finger. "And I don't want you to think that Fotheringay was an unfaithful servant. If you feel that way, I order you to forgive him."

Niko didn't know what to say. Fotheringay? Unfaithful? How?

"I hope you won't order *me* to forgive him." Becket's voice was too controlled. "I'd find it difficult. An undisclosed loyalty—"

"Is there an Englishman who isn't supposed to be loyal to the King? And hold that loyalty above any other loyalty, to all men, living or dead?" The king seemed more amused than anything else. He turned to Niko. "As you may recall, Sergeant Fotheringay was a problem for me. I couldn't *not* offer him a knighthood, under the circumstances, and, as I largely expected, he found that going back to the Fleet as a hero was more than a little . . . disruptive for his new company." The king's mouth twitched. "Although you'd think that a captain in my Marines wouldn't be so bloody deferential to a sergeant and—yes, yes, bring him in," he said, looking past where the knights sat. "The novices can wait."

Fotheringay dropped to one knee as he entered, rising instantly at His Majesty's gesture.

"Sit yourself down, too," the king said.

"Yes, Sire." Fotheringay sat.

"Any regrets, Fotheringay?" the king asked.

Fotheringay barely hesitated. "About asking Sir Niko for a position?"

"Well, man, what the hell else do you think I'm asking about? Yes, have you any regrets over that?"

"No, Sire."

The king's irritation vanished. "Very well, then," he said, gently. "And can you find it in you to speak your mind, and your heart? I know such things don't come easy to you—but we've discussed this once before, when I sent for you."

"Yes, Sire. I . . . I'm used to serving," Fotheringay said. "Lost that when I lost my captain on the *Serenity.*" He shook his head. "I spent a fair number of years watching his back, and . . . "

"And you've no objection to watching Sir Niko's." It wasn't a question.

"No objection, Sire. I'd prefer to."

"Well, good."

"If he'll still have me."

The king cocked his head to one side again, perversely reminding Niko of a hunting bird. "Why wouldn't he have you? Did you lie to your master?"

"Well, no. Not quite. I asked for a position, just like you told me to do, but . . . "

"You didn't tell him any more, as I also told you to. And, just as I'd predicted, he assumed you'd gotten yourself in some trouble, and didn't want to know about it, and just accepted you into his service." He raised a finger. "I wish all of what I had to do, to decide, was quite this easy." He took a long draw on his pipe. "So, that's settled. And I take it you would not think it beneath your new station to be his squire, rather than his servant?

Much the same thing, you know. Although the pay should be better."

Fotheringay didn't answer right away.

"Well, out with it, man, out with it."

"New station, Sire?"

"I told you that I'd knight you when you were retired from the Marines; I meant it." The king tapped on a sheet of paper at his elbow. "You're retiring, Sergeant, at the command and pleasure of your sovereign, and your sovereign is, among other things, a man who likes to keep his promises. And be still, Becket—he's getting the Order of the Guard, not the Order of Crown, Shield, and Dragon, and if there's one thing that continually irritates every other knight who serves this Crown, it's that you lot always act as though you're the only Order that matters. You're not."

The king reached out his hand, and one of the scribes quickly brought over an inkwell and pen; the king signed the sheet of paper with a few quick strokes. "Will that be enough for you, Fotheringay, or do I have to break out the Seal?" He turned to Becket without waiting for an answer. "And your novices. Are they ready to be knighted?"

"Ready enough. They'll have to go—"

"Yes, they'll have to go see Her." Mordred gestured to one of the scribes, who quickly rushed out of the room. "You'll have to make do with more . . . traditional servants, until I can order up another pair from Alton for you, to help you train Sir Niko—Scoville and Winslow are leaving for the Arroy now." He grinned. "Unless you find the need to say good-bye? And think that's worth delaying them?"

Becket actually grinned. "Delaying seeing Her? Just so they can take their leave of me? I wouldn't want them to bear ill will against me, not for that. If they resent me being a hard teacher, well, that's perhaps as it should be. Yes, they would be grateful on their way, but . . . "

"Yes, but they'd later think that their lives began the moment that they touched Her hand, and curse you for the lost hours, or even minutes. Auntie does have that effect on most—and She probably would on me, if She wanted to. I'm just as happy that She doesn't, all things considered. My family's been quite good about avoiding incest since the days of the Tyrant, and it would be best to keep it that way." The king sobered. "On to the other matter. Sir John wishes to be involved in this, and I'm disposed to have him join you; his judgment is generally good, and he's happier spending time in the open air, and has begun to pout."

The big knight grinned again. "I'll serve as you think best, Your Majesty. But part of that service is—"

"Yes, yes, part of it is telling your sovereign how he'll be best served by you, oftimes repeatedly." He turned back to Niko and Becket. "His only concern is our safety," the king went on. "And since I've promised to stay in the castle until Lady Ellen can join His Own . . . ?"

"Then you'll hear no objection from me, Sire," Sir John said. "Not on that."

The king cocked his head to one side. "I'd think you'd want to see her."

"Yes, Sire, I do." The big knight's face was impassive. "And if I could, consistent with my duty, I surely would. But that's not the issue here. Three of His Own should be enough to see to your safety, unless you're planning on entertaining more than usual—my concern is about Sir Martin."

Becket nodded. "Be a problem hauling what remains of this body up and down the hills of Colonsay."

Sir John shook his head. "That was not what I was speaking of. Servants for that, generally, and when not, well, I've a stronger back than most. My concern is putting you in danger when there's no benefit to it, none that I can see. Your courage isn't at issue, Sir Martin— but taking risks without benefit doesn't seem to me to be wise."

The king leaned forward. "But there is a benefit, and I can see it, even if you can't. You heard him. Sir Niko's education isn't finished, and I'm not disposed to change teachers. Seems to have worked out well enough. And if that means that Sir Martin gets to go along as the two of you chase down this Amadan Dubh—and whatever the hell else is going on Colonsay—well, that's your problem, and his." He eyed Sir Niko levelly. "I'm a suspicious man, by nature. Ascribe it to being almost murdered in my cradle by my late uncle. I've the feeling that many of the . . . strange events of the past year are linked, somehow—I just can't see what the pattern amounts to, and I'm not the only one who can't.

"If I had a way for you to prick at the heart of this spider's web, I'd do it, without a moment of regret, without a second thought, and leave this other matter alone, for the time being.

"But I don't. So you will handle this, whether it's part of it, or something else, and you can help Sir Martin train Sir Niko, as much as time allows."

Sir John nodded. "As you wish, Your Majesty," he said, and then he frowned.

"I thought we'd settled that," the king said.

The knight raised a hand. "No, Sire, not that. Just trying to figure out what else we need. Ship or ships, a wizard or two, a troop of Marines, and—"

"Enough." The king frowned. "I'm not going to bargain with you, John. Take what you need, and if you've any difficulty, say that you'll send the problem to me if you're not satisfied. As you would."

The knight nodded, and the king went on. "I don't much like this; I'd rather we could leave well enough alone. The Old Ones . . . well, most of them are gone now, or mostly gone. I've heard it said that they bred too much with us mortals, and that their blood has thinned; there are those who call what's left waterkin.

"Now, if there's a few true *gruagach* left in Scotland and Ireland, watching over the sheep and cattle, I've no problem with that; if the worst they do is spoil some milk when they're not attended to, then, well, let the Scots and the Irish give them their milk offerings, or not cry over spoiled milk. I'm not looking to make war on the race, what's left of it—and as you may remember, my many-times-great aunt is waterkin, herself, and ample proof that the old blood does not necessarily run so very thin." His lips drew themselves into a line. "But that tolerance does not apply to the *Caillach*, if she's still around, and it wouldn't apply to the *bean nighe*, either, and it most certainly does not apply to any one, of any race, who would enchant my people—*my* people—into madness and murder, not excepting this Fairy Fool."

"And then there's the politics, Sir," Sir John said.

The king frowned. "I'm rather more well aware of that than you are, Sir John. Be still."

Sir John sat motionless, his face holding no trace whatsoever of expression, then nodded. "I can keep a quiet tongue in my mouth, if that's your wish, Sire."

The king grunted. "Sir Martin's already figured it out, I'd expect."

Becket shook his head. "With respect, Your Majesty," he said, "I can see the general issue, but not the specific."

The king looked him over. "The specific, then: the Duke of New England is due to set sail on the eighth of Leeds, just under six weeks from now. I'd rather this matter be settled before that."

Niko would have to ask Fotheringay, later, what this was all about; it was well over his head. It was, obviously, something that he was supposed to know, and—

No. "Excuse me, Your Majesty, but I don't know what you and Sir John and Sir Martin are talking about." Let them think him a fool; it was still the right thing to say. To sit in silence and let his king think that Niko was smarter than he was would be a betrayal, and if revealing his own slackwittedness had consequences, well then, he would bear up under them.

Becket started to mutter a curse, but the king silenced him with a quick motion.

"It's not your fault, Sir Niko," he said, smiling. "You're not attuned to disloyalty—or, yes, John, to the possibility of disloyalty. To put it simply, Sir Niko: if the Crown can't deal with a rebellion this small and this close to Londinium, what thoughts do you think might enter my uncle's mind as he makes the long voyage to New England? I've no evidence of Uncle William's disloyalty, or he'd not be going back. But . . . " The king drew himself up straight, and rose from his chair, with a quick be-still gesture to Becket, keeping him in his seat while Niko and Sir John rose. "Sir Niko, Sir John, Sir Martin—rid me of this Amadan Dubh."

"Yes, Sire."

It sounded like a dismissal; Niko started to turn, but the king shook his head.

"No, you're not dismissed yet." He took a few steps forward and held out his hand. "Would you do me the favor of loaning me your sword? Oh, I'm only asking for your mundane sword, boy—I'm not suicidal."

Niko drew the scabbard from his sash, and presented the sword, hilt first, to the king. His Majesty drew the sword slowly, setting the scabbard aside. "Nothing fancy, eh? Plain, but serviceable," he said, with a grin. "Entirely appropriate, under the circumstances, given the subject in question." He turned to Fotheringay. "I'd prefer that this be done publicly and with proper ceremony, not quickly and in private. But not even my preferences are always decisive.

"Kneel, Nigel Fotheringay," the king said, his voice taking on a formal tone.

Fotheringay did so, and Mordred V tapped him once, lightly, on each shoulder.

"With this sword, I, Mordred Pendragon, King, do now dub thee knight of His Majesty's Guard," he said, quietly, slowly, not rushing the words. "It is a good and worthy order; be thou a good and worthy knight. Please rise, Sir Nigel."

The king slipped the sword back into the scabbard and tossed it to Niko, then turned back to Fotheringay.

"When I knight a man, it's traditional that I present him with a sword. And most of the time, it's for show, not for use—most of the time, but probably not this one. More than a fair selection in the armory—pick one that feels right, and if you don't find one that does, well, talk to the lord armorer, and see what he can do overnight." He gave Fotheringay a stern look. "That is a command from your sovereign—it's not a suggestion, Sir Nigel. I don't want to hear that I've given you some trophy to put over your mantel—"

"Doubt Sir Nigel has a mantel," Sir John said, rewarded by something between a smile and a glare from his sovereign.

"—but there's no time to do more than fit new grips to a prime Sheffield blade. There's enough of those, and one of them ought to serve. You four are to be billeted here tonight; you leave in the morning.

"Find the amadan dubh, and kill him," the king said. "Don't expend yourselves unless necessary. Try to avoid making it necessary. All of you." He met first Big John's eyes, then Becket's, then Niko's, and waited for a "yes, Sire" from each of them before he turned to Fotheringay.

"Watch Sir Niko's back, Sir Nigel," the king said. "But spare some attention for your own, if you can. And if you ever get tired of squiring for Sir Niko, you send word to us, and we will find another use for you."

"Aye-aye, Sire."

"Ever the sergeant, eh? No, don't bother correcting yourself; I didn't take it as impertinence." The king smiled. But it wasn't a pleasant smile. "*Now* you're dismissed," he said.

The king met Niko's eyes for a moment, and nodded, as though echoing Niko's thoughts.

Why rush Fotheringay's knighting? He would be no more faithful as Sir Nigel than he had been as Sergeant Fotheringay.

But it was obvious. The king thought it a distinct possibility that he was sending Fotheringay, and the knights—and the other knights—to his death, and would not withhold the honor that was due.

Niko met Fotheringay's eyes, and Fotheringay gave him his usual toothless smile.

Niko glanced behind him as he left; the king had already picked up his stack of papers, and was examining them closely.

INTERLUDE

Izmir

Revenge, so the Siciliani say, is a dish best served cold. My own disagreement with that is the fear that if it's left to chill, it will eventually spoil, and become impossible to eat.

Although, in every case I can think of, I would surely choke it down, and in the case of Alexander, I'd envy and resent the man who dined on that meal.

—Gray

Randolph stopped himself from wrapping his blankets more tightly about him, and watched through narrowed eyes as Smith came up the hatch, apparently to take the morning air.

The Izmiri coast loomed not only ahead of them, but all about them, as though threatening to come together and crush the ship. Marinarice lay at the north end of the sheltered harbor, and protected from both the sea and the winds and—with what Randolph thought of as a pitifully small garrison at Adakoy—from pirate raids, more or less. Most likely, it was the combination of not much of value to steal and the difficulty in raiding that had kept Marinarice safe from pirate raids for the past years, although even Guild ships made it a point to pay—and pay well—for the services of the local fishermen who supplemented their catch with reports of ship movements. Easy enough to catch a merchantman in the narrow passage out and into the Med proper. But, then again, it was prime hunting ground for the Blue Fleet's pirate patrols, as well, and it would have been comforting for Lieutenant Randolph to think that that was the cause of it.

He hadn't intended to find himself on the same trader as Smith, but it had happened nonetheless.

He really hadn't had any other choice, when he had followed Smith and his party to Kyrnia; there were no other Guild ships bound for Marinarice, and retracing his steps to Limmasol, and hoping to find a faster ship, leaving promptly, with the same destination, would have been far too optimistic. The Lord might be on the side of the righteous, after all, but He rarely saw to the details.

It had been a risk, of course, but a necessary one. Smith had left his men—and the girl—in Kyrnia, and while he seemed to give the deck passengers an occasional cursory look, it was the other stateroom passengers that seemed to draw most of his attention.

Of course, in one sense, they might as well have been on different ships—Smith had one of the staterooms below, while Randolph had taken deck passage, and had but a chalked rectangle on the raised poop deck to call his home for the journey; the foredecks were forbidden to deck passengers except for just after sunset and just before sunrise, when they were permitted to take what little exercise was possible, while separated from their higher-paying betters.

Smith stalked over to the quarterdeck, and mounted it without so much as a by-your-leave, something that grated on Alphonse Randolph—had the man no manners at all?—but didn't seem to bother the captain, despite him having to give constant attention to the wheel for the approach.

Randolph didn't think much of the captain. Guild sailors were supposedly experts at their craft, but Captain Hans—his surname was Lubeck, of course, from his clan, but the crew of the ship were all Lubecks, and he was known as Uncle Hans to all of the crew, and Captain Hans to the passengers—should not have tolerated a passenger on his quarterdeck, not on a tricky approach in a narrow channel, and never mind the discourtesy.

For once, the wind was this sailor's friend—it carried their conversation to him.

"I would guess it would be another hour before we dock, Captain?" Smith asked. His German was excellent, if perhaps overly classical.

"That would be hard to say, Herr Ibn Mahmoud," the captain said. Well, at least his eyes never left the waters while he talked to Smith, his voice laden with that preposterously gutteral Guild accent. "But quite possibly. Then again, I'm tempted to take one of the inner berths—things are a little too crowded dockside for my taste. Less time until we drop sail, of course, but more until we can get you properly to land. Not much more." He glanced over his shoulder at the sails.

He was flying far too few topsails for Randolph's taste, but he certainly knew his own ship better than Randolph did. A fat-bellied merchant wasn't a light and spry warship, after all, and Randolph didn't know this channel.

Still, you'd think that a man who made his living in these waters would know the channel, and know it well enough to maneuver his way through it with something better than a slow, wallowing lumber.

"I want to be on my way as quickly as possible," Smith said. "Waiting for a boat to take me ashore—"

"You may go ashore on the first boat, if you care to—"

"—is something I'd prefer to avoid," Smith said, reaching into his pouch and producing a coin.

The captain barely glanced down, and shrugged, then returned his attention to the water, making a quarter-wheel turn to port. Give the man that; he was constantly making fine adjustments to the course, and not spinning the wheel to and fro. Maybe he did know the waters better than Randolph had thought. "Fond though I am of good silver," the captain said, "and fonder yet of gold, I'd not care to get too close to another vessel, and the towboats in this harbor are sluggardly lots. I could signal for a boat to meet us, if you'd prefer."

"I'd prefer to debark on the dock itself," Smith said, adding another coin.

"Well . . ."

Smith started to move his hand back toward his pouch.

" . . . if that's your preference," the captain said, "I'll make it so."

Randolph hid his smile under his blanket. Smith wasn't half as clever as he, no doubt, thought himself. If the captain had intended to drop anchor at one of the outer berths, he was about ten minutes late in coming about. Lubeck had always intended to berth dockside, and had merely taken the opportunity to pry a little more money out of Smith, who was utterly oblivious to something so obvious.

The Turk sleeping in his chalked rectangle next to Randolph starting stirring, which was no concern to Randolph, but, once again, he also started snoring, and the painfully loud rasps drowned out the next traces of conversation, until the Turk subsided, and Randolph could hear them again.

" . . . one inquire as to your purpose in Marinarice?"

"Yes, one may," Smith said. "If one wishes to involve himself in matters beyond his station, matters which don't concern him, and matters that I'd prefer that any other man carry to his grave."

The captain smiled. "Then I must confess I'm not terribly interested, Herr Ibn Mahmoud." The smile dropped, for just a moment. "Nor, for that matter, am I interested in being threatened on my own quarterdeck, either."

Well, at least the man had some semblance of spine.

Smith cocked his head to one side, and dropped his hand to his sword hilt, and for a moment Randolph didn't know how it would go. The only sword he carried at his waist was the Sandoval, after all. But if he drew it, and killed—murdered—the captain, he could hardly destroy anybody and everybody aboard ship, as that would sink the ship itself.

Kill him, Randolph thought. Drawing a live sword always took something out of the man who wielded it, and the moment where Smith resheathed it would be Randolph's opportunity. Smith would be watching for movement from the crew, not the deck passengers.

But the hand dropped, and Smith nodded. "You're quite right, Captain Lubeck; you have my apologies." He bowed stiffly.

"Accepted, of course, Herr Ibn Mahmoud."

A practical man, Smith, Randolph decided. There was no reason to think that his enemy had no virtues, after all; self-deception was a luxury that he couldn't afford, no matter how many pounds of gold he wore beneath his clothing.

Patience, he counseled himself. And, perhaps soon, there would be an end to the need for it.

He buried himself back in his blankets, and pretended to go back to sleep.

CHAPTER 13
Pantelleria I

"Service, honor, faith, obedience. Justice tempered only by mercy; mercy tempered only by justice."

It's never easy, not that that matters. What matters to me is that it's rarely as simple as it sounds.

How can I be of service?

—Gray

Gray kept the rucksack with him, tied to the saddle before him.

Most of his own gear was still aboard the *Vergent*, back at Punta Karascia. It was silly, really. The rucksack was every bit as safe there, in his cabin, as it was here, as Lieutenant Carothers had put two Marines on guard at his door.

Gray had thought of leaving the Khan there, for obvious reasons, but had decided against it. He was not coming as a pauper begging for alms, but as a creditor, demanding payment, after all, and it wouldn't hurt to remind his debtor that he had ways of insisting, if necessary.

His mouth tasted of sand and his eyes were constantly stinging; the late afternoon wind blew hard, reminding him that the Arabs had called the island "Bent el Rhia"— "the island of the wind"—although other reminders were all about him, and he hardly needed to have the point driven home.

What plants there were on the side of the boastfully named Montagne Grande were small and twisted brush, only a few leaves spared by the winds. Down by the shore, the stunted trees were planted in sconces, protecting them from the winds; there was no such cover up here.

The castle at the top of the hill rose above him, close. Too close. Strange.

Either he was getting patient with age, or it had only taken an hour or so to make his way up the hillside. Which shouldn't have been so very strange, as the Montagne Grande was but a mile, as the crow flies, from the Punta Karascia, and even with all the twists and turns that the road took up the hill, it could hardly have amounted to more than twice that.

Still, the other two times he had visited the castle, it had taken the better part of a day to ride those one or two miles, as though the Wise preferred to keep himself more separate from the rest of the world than mere geography would allow.

That boded for a polite reception, if not necessarily a friendly one. It certainly meant that the proprietor was not intending to bar his entry.

As though in response to that thought, a gout of steam ushered forth from one of the cracks in the hillside, filling his nose with its hellish, sulphuric reek. It startled the small brown mare he had hired at the port into rearing, and it took all the horsemanship he had to remain on her back, and settle her back down.

Most other men, he thought, would probably have been thrown, but he hadn't been, quite.

Most other places he would have put this down to mere coincidence, but he was less disposed to see it here, both in the timing of it, and in it not quite having thrown him. It felt like a warning.

His hand itched for the feel of the Khan.

No, it was more than that. Both his hands did—the one that was gone even more than the one that remained. He brought his stump up to eye level. Very strange. He could feel himself moving his missing fingers, and the urge to scratch the itch of his absent palm was maddening.

But it was gone. He had long since accustomed himself to learning that absent parts of him could hurt just as much or more than the aches and pains of his body.

He was perhaps a hundred yards from the crest of the hill when the road began to lengthen in front of him; the castle seeming to grow just a little farther away with each of the mare's steps.

He pulled the reins, stopping the horse. "If you think that you can discourage me," he said, quietly, "then you're wrong. If you think to refuse to admit me, then think also on the possible consequences, and think on them carefully."

He let his fingers drop to the Khan's hilt.

So. The Wise is being shy, eh? Shall we see just how well it can hide from the two of us?

"If necessary," he said, deliberately speaking aloud, "we shall. I hope that it won't be necessary."

I've killed many a thing. Men, women, children, dark-lings, and deodands. Cities and cattle—but I've not yet killed one of the Old Ones. Perhaps today's the day.

"I hope not," Gray said. He kicked the horse into a slow walk, and while the road ahead didn't seem to shorten, it didn't lengthen, either.

Things had changed. The last time he had been here, the gates to the castle had stood open. This time, they were closed. Last time, the marching of phantom boots had sounded above his head, along the ramparts, and torches burned from their mounts in the walls.

Not this time. The massive gates stood closed, and the only sound in his ears, save from the snorting of his horse at the hitching post, was from the wind.

He stood in front of the gates. "Open them or not, as you please," he said.

Slowing, silently, as though turning on impossibly well-greased hinges, the gates swung open before him, and he walked quickly inside, and down the short road toward the keep.

Black was waiting for him, over on the steps to the keep itself.

As before, he was dressed in a mockery of the clothing of the Order—no silver piping along the cuffs, no sign of the Cross, no medallions laced into his boots.

If anything, he should have looked younger than he had last time; there was only a trace of graying of the hair at his temples, and his beard was a solid, inky black. His fingers toyed nervously with the slim stick that he always carried, and it was, still, the only weapon he displayed.

But, still, he looked older; there were wrinkles around his sunken eyes, and he seemed to be having trouble with his right hand.

"Hello, Gray," he said. "I'd say that you're welcome, but that would be a lie."

"I'm not here for welcome," Gray said. "But for repayment of a debt. Partial repayment."

"Ah." Black's smile was thin. "And with the threat of unleashing the Khan on me if I don't pay? And with no promise that there will be no further demands?" He tilted his head to one side. "That hardly seems just, all in all."

"It hardly seems just that Bear died saving your life, or whatever passes for life with you."

Black shook his head. "I seem to remember you—and he, and Cully—rejecting my pleas for aid and succor. Cully only came to follow Niko; you only came to my aid to follow Cully, and Bear only to accompany the two of you."

Gray nodded. That was true enough. "But, nonetheless, because we did that, you lived, and Bear died."

"True enough." Black sat down on the hard stone steps. "Then what would you have me do? Leave my island, and help you find what you seek?"

"Could you?"

"Hardly." Black toyed with his wand. "I'm old, Joshua, and hurting. I doubt that I'll ever recover, not fully, from the damage that those live swords did me, and even before that, I'd not dare leave my island—I haven't, since the end of the Age, when I was somewhat more . . . vigorous." He rose easily, giving the lie to talk of weariness. "Walk with me," he said.

The path around to the keep cut through the well-manicured grass on a broad curve that brought them underneath a sextet of apple trees, ripe with fruit. Wolf reached up and plucked two, then took a bite out of one, and offered the other to Gray, who declined.

"Oh, well," Wolf said, from around his mouthful. "Worth a try, I suppose." He dropped the other apple from his hand; it disappeared before it reached the ground. "What is it that you want, Gray?"

"I thought you could read my mind."

Wolf shrugged. "Well, yes and no. It would be more accurate to say that I can read your soul, but that's not quite right, either, and I know that you wouldn't believe me if I told you all of what I see there, so let's leave that be, for once. What is it that you want, Gray?"

"I want to know where Cully is."

"And you think I'd see that?"

"Are you saying that you can't?"

There was some permanent connection between the Wise and those who had visited him—or her, or them, or it—on Pantelleria, and Cully had been here several times; there had been enough of a link for Wolf to have contacted Cully—and Bear, and Niko, and Gray—when he had been attacked, and more: there had been enough for the Wise to have brought them here, in his final extremity.

"The trouble with you humans, Gray, is that you insist on making simple things complicated, complicated things simple, easy things difficult, and difficult things easy." He took another bite of the apple. "That said, it was sensible of you to come to me, rather than chasing about for Cully, hoping to pick up his trail. He can be devilishly hard to find." Black grinned. "And most fortunate, all in all—he's headed this way, and should be pulling into port shortly. A few days or so. And if that's all you have to ask . . ."

Gray didn't hear what the Wise had to say; he had turned, and was walking quickly toward the gate.

CHAPTER 14

Return to Colonsay

I think it was the day the York Rebellion broke out that I learned not to make quick judgments about people, a lesson that I should not have had occasion to learn again since.

I was but a year in service, and on leave, guesting with my uncle Charles on the fifteenth of York.

He was the second eldest son of my maternal grandfather, and had come into his inheritance during his active time in the Order. When he took retirement to the Inactive List, he became a rather successful importer of wine from the Continent, and had married what the family thought of as a

preposterously young and flighty girl, who pro-
ceeded to pop out an equally preposterous number
of babies. He spent short days supervising the ware-
houses, long afternoons at his club, and evenings
with his family.

It was hard to think of him as the knight that
they had called Red Charles; he had a round, beam-
ing face, framed only by wisps of white hair, and
an easy laugh.

On my previous visits, it had taken some persua-
sion for him to understand that I really did not
wish to interfere with his home life, but rather to
join it to the extent that I was welcome, but he
understood that well by this time, and when the
front doorbell rang, the two of us were down on
our knees on the rug in the sitting room with the
children, playing with a new kitten, while his young
wife stood over the lot of us, shaking her head half
in amusement, half in disapproval.

The bell rang, and the butler brought him an
envelope, which he opened. He read it quickly, then
looked up at me.

"All hell's broken loose; we're called, Martin," he
said, then turned to the butler. "No time for the
coach—get four horses saddled, and be quick
about it."

He paid no attention to the way that his wife
fled from the room, taking the children with her,
silencing their protests; he just walked to where his
swords hung above the hearth, and took them down.

Well, you couldn't expect much better from
women and children, I thought—until, moments

later, she met us at the door, struggling under the weight of his bags. It was only later that it occurred to me that either she had packed them in advance, or knew where he had left them, packed and ready to go.

I had seen him be affectionate with the children, but I had never seen him so much as lay his hand upon hers before. He reached out, took her hand, and pressed it briefly to his lips.

"I'm called—" he started to say, silenced when she laid a finger on his lips.

"Don't you worry about us," she said, her expression calm but somehow fierce, holding his hand for just a moment before she dropped it. "Not for a moment. I'll take care of things here."

He nodded, stooped to pick up his bags, and walked out the door, not looking behind. I followed.

She watched us from the door.

The next time I saw her, it was several months later, when I returned his swords to her, her dressed in widow's black. She accepted them with a grave nod, a word of quiet thanks, and without a whimper of complaint, and asked me but one question: "May I tell the children that he died honorably?"

Made me glad I'd never voiced my own misgivings about her; I'm not sure how I could have apologized for that.

—Becket

A sliver of moon hung low in the sky as the hull of the boat scraped noisily along the gravel just off the Strand. The mud flats stretched out in front of them, with Colonsay proper rising to the north, and Oronsay to the south. A boy who had been raised as a fisherman didn't have to look for a highwater mark to know that this was low tide, and that the mudflats would soon be underwater, separating Oronsay from Colonsay.

Niko stared intently at the strange shoreline, although he couldn't have said what it was that he was looking for. There was no trace of human habitation, which was understandable; the mile-wide mud-flats spent most of the day underwater, bridging the two islands only at low tide. It was theoretically possible to go between the two by boat at other times, but the natives never did. Not a seafaring folk, it was said, even though none lived far from it.

"Easy, there," Sir John whispered to the sailors. "We'll take it from here."

The bosun's mate grunted an aye-aye, and gestured to two of the sailors, who immediately shipped their oars and scrambled over the side to steady the boat, just after Niko.

There was no reason for him to wait. Getting in and out of a boat without tipping it over, after all, was something that he was more than passingly familiar with, and he gestured for Sir John to hand him his rucksack, which the big knight did.

The water was cold, and almost knee-deep.

"Back in the boat," Fotheringay said to the sailors. "We'll push you off." It was the work of a moment, and with the boat lightened of the weight of the knights and all of their gear, the boat easily and quietly backed, and came about, the sailors quickly rowing toward where the darkened mass of the Redoubt loomed, off in the night.

Niko led the way to the shore, vaguely irritated at the way that the other two splashed about too much. The idea was to make land on Colonsay stealthily; drawing attention could wait until the ship, with Sir Martin, the wizard, and the Marines aboard, anchored off of Scala-saig in the morning.

They emerged from the ocean, wet as rats. Niko shivered in the cold breeze, and clamped his jaw tightly together to keep his teeth from chattering.

"Easy, young sir," Fotheringay whispered. "I'll have you in dry clothes before long—and myself too, at that."

"And, with the wind blowing hard from the west, if we can find enough cover, perhaps we can have a fire," Sir John said.

Niko nodded to himself. He would have thought it too risky, himself, but when it came to woodsmanship, he would trust Sir John's instincts above his own.

There was no way to see it off in the dark, but the highwater of the Strand was always littered with drift-wood at low tide, and fires on Colonsay tended to be driftwood as often as the native peat. The smell of wood-smoke would excite no particular interest, although you could reliably expect that the natives would, in daylight, find smoke rising from some place unusual to be of more than passing interest.

Niko would have been tempted to protest, to argue that they should just get to it, but he had already had that discussion with Sir John, and been overruled.

Their timing had been just this side of perfect; the mudflats were dry enough to support the weight of their boots, and even Sir John, the biggest and heaviest of them all, barely sank to the ankles even in the dampest spots, as they made their way across the mud, toward where Hangman's Rock loomed ahead of them, in the dark.

They walked in silence. The sounds of their boots against the hard-packed mud and sand would not carry far, but you had to be careful about voices, Sir John had said. Be it castle, forest, or sea, voices would sometimes carry farther than you'd think that they would.

They made camp in the lee of Hangman's Rock, and after a few minutes of Sir John listening and watching, he gave a signal to Fotheringay, who quickly started the fire that he had already laid. The tinder crackled and popped, and before long it was a modest blaze that somehow gave off more warmth than light.

Sir John slipped off into the night, still in his rough clothes, while Niko dressed. The fire warmed Niko far more than perhaps it should have, as he stripped to the skin and dressed himself in his Order garments, from the boots up.

"Just as well," Sir John whispered from just behind him, "that we got some sleep before we came ashore." He was still in his rough clothes. "And all, alas, is quiet."

"Yes, it is." Fotheringay grinned. "Did you expect that the Amadan Dubh would be sitting on a rock outside of Garvard just waiting for us to come kill him, Sir John?"

The big knight grinned back. "Well, that would not have bothered me, if it had happened, I can honestly say. But, no; fortune is rarely so kind." He quickly stripped off his own rough clothes as he spoke, then hung them up himself on the side of the massive rock. He picked up one of his dirty boots, as though to bang it against the rock and rid it of the mud, then clearly thought better of it, and accepted a small stick from Fotheringay; he cleared the mud from it bit by bit.

Niko had already dressed, with Fotheringay's help, and the two of them waited patiently while the big knight bent to lace his own boots tightly.

"Well," he finally said, as he stood himself straight, "let's have at it." He gestured to the west. "There's a path that forks both to Garvard and Scalasaig, and if I've read the maps right, it passes by a croft on the way."

They caught the family asleep, just barely, while the wan gray light of premorning, the light that the Arabs call the wolf's tail, filtered weakly over the eastern horizon.

More accurately, Sir John was the one who did the catching asleep; the black house, larger than some but smaller than most, stood on a hilltop, with the sheep pen barely to the east of it, and Niko was sure that he and Fotheringay couldn't have approached so closely, not without giving an alarm. Niko was certain that even Sir John couldn't make his way past the pen without waking the sheep—nervous creatures they were—but, once again, he was wrong.

They only started bleating when Sir John's big voice boomed out, as the big knight stood but a few feet away from the rough-hewn doorway. "In the name of the king, come out of your holes, the lot of you."

That was Niko's and Fotheringay's cue, and they quickly ran around behind the house, repeating Sir John's words.

There was a long moment of silence.

"Again, I say—and for the last time—come out, the lot of you, or I swear we'll burn your thatch down about your ears," Sir John said.

That hadn't been part of the plan, and Niko wasn't sure what he should say—or even if he should say anything—as the occupants stumbled out, one by one, into the wan light.

Not a terribly threatening lot, by the looks of them. A thickset woman, holding an infant in one arm and a three-year-old on a hip; two boys, neither older than fourteen, and a girl, perhaps ten or twelve, shivering probably more from fear than the cold, despite the thinness of her patched shift.

"And where," Sir John asked, not gently, "is David Bella, the crofter?"

One of the boys started to say something, but silenced himself at a shake of the head of his mother.

"My husband," she said, her voice holding just as much fear as anger, "died at Kiloran."

"As you know," one of the boys put in.

"No." Sir John shook his head. "No, I did not. I've not taken inventory of the dead bodies of the traitors who tried to murder the baron and his family. That's, in part, what we're here for."

"Traitors?" She shook her head. "You'll find no treason here, or elsewhere on these islands. It was not our doing, but *his*."

"You were there?"

She didn't answer at first, but looked at Niko, as though expecting him to say something.

Niko didn't recognize her, not particularly; the McPhees of Colonsay looked much the same to him: dark, thickly built people. If he had spent much time among them, no doubt that he would have come to recognize them individually.

Was she part of the mass of madness that had gone insane on the beach?

Finally, she nodded. "Yes, I was, and I was taken by the pipes and drums as much as the others." She handed each of the small ones off to her sons. "I don't ask for or expect mercy for myself," she said, "but I do ask that you take me away before you take my life, or whatever else you want of me before you do that. I'll not beg for my life, but I will beg for that." She faced Sir John with apparent resignation. "Not in front of my children. Please."

"We shall see," Sir John said.

What? Was Sir John actually thinking of killing the woman? *No*.

"Wait," Niko said, moving between the big knight and the family. "I was there, Sir John. It wasn't rebellion, but madness, brought on by the Amadan Dubh, and—"

"And where is this Amadan Dubh?" Sir John asked, his voice dripping with scorn. He made an expansive gesture with his hand. "I see none such here; just a woman who has, with her own voice, in her own words, admitted to being part of the rebellion."

Niko turned to the woman. "Please—tell Sir John where he can be found."

She shook her head. "I can not. I would, if I could. I'll admit to feeding the *gruagach*, yes, but not consorting with that hellspawn. I'd heard rumors of it, heard distant piping, true, but that night was the first time that I'd seen him, and the first time that I've heard that he has *been* seen since before my grandmother was a baby."

"That won't do." Sir John shook his head.

"Then you'd best show us where you feed this *gruagach*, eh?" Niko more pleaded than asked. "If you speak truly, we'll show you mercy."

"Yes, sir," she said.

"No," the elder of the two boys said. "Not without your word on that. All of you. You'll leave my mother alone, if we help you."

"You think to bargain with us?" Sir John took a step toward the boy.

"Please, Sir John," Niko said, holding up his hand. "It's a fair enough bargain, at that." He turned back to the family. "Yes, you have our word on that. I am Sir Niko Christofolous, of the Order of Crown, Shield, and Dragon; you have my word that if you act faithfully, and loyally, all of your lives will be spared."

"I want *his* word," the boy said.

Fotheringay's hand came to his face, probably covering a grin. The old sergeant admired a certain amount of impertinence, and the boy clearly had enough of that.

Sir John nodded. "Yes; you have my word. Show us to this *gruagach*."

The boy looked to his mother, who nodded.

"I can't," the boy said. "I can show you to the stone in the meadow where we leave the milk, but that wouldn't do you any good."

"We'll decide what does good or not," Sir John said.

The mother started to say something, then stopped herself, but the boy just nodded.

"Then, perhaps, you'd better get some milk. Hurry, please," Niko said.

"Yessir."

The sun was well over the *gruagach* stone before Sir John emerged from the scrub and walked out into the meadow, shaking his head.

"You may as well come out," he called out. "From what I think I know about the *gruagach*, they'll show at night, if at all." He sighed as he produced a pipe from his pouch. "We're about done for the day . . . and me without a fire kit."

"I've got that handled, Sir John," Fotheringay said, emerging from where he had stretched out in the scrub. He gave his blanket a quick shake to dislodge the brush from atop it, then quickly folded it.

Niko got to his feet slowly, emulating Fotheringay.

Sir John had helped them chop brush. They had laid leather groundcloths for them to lie upon, and then Sir John had covered them first with blankets and then with brush, before stalking off into the gray mist to make himself disappear.

The three wide-faced cows watched for a moment as they rose and walked toward the low *gruagach* stone near the center of the meadow. Two immediately returned to their foraging, while one looked at Niko with what appeared to him to be irritation, and then turned away and joined the others. Their udders were bloated and heavy with milk, and it was probably past time for young Donald to be up with the yoke and buckets.

"Well, so much for that," Sir John said, crouching near where Fotheringay quickly made a small fire, and produced a lit stick. He puffed his pipe to life. "Maybe tonight, perhaps."

"Are you sure?"

Sir John shrugged. "Little to be sure about in this sort of hunting." He grinned from around the stem of his pipe. "But there's been one about, I'd think." He dipped a finger into the hollow of the stone. "Young Donald didn't clean it, you might have noticed, and if he'd left milk to rot in the sun, we'd have smelled that. Something's drinking it, and being thorough about it. Well, it's another place to hunt tonight—but, for now, I think a quick breakfast in Garvard would be the thing to do, and not just because I'd rather eat other than my own cooking, or Sir Nigel's. Doubt we'll have much difficulty finding a public house, eh?"

"How so?" Niko asked.

Sir John grinned. "Think about it."

"What he means to say, young sir," Fotheringay said, "is that with the *Reedy* dropping anchor off of Scalasaig just about now, and a company of Marines coming ashore under Sir Martin, there'll be runners passing word of that all over the island. News of that should beat us to Garvard, I'd think, and where does a townsman go to hear and tell the news?" He patted his ample belly. "And, even if not, well, I could easily tolerate surrounding some food, myself, and think it'd be the same for you. Got some jerky, cheese, bread, and a bottle of plonk in my sack, though; give you something to nibble on while we walk."

"We'll wait on the wine," Sir John said, leading the way.

Their kits had been hidden along the path down to the village; they quickly retrieved them, and made their way down the path.

"You seem quiet, even for yourself, Sir Niko," Sir John said, after they had walked for a while. "Deep thoughts, perhaps?"

Niko shook his head. "No."

"Well, out with it. You've got something to say, and it's best to just say it."

"As you wish, Sir John." Niko shrugged. "I didn't much like scaring that family, and—"

"Like? Liking has nothing to do with what you have to do, Sir Niko. And we're likely to have to do worse before it's all over," Sir John said. "It's, well, the nature of what we are, what we do." His voice was light and casual. "Just be happy that you've got me here, not Lady Ellen, say. Or Gray."

"Gray?"

Sir John gave him a long look. "Ask him about Vlaovic, sometime. Difficult call, and an ugly situation, and until I've had a city in revolt, I'll not criticize him for how he handled it. Worst I've ever had to do was in the Kush, and I'm told that they're writing ballads about that. '. . . and the Pashtus said that an Englishman's head will be paid for with heads five-score.'" He shook his head. His expression was grim, but inutterably calm. "After you do that sort of thing, boy, scaring a woman and a few children comes easy. Just as well the boy stopped himself. Thought for a moment that he was going to take a swing at me."

"And what would you have done?" Niko asked.

Sir John gave him a long look. "No choice, Sir Niko. We called them out in the name of the king. He's not to be disobeyed, and when we speak in his name, we're not to be, either."

Fotheringay cleared his throat, and the big knight turned to him in irritation.

"Well, what is it?"

"Begging your pardon, Sir John, and all, but I don't think Sir Niko would have let you kill the boy, and—"

"And you think he could have stopped me?"

Fotheringay stopped walking, and Sir John and Niko came to a halt, too.

"I don't know, Sir John," the old sergeant said. "I hope we never have to find out," he said, quietly. "But I'll tell you this—you turn to fight him, you'd best strike me down first. Failing that, watch to your back when you turn to him, because I'll be on it, and with steel seeking your heart or your throat—whichever's handier." His voice was calm and level. No trace of threat or braggadocio in his tone, despite his words. "I'll serve two masters. The king—and God save him, Sir John, God save him!—and Sir Niko. Not three. Not four. Not them and you."

"Nigel—" Niko started, but the big knight waved him to silence.

"No, Sir Niko. Let the man have his say. Go on, Sir Nigel," he said. "You were saying?"

"I was saying, with all respect, that I've got no objection to lighting your pipe, Sir John, or doing your laundry while I'm doing the young knight's. I'll treat you with the respect due your station, and not feel any the less for that. But the king himself told me to watch out for Sir Niko, and he didn't say, 'Nigel Fotheringay, you watch out for the young knight unless another knight raises a hand to him.'"

Sir John seemed to relax. "You know about me. You're a hard man, Nigel Fotheringay, but you're no Order Knight. Even without the Goatboy, you'd not have a chance against me, Fotheringay, not with sword, spear, or with bare hands."

Fotheringay stared intently at the big knight. "I'm not calculating my chances, Sir John. Just giving you fair warning. And if it needs to be handled here and now, well then, I'm at your service, sir."

"Do you really insist?" The big knight smiled. "So be it, then."

Niko stepped between the two. "Back away, Nigel. Now," he said. Fotheringay's right hand was down by his side, fingers curled. "Put the knife away."

"Sir Niko—"

"Now, Nigel," he said, his eyes locked on Fotheringay's. "And you keep your swords in their sheaths, please, Sir John."

"I've no desire for a fight. Not here and now, Sir Niko," Fotheringay said. "But I've no desire to back away from one, either. Not when it comes to you laying so much as an angry finger on the young knight. Two masters, Sir John. Not three."

"And you think to speak so to a knight of the Order? To this knight of the Order?"

Niko should have been scared, but there was a sense of calm at his core, as he turned to face the big knight.

"As you will, Sir John," Niko said. "I don't claim to know much about being a knight, much less a knight of the Order, but I think it has something to do with standing up for what I believe in, and I don't believe I'll let you kill Fotheringay."

"We don't need to have this out now—"

"I think that we do." Niko let his hand rest on Nadide's hilt. "Nigel—back away." He needed to sound authoritative, and tried to find the words. Oh: "That's not a suggestion." The king had used those words, and they felt right.

He more felt than saw Fotheringay step back.

Niko? What is it?

I don't know for sure, little one. I think, though, that we've got a fair chance of fighting Sir John and the Goatboy.

Oh.

His training was useless here. Watch the eyes, as Becket had taught him? Sir John had had the same training, and more years of practice. He wouldn't give away any intention with a quick narrowing of the eyes, nor with a sharp intake of breath, nor with a subtle tightening of the body that you could watch for, and react to.

It would be sudden, and Niko would have to try to react to it, rather than anticipate it. If it could be avoided, he would avoid it, even if that meant—

"Easy, Sir Niko," Sir John said. "You've my word I'm standing down." John of Redhook slowly, carefully, moved his hands away from his swords and crossed them over his chest. "Well, I'll say this for you, Sir Niko: you've got courage enough. Good sense, well, that remains to be seen." He drew himself up straight and bowed briefly toward Niko, and then to Fotheringay. "And if my choice here and now is to fight to the death with the two of you, or beg your pardon for my rudeness, then I've an easy choice. On one hand, we'd find two of His Majesty's knights dead, and useless to the king; on the other, we find old John Little having to top his sketchy breakfast with a swallow of pride. It's not a taste I much care for, but it won't be the first time I've dined so. So: I humbly beg your pardon, and apologize for offense given. I hope that's sufficient."

Niko didn't need to be told how to answer that. "Of course it is; I accept your apology."

"And will you take my hand, Sir Niko?"

"Of course."

Sir John's much larger hand had strength in it, and Niko had little doubt he could have brought it to bear, but Sir John's handshake was just firm.

"Nigel? I mean, 'Sir Nigel'? Will you accept my apology and take my hand, as well?"

Fotheringay had made his knife disappear. "No offense taken, Sir John," he said, as he accepted the handshake. "I'm not much for taking offense, truth to tell," he said with a toothless smile.

They were expected in Garvard, and Niko would have been able to work that out even if he hadn't recognized the crofter boy, which he did. The boy spotted them at the same time, turned, and walked quickly away; they followed him into the public house.

It was a low building, made of mudded stones. Above their heads, birds nesting in the thatch warbled, as though in warning.

He couldn't make out the Gaelic over the door of the public house, and cursed himself for his awkwardness with languages.

It was almost silent inside, no sound save for the crackling of the fire under cook pot in the hearth. If they had interrupted the conversation, they had done so before entering.

His eyes strained against the darkness of the common room. Light through the shutters striped the packed dirt floor and tables with the early morning sunlight.

So early in the morning it was not surprising that only half a dozen men sat at one of the tables. They crowded too closely together. Eyes settled on his for only a moment.

The publican rushed over. He was a thickset man, sharp nose projecting from under a pair of distinct but almost preposterously bushy eyebrows.

"Good morning to you," he said, his tone making the words a lie. "We've porridge and beer, and little else. Probably nothing nearly fine enough for such fine folks such as yourselves, but—"

"Porridge and beer will be fine," Sir John said. "And conversation." He nodded at Fotheringay, who moved a bench over until it was back up against the wall opposite the hearth, then picked up one of the rough-hewn tables, and set it down in front of the bench. Sir John set his swords down on the table and sat, his back to the wall, and gestured for Niko to sit next to him, which he did.

The publican rushed two bowls over, set them down on the table without a rattle, and rushed back through the open door to the kitchen, returning with another, and with a large clay mug. "I'll be back in just a wee moment with the rest," he said.

Sir John just nodded.

"Go ahead, Sir Nigel," he said. "See what you make of the local beer. I've heard that there's worse."

"There's always worse," Fotheringay said, then took a sip. "No matter how bad it is. But bad beer is, I've found, better than no beer at all—and, then again, there's much worse than this," he said, wiping his mouth with the back of his hand. "And I've no objection to being your taster, as well as the young knight's, Sir John."

The big knight chuckled. "You really think that we'll find Garvard a den of poisoners?"

If his voice was just a little too loud, nobody seemed to take notice.

"If I did," Fotheringay said, "despite being the tolerant man that I am, then I'd have an objection—a loud objection—and you can count on that, Sir John."

The publican returned with two more mugs, set them down, and scurried away, while the men at the table across from them seemed to be studying their own bowls and mugs with great intent.

At Sir John's gesture, Niko took a tentative sip. He was thirsty enough, but he had not acquired a taste for beer, which was perhaps just as well; a glass of wine was enough to make him sleepy.

"I'd heard that Garvard was known to be a talkative sort of town, and not quite so quiet," Fotheringay said, perhaps just a little too loudly.

Sir John shook his head. "Traitors, by and large, talk little when there's men loyal to the Crown about," he said, casually, if increasingly loudly. "And—"

"Sir." One of the men at the other table stood up, and shook off the hand of another, who had attempted to grab his sleeve, as he walked over.

The local was a big man, probably as tall as Sir John, although it was hard to tell while Sir John was sitting. His jaw was covered by a brush of uncombed black beard, but his cheek muscles were visibly tight.

"Sir," he repeated. "Private Miles McPhee, late of the Oban Guard, and no damned traitor, at your service. Sir."

"Sit you down, then, Private McPhee," Sir John said. "And have yourself one on the Crown."

McPhee seemed to hesitate for just a moment, but then he sat, and Sir John beckoned to the publican, who had suddenly appeared in the door to the back room.

"Glad to hear that there's at least one loyal man on Colonsay," Sir John said, then sipped at his beer, and as the publican dropped off another mug and scurried away, again, he gestured at McPhee to drink his.

"No disloyalty here, Sir . . . "

"John. John Little, of Redhook." Sir John smiled over his beer. "Not a relation, as far as I know, to the famous one."

"You're famous enough, Sir John," Miles McPhee said. "And, so it's said, famous for being a fair man, as well as a hard one." He hesitated for a moment. "Although I'd doubt that the Kali worshippers in the Kush would agree with the former."

Sir John shrugged. "What's left of them." The smile was gone from his face, and around his eyes. "Not something I'd much care to talk about. I'd rather talk about the—"

"Amadan Dubh." McPhee nodded. "That's all there's been talk about, since that night."

"Were you there?"

"No." He shook his head. "Not me. I don't plead any special innocence on that, mind. I would have been, though; I was abed, with the ague, and my wife watching over me. Never been all that thick with Calum Mary Machrins, either."

"No friend of yours?"

It was McPhee's turn to shrug. "He and I've never quite gotten along all that well," he said. "But it's a small island, and all; we're not enemies, if that's what you're asking, and I'd turn out for a barning at his croft, just as he did at mine, after mine burned down, and not think twice. Weddings? Well, that's another matter, I'd guess."

"And—"

"But I'd say this: he's a stingy man, and too quick with his sharp tongue and heavy hand, but he's no murderer, no rebel. None such on the whole island, I'd say—"

"And all of these loyal subjects of the earl and His Majesty were seduced by the pipes? By a piper that not one of them had ever seen before, who popped up at the shoreline, without any hint?"

"Now, I'm not saying that latter." McPhee raised a palm.

Niko started to say something, but silenced himself at a minuscule shake of the head from Sir John.

"And," Sir John went on, "you wouldn't want to say that the piper'd been seen before, and that it hadn't been mentioned to the baron." He had lowered his voice, and the softness of his words was somehow more menacing than the volume had been.

McPhee sipped at his beer. "I'm not sure why it should have been. If it'd happened, but . . . "

"But?"

"But. But . . . things happen here, and I don't know of a man or woman on Colonsay or Oronsay who would want to bother the laird about it. It's said that if you leave out an extra bowl of milk, sometimes, along with a skein of wool and a spinning wheel, you might find that you've slept better'n usual that night, and that it's all spun in the morning. So it's said."

"And why wouldn't you mention that?"

"Talk too much about such things, and they don't happen. So it's said. You hear music coming through the shutters of a night, you might want to listen to it, but that's about all. You don't want to top the missus, sure, as if you get her with child, the baby'll come too big and too early, and always, always have eyes of too deep a blue—so you just listen, maybe, and you let yourself drift off to sleep. Don't want to do much more; keep to yourself, is the way of it. You don't want to make no problems in this life, Sir John, not if you don't have to."

"Well, then we've a problem here. Rebellion—"

"Meaning no offense, Sir John, but there was no rebellion. You can blame the one whose name I'd rather not mention, if you'd like. I do. But—"

"But nothing," Sir John said. "Word's gotten out, Private McPhee. A rebellion on Colonsay? And none held to account for it—"

"Dozens of men, women, and children lie in their graves, and you say *none*?"

Sir John moved back from the table. "I'll speak as I see fit, and I'll ask you not to raise your voice to me, Miles McPhee."

McPhee took a long breath. "Then I'll give you my apologies, *Sir John*," he said, voicing the name and title as though it was half an insult. "But I'll say that it was not of their will that they tried to . . . to hurt the baron—"

"And his lady," Niko said. And Bear's mother.

"And my young master," Fotheringay put in. He was fiddling with his pipe. "Speaking just for myself, I don't take kindly to that, either."

"Aye, they tried to hurt the baron, and his lady, and Sir Niko; there's no dispute of that. But . . . but the baron—and his lady—have been nothing but kind and fair, as was his father before him. Yes, his father's father was called Laird Slataire, and it's said that my own grandfather was cuckolded by him.

"But Laird Giscard? There's no hatred there; if we're to be governed by outlanders, and we are, well, there's many worse and few better. But with the earl's soldiers tramping up and down the island, night and day, with swords in their hands and blood in their eyes, few'd want to admit to having heard anything, seen anything, known anything."

"Then somebody had best change his mind, Miles McPhee," Sir John said. "We've been sent by the king to deal with this Amadan Dubh. If he's gone, if he's fled, well then, we'd best pick up his trail. Because word of what's happened here has gone out, and if he's not brought down, there'll be those from New Londinium to Mumbai who will hear of what happened here and say to themselves that rebellions against the Crown will be tolerated, that those responsible for it will not be brought to justice, that the Crown forgives rebellion.

"The Crown, Miles McPhee, cannot forgive or forget or tolerate rebellion. Should every county, every barony, every grand duchy or satrapy be able to attempt rebellion, blaming it on some vanished local diety who others may not even believe in?

"I don't think so. I think that this must be settled soon, or His Majesty will have to take more serious action, and I'm afraid that the next knight of the Order sent will not be the likes of Sir Niko accompanied by myself, but perhaps more along the lines of Sir Joshua Gray. You've heard of Vlaovic?"

"Yes." McPhee nodded. "I've heard," he said, slowly, carefully, like a barefoot man picking his way carefully across a rocky beach. "And of other places—like Linfield, and even of Dunladen, in older times. But none in Scotland, not in living memory."

"Because there's been no damnable rebellion in Scotland, not in living memory," Sir John said. "That appears to have changed."

"And in the name of appearances, you'd kill every man, woman and child on the island?" McPhee shook his head. "That's not the Crown I've served, and I'll warrant it's not the one you do."

"It's not a matter of appearances, McPhee, but of reality. And the reality is that the Crown can't tolerate the appearance of rebellion."

Fotheringay's lips tightened, just a trifle, and he gave the smallest of nods. "Somebody had better be done for it," he said, "and it damn well had better be persuasive. The Oban Guard was in Szerbernica, when the Triune rebellion broke out. You look to be about the right age for that, Miles McPhee. Were you there?"

"No." McPhee shook his head. "I made my mark just after the Guard came home, sir. Heard the stories, though. Didn't much like them."

"Nobody much likes to hear them. Less to like being there—I'll tell you, after that, chasing down pirates in the Med was an easy cruise . . . " Fotheringay voice trailed off. "By comparison." He shook his head. "And instead of some governor who thought to work a better deal for himself with the Empire, imagine what happens if it's a French duke, or an Italian?"

"And centuries of loyalty counts for nothing?"

"Easy, man. It counts for much. It's us that are here, not Sir Joshua and the Khan, not the Corkies. You think that the king wouldn't sic the Irish on Scottish traitors?"

"Fotheringay—"

"I'll be still, Sir John, after I say this: it's right to have faith in the king's goodness, but we live in dangerous times, and only a fool would let treason go unpunished now, as much as ever. The king—and God save him—is no fool."

Miles McPhee raised a palm as Sir John started to speak. "I see your point," he said, still slowly and carefully. "I don't much like it, Sir Nigel, but I see it. If you'll meet me here this night, I'll see if I can help you find the one you seek. I make no warrantees of success, but I will swear to do what I can. On one condition."

Strange. McPhee was looking directly into Niko's eyes, not Sir John's. Perhaps that was because both Sir John and Fotheringay were looking at Niko, too, as though he had been the knight in charge of all of this, and Sir John had merely been speaking on his behalf.

"And that would be?" Niko asked.

"That you convey to His Majesty the king the greetings of Miles McPhee, and of the McPhees of Colonsay, his loyal subjects."

Niko nodded. It seemed little enough to ask, after all, and, of course—

"Done," Sir John said. "We meet tonight. At sundown. And where shall we meet?"

McPhee shrugged. "Matters little; it's a small island, and while I'll do the best I can, there's no guarantees, not when it comes to the Old Ones. Here would do."

"Then here it shall be." Sir John tossed a coin to the top of the table. "We'd best be on our way; we've much to do before then."

CHAPTER 15

Pantelleria II

There are those who say that bittersweet is better than no sweetness at all.
For all my failings, I am not one of those fools.
                                                    —Cully

It probably should have been a surprise that Gray was waiting for them at the Punta Karascia docks, but Cully found himself nodding, and smiling. It seemed right, somehow.

Gray stood out in the hot sun, on the worn boards, with apparent patience, seemingly oblivious to how all the dockside activity seemed to flow as far away from him, giving him a wide berth.

"Ah," Kechiroski said. "Sir Joshua has preceded us."

Cully turned to him, not bothering to try to conceal his irritation. "You expected him to? Strange that you didn't mention it to me."

Kechiroski hesitated but a moment. "No, Sir Cully, I didn't expect him to be here. But it makes sense, when you think on it. Just as the Admiral wasn't surprised that you decided to come here, there's no reason to think that Sir Joshua would be."

Cully didn't much like the idea of being so predictable, and he didn't think much of it, besides, so he just gave Kechiroski a nod, and gave quick instructions to have the girl brought up from her room, then climbed down the ladder to the dock, Guy right behind him, without so much as a by-your-leave.

Dockside at Punta Karascia was, thankfully, back to normal. The flotilla of Dar fellucas that had crowded the harbor last time was long gone, replaced by just a few small fishing fellucas, none of them flying the Scimitar and Star, and dwarfed by a Guild carrack, its naked mizzenmast boom swinging freely out in the wind.

That was just as well, and it would make it possible for the captain to allow some liberty, without having to worry about conflicts with the Arabs.

Still, there were no navy ships, which was strange—had Gray taken passage in the Guild carrack? And, if so, where was his gear? The only thing that he carried, other than his swords, was a small rucksack, slung over his right shoulder.

"Father Cully," Gray said, formally, with a bow. "Sir Guy."

"What are you doing here?" Guy asked, without so much as a polite greeting.

Well, somebody had to, but . . .

"I don't care for your tone, Sir Guy," Gray said, his eyes searching Guy's. "And I'd rather not share any disagreements we might have in public."

Guy started to say something—something stupid, no doubt—and Cully had decided to intervene. As much as the thought of Gray slapping Guy silly was amusing, it would hardly do, and it could happen.

But, instead, Gray simply reached his hand into his jacket, and produced a sheet of parchment, and handed it over to Guy. "I'm not going to insist that you call me Vicar, Sir Guy," Gray said. "But I do insist that you show due respect for my station."

Guy read the parchment at least twice, and then started to hand it back to Gray, sniffing in irritation when Cully took it.

Cully smiled. "I see," he said. "So you're my superior in the Order once more?"

"Superior, no, Father Cully." Gray didn't smile back. "Senior? Yes."

Trust Gray to make such a fine point, eh? "Well, then Sir Joshua, my senior, what are your orders?"

Gray gave one of his rare smiles. "Best to know what they are before you decide how to disobey them?"

"More or less," Cully said. "More like: best to know what they are before I decide whether or not to go along with them." He laughed, and clasped a hand to Gray's shoulder. "Although, truth to tell, it is good to see you,

Joshua," he said, both because he knew that the boy—that Sir Joshua would be warmed by him saying that, and because it was true.

Gray didn't answer for a moment. "As it always is for me to see you, Father." He glanced over Cully's shoulder, and his brow furrowed. "What is that?"

Cully turned. The sailors were bringing up Penelope's stretcher. Brave girl—she was biting on a rag to avoid screaming, and her quiet whimpers were barely audible above the sounds of the wind and the waves.

"*That* is a whom," Cully said, watching Gray's face go all blank and inexpressive at the implied rebuke, "and the whom is a very brave young lady named Penelope, to whom I am very grateful. We've much to discuss," Cully said. "I assume you've found quarters?"

Gray nodded. "I hadn't expected so many of you. But . . ."

"We'll see if there's room at the inn."

"Yes, Father Cully." Gray unslung the rucksack from his shoulder and handed it to Cully. "*She* said to give this to you."

He looked like he was going to say something more, but he just turned, and led the way.

"And you didn't try to get any more information from the Wise?" Cully didn't seem angry—more curious than anything else.

Gray shook his head. Despite the neutral tone, he still felt like a schoolboy, being upbraided. "It was difficult enough to get him to tell me you were coming."

Cully picked up the wine bottle and poured himself a third glass, ignoring Guy's scowl. "Well, that's for the morning, then," he said. "We could just ask, I guess."

"You've hope that the Wise will be of help? Just for the asking?" Guy's expression could hardly have been more scornful. Gray let his hand drop to the hilt of the Khan.

It would be interesting to see if my flame is stronger than that pitiful little saint's.

Cully caught the movement, and smiled over his wine-glass. "I've always hope, Guy," he said. "It's a bad habit, but I'm too old to learn better. But if I'm going to lean on something, it'll be a stout staff, not a wisp of hope for gratitude." He drained his glass of wine in a gulp, reached for the bottle, and stopped himself. "Leaning on hope is like relying on gratitude, decency, good sense. All of them exist, all of them I've seen, but not a one as reliable as a good piece of wood."

Kechiroski came out through the curtains, moving slowly and carefully, as though the rustling of them would cause an alarm. "She's sleeping, again," he said. He dropped down into the chair across from Cully, who had seated himself between Gray and Guy—likely through no coincidence.

The Montagne Grande rose above the slated roof of the *dammusa*, looming in the darkness. Guy looked at it for a moment. "I'm tempted to draw the Albert and dash up there right now. Seems to me that ingratitude for the help we've given him isn't right or proper."

"We?" Sir Guy was as irritating as ever. "I don't recall seeing you at the—"

"Shush. Be still, Joshua." Cully's face was stern. " 'We' is correct. It was three knights of the Order who saved the Wise, acting on behalf of the Order, of which Sir Guy of Orkney is a member, just as you are."

Kechiroski grinned. "Actually, Sir Cully, as I recall—and I was there—it was four knights of the Order. Were you omitting Sir Niko, or yourself?"

Gray was furious at the impertinence, but Cully just smiled. "Myself, actually," he said. "And I shouldn't have. Nor should I have omitted you, or Sigerson and Bigglesworth, or Fotheringay, simply because you're not of the Order."

Kechiroski shrugged, and cut himself off another bite of sausage, wolfing it down. "Makes no nevermind to me, Sir Cully; an ordinary seaman learns not to take offense—at least, from his betters."

Cully sat silent for a long moment. "I owe you apologies for offense I've given, albeit unintentionally, Sir Stavros. You've been a faithful servant of His Majesty, and a good companion."

Guy sniffed.

Gray was irritated, too, for reasons he didn't quite understand. Kechiroski's familiar tone with Cully was far more infuriating than it should have been, and Gray had the feeling that he had lost control of the discussion.

As you have. As you always do, around Cully. So pour yourself enough glasses of wine until it dissolves the irritation, the Khan said.

I don't think so.

Well, if you're not going to cut his head off, it's not a bad second choice.

Cully laughed. "Ah, I find that I've even missed that cursed Khan of yours." He smiled at Gray's start. "No, I'm not hearing him, Joshua—but I know what the Khan thinks is a solution to any irritation, and your dismissing him was written on your face as big as your letters on the chalkboard used to be. I take it I'm to live for the moment?"

Gray didn't know what to say to that.

I see no problem. Just tell him that you're too weak, and too much of a woman, to do what's necessary, if that involves raising your hand to Cully.

"Well." Sir Guy frowned. "All this talk is getting us nowhere."

Cully cocked his head to one side. "And what would you have us do, then?"

"I'd have us march up to the top of the Montagne Grande, first thing in the morning, and have some words with the Wise—and firm ones at that. He—"

"And you think the Wise is a man?"

Gray would have wanted to slap Cully silly. Baiting Sir Guy might be entertaining, but it was entertaining but one person: Cully.

Sir Guy's jaw clenched. "I don't care what he, she, or it is. It knows something, and it knows something that we simply must learn."

Gray expected some sort of argument from Cully, but the old man just shrugged. "Well, it's not up to me, after all, any more than it's up to you, is it?"

"I'm the senior—"

"And Joshua carries the abbot's vicarship." He held Sir Guy's eyes for a long moment, then turned to Gray. "The tradition is that when knights of the Order meet, the junior speaks first, so that he'll not be influenced by the words of his seniors, and can speak his mind freely and openly, and without his thoughts being molded by the others. While I think there could be an argument that my . . . recent return to service makes me the junior,

Sir Guy has accepted that as his role, by speaking his mind so openly, and—"

"Cully. Enough." It was one thing to love the man, but another to fail to notice that Cully had, once again, let his disdain for Sir Guy rule his mouth.

"—and I'm minded to accept that," Cully said, acknowledging the correction with the very slightest duck of the head. "I'll go next, and say that I'm frankly puzzled, that I'm no closer than I was a year ago to knowing what it is that's going on all about us, other than to say that I fear it, for reasons both obvious and subtle.

"As Sir Guy's senior, I'll say that I'm always tempted to do just the opposite of what he suggests, just because I hold his sagacity in less than high esteem, and I say that," he went on, raising a hand that surprisingly actually cut off Guy's beginning of a protest, "as a criticism of myself, more than him.

"So: I don't know. But I don't know what else to do, not here and now. The scent trail in Izmir ended with the Baba Yaga; we might pick up another in Hostikka, or anywhere near the Zone—or in the Empire."

"But you don't think so," Gray more asked than said.

"I don't know, Joshua. I just don't know." Cully's expression was incredibly sad under the mask of indifference and objectivity; Gray could see that, even if he doubted that Guy could. "Tell me again, what She said to you."

Gray shook his head. "Little, as always. She said that She had no Sight to help us, and little feeling as to what was going on." He smiled. "She said to give you the bag, and suggested that you not become accustomed to Her doing your laundry for you."

Cully smiled. "Nor should She. And what else did the Lady say . . . ?"

"And the rest was personal, between Her and me." He cocked his head to one side. "Or am I not to have a private word with Her?"

Cully didn't rise to the bait. "Yes, of course you are. So: we have no help from common sense, none from the Lady, and all sorts of wild geese to chase around not only the Mediterranean, but across half of Europe, while whatever is going on, goes on. My advice might surprise you: send me, unarmed and alone, to plead with the Wise, and when I'm turned down—and I shall be—take ship back to England, rendezvous with the admiral as we go, and lay it all before the king. I'll go to the Wise, as you already have, but what help you've been given was scant and niggardly. Going again so would be pointless, but likely harmless, unless we go in force, ruled by those with more anger than common sense. Doing it my way will cost us but a day."

And it might well cost them Father Cully, as well. But Gray could not and would not allow that to rule his decision.

"That would be giving up!" Sir Guy was almost shouting. "After all we've been through?"

Cully shook his head. "It's just service, Sir Guy.

"But I will say this: if we face the Wise in his—or her, or its—own home, we ought to go either as supplicants begging a favor, or as creditors demanding one, for there is no in-between here. It's up to you, Joshua. As your old teacher, I advise you: think carefully, and prayerfully, and then make your decision, Vicar."

It was all wrong. It shouldn't have been his decision; he just wasn't up to it.

Oaths were useless.

Mercy tempered only by justice; justice tempered only by mercy.

If there was something that the Wise knew, it wasn't just that they leave not knowing, but it wasn't safe to go try to demand anything out of the ancient one.

Was it avoidable? Of course. What was the right decision?

They were all looking at him, and he let his hand drop to the hilt of the Khan.

Go ahead, the Khan said, *take your tentative steps. Don't grasp the nettle firmly. Let it hurt you all the more that way.*

I don't have to go to the Wise; we can just leave.

Of course we can. Of course you can decide that. The Khan seemed more amused than disgusted. *I'm sure that the abbot would approve, after all, and—*

And you'd think to distract me with arguments that you know are false, and about which I care little.

I don't think to distract you at all. I'm trying, Gray, to help you face what you are: you're like me. We keep our friends close, and get our enemies closer, and we don't turn and walk away from either, not if we have a choice. So choose. Choose tentatively, as though you think that will make any difference, but choose.

"You've not spoken, Kechiroski," Cully said. "Your eyes watch everything while seeming not to, and I can't imagine that your ears are any less attentive. But your mouth is another matter—have you no words of advice?"

He gestured toward Gray. "The vicar would, I'm sure, want to consider your words, as well."

Kechiroski reached out a thick hand, and poured himself a glass of wine, then drank it with unseemly haste, as though fortifying himself for something dangerous.

"I'm not sure that I have many good words for this, Sir Cully. I'm just an old seaman, raised far beyond any estate I deserve, but I don't like either choice. I've been to the home of the Wise, and it scared me out of several years' growth. Truth to tell, Sir Cully, I'm beginning to wish that I had not been seconded into all of this, and had taken His Majesty's advice and returned to my homeland, to sit under an olive tree and sip at a glass of retsina.

"But I'll give you the seaman's answer: when you see a storm on the horizon, make your way as quickly as you can toward the nearest port away from the storm, and hope that it turns aside before it overtakes you."

Cully nodded. "So, Gray, you have two words of advice. Sir Guy says confront the Wise; Sir Stavros says make for the nearest safe port, by which I presume he means home. And you have my advice, too, such as it is—consider carefully, and make your own decision, because . . ."

"Because why?"

"Because the abbott was correct: you tend to defer far more to my supposed wisdom than is wise. If I thought I had any wisdom to offer in this, I would unmercifully prey upon your weakness in that. I've done that before; I shall do it again, when I think the situation warrants." His eyes went all distant; it was as though he was looking at something, or someone, far, far away. "She and I have had this discussion. I will not substitute Her judgment for my own. When I have no judgment to offer, and the decision seems to me to be balanced on the blade of a very, very sharp knife, I'll remind myself, I hope, once again, that it was She who told Ralph to give you this authority, and I shall hope and pray—and to the extent that I can, trust—that She decided wisely. So I'll say this to you, Brother and Father and Vicar, Joshua: whatever we do shall likely be the wrong thing. What we do, I fear, may matter, but it feels to me as though we play a game of chess, with the rules ever-changing, and an opponent who we can't see, but who is a hundred moves ahead of us."

"Very well," Gray said. "Once more to the Wise, but neither with threats nor pleas. We'll talk, and we'll listen. And then I'll decide what to do."

"In the morning, then."

"No," Gray said. "Now. If we're lucky, we'll arrive at daybreak."

Cully's mouth twitched. "Doesn't sound all that lucky to me, truth to tell."

Gray's thumb, as if of its own volition, fell to the Khan's hilt, and the mad, silent laughter of the Khan would have chilled his soul.

If he still had one.

CHAPTER 16

The Black Piper

There is much good that can be said about fear. It reminds you of your mortality, and the necessity to see to your salvation. It sharpens the wits, and the senses, particularly the sense of taste, as the steely taste in the back of the mouth is distinctive.

There are those who don't care for the taste, though. I'm one of them.

—Cully

"I don't like it," Becket said, finally. "Should have taken the company of the earl's troops, and the Marines, and that's just for a starter."

The sky was clear; the moon high, and the night wind blew from the northwest, and it chilled him to the bone. Not that Becket was unused to discomfort. Of all of his companions, pain and discomfort were the most constant and the most reliable.

Sigerson's expression grew even more neutral than usual. He shook his head minutely. His long face was even more taciturn in the pale moonlight than it had been in daylight, and the pallor was almost ghostly.

"No, I don't think so—with all due respect, of course, Sir Martin. For watching an empty meadow, this company is more than large enough. A company of troops?" Rising from his crouch, he stretched broadly. "No," he said, "I think not." His wand was in his hand, and he used the tip of it to scratch at his sharp chin, then returned it to his sheath. "This group may be too large, and have scared off the prey. I don't sense anything around, and I'm thought to be fairly good at that sort of thing."

"I've heard many say you are," Bigglesworth said, "and none say otherwise, sir."

The fawning of Sigerson's manservant—knighted or not—was irritating. "Sir Melrose—"

"No sirring for me, if you please, Sir Martin," Bigglesworth said, interrupting. "Just Bigglesworth, if you please—or Biggles, or boy, or whatever." It wasn't the first time he had corrected Becket on that matter, and each time he had done it with the same speed—and the same casualness that verged on impertinence. Or more than verged on impertinence. "Find the title a titch embarrassing, I do."

Sigerson grinned, and Becket let it pass. He didn't much care for the wizard, which wasn't unusual, or necessarily reflective of a fault of Sigerson's—Becket found most people irritating or worse, and wizards moreso than most people.

For some reason or other, the fact that Sigerson didn't look like a wizard made it worse, not better. Most wizards that Becket had had the misfortune to encounter were round and soft, probably a function of a largely sedentary existence. Sigerson, on the other hand, was tall and lean, and almost preposterously healthy—on their way up he had even volunteered to spell Sir John and the boy, who had declined, and taken turns carrying Becket up to the edge of the clearing.

Instead of the robes of a fellow of His Majesty's College of Wizardry, Sigerson was dressed in a preposterously plain and unadorned set of Marine utilities, although his two-inch-wide broad belt, instead of being weighted down with any gear, held only a preposterously small, preposterously slim leather sheath on one side, and a small leather bag on the other.

"Just be still, if you please," Sir John said. "Waiting a while longer will do no harm, and may do some good."

That was the first time that Becket had heard from him; Sir John had sat motionless through the night. While most of the rest of the men had taken their leave of the improvised blind behind Hangman's Rock to slip down the hill and relieve themselves, John of Redhook had simply sat, as though frozen.

Becket hadn't moved, but that had been a matter of necessity, rather than choice. Damn his legs.

The six of them were crowded in too closely for Becket's taste, although he could see the sense in it. If the Amadan Dubh were to find his way to Hangman's Rock, it was best that they minimize the number of places where he could stumble upon his hunters.

The local boy finally did something, other than sitting there.

He set his hand on Sigerson's forearm, then touched his index finger to his lips. Sigerson's man started to stir at that, and so did Fotheringay, but Sir Niko turned to Fotheringay while Sigerson turned to Bigglesworth, each of them giving the smallest of head shakes simultaneously, a duplicate motion that almost caused Becket to laugh out loud.

"It matters little," McPhee said, quietly. "If the—if he who you seek chooses to manifest himself, I'm sure he'll do it willy-nilly—on his terms, Sir Eric, not ours."

"And you think *he* would think he could take on a White Knight of the Order, and a Red?" Sigerson asked.

". . . and Sir Eric?" Bigglesworth put in.

McPhee shrugged. "About that, I'd not claim to know much. I don't claim to know much about the, about the Old Ones, and I'd not like to know more." Becket could more hear than see his frown. "But I've had the feeling that we've been watched for more than an hour, and my own feelings are the one thing that I do know much about. If I may?"

Becket wasn't sure if McPhee was asking him, but he nodded anyway.

Annoyingly, McPhee looked first to Sir John, who remained motionless, and then toward Sir Niko, who nodded.

What did McPhee think this was? Some sort of republic?

"*A bheil Gàidhlig agaibh?*" McPhee asked, as he turned back to Becket.

Well, of course he did, Becket said, and he said as much. "And Sir John does, as well."

"Then I shall—"

"But Sir Niko has damned little of it, and—"

"Then I shall speak in English, so Sir Niko will not misunderstand what I say. The Old Ones, it's said, find younger languages harsh on the ears, but I guess I shouldn't worry about offending the Dark Piper, eh?"

He rose slowly, and got to his feet, and cleared his throat. "You who watch, would you make yourself known?"

Silence answered.

If it was going to be that easy . . .

"Again, I ask you: would you make yourself known?" McPhee asked. "I'm known as Miles McPhee, and I'd have words with you, and perhaps more than words."

The only sound was the wind whispering through the rocks and grasses. Damned silly. They would encounter the Amadan Dubh on his terms, not on theirs, of course. Trap him?

How?

But you do what you can, of course.

McPhee reached into his tunic and with exaggerated caution, pulled out a small pipe, and brought it to his lips, pulling out a few tentative notes before going into a surprisingly low-pitched, slow tune. Becket couldn't place it, and he had thought himself more than passingly familiar with much of the music of the island, from his years with Giscard and Grace.

McPhee played for the longest time, and if patience hadn't been Becket's companion even longer than had been pain, he would have been more than a little impatient.

The pipes played on.

Over to his right, Sigerson seemed to stir, but out of the corner of his eye Becket could see Bigglesworth touch a finger to his master's sleeve, and the wizard subsided.

The pipes played on.

McPhee's tune had never been fast or note-filled, but it had slowed down, and lowered in pitch, until it suggested a dirge, perhaps, or something equally mournful. Easy enough to be mournful about something as useless as sitting on the edge of a clearing, waiting for the Amadan Dubh, who was clearly not going to show.

Kill me this Amadan Dubh, the king had said. But how were they to do that if they could not find him? Becket didn't care—as it didn't matter—that the king was notoriously impatient with failure. Becket was even more impatient with failure; the only excuse for a knight of the Order to fail was death—his own. And even that sort of failure could be a betrayal in and of itself, and to be viewed with suspicion until proven innocent.

Fools they were, fools they all were to trust the islander. Leading them out and up into the hills, only to sit through the night while nothing happened? Give time for the traitors in the coastal villages to flee? And flee they would—the Marines had no orders to prevent flight, and not enough numbers, even if they had such orders, to guard every stretch of beach from which a skiff or coracle could easily be launched.

Well, that could be handled. Fleeing traitors could be hunted down like the dogs that they were.

It made no difference. Patience would not be rewarded this night, but neither would reward issue from impatience. Plenty of time in the morning, after all and—

Wait. There was a sound. Another pipe—no, by God, another set of pipes!—off in the distance.

McPhee's playing slowly trailed off, and the other sounds became louder—no, not louder, but clearer. Each note with an edge on either side; each note pounding quietly, almost silently, in Becket's ears. Faster, and faster they came, and they played not only through his ears, but up and down his neck, and into his arms, and into the legs that had felt almost nothing but pain for years.

By God, he could feel long-flaccid muscles clenching and unclenching, and he found himself rising to his feet easily, effortlessly, without even a trace of the agony that had long been his constant companion.

Dance, the notes seem to say. Dance your joy, and your faith, and your life.

And dance he did.

He was not alone; the others were moving in the same slow gavotte that he was, save for Sigerson. Sir Niko swayed back and forth, and even Sir John danced to the tune, his long limbs preposterously graceful, absurdly awkward, both at the same time.

The sound filled Becket's ears, and his heart. As the pace picked up, his heart the faster and faster, in time with the song.

And then, off in the distance, Becket could finally see the hooded figure, standing at the far edge of the clearing— no, standing on the air, just above the far edge of the clearing, the long, pointed toes of his boots barely touching the grass from beneath the dark robes.

Dance, the song said. Dance faster and faster, and let it bring you to your destiny.

This time, Niko thought, we shall not be moved.

He had inserted the two small gobbets of wax in his ears at the first distant sound of the pipes, and pushed them in, hard, with his thumbs.

Despite what Sir Martin might have thought, his education had not completely escaped him—he remembered, from the *Odyssey*, that Ulysses had done the same thing, when resisting the call of the sirens, and had prepared himself.

Keep the music out of his head, yes; but don't reveal that to anybody, not in advance, for the world had a million ears, and you could never know which ones were listening.

Not ears, no—but hands. The world couldn't watch his hands at every moment.

So he danced, too. His movements were clumsy, but he was, after all just a clumsy outlander, and that would not be unexpected. Nadide would probably have noticed—surely she would have read his mind—but he didn't let so much as a finger rest upon her steel.

He would not have more than but a moment—and he might, if worse came to worst, not even have a moment—but he could try. The Amadan Dubh had escaped him the last time, despite his efforts. Was it that the combination, the union, the joining of him and Nadide that had frightened the Fairy Fool away? He simply didn't know, and there was no way of knowing.

Fotheringay danced, too. The squat little man would have looked almost comical under other circumstances, as his body twitch and capered to the music, only the tremors in his neck and clenched jaw indicating that he was fighting as hard as he could against the power, the magic, the majesty of the music.

And Becket was on his feet, too. Niko had never thought of Becket as a graceful man, but in his dancing there was a reflection of the man that Sir Martin had been in his youth.

It was Sir John who frightened him. As the big knight danced, he removed his sheathed swords from his sash, and dropped them to the grass, and moved away from them, toward the Amadan Dubh, his eyes never leaving the pipes as he moved, like a mouse hypnotized by a snake.

It was time to move. Or was it? Draw Nadide, run for Sir John's swords and throw the Goatboy to him, then attack the Fairy Fool simultaneously, with both of them joined to their companions, both of them with the full power of their swords, Red and White, upon them, break the spell and let the others—Bigglesworth, Sigerson, McPhee, and faithful Fotheringay—do what they could. That had to be the way of it—what was the other choice?

Wait until the Amadan Dubh could lay a hand upon Sir John?

No. It was time to move.

Now.

Nigel Fotheringay had always liked things simple. Life went better that way.

Even a complicated thing could be made simple, if you simply put your mind—and usually your back—to it. It had been that way from the day he had made his mark until, well, until recently. Being a Marine—private, corporal, and sergeant—had been difficult, true, more often than not. It had been, in its time, painful, boring, exciting, frightening, and many other things—but it had not been complicated.

Do what they tell you, then turn to and do more, and if you have a spare moment, you could take a breath and pray that the man beside you was doing the same.

And when it all went to hell around you—and that was one of the few things that you could count on this life: that it would go all the hell around you—just focus on your little piece of what was going on, and trust that that would be enough, because there wasn't a damned thing that you could do about it if it wasn't. Simple, see?

The lieutenant had always obsessed about how complicated it was to keep the company in training, and ready for action, and Fotheringay admitted that there was some truth in that. New recruits were clumsy as all hell, and utterly lacking in basic skills; too many of the experienced ones would allow themselves to go all sloppy and careless inside, and you could be all too easily fooled by a ship-shape uniform, if you didn't look. Train them all the same, and either the younger ones would step on the experienced ones, or the experienced ones would find it too easy and slack off. And there were always the thieves, and the slaggards, who would not see to their gear when nobody was watching.

So keep it simple. Beat the younger ones into shape, and make an example of a thief and the slaggards every now and then, and if there was a man whom you couldn't trust, in the long run, just be sure that he was the first one over the side, and let the pirates solve your problem for you.

Simple. Keep it simple.

And it was the same with the young knight. Fotheringay didn't know anything about training a knight of the Order, so he had done what he could: he kept the young knight's kit in shape, saw to his needs the way an officer's dogrobber should, watched his back, and if he felt bad about reporting on the young knight behind his back, well, His Majesty had given Fotheringay his orders, and it wasn't for the likes of Nigel Fotheringay to be saying if those orders were right. The only thing he had to do was keep his eyes on the task at hand, and his hands at the task on hand. But the rest of the world could take care of itself; Nigel Fotheringay, about whom not much good could be said, knew his place, and kept to his place.

But that did him no good, here and now.

The mad piper's tunes had invaded his mind, and his body, and his limbs moved to the music, and not of his own will. He could have, he supposed, thought himself not to blame, for all the others were in the same, leaky, boat that Fotheringay was, but perhaps it was not unreasonable of him to be more concerned that the boat was sinking than whose fault the sinking was.

Just give me one chance, he thought. One chance to strike at the Amadan Dubh, one chance to distract the Amadan Dubh from the young knight, and the others. He would ask no more of himself than that.

But it might be enough. It was his little piece of what was going on, and to do that little piece was all that he could expect of himself.

Fotheringay had no feeling, one way or the other, about Sir John, but he was famous for his skill with his hands and his sword, and the Goatboy was known to be a White Sword of great power—between Sir Niko and Sir John, if there could be but a moment of distraction, perhaps, if only Fotheringay could—

But he couldn't. His feet moved faster and faster to the tune, and he could not force his clumsy, wretched, damned, useless hands into his pockets where he had secreted the gobbets of wax that Sir Niko had slipped into his hand, and silenced any possible questions a quick touch of the fingertip to his lips.

Simple, but useless.

That was Nigel Fotheringay. The lieutenant would have been ashamed of him.

And then there was Sigerson, Sigerson thought.

That was the way that Eric Sigerson had always thought about himself, after all, in the third person. Perhaps it was that it helped him to maintain a wizard's necessary objectivity—not perfect objectivity, of course; that would be as crippling as a lack of emotional distance—or perhaps it was just that that was the way that he was.

To be a wizard was to be in the world, but not of the world. The forces that flowed above, below, around, and through the mundane world were always of great power, and the purpose of the wizard was to be a conduit for that great power—but only in the limited way; too much power was, as Saint Acton had wisely observed, corrupting. Manipulate it—but just enough of it, and not one whit more—and you could be a credit to your teachers, and your College; take one step toward the Black, and you would find yourself, inexorably, up to your neck in the darkness.

He could smell the blackness. The amadan dubh fairly reeked of it.

Sigerson did not try to resist it, of course. Not directly. Matching his skills and spark against the Black flame of the amadan dubh would have been pointless. Sigerson was only human, after all, and the piper was something older, and something perhaps more and less, at the same time.

He would let it flow about him. That was all he was capable of; that was all he would do, at the moment. Raging, fighting, resisting, struggling—there was a place in the world for all of that, but that was not his place, not here, and not now.

But he would do what he could, if no more.

He let his eyes sag shut, and applied just a hint of a spark, just a ghost of a cantrip, and let the music and the madness wash around him, as he had once seen his own master part a raging stream with the sharp edge of an oak leaf.

Not resistance—avoidance. Just the slightest of forces to push it all to one side.

Another man, he thought, would have regretted not been able to come to the aid of the others. After all, Bigglesworth had been his manservant since Sigerson had been a boy. Sigerson admired Sir Niko for his force of character and courage, and who could resist Fotheringay's dog-like devotion? Or the quiet courage that Sir Martin wore with such improbable, smelly dignity? He didn't know Sir John well, but, of course, Sir John was a knight of the Order, and more than worthy of the assistance that Sigerson would have offered, if he could.

But he had none. Anchored safely, the streams of music and madness and magic passing about him, he remained in a paradox: completely free, yet completely trapped, for the only place to move was into that stream of music and madness and magic passing about him.

Let the stream alter its course, and he could alter his. But in the eternal, frozen moment that it coursed about him, the only thing he had to offer was frozen independence and objectivity.

And if that could not be enough, that was as it was; Eric Sigerson had nothing more to offer.

And so it came, as it had to, to John of Redhook.

Every man, perhaps, thinks himself a paradox, and John was no different.

He thought himself a good man, but he had spent more hours on his knees with rosary beads in his hands than most sinners. He thought himself a gentle man, but burned bodies and seared souls lined his path through life, particularly in the Kush. He thought himself a humble man, but he took pride in his flawed gentleness, and his marred goodness, and it did not fail to occur to him more days than not that the king himself ofttimes treated John as a confidant, and would give an ear and an open mind to what he had to say.

And he had, after all, been selected to carry the Goatboy, and bear the soul of a saint through life, as both weapon and companion.

Of all the things he prided himself on, though, it was on his self-control. He was the servant of the king of his own choosing, by his own choice, as he was a member of the Order. Forget the sword—the powers vested in any knight of the Order were far too dangerous as it was, and in the loss of self-control could have effects that would harm the innocent.

Sir John had harmed the innocent enough for one life. He would threaten, bluster, and rage, yes—but he would do it because he thought it necessary, not because he could not control the temper that had caused a much younger John Little to flee Redhook.

He would control his body—but now his body was not his own. It danced, it moved, it capered to the sounds of the pipes.

From the neck up, he was still his own man. He could watch the others, and at least whisper to himself.

"Well, old boy," he whispered, his lips barely moving. "Let's see what you are made of, eh?"

Just a matter of getting his hand on the Goatboy. But instead of touching the steel of the Goatboy, his hand dropped to the sheath, and he found himself extracting both of his swords from their sash, and dropping them to the ground, leaving them behind as each step, each move, each turn brought him closer to the mad piper.

Yes, it had all come down to Sir John, and he had been tried in the balance, and found wanting.

There was one thing left to do: he prayed. Silently, not even moving his lips.

God, this humble sinner stands before You asking not for Your protection, not for Your blessing, not for Your forgiveness of my sins, though they be grievous and many.

I ask of you: just give me control of my body, Lord, just for three heartbeats.

I beg of You: let me get my hands on the throat of this Amadan Dubh.

And if not my hands, Lord, at least my teeth.

But yet his hands and feet moved to the sound of the pipes, and not to his own will, or his prayers.

Prayers are always answered; often the answer is no. John of Redhook knew that, and he tried to resign himself to that no as not only a possibility, but a reality.

But this time he more felt than heard the whisper of wind behind him, then the cold steel of the hilt of the Goatboy was warm in his hands, and in his mind, and in his heart.

John, the Goatboy said. That was all.

Just: *John*.

There was no time for more than that, because, yet again, about him, about them, the world changed.

CHAPTER 17

Breaking the World

*The world breaks us all. It shatters our bodies and
brutalizes our souls.*

*The question each of us—shattered body and
brutalized soul as a given—is: what to do next.*

—Gray

Cully was alone, as he walked through the castle gates,
and into the gathering darkness.

The others' horses were hitched next to his, but none
of them were there. Not even Penelope, who had been
brought up the long winding path to the castle in her

padded cart. For the life of him he couldn't have sworn when they went away, or how.

It was confusing being near the Wise. But, at least, it was usually private confusion.

Cully had expected that, of course. On his thankfully rare previous visits with the Wise, only once had he seen another human being, and that had been the last time, the time that Bear had been killed in front of his eyes.

He had expected it to all be the same as last time. And it almost was. The differences were annoying. Instead of the even, regular thumping of boots on the ramparts of his head, the footsteps were ragged, and irregular, as though they had been made by a dozen stumbling soldiers.

He looked for them, but it was already far too dark for him to have seen them even if they were there, and in all likelihood, it was just sounds, provided by the Wise, for his own amusement. It didn't amuse Cully.

He could have called out, but there was no point in that. He just followed the flagstone path around the donjon, past the barracks, and toward the hedge-rimmed plaza beyond.

That was where it had all happened. The way was lit by flickering torches, each one set not into a stone-lined hole that he would have expected, but into the grass. They sputtered and fumed and a few traces of their acrid smoke reached his nostrils, but there was no apparent heat; he held his hand, fingers spread widely, over one and paused for a moment.

No; no heat.

He walked on, and then he was in the plaza. The last time he had been here, bodies had been scattered across the stones, and the light of the noontime sun had beaten rightly down upon him.

But it had been empty of anything else. Yes, hedges had rimmed the plaza, and they were gone now, even though they had been evident but moments before.

It was the new thing that drew his attention. Rising off from almost the center of the plaza, a short tree rose barely head-high.

"It's an apple tree," a low voice murmured from behind him.

Cully turned slowly; there was no need to hurry.

The man facing him was about his own height and build, but not dressed as he would have expected. Instead of a mockery of the robes of the Order, he wore a gray woven sailor's tunic over calf-length breeches, the tunic belted with a length of rope, and carried a walking stick, on which he leaned heavily.

"Hello," the Wise said. His thinning hair was bound back in a sailor's queue, perhaps too tightly—the skin was tight over his temples. He seemed to have trouble breathing, although just a little.

It was the eyes that bothered Cully. They locked on his for a long moment, and seemed to see too much before they looked away.

"Hello," Cully said.

The Wise made no answer.

"Nicely done in distracting Gray the other day," Cully went on. "Did you think that would do more than buy a little time? Or were you waiting for me?" That sounded boastful, yes, but who cared how it sounded?

The Wise only shrugged.

And buying time? Time for what? Cully wasn't sure. If the Wise could be affected with force, that force wasn't going to come from an old man with a couple of swords.

Perhaps time for something else to happen, somewhere else?

The thought chilled him.

"Do you like the tree?" the Wise asked, ignoring him. "It's an apple. The seed came from Fallsworth." The Wise grinned. "No, I didn't go get it myself; but the wind brings many things to the Isle of Winds, after all. I thought it a fitting tribute to Bear. Don't you?"

Little enough; Bear had saved the Wise from a horrible death—or worse. What would a live sword with the soul of the Wise imprisoned in it have meant? And in whose hands?

He had a thought, for just a moment, but forced himself into the moment.

"Is it real? Or is it just some . . . illusion?" Cully waved his hand at the ramparts, from where the phantom stumbling sounds still issued. "Like all the rest. Like the hedge that was here but moments ago and now is gone."

"Oh, it's real. All of it is real." The Wise squatted, supporting himself with his walking stick. "Every bit of it. Just because you see things differently than others doesn't mean that you're being fooled, any more than they are."

"Or any less." Cully was skeptical.

"And that's true enough, as well." The Wise shook his head. "Shall we get right to the point? Or do you enjoy my company so well? Have you come as a supplicant? Or a creditor? Are you here to beg for help, or demand it?"

The others were gone; Penelope was alone in the cart, before the gate.

"Hello?" She hadn't seen them leave, but she had expected that. Cully had talked about his visits to the Wise's keep on the Montagne Grande on Pantelleria, as had Sir Joshua, and described what they had seen.

Interesting descriptions of the Wise. He apparently looked different to all who saw him, and while Cully and Gray had described him thoroughly, she wondered if they had ever noticed that they were largely describing themselves.

Well, what would she see? The girl that she had been, or the scarred wreck that she was?

There was no point in delay.

She forced herself to the edge of the cart, and lowered herself to the ground, standing as steadily as she could.

The pain was manageable, although the itching had intensified, yet again. Gentle Sir Stavros had spent hours gently massaging oils into her scarred flesh, and that helped, but she would, she was sure, always hurt, always itch.

Well, what could not be cured must be endured, and the open gates to the keep beckoned to her. She looked for a moment at her bag, wondering if there was any point in bringing it. Matching her paltry apprentice skills against even an ordinary of the College would have been futile, and she had every reason to believe that the Wise could deal with her pitiful little magicks with more ease than the Baba Yaga had done.

Very well, then: it would not be a threat, but a badge of her—low—office, and she would represent her College and her family and her companions as well as she could.

She slung the bag to her shoulder and walked slowly through the front gates.

It was strange. She obviously had been somewhat groggy on the trip of the side of the mountain, because she had the definite impression that the Wise was surrounded by stone walls.

But it wasn't. The wall around the house, gilded against the weather and heavily over laden with vines, was entirely reminiscent of her childhood at Everwood, complete to the decorative spikes topping the uprights. Oh, there were differences; the walls were much higher here, and the swung-open gate had no family crest upon it. But in some ways it felt the same.

She walked through, and wasn't sure whether to smile or to frown. Down the road, seeming preposterously lonely and small in the grassy vastness of the enclosure, Everwood stood.

The captain was not a poor man, but a town home was, by its very nature, much smaller than a rolling country estate, and the house sat all small and lonely in the middle of a vast lawn, with no outbuildings at all, not even the small stable that the captain maintained for both his horses and his carriages. It was as though her old home had been transplanted here, willy-nilly, without any sense of how silly it looked.

But it was, still, the image of Everwood, and that brought a smile to her lips.

"As I knew that it would," sounded from behind her. "Easy, Miss Penelope; don't turn quickly, for you might hurt yourself."

It wasn't the captain, although it looked entirely like him. The same tall, elegant form, with the same gentle expression above the carefully waxed goatee and mustache. And the same voice.

The false captain nodded. "No, I'm not him, nor pretending to be him. But I thought that a familiar appearance might be pleasant for you, Priyanka."

The use of that name was a false note, and if she had had any doubt that it was the captain, it would have dispelled that entirely. He would have called her "Miss Penelope."

"As was my intent. I would like to reassure you—and perhaps I have other motivations, as well; neither human nor other often does things for only one reason—but I wouldn't try to fool you in such a clumsy way. I just wished to treat you gently, for you have been badly used." He looked at her face without any sign of the distaste at her scarring that she was trying to become used to. "I can fix that, you know."

She nodded, as an acknowledgment, not as an agreement. "I am Penelope Priyanka Miller," she said. "At your service."

"I know," he said, rather than introducing himself. "Apprentice of His Majesty's College, companion to Sir Cully of Cully's Woode, beloved daughter of Martin Miller and Hemashri Miller, and other things. I'd say I'm pleased to meet you, but I'm not always one for the proper forms—as I prefer my privacy, these days, and you and your companions have impinged on it, to be blunt."

"Where are the others?"

"Oh, they're here, even if you don't quite notice them. I certainly do. The knights are all one of a kind, even though each one of them thinks himself so very different. All three of them are having much the same discussion with me. Kechiroski and I are having our own talk at this very moment, which I suspect you won't find is all that much like yours."

He reached for her hand, slowly, tentatively, just as the captain had on the rare occasion that he had done so.

She let him take it.

"Would you care to accompany me into the house?" he asked. "You'll find it entirely familiar, save for the staff. I don't think you'll actually see anybody, although the odors of turmeric and cooked apples may be somewhat familiar to you. As might the sounds, if the kitchen door just happens to be open. I certainly can promise you a dish of something quite familiar and pleasant—if you care to partake."

She knew better. "I've been told that if I let so much as a morsel of food pass my lips, I'll have to remain here."

"That is entirely possible." He nodded. "And would that be so very bad? I rarely give my word on anything— it has a tendency to bind my actions more tightly than it does for humans—but I can give you my word that you would find remaining here entirely pleasant, and quite interesting, all in all." He shrugged. "And you might find, should you leave someday—and then make no promises on that account—that your bag would be filled with things more useful than it is now, just as your mind would be filled with skills far more puissant than you're likely to have, even after years of study, and then even at the height of your cycle."

Distraction. That's what it was; he was trying to distract her, but from what? Was he doing the same thing with the others? And to what end? With what goal? It didn't make any—

Wait.

"Hello?"

There was no answer. Sir Guy let his hand drop to Albert's hilt.

Patience, Guy, Albert whispered in his mind. *Patience is a virtue, and you've none too much of it.*

That was true enough, and he ducked his head, grateful for the correction. He was, after all, a sinful man.

He stalked across the compound.

Strange place, and not at all what had been described to him. The walls, which from the outside had appeared to be stone, were built of rough-hewn logs, like the palisades that settlers in New England built against the depredations of the native saracens. The tops of the poles looked freshly cut, and sap dripped down their sides. His admittedly keen vision could see armies of ants marching to and from it, as though carrying the drippings away to their nests.

Very strange. What was the purpose of it? Why put up logs to rot inside the stone walls? Or had the builders put up a stone facade on the outside of log walls? If the stone walls weren't enough to stop wind or invaders, what possible use could a log palisade do inside stone walls?

It didn't make sense, and he was more than vaguely irritated with Cully and Grayling for not having mentioned this. They had been typically evasive in describing the Wise's habitation, and while he had pressed them, they had been—again, typically—useless, as had Kechiroski.

Maybe this was a change since the three of them had last been here?

But while the logs appeared freshly hewn, they couldn't have been all that new; dozens of sparrows and gislings were nesting in the interstices, and their songs probably should have cheered him, but didn't.

The cobblestone path twisted across the lawn, green and flat as that on a thousand-year-old estate in Pendragonshire, toward the main house, and Sir Guy's boots clicked against the hard stone as he walked.

An impressive looking house, indeed; the high archway and open windows seemed almost Grecian, although the overgrowth of vines had a definite English flavor to it—if he'd had to guess, he would have guessed fourteenth century or so. Quite pleasant.

Strangely, right out in front of the main entrance of the keep, a small tree stood, no more than twice Sir Guy's height.

The branches were heavily laden with deeply ripe apples, although, surprisingly, there was no windfall below.

"It's an apple tree," a low voice murmured from directly behind him.

He turned, reaching for Albert, but stopped the motion. The other man was at least a dozen feet away, and had his hands held out in front of him, fingers spread widely, in an unmistakable call for peace.

"Hello," the Wise said. His voice was low and pleasant, much as Sir Guy's own.

Sir Guy had to admit that he—if it was a he, rather than an it—was a well-made fellow; he was perhaps a touch shorter than Sir Guy, and his face had a few more lines and was topped with slightly less hair, but the Wise was a handsome sort, with a strong chin and a beneficent expression, perhaps somewhat like Sir Guy's own.

That said, Sir Guy was less than pleased with the Wise's choice of garments—his tunic and robes appeared to be an imitation or mockery of the robes of the Order, though they had no piping along the cuffs, and no sign of the Cross or any other insignia at all.

But at least the Wise was unarmed, at least with physical weapons—his sash was empty of anything except a slim white stick, vaguely reminiscent of a wizard's wand, although longer.

"Greetings," Sir Guy said. "I am Guy of Orkney, sworn knight of the Order of—"

"Do you like the tree?" the Wise asked, rudely interrupting him without so much as a by-your-leave.

"I've no opinion on such matters," he said. "I've come here to talk with you about matters of interest, sir. And it appears you have the advantage of me, and I would appreciate you properly intro—"

"It's an apple," the Wise said, as though Sir Guy couldn't see that for himself. He started to let his hand drop to Albert's hilt, but stopped the motion. There would be opportunity enough for that, were such necessary.

"Yes, I've seen apple trees before, sir. But I—"

"The seed came from Fallsworth."

"And what of that? Is there something special about Fallsworth apples that should concern me? Are these such wondrous apples that they should be of great interest to a knight of the Order who is on mission? I've come here to—"

The Wise grinned. "No, I didn't go get it myself; but the wind brings many things to the Isle of Winds, after all."

"As the wind of the ship's sails brought me to this island. And I—"

"I thought it a fitting tribute to Bear."

It was maddening. This . . . this Wise was unable to let Sir Guy get a sentence out without interrupting. If Sir Guy hadn't been a man of calm disposition, he might have sworn out loud.

And Bear? "I would prefer to discuss the matter that has brought me here," he said, carefully, "but if you wish to bring up the late Sir David Shanley, it would suit me better if you spoke of him more formally, and not use the common name that many of his brothers used."

"Don't you?"

"No," he said. "I've always been one for more formality, and think none the less of myself for it." He looked about. "But there are some strange things happening hereabouts. What's the meaning of this palisade? Of this apple tree from which the fruit doesn't fall? And where are the others?"

Was this some sort of deception? Sir Guy knew who the Father of Deception was, and it was not impossible that the Horned One could manifest himself in such a pleasant and handsome form.

"Oh, it's real," the Wise said, answering his thoughts rather than his words. Sir Guy didn't much like that. "All of it is real."

"As is your impertinence, sir. And your rudeness. I've introduced myself quite properly, and I find your refusal to do the same quite rude. Don't you?"

"Every bit of it." The Wise shrugged, as though to say that he wasn't bothered by his own improper behavior, even though he had admitted it.

"And I see simple courtesy as something that both the high and the low ought to practice."

"Just because you see things differently than others doesn't mean that you're being fooled—"

"It's difficult and dangerous to try to fool a knight of the Order, sir."

"—any more than they are."

"And you'll not distract me from my task with your banter."

"And that's true enough, as well." The Wise shook his head. "Shall we get right to the point? Or do you enjoy my company so well? Have you come as a supplicant? Or a creditor? Are you here to beg for help, or demand it?"

The Elder laughed. A far-too-familiar laugh; Kechiroski remembered it from a time when he wasn't Kechiroski. "Nissim al-Furat, Stavros Andropolonikos, Stavros Kechiroski, Sir Stavros Kechiroski—it's all the same to me. I know where your loyalties are; and they stem from who you are. Who you really are, and not who you appear to be."

The Wise had appeared in the form of Shayk Tzidiki, complete with robes, *kafiyeh* and *agal*, and the fierce expression beneath it, relieved only by the gentle, knowing eyes.

His training, under the careful tutelage of the لجنة نزع السلا, was still with him; he set a puzzled expression on his face, with just a trace the fear beneath it, the way any innocent man suspected of some horrible crime would do.

"Very nicely done, indeed, Nissim," the Wise said. "But hardly the point. If you'd care to posture for a while, I certainly have time. At least here and now; I can't speak for you. But you do neither of your causes—the one that you effect to support, and the other—any good at all that I can see by the delaying such matters. So don't bother doing that."

The Wise took another puff from his hookah. "I'd say I'm a patient man, but human values like patience don't quite apply to me; and I'm not a man." The Wise held out a tray of sweetmeats. "Eat a little, smoke a little, and if you're posing as Stavros Kechiroski at the moment, have a nice glass of retsina; if you're being Nissim al-Farat in this instance, perhaps some other intoxicant."

Stavros hadn't noticed the glass of retsina on the table before him before; he downed it in one quick swallow.

He had instructions as to what to do if his disguise was discovered; there was a capsule still hidden beneath his clothing. His fingers fondled it. No reason not to take advantage of it; he had filed his most recent report in a hidden nook at the port. His death would be a loss to his brothers—but perhaps they would find a way to make some gains out of it.

"Go ahead." The Wise made an expansive gesture that would have been entirely in character for the shayk he was imitating. "In fact, I'll promise you this: if you do not swallow that capsule immediately, I'll reveal your identity to all of the others, immediately. And give them cause to believe me. I can be very persuasive, when I'm of a mind to."

Kechiroski retrieved it, brought it to his mouth, and shattered the glass between his teeth. The end would come soon, but—

But no. Instead of the expected sharp shards of glass in his mouth in a bitter taste on his tongue, it was merely an Injan candy, redolent of honey and persimmon.

"Well, so much for that." The Wise shook his head. "Yes, you've eaten food I've provided you, and you'll remain here as long as I choose. This is my place, and that we shall proceed here, you and me, as I choose, not you. Shall we talk openly now?"

There was no point in evasion; the Wise knew much. He might as well—but he felt a sense of triumph that his work for the committee had been done in faith and ignorance, not knowledge that could be extracted from his body with torture, no matter how long the torture, nor from his mind.

Why was the Wise being so helpful? Could it be that—

"No, it couldn't be. I tried to stay out of human affairs, and the battle between Crown, Empire, and the Dar are entirely human affairs, from my limited point of view. If I were to show a favorite, it would be—well, leave that be; I have no favorites among you. A certain amount of fear of some of the tools that some of you wield, yes, but fear and favor are such . . . different words, don't you think?"

If the Wise was not involved in the affairs of this world, then why the hesitance? Why project such an image of disinterest when he—or she, or it, or them, or whatever it was—was passionately interested in staying out of whatever was going on?

Why?

"It's something not quite human," he said, throwing away half a lifetime of habit, letting himself think aloud. "Amadan Dubh, swords, darklings, and all the rest—it isn't just the Empire, or something similar. It's something much larger."

Not a challenge to the Dar, not the Empire tentatively seeking out weakness in both Crown and Dar—but a distraction to all, that's what it was. That's what it had to be. Setting off a war between Dar, Crown, and Empire, and who would benefit?

Kechiroski didn't know, but he had a suspicion.

More: the Wise knew precisely what it was. And, for whatever reason, was not only disinterested in it— disinterest could be mended with a threat—but was terrified of it, and feared getting involved in it.

By the Beard—

He rose to his feet. "Gray! Sir Joshua Grayling!"

The Wise smiled. "He can't hear you. Nobody can hear you. Nobody will ever hear you. It's all happening right now." He shook his head. "You've been looking in all the wrong places, all of you, and he's quite effectively distracted you. All of you." He cocked his head to one side. "And for his next move, it's precisely too late to stop it. I'm sorry. Not very sorry, but sorry nonetheless."

"It's an apple tree," Black said. Others could call him the Wise; Gray preferred the name that had been given to him.

Black hadn't been waiting on the steps of the main building of the keep; Gray had gone around back to the plaza behind, to find Black half sitting on a waist-high stump of a branch, half leaning against the bole of the tree.

"I've seen apple trees before," Gray said.

As before, Black looked familiar, but disturbingly different. Dressed in Order robes, yes, but without piping and insignia, and no swords whatever thrust through his sash—not even the wandlike stick that Black had been playing with the last time, which Gray assumed was hidden inside his robes, along with Black's right hand.

Other than that, he was changed but a little. Hair still black as the raven, shot with a bit more gray; beard close-trimmed and neat, like Gray's own.

Black rose from the steps, the apple held out in front of him. "Hello," the Wise said, proffering the apple. "Do you like the tree?"

Gray almost smiled. "An apple from the Tree of Knowledge of Good and Evil? I think it's forbidden." Although, truth to tell, he felt that he already had more than a taste of that.

"It's an apple." Black shrugged, as though to say, *just an apple*. "The seed came from Fallsworth. No, I didn't go get it myself—"

"You should have gone yourself. You should have gone to lay a wreath and say a prayer over Bear's grave."

Black shrugged. "The wind brings many things to the Isle of Winds, after all. I thought it a fitting tribute to Bear. Don't you?"

"I think you're trying to distract me," Gray said. "I think that you know something that I need to, that you can do something that I'd want you to do, and I think you're stalling, Black. Do you think your deception will work for me?"

Black's brow wrinkled at the word "deception."

"Oh, it's real. All of it is real."

"As are the matters I've come to ask you about." He wished he had the wit or the knowledge to put all the pieces together, but he didn't. All he had was the responsibility to do that which was right.

"Every bit of it," Black said.

But then there was what the Lady had said to Gray.

And if you should see that faith, wisdom, and justice are insufficient, and since you believe with all your heart that you are a man who has sacrificed his soul, and are without honor, that leaves you one virtue left.

"And that's true enough, as well."

Mercy. But upon whom? Upon the Wise?

The steel of the Khan was but a fraction of an inch from his hand. The Wise had almost fallen prey to lesser Red Swords—and here, in his weakened state, could he stand against the combination of Gray and the Khan?

No.

The Wise shook his head. "Shall we get right to the point? Or do you enjoy my company so well? Have you come as a supplicant? Or a creditor? Are you here to beg for help, or demand it?"

"I demand it," said Sir Guy. "In the name of the king, and of the Order of Crown, Shield, and Dragon."

"And if I do not adhere to your demand?"

Gray had said that he would decide what was to be done. But Gray wasn't here—or, if he was, Sir Guy couldn't see him. It was Sir Guy's choice, and he would make it as a knight should.

"Then ready yourself, whoever you are," Sir Guy said, as he let his hand drop to Albert's hilt.

Be careful, Guy.

"You think to defeat me here, in this place?"

Sir Guy shook his head. "I know not what this will bring, but I'll do as I see best, and let the future bring what it will."

"So be it."

"Demand," said Cully. "You've got your reasons for not sharing what you know, what you can do. I don't give a tinker's damn for those reasons."

"And with a mundane sword, you think to defeat me? When it took almost a dozen swords of the brightest Red? What would your Lady say to that silly idea?"

"Oh, you make it easy for me." Cully smiled, as he drew both of his scabbards, gripping the swords by their hilts, and letting the scabbards fall away. "I'm not required to win, am I? Never took an oath to that effect."

"So why fight? Why dash yourself to bits against me? What would the lady Morgaine think of that? Do you think she would hold you in higher esteem, or lower?"

The words didn't matter, but they were reason in and of himself. No, of course, he had no chance to defeat the Wise, not in his own place—but he did have a chance to distract a little of the Wise's attention, at least, and give Gray the opportunity to do the necessary.

Whatever the necessary might be.

And if that meant that Cully would not, once again, have to stand over a dead body of another of his lambs, but could lie down next to them, well, then, so much the better.

It's in your hands, Joshua; may they be better than my old trembling ones.

He drew himself up straight. "I am Sir Cully of Cully's Woode, sirrah," he said, "and I'll not let Her name sully your lips, whoever or whatever you are." Enough planning, enough reasoning, enough scheming.

Let it come down to this.

"I come to beg," Gray said, dropping to his knees before Black. "To beg for mercy," Gray said, as his hand fell to the hilt of the Khan. "Mercy for what remains of my soul, if anything; mercy for you; mercy for all."

We live again, the Khan said.

"A strange form of begging, with your hand upon the Khan."

No. More and less than that. In one moment of unfettered rage, the Sandoval had turned Linfield into a more than century-long horror.

There was greater power and greater evil in the Khan. Enough to slay the Wise?

Perhaps; perhaps not.

Enough to turn this island into something that would make Linfield a mild inconvenience by comparison?

Yes.

And if Black were to strike him down as he drew, well then, that would be mercy, wouldn't it? A mercy on all those who would be affected by Pantelleria, the island of the winds, turned into a Hell on Earth, wouldn't it?

And yes, it would be a mercy on the soul of Joshua Grayling, who would not leave such behind as his legacy, who could burn in Hell thinking that, at least, there was one sin that he had been stopped from committing.

"You can stop me, Black. You can show me that mercy, that justice."

"Wait—" Black's face had gone ashen. "I can't—I. He."

"Lost your way with words, have ye?"

Do it now, Joshua. Let us live again, and let—

"No. I can't—I can't say, but I can send you to where it all is happening. But it's too late, Joshua. It won't do any good."

"Who are you to say what will do good? Who am I?"

Let it end, now. The Wise had ample time to strike him down before he drew the Khan; there was no point in talking, not any more.

He started to draw the Khan from his sheath.

But in an eyeblink, he had fallen into madness and darkness, lasting but a moment, or forever.

CHAPTER 18

The Return

This is what we do. This is who we are.

—Becket

It would not be enough, John thought, but it would be all that they could do.

It was the light. It was always the light.

By himself, as John of Redhook, light was just the way of, well, seeing things. By himself, as the Goatboy, light was something of memory, while he waited in the warm dark.

Together, it was something else. John had never noticed flickering stars above shone down with the light that was not merely a dim white, but subtly colored with attenuated reds and oranges of distant stars. The Goatboy had, back when he had a body of his own. Yes, the Goatboy had been a goatboy, not a shepherd, but after a long day of herding the goats to and from the baron's pens, he had upon occasion taken his meal up away from the keep, and up onto the hills overlooking Llwinderw. Serf he had been, yes, and a landless one at that, but he had long since been uncollared.

And his eyesight had been keen, in his youth. He had no book learning, and the only names for any of the stars that he knew were the ones that he had given them. But he remembered.

The colors were all the more when the two of them were one than they had ever been separately. How could John have never noticed the colors at all, or the Goatboy thought them dim and faded? It wasn't just the stars above—the night did not rob any colors; it merely hid them. The lush green of the meadow, stained and scarred with the burned yellow where the sheep had relieved themselves; a million different browns of the bushes. And not just the colors of nature—but those of humans. There was something beautiful about the colors in a human face—whether it was the clear and dusky complexion of young Sir Niko, or even the florid redness of the burst veins in Fotheringay's nose.

But the best of the colors were the ones that they felt, rather than saw. There were those who said that the difference between the whiteness of a White Sword and the redness of a Red was meaningless. Those had never seen what the two of them, joined into one, could now see: the rich and fiery and frightening redness of the union of Niko and Nadide, blazing to their right as they circled about the Amadan Dubh, orbiting his foul blackness while Goatboy and Sir John blazed white, white and pure, their light stopped but inches away from the foul blackness of the mad piper.

And it was not just their own light. Light flowed from the stars above, and from the world around them, filling their muscles and nerves and bones with a fire that was something of pleasure, something of pain, and everything of much more.

It is your clothes, your clothes I am washing, the pipes sang. And it was a lie. Oh, the dark piper was not without power; as had been the case for young Sir Niko, they were trapped in real time, not the fast time that had been the final astonishment for the butchers of the Kush.

They raised the sword that was not merely the Goatboy anymore above their head, and beat down upon the blackness. Again, and again—

But that was not enough.

So they burn hotter, and brighter. Hotter and brighter than they ever had before; once, in the Kush, they had let their joined flame burn almost as bright, almost as hot.

But that would not be enough. Maybe there would not be such thing as enough.

If they had been separate minds, of separate souls, they would have discussed it, they would have decided to keep beating down upon the darkness, not because it was written that the light would conquer the dark—although it surely was written—but because they could not retreat from the foulness. Leave the madness behind them? Try again in some other way on some other day?

No. They let their white flame grow brighter and brighter, aware of the damage that it was doing to both steel and body, but not caring.

The dark would fall before the light.

And yet it did not. No matter how hot they burned, how bright their light shone, it stopped at the edge of the darkness, and the pipes played on.

So they burned brighter, and hotter, knowing that it would not be enough.

It was always the same; but it was always different. Breathing was difficult, almost impossible; in the slow red time, his heart pumped hard, but too slowly, in his chest. His body—their body—obeyed as quickly as it possibly could, but mere fleshy muscles could only move it so fast, and recover only too slowly.

Sir John would take the dark piper from the front; Niko ran across the meadow, trying to circle around.

Through his wax-clogged ears, the notes of the piper reached him, but they were just notes, the slow dirge becoming merely a long wail that barely reached their mind, and touched their heart and soul not one whit.

It was always the same; but it was always different. This time, they did have their speed, but as they tried to wheel around, the soles of Niko's boots slipped on the grass, his feet shooting out from beneath him.

He could almost hear the dark piper smile, but he caught the fall on his left elbow, and didn't for a moment release his clamped grip on Nadide's steel, the grip that kept them one.

He sprung back to his feet, to their feet, letting their fear and anger turn all red and steely.

And the dark piper but laughed.

The notes of his pipe came faster and faster, and while Niko did not know how, they spoke to him: *Run, rabbit run. You can still escape from the trap*, they lied.

He wasn't sure how he knew it, but with the piper concentrating upon him, the others had been released from its spell. The dim spark of Sigerson flared across the meadow, and beat down against the blackness—

But it was like sparks from a campfire extinguishing themselves in a lake. No effect at all.

They reached inward, and outward, and let their fire burn until their redness was almost as bright, almost as painful, almost as shattering as the White flame from Sir John and the Goatboy.

But it wasn't enough.

Very well; so be it. Let there be more.

His legs failed him as the pipes became nearly music, and not strings pulling his muscles; Becket fell to the grass. He wasn't sure, but he thought he might have heard or felt bones snap in his right foot, but it didn't matter.

He crawled across the ground, fingers tearing at grass and soil, toward the Amadan Dubh. It would have been nice to have had some help from his traitor legs, from his useless knees, from the shattered feet, but what of that? He had hands, and gripping the soil forced grit and grass beneath his fingernails, what of that?

His eyes were closed against the brightness of the white and the red, but he didn't need eyes. He didn't need legs. He had hands, and he had his swords in his sash.

But it wouldn't be enough. It wouldn't have been enough if he were a quarter century younger, legs like wooden pilings, the strings that he'd had in youth.

But what was it? It was what a knight could give: everything he had.

Becket pulled himself along.

The moment had come. And the moment had found Sigerson wanting. It was one thing to let the magic and the madness wash about him; it was quite another to relieve it. Three steps forward, two to the side, and he could deflect it about Bigglesworth, and McPhee, as well as Fotheringay and Becket.

But that was all he had.

Even through his jammed-shut eyelids, the light was blinding, but it was not enough, either. The darkness expanded—slowly, painfully, hesitantly, yes—but it expanded nonetheless.

What fools they had all been. They had not been hunting the Amadan Dubh; it had been hunting them, and waiting for them to assemble all in the right place, all in the right time. And now the trap was sprung, and while Sigerson had a high opinion of himself, he knew it was not for him. It was for the knights.

And not just one—and not just two. Three knights of the Order; two of them with live swords. They were the prey; Sigerson and the others were merely dessert.

And who would set such a trap?

There was one; but he should have been long dead.

Gray never knew how long it had been, or how far he had fallen. Not that it mattered; but it would have been nice to know.

He landed hard, on his side, in the dark. Sounds of the pipes pervaded his mind, and it was with his last bit of self-control that he got the Khan into his hand.

We live again.

They were one, once again. Sharper, brighter, and darker than ever before, more alive, and more real.

It was wonderful. It was wonderful to have flesh again, and not merely be imprisoned in the cold steel, and it was every bit as wonderful to be freed of the fleshy prison of the crippled body of Sir Joshua Grayling.

He was, once again, more than a sword, far more than human, and that could be but the beginning.

Where was he? Even the Gray Khan didn't know—although he knew some of the others. Some were strange, but Gray's companions—well, they could have felt them if they hadn't seen them, as they fell across the meadow, trapped in their slow time, while their fires burned.

All of them were there: Father Cully, the girl Penelope—and even Sir Guy and Albert, flaming into white incandescence more in his mind than in his eyes.

And not just them. Two others beat down against the blackness, and there was no mystery as to who they were. He had seen the dim red of Niko and Nadide on two occasions before. He had never before been present when Sir John had drawn the Goatboy—it had been Sir Robert Linsen who had carried the Goatboy at Vlaovic, after all, and who had reduced Gray's pitiful little bit of justice against the rebels to something far less than the Gray Khan would have enjoyed—the Gray Khan knew the Goatboy's flame as well as he did that of the Nameless.

You could say or feel what you would about the vapidity of those silly saints, but each of them was distinctive, just as each of the true swords, the Red Swords was.

But the greatest joy was the darkness. It huddled at the center of the meadow, beating back both the White and the Red.

How wonderful. No, there was nothing of wonder in its stinking blackness—there was nothing of joy in its corruption and madness. But it was strong; it was powerful. It could resist the power of both Nadide and the Goatboy, and even adding the pallid white light of Albert would be no match for it.

It was, after all, what both Gray and the Khan had always wanted: an opponent worthy of the fullness of their power, and their glory.

And it was only a minor irritation that Father Cully stood before him, before them, his mouth moving slowly, his face creased in concern, his eyes wide. They had been through this before; and the part of them that was Gray had been weak. This time, they would not be so weak—but handling Father Cully could wait until the dark enemy was handled.

He could have fought with himself over whether or not to strike Cully down, but there was no point in that, no point in battling with himself. That could wait for later.

After all, Cully was just a human, and hardly a foe worth thinking of; let the strength that was the Khan and the sentimentality that was Gray work that out later. It didn't matter what they decided; what mattered was the dark piper.

It was the work of but a heartbeat to step to one side, to slip away from Cully, and to bring all that they were to bear on the darkness.

Vlaovic—hah. Linfield—nothing. Bring down the darkness upon this darkness, and let the world know of the power and the glory of the Gray Khan.

They let the redness build within them, and poured it out into the darkness, beating back, further and further, as the hymn of power within them, saying a louder and purer song with every passing moment.

"No," Cully shouted.

But it was, as the Wise had said, too late. Gray slipped to his right, seeming to gain in size and strength as he moved.

But it was different, this time. The last time that Cully had seen Gray take the Khan in hand, the light had been blindingly red. This time, it was red enough, but there was a darkness mixed with the light that chilled his heart more than blinded his eyes.

The grass beneath Cully's feet began to curdle, to twist and grow, thin blackened fingers reaching out to grasp at his boots, trying to anchor him in place.

The sword was in his hand, and he hacked at the grass with every step.

"Joshua, no." There was no doubt in his mind that Gray and the Khan could destroy the Amadan Dubh—but at what price? Turn all of—

—Oh my God. They were on Colonsay, just miles from the Scottish coast. How far would the destruction go? Just over the island? To Islay on the mainland? And could it stop there? Would it stop there?

No. Madness and magic from the Amadan Dubh was a bad thing, a horrid thing, a terrible thing—no question of that. But to lay waste to how much? To how many?

There were worse things than defeat; a victory that would blacken the soil for miles, perhaps a hundred miles, was one of them.

The Wise had done them no favor by bringing them here. Why had he done that?

"Joshua, Joshua—you must stop."

But the flame, the horrid red and black flame, grew brighter.

And the pipes played louder.

It is my shirt, and your shirt, and his shirt, and all their shirts that I am washing, the pipes said.

Madness.

"Joshua, Joshua—as you love me, stop."

There was but one thing to do. And Sir Cully of Cully's Woode, sworn knight of the Order of Crown, Shield, and Dragon, did it.

It had begun slowly, and was all over in a moment.

Niko found himself standing in the predawn light of the clearing. He never did remember how—or why—he had sheathed Nadide, but she was in her sheath, and in his sash.

The dead were scattered about the clearing. Sir John's body was still smouldering, and the breeze brought the horrible smell of cooked flesh to Niko's nostrils. It was all he could do not to retch.

Nor was Sir John the only one.

Niko knelt beside Becket. He was unmarked—Niko felt for a pulse at his throat, hoping.

No. The body was already cold.

All of the rest, save two, had fallen, but some of them were still breathing—the girl, Sigerson, Bigglesworth, a local whom Niko didn't recognize.

Sir John was dead; Sir Guy was dead; Sir Martin was dead; and Sir Cully wept over Gray's body.

That left Sir Niko in charge. He should do something, he knew, but he wasn't quite sure what. Becket wasn't there to tell him, after all, and he didn't know.

Fotheringay stood over the smoking heap of black robes, idly wiping his dagger back and forth on his sleeve. Their eyes met, briefly, and Fotheringay just nodded.

Part of Niko wanted to laugh. Two knights of the Order—a Red and a White—and then two more, one of each, and who had done for the Amadan Dubh?

Nigel Fotheringay, of course.

Fotheringay's lips moved. But Niko didn't need to hear the words to know what they were.

"Just doin' me duty, young sir." It was a rare moment that Fotheringay allowed himself an expression that wasn't bland, as he kicked the body of the Amadan Dubh. "King tol' me to watch his back, you bloody git. Didn't tell me not to put a knife in yours."

But it wasn't a day for laughter, as Cully knelt over the body of Sir Joshua Graying, the Khan lying inert on the grass, with Cully's own bloodied sword behind it.

"No."

Niko turned at the sound of Sigerson's voice.

The wizard looked much the worse for wear. "It could have been worse," he said. "But it's not a good day at all." He looked out to the sea. "If I've read this aright, it's as bad a day as there's been in closer to a millenium than far from it." He cocked his head. "Have you any ideas what we ought to do, Sir Niko?"

"Gather the swords—but don't touch them with your hands."

The obvious thing to do was to make for Alton, and the Order, but they had already done the obvious.

"Nigel."

"Yes, Sir Niko?"

"Get Cully on his feet. We're going to get moving."

"Yes, Sir Niko. Would you mind me asking where?"

That was obvious, but there was no reason not to state the obvious. "The Lady, Nigel. We're going to see Her."

Fotheringay nodded, but he didn't move right away. "Thought so. Mind me asking a favor? If it isn't too much trouble?"

"Go ahead."

"I wouldn't want you to stay your hand, mind, and I wouldn't ask that, sir. But if it turns out to be convenient, you think maybe you could try to arrange for me to do for whoever it was that killed Sir John?" Fotheringay shrugged. "I'll confess that I'm a sentimental man, and I was passingly fond of the good knight."

"We'll see," Sir Niko said. "Enough talk; we need to get to a boat, and get to the mainland. Quickly."

"Yes, Sir Niko."

AFTERWORD I

DuPuy

When you don't know what to do, DuPuy had long since decided, you do what you can.

He hadn't had anything that made more sense to do, so he headed homeward. Perhaps His Majesty would have the good sense to relieve a useless old man of something that he was clearly no good at.

In the meantime, well, the *Lord Fauncher* was headed homeward, and almost home, at that. Round Brest, and make for Plymouth. Favorable enough wind—and he would have a favorable enough wind, or know a good reason why—and while Winters wasn't the navigator that DuPuy had been in his youth, surely the man could get the *Lord Fauncher* and DuPuy to Londinium more quickly than the overland route could.

And, if not, a few more hours wouldn't matter. Besides, it was good to have the wheel in his hands for awhile.

Probably the last time, at least for a navy ship. The pay of a commissioner was, well, preposterously high. Not enough to purchase a merchantman outright, no—at least not one worth having—but once HM shed DuPuy of the honors that he didn't deserve, he could go hat in hand, if necessary, to a banker in the City, and see what might or might not be done.

Things to do before then, of course. Had to see that Emmons was properly settled, and protected from DuPuy's disgrace.

Track down the source of the live swords, HM had said, and DuPuy had given it his all—but that, demonstrably, had not been good enough.

Pins in his stateroom; dispatching agents here and there, and the only damned thing he knew was that Cully and his crew might be near something useful, but surely didn't need DuPuy to either succeed, or fail. Didn't much matter.

The wind picked up just a touch, and came from a point or so closer to west-norwest than the pure norwest it had been. If it had been his quarterdeck, there would already be rope monkeys going aloft to trim the sails accordingly, but it wasn't his quarterdeck, after all, and—

"Topmen aloft" piped from behind him.

Well, so much for even his private complaints about Winters, eh? He turned to see the Captain standing on the main deck, briefly touching a finger to his hat in what would have been a mockery of a salute, if it hadn't been from the captain, and if DuPuy—Simon Tremain DuPuy, if you please—had deserved a salute.

"Permission to come up, sir?" Emmons asked, from his usual position just below the quarterdeck, waiting.

"Shouldn't you be asking the captain, Lieutenant?"

"I did, Admiral. He said that you had the deck. Sir." His boot face was firmly in place.

"Well, come on up, then. What is it?"

"There's something in the distance, three points to port of the bow."

"And the watch hasn't seen it?"

"I've got good eyes, and a good glass, and, well, there shouldn't be anything..." Emmons had his glass in hand. "I think you should see—"

"Pirates, Mr. Emmons?" DuPuy asked, smiling. "I'm sure that Captain Winters is keeping a good watch, but these are hardly the waters—"

"Nossir." Emmons face was even more expressionless than usual. If such a thing were possible. "Not pirates. Not a ship at all, Admiral."

"Not a ship?" They were miles from land, and it should be a good two hours before they'd spot any coast in front of them, and then only if the wind kept up.

"Nossir."

Emmons handed him the glass.

DuPuy's eyes weren't that of a younger man, and it took some time for him to make out what the mass might be.

"An island, Mr. Emmons."

"That was my thought, Admiral."

Not a new island off the coast of England. No. An old island.

A very old island.

"I see," DuPuy said, pleased that his voice was still calm. "Would you be so kind as to do something for me, Mr. Emmons?"

He was already loosening his tie, and getting the chain holding key to the strongbox from his neck. "There's sealed orders in my strongbox; I'll want the captain to witness their opening. Bring them—and a knife; I'll pin them to the deck myself, by God, lest they blow away."

Emmons took the key, but shook his head. "I think the stateroom would be more appropriate, Admiral. If you don't mind my saying so. There's plenty of time, sir."

"Too damn little, and plenty. So be it; on your way." DuPuy nodded, and as Emmons made his way down the ladder with unseemly haste, he called out to the captain. "Captain! Would you be so kind as to have an officer take the deck and then meet me in my stateroom?"

"Immediately, Admiral."

"No rush—I'd like you to come about, and set course for Brest. See to that, if you please, then please join me."

Plenty to think about over the next few minutes. Sail toward the island? He had dismissed that in an instant. There was no chance that one ship, and a single company of Marines was enough. Hell, there was more than a chance that all His Majesty's forces, land and sea, weren't enough. It might already be too late.

The second officer relieved DuPuy of the deck, and the steersman took the wheel.

It wouldn't be official until he broke the seal of the orders, of course, but his mind was several steps beyond that. Turn the ship, of course; the way to Portsmouth was surely blocked.

Put in at Brest, and raise every ship that he could, for a starter.

And what next? Well, he would just have to see.

DuPuy turned in irritation at the knock. "Well, come in, dammit."

It was Winters, of course. "You sent for me, Admiral?"

"I'd appreciate you reading these orders, and then getting your scrivener in here—and any officer who you don't need who can hold a pen. Lots of orders to write, captain."

Winters barely glanced at the orders, and then smiled. "I don't suppose you'll be complaining about me calling you by your rank anymore, Admiral."

DuPuy forced a smile. "I think not."

"We're on course for Brest. I'd guess . . . three hours, if the wind holds, before we put in. I've taken the liberty of ordering courier pennants aloft—I'm assumed you'll have orders to send."

"Yes, I think I might. We'll put in at Brest—we'll start there. Raise every man and ship we can there, and send for more, in all directions—the way to Londinium is likely blocked, but there are other directions, and other ports."

"Aye-aye, Admiral." Winters drew himself up straight. "Is there anything you'd like me to tell the crew, Admiral?"

DuPuy shrugged. "There's no reason that they ought not to know, Captain. You tell them. Tell them we're sailing against Avalon—against the Tyrant Arthur, and his minion, Merlin. It appears that they're back. Mallory seems to have had it right; Mordred the Great didn't kill them quite well enough. It appears that we've been delayed to this party—and through some cleverness, at that."

All of it. He still couldn't see the whole picture, but it was falling together—distractions, an attempt to set Crown against the Dar, Ghost Dancers in the colonies; darklings on the Continent.

Very nicely done, he thought. Delay and distract, while the real enemy moved quietly, readying himself.

Were they already in Londinium? Quite possibly—no, almost certainly.

And His Majesty? Well, if His Own couldn't see to His Majesty's safety, there was nothing that DuPuy could do about that, not now.

But a sailor—a sailor again, dammit—would do what he could.

Every little bit of it.

"We'll fix that, Admiral."

Grand Admiral Sir Simon Tremaine DuPuy, by the Grace of God and Appointment of His Majesty, Mordred V, the Commander in Chief of all of His Majesty's Forces, nodded. "We will most certainly try, Captain Winters. Hoist battle pennants."

"Aye-aye, sir."

AFTERWORD II

Her

He would have preferred to have gone alone, of course. But the others were necessary, and in this lifetime, you don't always get what you prefer, something that Cully knew better than any other.

Besides, he couldn't have done this by himself, at least not until they reached the Arroy. There were picket lines stretched at all the known approaches to the Bedegraine, and the town of Bedegraine itself had fallen immediately to the invaders from the sea.

Too many years of peace. Too many years of letting town walls fall for lack of repair, too little repair for lack of an enemy to repair it against.

Too many of them.

So they came in through Linfield, and left their horses and their gear at the edge of the Bedegraine, then walked into the forest, single file, with Cully in the lead, followed by Sigerson and his man assisting Penelope, with Fotheringay, burdened with the pack wrapped in blankets next, and Sir Niko bringing up the rear.

There was no point in rushing, not anymore. Let them be pursued into the Arroy, if that's what the others wanted. If Her defenses weren't up to the task, another few hundred soldiers wouldn't make any difference.

Besides, it was good to do something ordinary. It was good to do something, and it was good to know that when they reached a fork, it didn't much matter which path they took.

He always chose the easier one. It didn't make any difference.

Still, there was something not unpleasant in the gradual way that the Bedegraine gave way to the Arroy.

It spoke of Her safety, for one. And, of course, even though neither the Bedegraine nor the Arroy were his long-lost, much beloved Woode, both were forest, after all, and the smell of rotting humus an earthy perfume, was something that could distract him as long as he didn't think about Gray.

He tried not to think about Gray.

He failed.

The others were silent behind him.

It was, by his calculation, somewhere near noon, but there was no way to spot the sun for even a moment through the leafy canopy; what light that trickled down was wan and directionless, giving no warmth or guidance.

It was the silence, mainly, that persuaded him that they had reached the Arroy proper.

He reached back into his rucksack and took out the hairbrush that he had noticed but a few days before. This time, he would not stop to bathe and make himself presentable, but he could, at least, appear before her with properly brushed hair.

He stopped. He didn't know how he knew, but She was over the next rise.

He turned to the others. "Would you," he asked, "would you please give me a moment or two with Her before you join us?" They would have to see Her, of course. But . . .

It was, of course, Sir Niko who answered. "Of course, Sir Cully. We'll wait for your call."

He gestured at Sigerson and Bigglesworth, who carefully lowered Penelope to the blanket that Fotheringay had spread for her on the ground.

As Cully topped the rise, he thought himself mistaken. There was no sign of Her, just a path leading down into a valley, filled with stones.

"I'll not ask you to sit table with me this time, Cully," She said from behind him.

He turned. She was, as she always was, quite perfect.

"My Lady," he said, dropping to a knee. "I'm relieved to find you well."

"Are you indeed?" Her voice, even after all these years, was still the surprise that it had been when he had knelt before her as a novice: half an octave lower than it should have been, sweet but not to the point of cloying, bracing as a cold stream.

Her perfect lips, the color of fresh blood, parted in a smile.

But there was nothing to smile about.

"Well, no," she said, "there is always something to smile about. Not as much as one would wish."

"No, my Lady, not as much as one would wish."

"Do you hate me, Cully? I sent him to you."

"You send all my lambs to me, my Lady, and I butcher them all, don't I?" He would not let his voice break, not in front of Her. "And why should it have been different with Joshua? Why should he have been so different from all the others?" He raised his hands before his face. "Merely because I slew him with my own hands, with my own sword, without giving him a moment to repent his sins?"

"You think your God would send such as Joshua to Hell, Cully?"

"I don't judge God, my Lady. I judge myself, and perhaps—"

"And more than perhaps you judge Me." She nodded. "Which is, I suppose, as it should be." She touched two fingers to Her own lips, and then to his.

She had never before touched him without his permission. It was all he could do not to seize that perfect hand, clamp his fingers around that perfect wrist.

"And then what, my Cully? And then what? Force my lips to yours? Or wring my slender neck? Or both?"

There was but one answer to that. "Neither, Lady." He forced himself to rise. "Do you need protection?"

She shook her head. "I'm safe here, and, should that change, I should be able to retreat from the world, from this world. But you didn't come to see to My safety. Did you?"

He shook his head. "I don't think it's safe to try for Alton, and the way to Londinium and the College is likely watched, and guarded."

"You want me to fit the swords to your companions?"

"Yes. Can you? Will you?"

She frowned. "Yes, and yes. Sigerson won't do, though; the fire of any of the live swords would burn out his spark, and he'd feel the lack of it more than, than one would miss—"

"Would miss a hand?"

She swallowed hard, and nodded. "Yes. More than one would miss a hand. You think Penelope for the Goatboy, perhaps?"

He shook his head. "No. For Albert. The combination of Sir Guy and Albert eased her pain. Perhaps Albert can do so alone."

"I'm not sure she'd be the ideal choice—"

"And you see others?" he asked.

"No," she said. "Well, that leaves Bigglesworth and Fotheringay for the Khan and the Goatboy—"

"Bigglesworth for the Goatboy, yes. At least for the time being."

"And Fotheringay for the Khan?"

"Hardly."

She smiled. "Of course not. You'll carry the Khan, won't you?"

"Of course, my Lady."

Once more, She touched Her fingers first to Her own lips, and then to his. "So be it, my Cully."

"I'll go get the others. If this is to be done, t'were best done quickly."

"There's time enough for one more question of you, isn't there?"

He forced a smile. "And, yes, for one more answer, Morgaine. And the answer, as You know, is yes. Yes, You are my Lady, as you always shall be."

"I know. I just wanted to hear it one more time, from your lips."

It was easy to turn away from Her, and not just because it was but for a moment—it was because the Khan, and his own doom, waited.

"As will I, my Cully," she said, her voice so low that for a moment he wondered if she had meant the words for his ears.

But it was only for a moment.

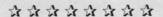

IF YOU LIKE...
YOU SHOULD TRY...

DAVID DRAKE
David Weber

DAVID WEBER
John Ringo

JOHN RINGO
Michael Z. Williamson
Tom Kratman

ANNE MCCAFFREY
Mercedes Lackey

MERCEDES LACKEY
Wen Spencer, Andre Norton
Andre Norton
James H. Schmitz

LARRY NIVEN
James P. Hogan
Travis S. Taylor

ROBERT A. HEINLEIN
Jerry Pournelle
Lois McMaster Bujold
Michael Z. Williamson

HEINLEIN'S "JUVENILES"
Rats, Bats & Vats series by Eric Flint & Dave Freer

**HORATIO HORNBLOWER OR
PATRICK O'BRIAN**
David Weber's Honor Harrington series
David Drake's RCN series

HARRY POTTER
Mercedes Lackey's Urban Fantasy series

THE LORD OF THE RINGS
Elizabeth Moon's *The Deed of Paksenarrion*

H.P. LOVECRAFT
Princess of Wands by John Ringo

GEORGETTE HEYER
Lois McMaster Bujold
Catherine Asaro

GREEK MYTHOLOGY
Pyramid Scheme by Eric Flint & Dave Freer
Forge of the Titans by Steve White
Blood of the Heroes by Steve White

NORSE MYTHOLOGY
Northworld Trilogy by David Drake
A Mankind Witch by Dave Freer